Children of the Market Place

Edgar Lee Masters

Contents

CHILDREN OF THE MARKET PLACE

BY

Edgar Lee Masters

TO GEORGE P. BRETT

CHAPTER I

I was born in London on the eighteenth of June, 1815. The battle of Waterloo was being fought as I entered this world. Thousands were giving up their lives at the moment that life was being bestowed upon me. My father was in that great battle. Would he ever return? My mother was but eighteen years of age. Anxiety for his safety, the exhaustion of giving me life prostrated her delicate constitution. She died as I was being born.

I have always kept her picture beside me. I have always been bound to her by a tender and mystical love. During all the years of my life my feeling for her could not have been more intense and personal if I had had the experience of daily association with her through boyhood and youth.

What girlish wistfulness and sadness there are in her eyes! What a gentle smile is upon her lips, as if she would deny the deep foreboding of a spirit that peered into a perilous future! Her dark hair falls in rich strands over her forehead in an elfin and elegant disorder. Her slender throat rises gracefully from an unloosened collar. This picture was made from a drawing done by a friend of my father's four months before I was born. My old nurse told me that he was invalided from the war; that my father had asked him to make the drawing upon his return to London. Perhaps my father had ominous dreams of her ordeal soon to be.

They pronounced me a fine boy. I was round faced, round bodied, well nourished. The nurse read my horoscope in coffee grounds. I was to become a notable figure in the world. My mother's people took me in charge, glad to give me a place in their household. Here I was when my father returned from the war, six months later. He had been wounded in the battle of Waterloo. He was still weak and ill. I was told these things by my grandmother in the succeeding years.

When I was four years old my father emigrated to America. I seem to remember him. I have asked my grandmother if he did not sing "Annie Laurie"; if he did not dance and fling me toward the ceiling in a riot of playfulness; if he did not snuggle me under my tender chin and tickle me with his mustaches. She confirmed these seemingly recollected episodes. But of his face I have no memory. There is no picture of him. They told me that he was tall and strong, and ruddy of face; that my beak nose is like his, my square forehead, my firm chin. After he reached America he wrote to me. I have the letters yet, written in a large open hand, characteristic of an adventurous nature. Though he was my father, he was only a person in the world after all. I was surrounded by my mother's people. They spoke of him infrequently. What had he done? Did they disapprove his leaving England? Had he been kind to my mother? But all the while I had my mother's picture beside me. And my grandmother spoke to me almost daily of her gentleness, her high-mindedness, her beauty, and her charm. I was raised in the English church. I was taught to adore Wellington, to hate Napoleon as an enemy of liberty, a usurper, a false emperor, a monster, a murderer. I was sent to Eton and to Oxford. I was indoctrinated with the idea that there is a moral governance in the world, that God rules over the affairs of men. I was taught these things, but I resisted them. I did not rebel so much as my mind naturally proved impervious to these ideas. I read the ***Iliad*** and the ***Odyssey*** with passionate interest. They gave me a panoramic idea of life, men, races, civilizations. They gave me understanding of Napoleon. What if he had sold the Louisiana territory to rebel America, and in order to furnish that faithless nation with power to overcome England in some future crisis? Perhaps this very moral governance that I was taught to believe in wished this to happen. But if the World Spirit be nothing but the concurrent thinking of many peoples, as I grew to think, the World Spirit might irresistibly wish this American supremacy to be.

And now at eighteen I am absorbed in dreams and studies at Oxford. I have many friends. My life is a delight. I arise from sleep with a song, and a bound. We play, we talk, we study, we discuss questions of all sorts infinitely. I take nothing for granted. I question everything, of course in the privacy of my room or the room of my friends. I do not care to be expelled. And in the midst of this charming life bad news comes to me. My father is dead. He has left a large estate in Illinois. I must go there. At least my grandmother thinks it is best. And so my school days end. Yet I am only eighteen!

CHAPTER II

I am eighteen and the year is 1833. All of Europe is in a ferment, is bubbling over in places. Napoleon has been hearsed for twelve years in St. Helena. But the principles of the French Revolution are working. Charles is king of France, but by the will of the nation first and by the grace of God afterward. There is no republic there; but the sovereignty of the people, the prime principle of the French Revolution, has founded the right of Charles to rule.... And what of England? Fox had rejoiced at the fall of the Bastille. Coleridge, Wordsworth, and Southey had sung of liberty, exulting in the emancipation of peoples from tyranny. Then they had changed. Liberalism had come under the heel again. Revolution was feared and denounced. Liberal principles were crushed.... But not for long. We students read Shelley and Byron. They were now gone from earth, eleven and nine years respectively. They had not altered their faith, dying in the heyday of youthful power. Would they have changed at any age to which they might have lived? We believed they would not have done so. But what of England? It is 1833 and the reform bill is a year old. The rotten boroughs are abolished. There is a semblance of democratic representation in Parliament. The Duke of Wellington has suffered a decline in popularity. Italy is rising, for Mazzini has come upon the scene. Germany is fighting the influence of Metternich. We students are flapping our young wings. A great day is dawning for the world. And I am off to America!

What is stirring there? I am bound for the Middle West of that great land. What is it like? Shall I ever return? What will my life be? These are my reflections as I prepare to sail.

I take passage on the *Columbia and Caledonia*. She is built of wood and is 200 feet long from taffrail to fore edge of stem. Her beam is 34-1/2 feet. She has a gross tonnage of 520 tons. She can sail in favorable weather at a speed of 12 knots an hour. I laughed at all this when, something more than twenty years after, I crossed on the *Persia*, 376 feet long, of 3500 tonnage, and making a speed of nearly 14 knots an hour, with her 4000-horse-power engines.

It is April. The sea is rough. We are no sooner under way than the heavy swell of the waves tosses the boat like a chip. The prow dips down into great valleys of glassy water. The stern tips high in the air against an angry sky. The shoulders of the sea bump under the poop of the boat, and she trembles like a frightened horse under its rider. I have books to read. My grandmother has provided me with many things for my comfort and delight. But I cannot eat, not until during the end of the voyage. I lie in a little stateroom, which I share with an American. He persists in talking to me, even at night when I am trying to sleep. He tells me of America. His home is New York City. He has been as far west as Buffalo. He gives me long descriptions of the Hudson River, and the boats on it that run to Albany. He talks of America in terms of extravagant eulogy. The country is free. It has no king. The people rule. I have read a little and heard something of America. At Oxford we students had wondered at the anomaly of a republic maintaining the institution of slavery. I asked him about this. He said that it did not involve any contradiction; that the United States was founded by white men for white men; that negroes were a lower order of beings; that their servitude was justified by the Bible; that a majority of the clergy and the churches of the country approved of the institution; that the slaves were well treated, much better housed and fed than the workers of Europe; better than the free laborers even in America. His thesis was that the business of life was the obtaining of the means of life; that all the uprisings in Europe, the French Revolution included, were inspired by hunger; that the struggle for existence was bound to produce oppression; that the strong would use and control the weak, make them work, keep them in a state where they could be worked. All this for trade. He topped off this analysis with the remark that negro slavery was a benign institution, exactly in line with the processes of the business of life; that it had been lied about by a growing fanaticism in the States; New York had always been in sympathy, for the most part with the Southern States, where slavery was a necessary institution to the climate and the cotton industry. He went on to tell me that about a year before a maniacal cobbler named William Lloyd Garrison had started a little paper called *The Liberator* in which he advocated slave insurrections and the overthrow of the laws sustaining slavery; and that a movement was now on foot in New England to found the American Anti-Slavery Society. And that John Quincy Adams, once President, but now a senile intermeddler, had been presenting petitions in Congress from various constituencies for the abolition of slavery in the District of Columbia. This would be finally squelched, he thought. New England had always demanded a tariff in order to foster her industries, and that policy trenched on the rights of the states not needing and not wanting a tariff. While slavery did not in any way harm New England, she intermeddled in a mood of moral fanaticism.

I was much interested in these revelations by Mr. Yarnell, for such was his name.... One morning we began to sense land. We had been about three weeks on the water. We were nearing the harbor of New York.

CHAPTER III

Yarnell was a man of about thirty. He seemed very mature to me. In fact he was quite a man of the world. I had told him my destination, and asked him how best to reach it. He had given me some information, but it was not wholly clear. He advised me to ask for direction at the Franklin House, which he recommended to me as a comfortable hotel.

As we came into the harbor we stood on the deck together while he pointed out the places of interest. I was thrilled with its beauty and its extent. The day was mild. A fresh breeze was blowing. May clouds floated swiftly in the clear sky. I felt my blood course electrically in expectation of the wonders of New York. It was now lying before me in all its color and mystery. Boats of all kinds passed us. There was a tangled thicket of masts at the piers. I discerned gay awnings over a walk around a building near the water. Yarnell said this was Castle Garden, where many diners came for the excellence of the food and the view of the harbor. I could begin to see up the streets of the city beyond the Battery. But there was a riot of stir and activity, in expectation of our boat.

I disembarked and hired a hack. I was traveling with a huge valise. This the hackman took for me. Yarnell came up to bid me adieu, promising to call upon me at the Franklin House. The fare was twenty-five cents a mile. The hotel was at 197 Broadway. Was it more than a mile? I did not know. I was charged fifty cents for the trip. I was not stinted for money, and it did not matter. I paid the amount demanded, and walked into the hotel.

How simple things are at the end of a journey and a daily restlessness to arrive! My valise was taken to my room. I went with the negro porter. I looked from my window out upon Broadway. The porter departed. The door was closed. My journey to New York was over. I was alone. I began to wish for Yarnell, wish to be back upon the boat. Above all I began to sense the distance that separated me from England and those I loved. Here was the afternoon on my hands. Should I not see something of the city? When should I start west? I took from my pocket the letter written from Illinois by the lawyer, who had advised this journey and my presence at Jacksonville, for that was the town where my father's estate was to be settled. For the first time I was conscious of the fact that difficulties probably stood in my way. The letter read: "Claims are likely to be made against the estate that require your personal attention." What could it mean? Why had my grandmother said nothing to me of this? She had seen the letter. I began to wonder. But to fight down my growing loneliness I started out to see the city.

As I passed up the street I bought **Valentine's Manual** and glanced at it as I walked. How far up did the city extend? The manual said more than thirteen miles. I could not make that distance before dark. A passerby said that there was a horse railway running as far as Murray Hill. But I strode on, arriving in a little while at Washington Square. Beyond this I could see that the city did not present the appearance of being greatly built. On my way I passed the gas works, the City Hall, many banks, several circulating libraries, saw the signs of almost innumerable insurance companies. But the people! They were all strange to me. So many negroes. My manual said there were over 14,000 negroes in the city, which, added to the white population, made an aggregate of more than 200,000 souls. I sat for a while in the Park and then retraced my steps.

On my way back I stopped at Niblo's Garden at Broadway and Prince Street. It was a gay place. People were feasting upon oysters, drinking, laughing, talking over the affairs of the day. Here I partook of oysters for the first time in my life. I walked through the grounds, looking at the flowers. I stared about at the splendor of the paintings and the mirrors in the rooms. Then like a ghost I resumed my way to my hotel. Why? There was nothing there to call me back. Yet it was the only home I had, and the evening was coming on.

Instead of stopping at the hotel, I went on to Castle Garden. I decided to dine there. I could look over the harbor and the ships. It was a way to put myself in touch with England, to travel back over the way I had come. I found a table and ordered a meal.

I became conscious of the fact that the captain of the **Columbia and Cale-**

donia was at a near table with a gay party. They had wine, and there was much merriment. This abandonment was in contrast to the serious, almost dark spirit of a party at another table. This was composed of men entirely. I had never seen such faces before. Their hair was long. They wore goatees. They were strangely dressed. They talked with a broad accent. Excitement and anger rose in their voices. They were denouncing President Jackson. The matter seemed to be a force bill, the tariff imposed by New England's enterprise, the duty of the Southern States to resist it. They were insisting that there was no warrant to pass a tariff law, that it was clearly a breach of the Constitution, and that it should be resisted to the death. There was bitter cursing of Yankees, of the greed of New England, of its disregard of the rights of the South.... But out upon the harbor the sea gulls were drifting. I could hear the slapping of the waves against the rocks. And in the midst of this the orchestra began to play "Annie Laurie." The tears came to my eyes. I arose and left the place. My mind turned to a theater as a means of relief to these pressing thoughts. I consulted my manual, and started for the American theater. It was described as an example of Doric architecture, modeled after the temple of Minerva at Athens. I found it on the Bowery and Elizabeth Street, bought a ticket for seventy-five cents and entered. The play was *Othello*, and I had never seen it before.

I could not help but overhear and follow the conversation of the people who sat next to me. They were wondering what moved Shakespeare to depict the story of a black man married to a white woman. Could such a theme be dramatized now? How could a woman, fair and high-bred, become the wife of a sooty creature like Othello? Was it real? If not real, what was Shakespeare trying to do? And much more to the same effect, together with remarks about negroes and that slavery should be let alone by New England, and by everyone else.

The play was dreary to me, played listlessly where it was not ranted and torn to tatters. I sat it through and then went back to my hotel.... The loneliness of that room as I entered it has never left my memory. For long hours I did not sleep. The city had 600 night watch, so the manual said, and I could hear some of them going their rounds. At last ... I awoke and it was morning. I awoke with a sense of delight in the strength and vitality which sleep had restored to me.... I went below to breakfast and to find the way to travel to Illinois.

CHAPTER IV

The clerk of the hotel told me that the best route was by way of Albany, the canal, the Great Lakes to Chicago; that when I got there I would likely find a boat or stage service to Jacksonville. I could leave at noon for Albany if I wished. Accordingly, I made ready to do so.

I was entranced with the river boat. It was longer than the *Columbia and Caledonia*. And it was propelled by steam. It had the most enormous wheels. And no sooner were we under way than I found that we were gliding along at the rate of twenty miles an hour. The swiftly passing hills and palisades of the Hudson served to mark our speed. There were great saloons, lovely awnings under which to read or lounge, promenade decks. And there was a gay and well-behaved crowd of passengers.... At dinner we were seated at long tables, and served with every luxury. And the whole journey cost me less than seven shillings.

On arriving at Albany that night at about nine o'clock I found myself in the best of luck. I could get passage on a canal boat the next morning for Buffalo; rather I was permitted to sleep on board.... I got on and retired. I awoke just as the boat was beginning to start. I had never seen anything like this before. The boat was narrow, sharp, gayly painted. It was drawn by three horses, each ridden by a boy who urged the horses forward. We traveled at the great speed of five miles an hour.

But it was delightful. We were more than three days going from Albany to Buffalo. The time was well spent. The scenery was varied and beautiful. All the while we were climbing, for Lake Erie, to which we had to be lifted, was much above us. We went through lovely valleys; we ran beside glistening streams and rivers; we wound around hills. The farms were large and prosperous. The villages were new, fresh with white paint and green blinds, hidden among flowers and shrubbery.

You see, I am eighteen and these external objects realize my dreams and stimulate them. I do not know these people. They are frank, talkative, often vulgar and presuming. But they are friendly. There is much merriment on board, for we have to dodge down frequently to save our heads from the bridges which the farmers build right across the canal. The ladies have to be warned and assisted. There are narrow escapes and shouts of laughter. And when the dinner bell is rung by a comical negro every one rushes for the dining room. I am introduced again to the American oyster, raw, fried, and stewed. It is the most delicious of discoveries among the new viands. Then we have wonderful roast turkey, chicken, and the greatest variety of vegetables and sweets. I am keeping a daily record of events and impressions to mail to my dear grandmother when I shall arrive at Buffalo....

Sometimes I get tired of the boat. Then I go on land and run along the path behind the horses. A young woman on her way to Michigan to teach school joins me in these reliefs from the tedium of the boat. We exchange a few words. But I see that I am not old enough for her. I have already observed her in confiding conversation with a man about the age of Yarnell. And soon they go together to trot along the path, to stray off a little into the meadows, or at the base of the picturesque hills.... I am interested in the talk of the passengers, and cannot choose but follow it at times.... One man has been reading the *New Yorker*, printed by H. Greeley and Company. I learn that Horace Greeley is his full name, and he comes in for a berating at the hands of a man with one of the characteristic goatees that I first observed at Castle Garden. The Whigs! I had always associated this party with latitudinarian principles. Now I hear it called a centralist party, a monarchist party. A voluble man, who chews tobacco, curses it as a mask for the old Federalist party, which tried to corrupt America with the British system, after it had failed as a combination of Loyalists to keep America under the dominion of Great Britain.... This is all a maze to me, at least so far as the American application is concerned. Then the man with the goatee assails New England, and calls her the devotee of the soured gospel of envy which covers its wolf face of hate with the lamb's decapitated head of universal brotherhood and slavery abolition. Surely there is much strife in America.... Also again President Jackson, the tariff, and the force bill! And will South Carolina secede from the Union on account of the unjust and lawless tariff? New England tried to secede once when the run of affairs did not suit her. Why not South Carolina, then, if she chooses? Another man is reading a book of poems and talking at intervals to a companion. I hear him say that a Mr. Willis is one of the world's greatest poets. I glance at the book and see the name Nathaniel Parker Willis. Also it seems Willis is the editor of one of the world's greatest literary journals. It is published in New York and is called the ***New York Mirror***.... It is all so strange. Is it true that in this country, so far from England, there are men who are the equals of Shelley and Byron, or of Tennyson, whose first book has given me such delight recently?...

We near the journey's end. At Lockport we are lifted up the precipice over which the Falls of Niagara pour some miles distant. We are now on a level with Lake Erie, to which we have climbed by many locks and lifts over the hills since we left Albany. Soon we travel along the side of the Niagara River; quickly we drift into Buffalo.

CHAPTER V

Buffalo, they told me, had about 15,000 people. I wished to see something of it before departing for the farther west. For should I ever come this way again? I started from the dock, but immediately found myself surrounded by runners and touters lauding the excellences of the boats to which they were attached. The harbor was full of steamboats competing for trade.... They rang bells, let off steam, whistled. Bands played. Negroes ran here and there, carrying freight and baggage. The air was vibrating with yells and profanity.... But I made my escape and walked through the town. It had broad streets, lovely squares, substantial and attractive buildings and residences. And there was Lake Erie, blue and fresh, rippling under the brilliant May sun. I had never seen anything remotely approximating Lake Erie.... "How large is it?" I inquired of a passerby. I was told that it was 60 miles wide and 250 miles long. Could it be true? Was there anything in all of Europe to equal it? I could not for the moment remember the extent of the Caspian Sea. And I stood in wonder and delight.

As I left the dock for my walk I had observed the name *Illinois* on a boat that had all the appearances of being brand new. I walked leisurely toward the dock so as to avoid the touters as much as possible while I was overlooking the boat. I liked it, but would it take me to Chicago? The gangplank was lying on the dock and near it stood what seemed to me to be the captain and the pilot, around them touters and others. I edged around to the captain and asked him if the *Illinois* would take me to Chicago. "In about an hour," he said with a laugh. Immediately I was besieged by the runners to help me on, to get my baggage, to serve me in all possible ways. I couldn't hire all of them. I chose one, who got my valise for me, and I went aboard.

It was a new boat, and this was its maiden trip. All the stewards, negroes, waiters were brisk and obliging, and bent on making the trip an event. The captain gave parties. He was a bluff, kindly man, who mingled much with favorite passengers. Wine flowed freely. The food was abundant and delicious. We had dances by moonlight on the deck. A band played at dinner and at night. The boat was distinguished for many quaint and interesting characters. I enjoyed it all, but made no friends. I did not understand this free and easy manner of life. The captain noted me, and asked if I was well placed and comfortable. Various people opened conversations with me. But I was shy, and I was English. I could not unbend. I did not desire to do so.

We docked at Erie and at Cleveland, both small places. We came to Detroit, the capital of Michigan. On the way some one pointed out the scene of Perry's victory over the hated British. We passed into Lake Huron.

Then later I was privileged to see Mackinac, an Indian trading post. I viewed the smoking wigwams from the deck of the *Illinois*. Here were the savages buying powder, blankets, and whisky. The squaws were selling beaded shoes. The shore was wooded and high.... I looked below into the crystalline depths of the water. I could see great fish swimming in the transparent calms, which mirrored the clouds, the forests, and the boats and canoes of the Indians.... We ran down to Green Bay, Wisconsin. Here too there were Indian traders.... We went on to Milwaukee. As there was no harbor here a small steamer came out to take us off. I went ashore with some others. A creek flowed from the land to the lake. But the town was nothing. Only a storehouse and a few wooden buildings. Soon we proceeded to Chicago. I was told that the northern boundary of Illinois had been pushed north, in order to give the state the southern shores of the great lake, with the idea of capturing a part of the emigration and trade of the East. This fact eventually influenced my life, and the history of the nation, as will be seen.

Chicago had been a trading post, and to an extent was yet. The population was less than 1000 people. There was a fort here, too, built in place of one which had been destroyed in a massacre by the Indians. There was much activity here, particularly in land speculation. Not a half mile from the place where we landed there was a forest where some Indians were camping. I heard that an Indian war was just over. The Black Hawks had been defeated and driven off. But some friendly remnants of other breeds were loitering about the town.

Carrying my valise, I began to look for a hotel for the night. Also, how and when was I to get to Jacksonville? A man came by. I hailed him and asked to be driven to a hotel. He walked with me north toward the river, past the fort and landed me at a hostelry built partly of logs and partly of frames. Surely this was not New York or Buffalo! As I came to the hotel I saw a man standing at the door, holding the bridle bits of an Indian pony. He came into the hotel soon, evidently after disposing of his charge. At that moment I was asking Mr. Wentworth, the hotel manager, how to get to Jacksonville. The man came forward and in the kindest of voices interrupted to tell me what the manager evidently could not. "I am going there myself to-morrow," he said. "You can ride behind. The pony can carry both of us." I looked at my new-found friend. He had deep blue eyes, a noble face, a musical and kindly voice. He looked like the people I had known in England. I was drawn to him at once in confidence and friendship. He went on to tell me later that he had been in the Black Hawk War; that he had been spending some time in Chicago trying to decide whether he would locate there or return to Jacksonville. He had been offered forty acres of land about a mile south of the river for the pony. But what good was the land? It was nothing but sand and scrub oaks. Unless the town grew and made the land valuable as building property, it would never be of value. For farming it was worthless. But around Jacksonville the soil was incomparably fertile and beautiful. He had decided, therefore, to return to Jacksonville. His eyes deepened. "You see that I am attached to that country." He smiled. "Yes, I must go back. Some one is waiting for me. You are heartily welcome to ride behind." How long would it take? A matter of five days. Meanwhile he had told me how to reach there independently: by stage to a place 90 miles south on the Illinois River, then by boat to a town on the river called Bath, then cross country to Jacksonville. I began to balance the respective disadvantages. "My name is Reverdy Clayton," he said, extending his hand in the most cordial way. I could not resist him. "My name is James Miles," I returned with some diffidence. "James Miles," he echoed. "James Miles ... there was a man of that name in Jacksonville, poor fellow ... now gone." "Perhaps he was my father ... did you know my father?" I felt a thrill go through me. Was this new-found acquaintance before me a friend of my father's? It turned out to be so. But why "poor fellow"?

Clayton was not over thirty-two, therefore my father's junior by some years.

How well had they known each other? We went to dinner together. We were served with bacon and greens, strong coffee, apple pie. It was all very rough and strange. But Clayton told me many things. He knew the lawyer Brooks who had written me. Brooks was a reliable man. But when I pressed Clayton for details about my father he grew strangely reticent. I began to feel depressed, overcome by a foreboding of wonder.

After dinner we separated. Clayton had errands to do preparatory to leaving and I went forth to see the town. What a spectacle of undulating board sidewalks built over swales of sand, running from hillock to hillock! What shacks used for stores, trading offices, marts for real estate! Truly it was a place as if built in a night, relieved but little by buildings of a more substantial sort.... Drinking saloons were everywhere. I heard music and entered one of these resorts. There was a barroom in front and a dancing room in the rear. The place was filled with sailors, steamboat captains and pilots, traders, roisterers, clerks, hackmen, and undescribed characters. Women mingled with the men and drank with them. They dressed with conspicuous abandon, in loud colors. Their faces were rouged. They ran in and out of the dance room with escorts or without, stood at the bar for drinks, entwined their arms with those of the men. In the dance room a band was playing. A man with a tambourine added to the hilarity of the music. It was a wild spectacle, unlike anything I had ever seen. No one accosted me. I could feel a different spirit in the crowd from that I had seen on the boats or in New York. There was no talk of politics, negroes, force bills. They did not seem to know or to care about these things. It was a wild assemblage, but without meanness or malice. They were occupied solely with a spirit of carnival, of dancing, drinking, of talk about the arrival of the *Illinois*; about the price of land and the great future of Chicago. "It's as plain as day," said a man at the bar. "Here we are at the foot of the lake. The trade comes our way. The steamboats come here from the East. Look at the country! No such farm country in the world! Why, in twenty years this town will have a population of 20,000 people. It's bound to." How could it be? How could such a locality ever be the seat of a city? So far from the East. And nothing here but wastes of sand!

I left the place unnoticed and returned to the hotel. I sat down drearily enough. The feeling that I was far from home, far even from the civilization and the charm of New York came over me with depressing effect. I began to wish that Clayton would appear. I had not decided to accept his kindly offer. I must be off to-morrow. The air seemed oppressive. Was it so warm? I put my hand to my brow. It was hot. Perhaps I was not well. The trip I had just ended was after all wearisome. I had not slept well some nights. I sensed that I was fatigued. What would a ride of more than 200 miles on a pony do to me? But on the other hand I had the alternative of 90 miles by stage. For the first time I began to feel apprehension about the days ahead.

While I was thinking these matters over Clayton came in. He supplemented my doubts by telling me that if I was not used to riding, a journey of such length would make me lame; at least a little. I then decided that I would take the stage, and the boat. The next morning, promising to see me in Jacksonville and offering to befriend me in any way he could, Clayton bestrode his pony and was off. In an hour I was rolling in the stage toward the Illinois River....

CHAPTER VI

We were some hours getting through the sand. Then we came to hilly country overgrown with oaks and some pines. Later the soil was rocky. We skirted along a little river; and here and there I had my first view of the prairie. The air above me was thrilling with the song of spring birds. I did not know what they were. Some of them resembled the English skylark in the habit of singing and soaring. But the note was different.

My head felt heavy. I seemed to be growing more listless. But I could not help but note the prairie: the limitless expanse of heavy grass, here and there brightened by brilliant blossoms. All the houses along the way were built of logs. The inhabitants were a large breed for the most part, tall and angular, dressed sometimes in buckskin, coonskin caps. Now and then I saw a hunter carrying a long rifle. The wild geese were flying....

Some of the passengers were dressed in jeans; others in linsey-woolsey dyed blue. As we stopped along the way I had an opportunity to study the faces of the Illinoisians. Their jaws were thin, their eyes, deeply sunk, had a far-away melancholy in them. They were swarthy. Their voices were keyed to a drawl. They sprawled, were free and easy in their movements. They told racy stories, laughed immoderately, chewed tobacco. Some of the passengers were drinking whisky, which was procured anywhere along the way, at taverns or stores. The stage rolled from side to side. The driver kept cracking his whip, but without often touching the horses, which kept an even pace hour after hour. We had to stop for meals. But the heavy food turned my stomach. I could not relish the cornbread, the bacon or ham, the heavy pie. When we reached La Salle, where I was to get the boat, I found myself very fatigued, aching all through my flesh and bones, and with a dreamy, heavy sensation about my eyes.

The country had become more hilly. And now the bluffs along the Illinois River rose with something of the majesty of the Palisades of the Hudson. The river itself was not nearly so broad or noble, but it was not without beauty.... More oblivious of my surroundings than I had been before, I boarded *The Post Boy*, a stern wheeler, and in a few minutes she blew the most musical of whistles and we were off....

The vision of hills and prairies around me harmonized with the dreamy sensations that filled my heavy head and tired body. I sat on deck and viewed it all. I did not go to the table. The very smell of the food nauseated me. I do not remember how I got to bed, nor how long I was there. I remember being brought to by a negro porter who told me that we were approaching Bath where I was to get off. I heard him say to another porter: "That boy is sure sick." And then a tall spare man came to me, told me that he was taking the stage as I was, and was going almost to Jacksonville, and that he would see me through. He helped me in the stage and we started. I remember nothing further....

I became conscious of parti-colored ribbons fluttering from my body as if blown by a rapid breeze from a central point of fixture in my breast. Was it the life going out of me, or the life clinging to me in spite of the airs of eternity? My eyes opened. I saw standing at the foot of the bed, an octoroon about fourteen years of age. She was staring at me with anxious and sympathetic eyes, in which there was also a light of terror. I tried to lift my hands. I could not. I was unable to turn my body. I was completely helpless. I looked about the room. It was small, papered in a figure of blue. Two windows stared me in the face. "Where am I?" I asked. "Yo's in Miss Spurgeon's house ... yo's in good hands." At that moment Miss Spurgeon entered. She was slender, graceful. Her hair was very black. Her eyes gray and hazel. Her nose delicate and exquisitely shaped. She put her hand on my brow and in a voice which had a musical quaver, she said: "I believe the fever has left you. Yes, it has. Would you like something to eat?" I was famished and said: "Yes, something, if you please." She went out, returning with some gruel. Turning to the octoroon she said: "Will you feed him, Zoe?" And Zoe came to the chair by the bed and fed me, for I could not lift a hand. Then I fell into a refreshing sleep. I had been ill of typhoid. Had I contracted it from the oysters, or from food on the steamer? But I had been saved. Miss Spurgeon had refused to let the doctor bleed me. She believed that careful nursing would suffice, and she had brought me through. But I had a relapse.

I was allowed to eat what I craved. I indulged my inordinate hunger, and came nearer to death than with the fever itself. But from this I rallied by the strength of my youth and a great vitality. All the while Zoe and Miss Spurgeon watched over me with the most tender care. And one day I came out of a sleep to find Reverdy Clayton by the bed.

A father could not have looked at me with more solicitude. His voice was grave and tender. His eyes bright with sympathy. "You will soon be well again," he said. He took my hand, sat down by me, cautioned me not to worry about my business affairs, told me that nothing would happen adverse to my interests while I was incapacitated, that Mr. Brooks was guarding my affairs and that they were not in peril.... And it turned out that Miss Spurgeon was his fiancee, that it was to her that he had returned from Chicago. They were soon now to be married. I asked him if Zoe was a slave. He laughed at this. "No one born in Illinois is a slave," he said. "This is a free country. Zoe was born here."

Miss Spurgeon came in and I could now see them side by side. They seemed so kind and noble hearted, so suited to each other. I loved both of them.

I was stronger now, was sitting up part of each day. I reached out my hands and took their hands, bringing them together in a significant contact. Miss Spurgeon bent over me, placing a kiss upon my brow. "You are a dear boy," she said. And Reverdy said: "The Lord keep you always, son." Their eyes showed the tears, and as for me my cheeks were suddenly wet. Then from what they said I learned that Reverdy had been gone many months, that Sarah, for that was her name, had been in great anxiety, that Reverdy had just got out of the service the morning I had seen him in Chicago; and that he had speculated on staying there a while for the purpose of improving his fortune with a view to his marriage. But now having returned, they were to be married soon. What had been the delay thus far? They were waiting for me to get well. I had interfered, no doubt, with the wedding plans, with the arranging and ordering of the house for the wedding. But they said they wished me to be present. Sarah thought there was something well omened in my meeting with Reverdy in Chicago, and in the fate that had brought me to her house, and she wished to fulfill the happy auspices to the end by having me for the chief guest at the wedding. But how had I come to this household?

The stranger who had helped me on the boat at Bath had turned me over to a young man named Douglas who had brought me here, because of the poor comforts at the inn of Jacksonville. Douglas had been here but a few months himself, having come from the state of Vermont. He, too, had been ill of the same disease; had been confined under wretched circumstances at Cleveland on his way west; had nearly died. When he saw me he was moved to do the very best for me. He had brought me to Miss Spurgeon's and pleaded with her to take me in. And she had consented to the ordeal of my care, because Zoe insisted upon it, offering to take the burden of waiting upon me and watching over me. The Spurgeon house was quite the best in this town of 1000 people. Sarah's father and mother were both dead, and she was living here with a grandmother, a woman now of more than eighty, whom I did not see until I began to go about the house.... Meantime Zoe's face and manner became clearer to me day by day. She was not very darkly hued, rather lighter than the Hindus I had seen in England. Her hair was abundant and straight. Her lips were full but shapely. Her nose rather of a Caucasian type. Her voice was the most musical one could imagine. And she sang--she sang "Annie Laurie" at times in a voice which thrilled me. There was grace in her carriage, charm in her gestures and movements. And she waited upon me with the affection of a sister.

As I grew better Mr. Brooks came to call upon me. And at last I went to his office to talk over the matter of my father's estate. It was now July and the heat was more terrible than I had ever conceived could prevail outside of a tropical country.

CHAPTER VII

Sarah and Zoe followed me to the door the morning I went to see Mr. Brooks. Cholera had descended upon the community and they begged me to go to Mr. Brooks' office and return at once, and not to be in the sun any more than was necessary. I had no fear. Having come from so serious an illness I did not feel that another malady would attack me soon. As I walked along I could see that the boundless prairie was around me. I inhaled the spaciousness of the scene. I could see the deep woods which stood beyond the rich prairies of tall and heavy grass. The town was built roughly of hewn logs. It was like a camp of hastily constructed shacks. But a college had already been founded. It had two buildings, one of logs and one of brick. I looked back to see that the Spurgeon house was substantially built, with care and taste.... Mr. Brooks' office was in one of the log structures about the square. One entered it from the street. I counted the signs of eleven lawyers on my way. The tavern where I had stayed, except for Douglas and Miss Spurgeon, was a most uninviting place.

Mr. Brooks sat behind a rude table. Back of him on a wall were a portrait of Washington and a map of Illinois. On the table there was a law book of some sort. Altogether there were three chairs in the room. The floor was made of puncheon boards, and was bare. Flies buzzed in the air and at the rude windows. I felt strong when I left the house. Now I was not sure how long I should feel so. Mr. Brooks invited me to have a seat; and after a few words about the heat and the cholera he began to tell me stories of the people and the country. "Some years ago," he said, "a man came to this country, I mean over around the river country which you saw when you took the steamboat at Bath. He didn't have anything, but he was ambitious to be rich. How could he do it? Well, you can work and buy land with your savings, and land here under the Homestead Act has been $1.25 an acre since 1820;

still that may not put you ahead very fast. And if you're ambitious you want to get rich quick. That's the way every one here feels who is bent on getting rich. Money is not as plentiful as land; and if land is only $1.25 an acre it takes $800 to get a section. That's a lot of money to a man who has nothing. This land around here is rich as the valley of the Nile. It is six feet or more of black fertility. I'll bet that some say it will be worth $50 an acre."

I began to wonder why these Americans talk so much. I had observed it everywhere. Here I was come on a matter of business, of my father's estate; and the lawyer with whom I was forced to deal was talking to me interminably of things that had nothing to do with it. But I was young and strange, and not very strong; and it did not occur to me to show impatience with him. And so he went on.

"This man was fine to look at, prepossessing and engaging. He looked like a driver, a man of his word too. And one day when he was standing on the street here he was approached by a stranger who began to get him into conversation. You see, we don't have slavery here as a regular thing. The negroes are sort o' apprenticed-- free but apprenticed. But under pretty severe laws, have to be registered, can't testify, and so forth. This state is part of the Northwest Territory which was made free by the old Confederate States in 1787; but we actually had an election here eleven years ago to make it slave. And the people voted it free. Anyhow we have negroes here; and the people are from Tennessee, Kentucky, Virginia, and the Carolinas where they do have slavery, and we're all beginnin' to be scared over the agitation. Now this stranger was a Southerner and any one could see he was; but of course didn't look different from some of our own people. So this stranger began to talk to this man and ask him if he was married, and he wasn't; and asked him if he would like to make some money, which of course he did.

"And finally the stranger said that he had a daughter that he would like to introduce, and asked this man to come with him a mile or so, and if he liked the girl he would pay him to marry her. They started off and found the girl. She was a mulatto or octoroon as they say, and as pretty as a red wagon. You see the stranger was pure white and from New Orleans; but the mother of the girl was a slave and they say kind of coffee colored. And the upshot of it was that the stranger offered this man $2500 to marry the octoroon. What he wanted to do was to place her well. He didn't want her to run the chance of ever being a slave, as she might be in the South.

He was her father and he naturally had a father's feeling for her, even if she was an octoroon. And this stranger said that he had been around town and the country for some days looking at prospective husbands and making some inquiry, and that he had found no one to equal this man. The man liked the octoroon, the octoroon liked the man. And they struck a bargain. The man got his $2500; he married the girl on the spot. The stranger disappeared, and was never seen or heard of again. It all happened right there. The man bought land, he got rich. He was one of the best men I ever knew, and one of my best friends. The octoroon died in childbirth, leaving a daughter still living and in this town. The man died recently. His name was James Miles. He was your father. And Zoe is your half-sister, and wants to share in the estate, and that's why I sent for you."

The flies began a louder buzzing at the window. The heat had increased. I looked through the open door and saw a man fall over, whether from heat or cholera I could not tell. I was by now weary and faint. I said: "I do not know what to say now. If we can agree, I mean if we are allowed to agree, Zoe and I will have no trouble. I am getting faint. And I shall come again." With that I arose and walked weakly from the room.

CHAPTER VIII

What were my thoughts after all? Was I ashamed of my kinship with Zoe? With this human being who had nursed me so tenderly through my illness? Did I begrudge her the interest which she had, of right, with me in our father's estate? She was as closely connected to him by ties of blood as I was. These things I reflected upon as I felt course through me a deep undercurrent of regret.

Was it my mother? Her face came before me as I had learned to know it from her picture. Yes, that seemed to be it. My mother had not been honored. How could my father for any ambition, for any exigency of circumstance stoop to a marriage of this sort, with the memory of my mother still fresh in mind, if not in heart? Ah! that was it! Did he keep her in his heart? My grandmother's reticence about my father began to fill in with significance of this sort. She knew that he had married the octoroon not many years after my mother's death. She resented it and she preserved silence about him, while keeping me ignorant. Thus without any preparation for the disclosure, I had encountered it at full speed in my career. Reverdy had, no doubt, alluded to this matter when he spoke with such feeling of my father in Chicago. "Poor fellow," he had said. Did my father suffer for this marriage? What was his secret? Why "poor fellow?"

With these thoughts I entered the house. I could sense that they knew that I should return with the secret which they had kept from me. Zoe was not in sight. Sarah's grandmother sat in her chair by the window and called me to her. "Come here, Jimmy," she said. "You're a nice English boy. You know we are all English. My father and mother were English ... well, to be truthful, my father was half Irish. His mother was Irish. And that makes us all friends, no matter how much we fight. We fight and get over it. My husband was in the Revolutionary War; and he's dead and gone long ago; and here I am in this new country of Illinois with Sarah and a son-in-law soon to be ... and maybe as lonely sometimes as you are. Sarah's mother was my pride and she's dead a long time too, but I don't get over that.... What's the matter, Jimmy? You've had bad news. O, yes, it had to come. You know now about Zoe. Well, remember that pretty is as pretty does. For that matter, she is pretty enough, and good enough too. Change her skin and any boy would be proud to be her brother. That's what a little color does. And yet the good Lord made us all, white as well as black. I have always liked the colored people. I liked them in Tennessee, and I hated to see them mistreated whenever they were. But I'm like a lot of others, I don't know what we are going to do with so many of them; and I say let the southern people run their own business and not try to intermeddle in the business of the Almighty. If He hadn't wanted slavery He could have prevented it. As for me, I don't want no slaves. Every one to his own way. Reverdy's father came down from Tennessee too. He emancipated all his slaves before coming. He grew to hate slavery. He brought one old nigger woman with him to Illinois. She's here yet, on a farm not more than fifteen miles away. And Reverdy's father provided for her, and left a little fortune to Reverdy ... more than $600, and that gives him a start."

The old lady talked on in this manner without a pause.

Just then Reverdy and Sarah came in. They had been for a walk. Sarah had gathered a bouquet of wild flowers. They took in the scene, evidently divined the subject of our talk. For Reverdy sat down and began with gentleness to pick up its threads. "You have been told, James, I hope, that Zoe is not trying to take anything from you. She will make no fight on your father's will." ... "Will," I echoed. "There was a will then?" "Didn't Mr. Brooks tell you?" ... He hadn't told me. He had scarcely had the opportunity. But if Zoe had been remembered in the will what was the danger now? "No, your father was fond of Zoe ... he remembered her; but not to the same extent that he remembered you. She gets $500 of the estate and you get the rest. But the hitch is here: we have eleven lawyers in Jacksonville and another one studying to be a lawyer; this newcomer, Douglas. And they are as hungry as catfish after a hard winter. And Mr. Brooks feared that some of these fellows would try to stir up a little business by using Zoe to attack the will, and he thought it was best to get it settled. He was a good friend of your father's, liked him, and he wants to see his wishes carried out. Your father was one of the best of men. It's a great loss to the community ... his death."

But as Zoe was my sister why should she not have some of the land that my father left? Should her dark skin deprive her of that? My father had evidently thought so. But now I could settle the estate by enforcing the will, or I could divide the estate with her equally. Could I enforce the will after all? I knew nothing of such things. I hadn't asked Mr. Brooks' advice about anything. There I sat then going over these matters in my mind, in a kind of weariness and sickness of heart. I had heard of cases where wills had been rejected for fraud or lack of mind on the part of the maker. Was it possible that my father's mind was disturbed? What fraud could have been wrought upon him? I, the chief beneficiary, had not influenced him; no one could have done so for me. What then?

Zoe came in now and began to spread the table. There was only the one large room downstairs beside the kitchen. But I loved its comforts, its quaint and substantial furnishings. All brought from North Carolina originally, Mrs. Spurgeon said. There were silver spoons, hand wrought; and blue china, and thick blue spreads for the table. There were three rooms upstairs. The beds were posters, built up with feather beds in the cold weather; spread now with thick linen sheets. Mrs. Spurgeon had woven some of these things. Her loom stood yet in one of the outhouses, on occasion set up in the living room when she brought herself to the task of weaving, rarely now. She was too old for much labor. Sarah helped Zoe with the meal. Reverdy stayed to share it with us. But I had learned that he lived at the tavern, though he disliked it thoroughly.

Some nights later I asked Zoe to walk out with me. She was timid about the rattlesnakes which she said were everywhere through the woods and the grass, sometimes crawling into the roads. There were wildcats and wolves too in the timber; but they were not so likely to be encountered now as in the winter time. I had a pocket pistol, and taking up a hickory stick that was in the corner, I urged Zoe to allay her fears and come. Sarah joined me in prevailing upon her. Zoe doubtless knew that I wished to talk with her about the estate; and at last she walked with me out of the house and into the road.

After a few minutes of silence I asked her about my father: what were his spirits; his way of life; where did he live; did she live with him? Then Zoe told me some of the things I had learned from Mr. Brooks. And as her mother had died when Zoe was born she had been taken by Mrs. Spurgeon to raise. She said that her father, my father, had lived a part of the time at the inn, and a part of the time at his house on the farm; that during the last two years of his life she had seen more of him than formerly, though he was often in St. Louis, and even New Orleans. And she added with hesitation that he drank a good deal at the last, and was often depressed and silent. "Was he kind to you?" I asked. Zoe said that he was never anything but kindness, and that he provided her with comforts and with schooling whenever any one came along to teach the children of the community. I had already seen around the house a copy of the *Spectator*, and Pope's poems. Zoe told me that she had read these books, part of them over and over, and that she had had a teacher the year before who had helped her to understand them. I began to delimn Zoe as a girl of intelligence. Of vital spirits she had an abundance.... The night was very warm and of wonderful stillness, no breeze. We heard the cry of what Zoe called "varmints" in the woods. A night bird was singing. She told me it was the whippoorwill. I never had heard a more thrillingly melancholy note. Once Zoe stepped upon a stick in the road. Thinking it was a snake she gave a cry and leaped to one side. But I calmed her and we kept our way.... I had never seen the stars to the same advantage, not even on the ocean. They were spread above us in infinite numbers, and of remarkable brilliancy. And there was the prairie, stretching as far as the eye could penetrate into the haze of the horizon, except where a distant forest rimmed the edge of the visible landscape. Zoe took up my remark about the spaciousness of the country with telling me that young Douglas had been to supper a few nights before I had come to myself out of the fever, and that he had said that the prairie affected him as liberty would affect an eagle released from a cage; and that he looked back upon the hills of Vermont as barriers to his vision. "He is nearly your age," said Zoe; "only two years older. You will like him; every one does. No one can talk like him that I have ever heard."....

At last I brought forward the subject of our father's will. Zoe was silent for a moment, for my specific question was what she wished to have done. Then she said: "It's all foolishness. These lawyers here have been bothering me to get me to fight the will, and trying to get me to break the will because my pa drank. I know he drank, but I don't see what difference that makes. He always knew what he was doing, so far as I know; and even if he didn't I'd never say nothin' about it. I know my place; and things is gettin' worse about colored folks, and less chance for a colored girl to marry a white man even if she wanted to, 'specially if I knew he was marryin' me to get my land. I'm satisfied with the will the way it is and always have been, or any way you want it, Mr. James. I know my place, and that there is a kind of curse on me for bein' dark skinned; and I think my pa was mighty kind to make the will the way he did. This **5000** acres he left is worth a lot of money, more than $5000 Mr. Reverdy says; and if I had what the will gives me I'd have $500, and what would I do with it? For I've always got to work anyway."

Suddenly we saw lights ahead in the road and heard the rattle of wheels. It was the stage coming into Jacksonville. It was upon us almost at once. The lights of the lantern made us blink our eyes. We stepped to one side. A voice called out: "Well I'll be damned if there ain't a white feller strollin' with a nigger!" "Shut your trap," said the driver, and the stage rolled rapidly away from us.

My mind was suddenly made up as to the farm by the remark falling so brutally from these unknown lips. I took Zoe's hands. I drew her to me. She was weeping. Was not one half of her blood English blood? Yes, and what Englishman would not resent with tears an insult which he could neither deny nor punish? But I would punish it. Zoe should have her rightful half.... And silently we walked back.

CHAPTER IX

The next morning the alarm over the cholera is more intense. All kinds of horrifying stories go the rounds. News has been brought by passengers on the stage that a man and his wife, living near the Illinois River, died within an hour of each other. They were well at dawn. At noon they were both under the black soil of the river's shore, buried by three stalwart sons, who carried their bodies in the bed clothing and let them down by it into hastily made graves.

Something has happened here. The stage driver who silenced the rowdies last night is stricken this morning at the tavern. He is dead. By noon he is buried in the village cemetery where the ashes of my father lie.

Mrs. Spurgeon thinks that Reverdy should leave the tavern and come here with the rest of us. I am to take the word to him when I go to see Mr. Brooks. She has seen the ravages of cholera before. There is nothing to do but to be careful about diet, keep cheerful, and surrender to no fears. I am not in the least alarmed. But the negroes are panic stricken. They are calling upon the Lamb to save them. They are singing and wailing. They are congregating at the hut of Aunt Leah, an aged negress, who is sanctified and gifted with supernatural power. Zoe is not in fear, and Sarah goes about the duties of the day with calm unconcern.

I am off to see Mr. Brooks again. The streets are almost deserted. The faces of those I meet are white and drawn. Mr. Brooks acts as if his mind is stretched out of him in apprehension. Yet he is in his office ready to pick up what business may come his way; and he is waiting to see me.

I tell Mr. Brooks at once that I want to divide the property equally with Zoe. He thinks, evidently, that I have weakened before the mere prospect of a contest; and he assures me that the estate can be settled as my father intended. Well, but can this plan of mine be carried out? As easily as the other, he says, and of course more bindingly if there can be a difference. For he had intended to have the court decree a sale of the property and divide the money under the sanction of the court. But according to my plan Zoe could get no more; and therefore no one could object to it.

I am curious about my father. What is the danger of a contest, even if Zoe could be brought to make one? Mr. Brooks tells me that my father was drinking heavily toward the last; that he looked aged and worn. His hair had turned white, though he was only forty. He acted like a man who had a corroding sorrow in his heart. When he took the cold it developed rapidly into lung fever. He was dead in three days. His will was made just as he took to his bed at the tavern. There were stray scamps about Jacksonville who would swear to anything. And though Zoe was a colored girl, and notwithstanding the character of such witnesses in her behalf, a case so composed might be troublesome. Then there was the treasure at stake; and the hunger of lawyers and maintainers. Well, I had settled it. None of these wolves should have a chance. Mr. Brooks scrutinized my face with large, pensive eyes. After a silence he said: "You are the boss; but I want you to know that the will can stand. I will guarantee to win the case if there is one." "Can we see the farm?" I asked. "And my father's grave?" Mr. Brooks brought up his buggy and we were off.

But first I wished to find Reverdy and give him Mrs. Spurgeon's message. He had gone out to his little farm. He was raising a crop, having returned from the war just in time to get it planted. It was only a little out of our way, and we could stop there on our return.

Almost at once we came to the cemetery, a crude enclosure, fenced with rough pickets, evidently split with the ax. Mr. Brooks led me to the spot.

Weeds abounded everywhere. The grasshoppers were flying before our steps. A long snake glided away from my feet as I stepped near the yellow clay which tented the body of my father ... and Zoe's father ... the husband of my lovely mother, so long dead. Here was the soldier of Waterloo, the adventurer into this Far West, the man who had died with some secret sorrow, or some sorrow for which he found no words or no confidant. Above me was the blinding sun, before me the prairie, at my feet this hillock of clay, where weeds had already begun to sprout. Mr. Brooks watched me; and seeing me move he started on; and I followed him through the broken gate to the buggy.

It was two miles to the log house which my father had built on his land. We drove up and went in. A tenant named Engle was living here with his wife and numerous children. Some of them crowded around us; others ran and hid, afterwards peered around the corner, timid and wild. Engle was not there; but his wife came from her washing to tell us where he could be found, what he was doing. When Mr. Brooks revealed to her who I was she stared at me with simple wondering eyes, drying her hands the while upon her apron. She was terribly upset by the reports of the cholera. Besides ... she went on: "There's a right smart lot of lung fever this summer. I 'low the men let their lungs get full of dust in the barn or somethin'. And I never did see the like of bloody flux among the children, and the scarlet fever too. We never had nothin' like that in Kaintucky. But I says to my man this mornin', there ain't nothin' to do but to stick it out. When yer time comes I guess there ain't no use ter run. And people do die in Kaintucky, too."

We proceeded to drive around the entire acreage. It took us some hours. Always the prairie, boundless and colorful. Miles of rich tall grass, sprinkled everywhere with purple, brick red, yellow, white, and blue blossoms! Billows of air drove the surface of it into waves. It was a sea of living green.

We passed forests of huge oak and elm trees, which grew along the little streams. There were many fields of corn, too, tall and luxuriant; and wheat ready for harvest. We came upon Engle at last. He wanted me to come close to see the corn. I got out and stood beside it, stroked its long graceful banners, turned up the dark soil with my boot and saw how rich and friable it was. And all this was mine, mine and Zoe's.

My imagination took fire. My ambition rose. I resolved to study the whole agricultural matter, and to reduce these acres in their entirety to cultivation. I would raise cattle and sheep. I would build fences. Above all I would make a house for myself. Here was my place in life and my work. No delay. I should begin to-morrow with something directed to the general end.

Returning we went past Reverdy's farm. But he had finished his work and gone to town. Accordingly we speeded up. When I arrived home I found Reverdy already there. But he would not leave the tavern. He gave no reason in particular. He said he was as safe there as anywhere; and it was more convenient for him.

But there was much doing. Sarah and Zoe were mixing the ingredients of a cake. A turkey was roasting; we were going to have a guest for supper. Douglas, the law student, the new school teacher, was coming; and all was delighted expectation. "For," said Mrs. Spurgeon, "I reckon we ain't never had such a young feller before around these parts. Talk! You never heard such talk. It flows just like the water down hill. And there never was a friendlier soul. I never thought they raised such people up in Yankeeland as him. You can bet he'll make his mark. He'll be a judge before he's ten years older; and they do well to get him here. And what I say is: where did he get his eddication? He is an orphan too, like you, James ... raised by an uncle so far as he had a raisin'. But the uncle fooled him. He promised him an eddication, and then went back on it. And what does young Douglas do? He busts away. He gets awful mad and comes west to make his fortune. Make a young feller mad, hurt him good and plenty, and if he has the right stuff you make a man of him. I've seen it over and over. When a young feller's mad and disappointed, if he's got the right stuff in him, he gets more energy, like a kettle blown off. They do, unless they sulk. Now there's other types. There was your poppy; he warn't mad and he didn't sulk exactly, and yet there was somethin'. He seemed to simmer and stew a little. But he left five thousand acres of land. Maybe he was one of these here big speculators like as is all over Illinois now, that has some kind of a different secret, and makes a big success some other way. You can never tell. But you see when Douglas came here he landed from Alton down here at Winchester and went right to work makin' a few dollars at a auction where he was a appraiser. And he worked at his trade too. For he's a cabinet maker. Yes, sir, he has a trade. With all the books he's read he has a trade. And now he's up here to look over the ground; for they say he's comin' here next spring to practice law, and even then he'll be only twenty-one."

Surely, this was a land of haste, of easy expedients. I did not know a great deal about the legal education of an English lawyer; but enough to appreciate the difference between the slow and disciplined training there and the rapid and loose preparation which I heard Mrs. Spurgeon describe with so much pride. I went into the corner of the room to write a letter to my grandmother.

CHAPTER X

This is the letter that I wrote:

"Dear Grandmama: I cannot describe to you the conditions that surround me. The boundless extent of the country, the wildness and beauty of the prairies, the roughness of this frontier town, above all the people themselves. The house I am living in is unlike anything you ever saw; but yet it is very comfortable. And my hostess, Mrs. Spurgeon, as well as her granddaughter, have treated me with all the consideration that my own kindred could do. I was very dangerously ill and they took care of me with wonderful solicitude; particularly Zoe, who nursed me and scarcely left my side. Now I am well, or nearly so, and they insist on my living with them. I pay two dollars a week, or about eight shillings. And everything is clean and nice; the food very good, delicious bacon smoked with hickory wood; but altogether the diet is unlike what I was accustomed to in England. It all seems like a story, first that I should meet Reverdy Clayton when I landed in Chicago from the steamboat which had brought me from Buffalo. He offered to bring me here on his Indian pony. But I was afraid to risk so long a ride, especially as at that time I was beginning to feel very badly. Then it is strange that I should get here and awake from an illness so serious in the house of Mrs. Spurgeon, whose granddaughter Sarah is going to marry Reverdy ... one never knows whether to attribute these things to Providence or to the accidents of life.... Perhaps you were right never to tell me about my father's marriage to the octoroon girl; but you must have known that I would find it out on arriving here. It has caused me much thought, if not disturbance of mind; but I have worked out my problems, perhaps impulsively, but still to my own satisfaction. Zoe is about the color of an Indian from Bombay. She is a beautiful girl, and shows her English blood in her manner and her active mind. I do not believe that there was the slightest danger that she would have attacked the will; but many considerations moved me to divide the estate with her equally. She took care of me with the most affectionate interest when I was ill. Besides, the land is not worth so very much, and one half of it will give her no fortune to mention. She is in danger even now, and the future for her is not reassuring. Illinois is supposed to be free territory, but it is not so many years ago that a vote was taken in Illinois to have slavery here, and it was defeated by no very great majority. And now the Illinois laws are rather strict as to colored people. The country is beginning to be feverish about the slavery question. I saw evidence of this in New York and on the way here; though just in this place the matter is not so much agitated. Yet the other day a copy of a periodical arrived here called *The Liberator*, and it made much angry talk. I will not tire you with this subject, dear grandmama, but only say that the effort here and everywhere in America seems to be directed toward hushing the matter up. But to return to Zoe: if her mother's father wished to secure the mother against misfortune by bringing her north and marrying her to a white man (my father, as it turned out) why should not I, her half-brother, try to protect her against the future that her mother might have incurred? I reason that I have taken the place of Zoe's grandfather, and must do for her what he tried to do for Zoe's mother. This inheritance of duty comes to me as the land comes to me, without my will. Zoe's grandfather gave my father his start, gave him the $2500 bonus to marry Zoe's mother. I think, in considering what share of the estate Zoe should have, these things cannot be ignored. Of course I don't know exactly how much of the $2500 went into this land. From things I have heard I think my father spent money freely; he went about a good deal and was not as temperate as he should have been for his own health and prosperity. Something was evidently preying upon his mind. Anyway, I have decided the matter, and I hope you will approve of me. I went to father's grave this morning, and it made me sad. Afterwards Mr. Brooks, the lawyer, drove me to the farm and around most of it. I am going to take hold of it at once. This country is growing rapidly, and I mean to do what my father didn't exactly. I am going to be rich; that is my ambition. And I must think and work. I am well again, or nearly so, and full of hope and plans, though sometimes lonely for you and for England. Some day I shall come back to see you. My love to you, dear grandmama. And do write me as often as you can.

"Affectionately, James."

And that evening Douglas came. He was of the smallest stature, but with a huge chest and enormous head. His hair was abundant and flowing, tossed back from his full forehead like a cataract. His eyes were blue and penetrating, but kindly. His face rather square. His voice deep and resonant. His words were clearly spoken, and fell from his lips freely, as if he were loosening them into a channel worn by long thinking. His ideas were clearly envisioned. He had read books of which I had never heard. But apart from books his sallies of wit, the aptness of his stories and allusions quite dazzled me.

Though he was but two years my senior, I felt like a boy in his presence. His maturity and self-possession and intellectual mastery of the hour kept me silent. He recalled what he had done to bring me to the comforts of Mrs. Spurgeon's house when I arrived in Jacksonville, ill and helpless. After that he did not exactly ignore me, but I seemed not to enter into the association of his ideas or their expression. He talked of the country. There was the matter of Texas, a territory half as large as central Europe. But if Texas seceded from Mexico he wished the country absorbed into the domain of the United States. Texas has a right to secede. All governments derive their powers from the consent of the governed. Let moralists and dreamers say what they would, the course of America was toward mastery of the whole of North America. Yes, and there was Oregon. If the Louisiana Purchase of 1804 did not include Oregon, what of the Lewis and Clark expedition; what of the founding of Astoria by Mr. Astor of New York, on the shores of the Columbia River; what of the restoration of Astoria to the United States in 1818 after it had been forcibly seized by Great Britain in the War of 1812? Douglas looked forward to the day when Great Britain would not have an inch of land from the Gulf of Mexico to the North Pole, and from the Atlantic to the Pacific. All of this vast territory should be the abiding place of liberty forever. Homestead laws should be passed with reference to it, and settlers invited to reduce it to cultivation. It should be tilled by millions of husbandmen, the most intelligent and progressive of the world. It should be crossed by railroads and canals. Already there were the Mohawk and Hudson railroad, the Boston and Albany, and the Baltimore and Ohio. Illinois should have railroads and canals; the rivers and harbors should be improved. Lake Michigan should be connected with the Mississippi River by a canal joining Lake Michigan with the Illinois River.

What was it all about? National wealth as a foundation for education, power, the supremacy of the white stocks having the greatest vitality.

Zoe was waiting upon the table, occasionally sitting down to take a bite. Douglas neither saw her nor was he oblivious of her. He talked ahead, referring now to the slavery question. He believed the North should leave the South alone. He had seen the reformer, the intermeddler, in his native lair in Vermont. Who had brought into this remote and peaceful town that copy of Garrison's *Liberator*? He was a half-cracked busybody. People who had no business of their own made the business of other people their business. He would put all such drivelers to work upon the roads, and thus make them contribute to the nation's wealth. He referred to the works of Jefferson, which he had read, to the *Federalist*, which he had read, and to much else, of which at that time I did not know a line. I studied Reverdy's face to see whether or not Reverdy concurred in what Douglas said. I had confidence in Reverdy, and was willing to go along with Douglas if Reverdy approved of these programs; although my English blood was stirred to some extent by Douglas' evident hostility to Great Britain. I sensed that Reverdy did not wholly agree with Douglas in all his theories and plans. But Reverdy knew that he could not cope with such a whirlwind as this dynamic logician. He therefore at times smiled a half disapproval, but did not express it. For myself I found my mind consenting to the magic of Douglas' vision. I did not relish the idea of England's surrendering Oregon; but, on the other hand, since my fortunes were cast in the United States, did it not behoove me to draw upon the country's increasing prosperity and to help to increase it? Texas did not matter. I did not fancy the institution of slavery. It grated upon my sensibilities; but I had a very slight understanding of it in the concrete. I was glad that England was rid of it. I had never admired the Wesleys, the Methodists; but I was glad to give them credit for what they had done to relieve England of such an abomination. I rejoiced that more than seven years before I was born Clarkson and Wilberforce had brought about the abolition of this traffic from the land of my nativity and its dependencies.

Then here was Zoe. If I was indifferent to slavery I had to be logical and be indifferent to her becoming a subject of barter. At least what, but a sentimental reason, could I set up against the enforced servitude of Zoe? What did it matter in point of justice and civilization that the South could not carry on her commercial interests without slavery? Was trade everything? Were the merchants the leaders of civilization? Were merchants to be permitted to do what they chose in order that they might create wealth for themselves, or even the nation? In a word, was wealth everything? My Adam Smith had said no, and I had already read that. He had classified banks of issue, colonialism, and slavery, as well as some other things as equal parts of a mercantile program. I was, therefore, inclined to dissent from any plan that included any one of these things. And still I was swept along by the torrent of Douglas' thinking. His vision enthralled me. His outlook upon the country, its increasing power and wealth, fascinated my imagination. Was I not resolved to be rich myself? And for moments I was under the spell of his great power. He was a world thinker, but with his own country forefronted in the playing of a colossal part. It appealed to my English blood, that blood which does great deeds through great vision, and then repents the iniquities along the way and corrects them at last. And who was Douglas in spirit? Nothing less than the English genius. And so my feelings were mixed, but admiration for him predominated. I felt his edge and did not like it; his audacity and resented it; his power and rebelled against it; his brusqueness and shrank from it; his emphasis upon power and supremacy, and felt that he might be overlooking finer powers and more lasting triumphs. But his eyes were full of kindly lights, in spite of their intellectual penetration; and he was charming to the last degree.

He stood up. I was a head taller than he. But his torso belonged to a giant, and his head. We all arose. And after a time, saying that he was spending his evenings in the study of law, he took his leave.

CHAPTER XI

The autumn was coming on. The cholera had abated. The air was cool and fresh. The country was taking fire from the colors of the changing year. And I was feeling more rugged than I had ever felt in my life.

As I have said, a college had already been founded in Jacksonville. Indeed, some years before my coming the one brick building on the campus had been constructed; and before that the log hut, also on the campus, in which the young president and his pretty wife had spent their first winter here in 1829. Reverdy told me that he had helped to hew and place the logs. I had become acquainted with Mr. Sturtevant, the president; for he was eager to hear of England, and Oxford and Eton. I was fascinated with this experiment of a college in the wilderness. He loaned me many books; and I often spent an evening at his house.

In September I decided to go out to the farm and live with the Engles. I had many plans for the spring which could be better attended to on the ground; and then I was getting ready to build me a house. Reverdy knew where to find the logs, how to prepare them. He knew where to get men to help him, and I was glad to leave these things to him. Mr. Brooks had already commenced proceedings to settle the title to the land, dividing it between Zoe and me. This was off my mind. I had men building fences, plowing. I was buying horses, cattle, hogs. In all these things Reverdy was an incalculable help. I could not have succeeded without him. He knew horses and he helped me to honest dealers.

One day I was walking over my land. I came to a beautiful grove of trees by the brook. And there in the midst of it was a log hut. I pushed the rude door open and entered. There was but one room. It had a fireplace needing repair. I saw a ladder in the corner, climbed it through a loft hole and looked into the loft. The rafters were rough and crooked, made only of undressed poles. I could see daylight through the shingles. The floor was of hewn planks. But I was elated. Why not come here to live? I did not like the Engle children. They were too numerous. I had no privacy there. But here! I could be to myself. I could make myself more comfortable than I was at the Engles'. I could have what food I wanted. I could kill game, for the country was full of it. I could bring my books. I could be a lord.

I hurried back to town to tell Reverdy; to ask him to help me to mend the fireplace, and to put the house in condition for the coming winter. Reverdy looked at me in astonishment. How could I stand the loneliness? Did I know what I was getting into? Could I take care of myself entirely? What if I fell ill again and in the middle of the winter, when the ways were snowbound?

I thought of Zoe. Why not take her with me? I could teach her. She could run the house. Reverdy looked at me with a certain dubiety. Sarah would hate to part with Zoe. Perhaps there were other things; but he did not express them. However, nothing could deter me.

Zoe was delighted with the plan. She wanted to get away, to be with me, since I wanted her. Besides, Reverdy and Sarah were to be married in a few days. He was coming to the house to live and that would make a difference in the conveniences. And Mrs. Spurgeon, as far as I could judge, was not averse to Zoe's departure. Thus it was to be as I wished.

Reverdy left off the work on my new house to help me repair the hut. We had to make a hearth. For this I found stones by the brook. We stopped the chinks between the logs with heavy, tough clay. We mended the holes in the roof. We repaired the floor. I bought beds and bedding, utensils for cooking, a rifle, an ax, and some other tools. I stocked the house with provisions. And in a week I was installed, listening at night to the cry of the wild animals, wolves and foxes and owls; and the song of late whippoorwills when an access of lingering summer warmed the midnights. I chopped my own wood. I killed quails and squirrels, and roasted them. I tried my hand at making cornbread. And I awoke in the delicious mornings, exuberant and happy. Zoe had not come to me yet, for she was staying on at Mrs. Spurgeon's until Sarah was married. And at last the wedding was celebrated.

I shall never forget that night. It was unlike anything of which I had ever heard. The town minister performed the ceremony. Mr. and Mrs. Sturtevant were present. Douglas had been invited; but whether he failed to get the message, or whether his new duties of teaching at Winchester prevented him from coming I do not know. We missed him greatly. An emergency arose in which his courage and gift of speech might have been of use. I can imagine how he would have handled the crowd that assembled outside while the wedding was in progress. In short, we were treated to a shivaree, or ***charivari***.

No sooner had the clergyman pronounced the final words than the most unearthly noise broke loose right at the door. There was the sound of tin pans, kettles, horns, drums; and this pandemonium was punctuated by the firing of shots and the throwing of stones at the door and gravel upon the window panes. Sarah, already flushed from excitement, took on an expression of alarm. I thought that we had been attacked by a band of Indians bent upon massacre. The clergyman, however, smiled. And Reverdy left the side of his bride and went to the door.

He flung it open. And there burst upon my vision the wildest assemblage of faces I had ever seen. Some were blacked to resemble the negro. Some were painted to look like the Indian on the warpath. They were dressed fantastically, in a variety of colors, with feathers in their hair or hats or coon caps. They leered, grinned from ear to ear. They yelled, and again began to beat their pans and kettles and to fire their rifles. Sarah put her fingers to her lips in a gesture of terror, of violated privacy. But after all this was but the frontier's hymeneal chant, the festivities of the uninvited wedding guests. To quiet them it was necessary to ask them to partake of the wedding delicacies.

They pushed and writhed into the room. Some of them were half drunk. They trod upon each other. What they might have done if Reverdy had not managed them out of the kindness of his heart and with a certain adroitness is past conceiving. It seemed to me that a riot was on the point of breaking loose at any minute. But having satisfied themselves, they began to file out. Some lingered to wish the bride and groom a happy life. Reverdy spoke with each one in such friendliness of voice and manner, in which there was neither nervousness nor resentment. He took it all as a matter of course. But Sarah was visibly distrait. I could see that she was relieved as they began to depart. A few yells, a few intermittent shots marked their going away. Then all was silent. The guests now began to leave. And as I was going back to my hut for the night I came to Reverdy and Sarah to bid them God-speed. I had never seen Sarah look so charming. Her bridal dress was made of striped calico. She had a bonnet to match. Reverdy had a new suit of blue jeans. He looked handsome and strong. And he turned his eyes upon Sarah with a look of protecting tenderness. I took their hands in mine to emphasize my blessing with the closeness of affectionate contact. Sarah kissed me on the cheek; and I left, bestriding my horse at the gate, and riding through the darkness to my hut.

Zoe was to come to me the next morning.

CHAPTER XII

The next morning while I was sitting near the door, cleaning my rifle, I heard the soft pounding of a horse's hoofs on the heavy sod, and looking up saw Reverdy and Sarah. He was in the saddle, she was riding behind. I was about to ask for Zoe when I saw her peeping mischievously around the shoulder of Sarah, showing her white teeth in a happy smile. It was not Reverdy's Indian pony that was carrying so many travelers, but a larger horse. They all got down and came in to see my hut. Sarah was greatly pleased with it, and Zoe could not contain her delight. Reverdy and Sarah were on their way to Winchester to pay a brief visit to Sarah's aunt. They were soon off, Reverdy giving me the assurance that it would only be a few days before he would again be at work on my new house. Meanwhile the other men would continue getting the logs.

Zoe did not delay a minute in taking charge of the house. I had not cleared the breakfast table. She did so, then made my bed. I told her to spread it with clean sheets as it was to be hers now, but she would not hear to this. She was afraid to be on the ground floor where an intruder could walk in upon her, or a stray wolf push the door open and wake her with its unfriendly nose against her cheek. I told her then to look at the loft. She climbed the ladder and took a peek, descended with the remark that she liked it and would take it for hers. Almost at once we had perfect order in the hut.

Zoe cooked, and cleaned the rooms. I was busy with my new dwelling. I killed enough game to keep us in meat. Sometimes standing in the doorway I could bring down a deer. Then we had venison. But we were never without quail and ducks and geese. Zoe made the most delicious cornbread, baking it in a pan in the fireplace. The Engles brought us some cider. I had bought a fiddle and was learning to play upon it. We never lacked for diversion. In the evenings I played, or we read. My days were full of duties connected with the new house, or the crops and improvements for the next year. And spring would soon be here.

I was beginning to be looked upon as a driving man. They had scoffed at me as a young Englishman who could not endure the frontier life, and who knew nothing of farming. But they saw me take hold with so much vigor and interest that I was soon spoken of as an immediate success. My coming to the hut and living and doing for myself had helped greatly to confirm me in their esteem. I saw nothing hazardous or courageous in it. As for the daily life I could not have been more happily placed.

The fall went by. The winter descended. The brook was frozen. I had to break the ice with the ax to get water. I had to spend an hour each day cutting wood for the fireplace and bearing it into the hut. These were the mornings when the cold bath, which I could never forego, no matter what the circumstances were, tested my resolution. For I was sleeping in the loft where the bitter wind fanned my cheeks during the night. Zoe had found it too rigorous, and preferred the danger of an intruder to the cold. Even snow sifted on my face from rifts in the shingles which we had overlooked. But nevertheless I adhered to the morning lustration, sometimes going to the brook to do it. I had never experienced such cold.

Yet the months of November and December, which at the time I thought were the extreme of winter weather, were as nothing to the polar blasts that poured down upon us in January and February. I had no thermometer. But judging by subsequent observations I am sure that the temperature reached twenty degrees below zero. I took no baths in the brook now but contented myself with a hurried splash from a pan. At night I covered myself with all the blankets that I could support. I protected my face with a woolen cap, which was drawn over the ears as well. Zoe, though sleeping near the immense fire which we kept well fed with logs, got through but a little better than I. We heated stones in hot water to take to bed with us. All kinds of wild animals coming forth for food were frozen in their tracks. I found wolves and foxes in abundance lying stiffened and defeated in the woods. Some nights, seeing the light of our candle they would howl for food and shelter; and I heard them run up and down past the door, wisping it with their tails. Then Zoe would cling to me. And I would take up the rifle in anticipation of the wind opening the door and admitting the marauder. We were snowbound the whole month of February. I had to shovel a path to the brook. But it was out of the question for any one to go to town, or for any one to come to us. And of course during these bitter days nothing was done on my new house. The logs were all cut. They stood piled under the snow, except for a few that had been put in place.

One brilliant morning in the last of February I had gone to the brook for water. The cold had moderated to some extent. But the snow remained deep in the woods and on the fields. For though the sun shone, the sky was nevertheless hazed with innumerable particles of frozen mist, having the appearance of illuminated dust, or powdered mica. Somewhere in the depths of this screen I heard the joyous cry of a jay. And Zoe, who was by my side, said that spring was at hand.

The next day the air was milder. Soon the snow began to melt. We heard musical droppings from our eaves. The brook broke from its manacles. I could see patches of dead grass and dark earth between the disappearing snow on the fields. At break of day we heard the chirrup of the chickadee, the sparrow. I now resumed my plunge at the brook. And as we were depleted of cornmeal and other provisions, Zoe and I went to town, riding one of the horses which Engle had brought over to me. Bad news waited us here. Mrs. Spurgeon had died during the bitter weather, about three weeks before. Sarah was very much depressed. And Reverdy seemed almost as unhappy over the loss.

He had much to do, but he would now set to work upon my house.

Soon he came out bringing the men. I had made a drawing for the work and I was much about watching to see that it was followed. We could have had bricks for the chimney, though it was a good deal of labor to haul them. But why not a chimney of stone? There were plenty of stones of adequate size along the bed of the brook. And so we used them. But I did buy lumber for the floors. I sent to St. Louis for the kind of doors I wanted, and windows too. I was having a house built with regard to roominess and hospitable conveniences; a large living room, two bedrooms, a dining room, a kitchen, downstairs. The second floor was to have four chambers. I had selected a site back from the road. It was in a grove of majestic oaks, not far from the brook and the hut. The work progressed none too rapidly. Some of the men had to be away at times to attend to their farming. As for myself I had learned to plow, and was at it from early morning until sundown. I had many laborers working for me, plowing, sowing, building fences, clearing; in a word, reducing the land to cultivation. It was a big job.

I had won the respect of the community by the energy with which I had undertaken the task. The neighbors said I was an improvement on my father. They wondered, however, if I would be as far-sighted and acquisitive as he, if I would add to what I had or lose it.

In March I had a letter from my grandmother. She expressed pride in me for what I had done, approved the spirit I had shown towards Zoe. She was a great admirer of Wilberforce; and as she disliked America for its separation from the Crown she wished the institution of slavery no good on these shores. But she was disturbed about the conditions in England and Europe. The old order seemed to her to be crumbling. Revolution might break forth. The middle classes in England, having secured their rights, as she expressed it, the laborers were now striving for the franchise. Chartism was rampant. What would it all come to? Was England safe against such innovation? But how about America, if the colored people were given freedom, not of the franchise merely, but in civil rights of property and free activity? But contemporaneous with this letter, two events came into my life of profound influence. One was my meeting with Russell Lamborn, the son of one of Jacksonville's numerous lawyers. And the other was an extraordinary debate between a Whig politician named John J. Wyatt and young Douglas. It was at the debate that I met Lamborn.

Douglas had finished his school teaching. He had been licensed to practice law, though not yet twenty-one years of age. He had opened an office in the courthouse at Jacksonville. His sharp wit, pugnacity, self-reliance, had already excited rivalry and envy. He had suddenly leaped into the political arena, carrying a defiant banner.

Affairs in America were no more tranquil than they were in England. President Jackson had stirred the country profoundly by his imperious attitude toward the banking interests on the one hand, and the matter of South Carolina's nullification of the tariff law on the other hand. This had weakened the Democratic party in Illinois. And as there was to be an election in the fall of state officials, it was necessary to success to satisfy the electorate that President Jackson had not betrayed his leadership.

Bantering words went around to the effect that Douglas was seizing the opportunity of this debate to make himself known, to get a start as a lawyer, and a lift in politics. When a chance to make a hit fits the orator's opportunity and convictions, it would be difficult for a man of Douglas' enterprise and audacity to resist it.

For Douglas had, in spite of everything, captured the town. His name was on every one's tongue. He had lauded President Jackson and his policies with as much fervor as he had with virulence and vehemence denounced the humbugging Whigs, as he had characterized them. The village paper, a Whig publication, had sat upon him. It had dubbed him a turkey gobbler, a little giant, a Yankee fire-eater. But Douglas gave no quarter to any one. He returned blow for blow. He had become a terror. He must be subdued.

John J. Wyatt, a man of ready speech, in the full maturity of his powers, a debater and campaigner, a soldier in the War of 1812, and a respected character, was to lay the adventurer, the interloper, low! He was elected to the task. Was Douglas a youth? No. He was a monstrosity. He had always been a man. He had never grown up. He had simply appeared in this part of the world, a creature of mature powers. Yet Wyatt would subdue him.

We were all in anticipation of the contest. It was to take place in the court-house. What was the subject? Anything. Everything. Chiefly Whiggery and Democracy. I came into town bringing Zoe and leaving her with Sarah. Reverdy and I went together. Here I met Russell Lamborn. He sat on one side of me and Reverdy on the other.

I shall never forget this night. Wyatt opened the debate, and he closed it. The question was: Are the Whig policies best for the country? Douglas had the negative and, therefore, but one speech. Was it fair? Had not the young man given away too much? No, for Douglas proved a match for two or three such minds as Wyatt's. He humiliated to the last degree the older, and at first confident, antagonist.

It was the most extraordinary exhibition of youth and dash and confidence and ready wit, and knowledge and dialectic handling of difficult matter. It furnished the groundwork of my education in the history of American politics up to that time. It led into almost every possible matter of constitutional law and party policy.

Wyatt talked for an hour. He jeered at Douglas. He referred to his diminutive stature. He spoke ironically of his work as a cabinet maker, and advised Douglas to stick to it and leave the profession of the law alone. He characterized him as a strolling fellow who was trying to break into the favor of the community with an impudence as effective as burglar's tools. What did Douglas know of law? Who would trust his interests to a lawyer so inexperienced? When had Douglas had time to master its simplest principles? Who could not see through Douglas' thin scheme to attach his fortunes to the chariot of the great but misguided Jackson? Why had Douglas leaped to the defense of Jackson in this community, like a fice coming to the aid of a mastiff? Why, if not to get a bone for his own hungry stomach? Everything in the way of a taunt, a slur, a degrading image, a mockery of youth's ambition, an attack upon obscurity trying to rise, were thrown by Wyatt at Douglas. All the while Douglas sat imperturbed, his head at a slight angle, which gave him the appearance of attentive listening; and with a genial smile on his face that was lighted a little with ironic confidence. Then Wyatt sat down amid great cheering.

Reverdy thought that Wyatt had overdone himself, had forfeited to a degree the sympathy of the audience. There was no call for such rough handling of a young man. The feelings of the crowd reacted. And as Douglas arose he was given a loud reception. For there were Democrats enough in the room. But though Douglas looked like a man while seated, he seemed a boy when he stood up. His stature told against him. But as soon as he spoke the first word the silence was profound. The voice was the voice of a man, and a strong man. It rolled over our heads with orotund volume. The clearly syllabized words fell upon delighted ears. He caught the crowd at once.

Who would dare accuse him of subserviency to Jackson or to any man, for bread or for position? He differed from Jackson about the tariff, and all Jacksonville could know it. He agreed with Jackson about the bank, and the whole country would come to approve Jackson's course. Was nullification right? Perhaps Jefferson knew as much about that as Mr. Wyatt. Let the laws of the Constitution be obeyed and nullification would never be provoked. What had created nullification? The vile policies of the humbug Whig party, the old monarchist harlot masquerading in the robes of liberalism. How did these people dare to use the name of Whig, how dare to resort to such false pretenses, when it was common knowledge that the personnel of that party, having been put down as Federalists for gross usurpation and monarchist practices had, being forced to change their skin, adopted the title of the liberal party of England, remaining more Tory than the party that tried to destroy American liberty during the Revolution? And now this Whig party like a masked thief was abroad in the land to pick up what spoils it could, and to take from trusting hearts sustenance for its misbegotten existence. It was already beginning to coquette with the slavery question, hoping to deceive the people with humanitarian and moral professions. Very well! If it was the Good Samaritan it pretended to be let it give up its bank and its tariff, which took enough money out of the mouths of the poor to feed all the niggers in the world. Let the whiner about wrongs quit his own wrongs. Let the accusing sinner repent his own sin. Let the people of New England pluck the pine logs from their own eyes before talking of hickory splinters in the eyes of the South.

And then Douglas took up the history of the formation of the Union. What went into the Union? Sovereign states. Who concluded a treaty of peace with Great Britain after the Revolution? The thirteen sovereign states that had waged the war. Who formed themselves into the Confederate States, each retaining its sovereignty? The same states. Who left that union and formed the present Union? The same states. What did they do? They retained all the sovereign powers that they did not expressly grant. They never parted with their sovereignty, but only with sovereign powers. Where does sovereignty reside under our system? With the people of the states. What follows from all of this? Why, that each state is left to decide for itself all questions save those which have been expressly given over to Washington to decide. Who is trying to nullify these inestimable principles and safeguards? That is the real nullification. The humbug Whigs, who would like to centralize all authority at Washington ... "and Mr. Wyatt here in this new country, among people of plain speech and industrious lives, is the spokesman of these encroaching despotisms, which he has vainly attempted to defend to-night. He dares to assail the great name of Andrew Jackson. He would like to overcome the state sovereignty which permits Connecticut to raise cranberries and Virginia to have negro slaves, which leaves Kentucky with whisky and Maine with water, if Maine ever chooses so. He does not know that the French Revolution was waged for the great principle of the people to rule; and he fails to see that the whole world is coming to accept that doctrine. With the growing wealth and power of the North, of Illinois, it is necessary that the rights of the individual and local communities and of the small states as well as the large states should have the effectual counterbalance of state sovereignty to protect them against the ambition of centralists, who are money grabbers wrapping themselves about with the folds of the flag and with the garments of superior holiness."

He wished to see Illinois crossed by two railroads, from north to south, and from east to west. He would see the Illinois and Michigan canal completed, so that the great lake at the north of the state would be connected with the Mississippi River and with the Gulf of Mexico. What did it mean? The state would fill up with earners of wealth. Lands would increase in value. Cities would be built. As for himself, he would do his utmost to bring these benefits to the state.

By what authority was his right challenged to come to this state to make his home; and to this town to follow the profession of the law? Was there any one present who did not wish him to strive for these achievements for this western country? Perhaps Mr. Wyatt objected. No matter. He was here to stay. He had left a land walled in by hills and mountains, where the eye was deprived of its use in forming a vision of the world. Here he had found his mind liberalized, his vision quickened. Here he had found a hospitable people, inspired with hope of the future. And he was glad he had cast his lot with theirs. He had grown in this brief time to feel that they were his people. And he asked them to adopt him as their son, trusting him not to forget his filial duties.

The crowd was completely amazed at the vigor and fluency of Douglas' speech. Such applause arose that Wyatt was visibly embarrassed as he stood up for his rejoinder. He saw that Douglas had carried the day. He made a feeble attempt at reply. He tried satire; but it fell on unreceptive ears. He dropped denunciation. He dared not attempt that. He took up logical analysis. It left the audience cold. He pecked timidly at the doctrine of state sovereignty. Then voices began to question him. He shifted to Jackson. But the audience would not listen. After using one half of the hour allotted him for a conclusion, he sat down half wilted and discomfited.

A storm of cheers arose for Douglas. He was surrounded by a host of admirers. And I saw him now in a new phase. He was winning and gallant, of open heart, of genial manner. When he saw me he smiled a warm recognition. I went to where he stood to offer my congratulations. I asked him to come out and see me, and have a meal with me. He was already mingling with the young people of his own age at dances and in sports. That had been his custom at Winchester. He was glad to come, inquired the way. He was very happy. He knew that he had won his spurs this night. And from thenceforth he was a notable figure. Had anything just like this ever occurred in England? I had never heard of it. I should certainly write my grandmama of this event.

CHAPTER XIII

Russell Lamborn left the courthouse with Reverdy and me. He lingered at the gate as if he wished an invitation to go into Reverdy's house; but Reverdy did not invite him. He would have asked Douglas to come in for the remainder of the evening, such as it was, except for Sarah's condition.

Douglas had quite carried Reverdy away. And yet there lurked in him something that was not intellectually convinced and morally satisfied. I felt a little the same way. I did not know how to describe my state of mind. With Douglas' vision of the country, his hopes for it, the part he wished to play, I felt my English blood stir. But was there enough moral depth to him? Did he reckon enough with the forces which made for culture, enlightenment? Was he really high-minded? Did he not have the gesture and the touch of the magician, the abandonment of the indifferent demigod--indifferent to the higher and the deeper currents of man's life? I tried to formulate some of these nebulous ideas to Reverdy, but found myself running into denials, facts of contradiction in Douglas' attitude and thinking. Reverdy was equally unable to state the case against Douglas, which he felt a keener critic of thought would easily do. Meanwhile young Lamborn stood with us while we fumbled these doubtful things. He seemed reluctant to leave. I wondered in a vague way what kept him from going. What did he want?

And when Douglas did come to see me, which was within a few days of the night of the debate, Lamborn came with him. It was in the afternoon and they were on their way to a country dance. I could not help but observe that Lamborn had been drinking. What a strange taste--this whisky drinking! We did it in England, to be sure. But here it was done everywhere and at all hours and in all degrees of immoderation and vulgarity. Lamborn, however, was not unduly under the influence of drink; he was rather laughing and genial and humorously familiar. Douglas had doubtless taken as much as Lamborn, but he was quite equal to resisting its relaxing effects.

Douglas and I sat under a tree by the brook. The buds were coming out. There was the balmy warmth of spring in the air. I had a chance now to revise my first impressions of him. His charm could not be denied. His frankness, the quickness of his thought, his intellectual power, his vitality, his capacity for work, the tireless-ness of his energies, were manifested in his speech, his movements, the clear and rapid glances of his eyes.

At the same time I found angles to him. I sensed a ruthlessness in him. I saw him as a fearless and sleepless antagonist, but always open and fair. There was only once when his nature broke ground and revealed something of his inner self, some-thing of a sensitiveness which suffers for subtler things and penetrates to finer un-derstandings. This was when he was telling me of the effect of his uncle's broken promise to educate him. He had suffered deeply for this; and he was sure his whole life would be influenced by it. It had stirred all the reserve ambition and power of his nature. It had thrown him forward in a redoubled determination to overcome the default, to succeed in spite of the lost opportunity.

Hence he had read many books. He had studied the history of America, and other countries as well. His mind ran to statecraft. He thought of nothing else. He sensed men as groups--thinking, desiring, trading, building--and for these ends or-ganized into neighborhoods, villages, cities, and states. His genius, even then, was interested in using these groups for progressive ends, such as he had in view. He was a super-man who sees empires of progress and achievement for the race through the haze of the unformed future, and who takes the responsibility of carving that future out and of forcing history into the segment that his creative imagination has opened. He would guide and make the future, while serving men.

Here he was then just past twenty-one, born on April 23d, the reputed birth-day of Shakespeare; young, and yet old with a maturity with which he was invested at his entrance into the world. He was in every way a new type to me. We were mutually drawn to each other. I knew that his courage could never stoop to little-ness. His integrity, even when his judgment might err, seemed to me an assured quality of nature. As for me, he doubtless thought that I was one of the coming men of the community. Whatever I was, I was dependable. If I should become attached to him he could rely upon me in case of need. This, I think, made him regard me at this early stage of our friendship as a person not to be neglected in his business of creating adherents. When I spoke to him in terms of wonder and congratulation of his defeat of Wyatt, he took it with a smile and as a matter of course. He had found it an easy thing to rout Wyatt. Wyatt had stirred his fighting blood; and everything pertinent to the discussion had come to his mind in the heat of the debate....

And now we began to hear the sound of a fiddle, scraped in a loose and erratic fashion and giving forth an occasional note of a tune. I looked around and saw Lamborn sitting in the doorway of the hut. Zoe was near him, laughing at his half-drunken attempts to manage the instrument. Douglas looked up. A quick smile shot across his face. He glanced into my eyes in a searching manner which mystified me and sent a sudden thrill through me. What was he thinking? Surely he knew of my relation to Zoe. I caught out of his expression the prejudice of the time against the social equality that I was maintaining in standing by Zoe and having her with me. I had not shirked my heritage. Perhaps Douglas admired me too much to speak what was in his mind; or perhaps he was too much of the politician to trench upon ground so personal. At all events, we were silent for a moment. And then Douglas called to Lamborn. It was time to go. Lamborn rose to his feet, swaying a little as he did so, and came to where we sat. He looked me over in a scrutinizing way, then shot forth his hand for me to take it. It was an awkward act and out of place! Yet I felt compelled to give him my hand. And with good-bys they bestrode their horses and were gone. I began to have ominous reflections.

I went to the hut and asked Zoe what Lamborn had been saying to her. She laughed and seemed reluctant to tell me. I pressed her then; and she said that he had followed her through the house and tried to kiss her; that she had come around to the front door so as to be in sight of Douglas and me; then that Lamborn had taken the fiddle down and had begun to play it.

All the possibilities of Lamborn's attitude dawned on me instantly. How dearly might I pay in some way for my father's desire to be rich! If Douglas had taken his initial hurt in life from his uncle's failure to educate him, I had begun the weaving of my destiny with these threads which my father had bequeathed to me. What would my complications be if Zoe eloped with a wild fellow like Lamborn, bringing his personality into the texture of my affairs; the matter of this land, and Zoe's interest in it? I could sense ahead an unending difficulty, an ever deepening annoyance, or even tragedy. Had I gone too far in dividing the estate with Zoe? For the first time the presence of the negro in the state, the complications that it created, were forced upon me concretely and with impressive effect. My heart registered a vague apprehension. I warned Zoe against Lamborn, and decided that he should not come about me again.

The work on my house was now progressing rapidly. I wished to move into it on my birthday, June 18th. I watched its completion day by day, and in addition I had much to do around the farm. I had made a start with a few calves toward raising cattle. In every way I was forging ahead as fast as I could. But my greatest delight was the house. I wanted to make it as beautiful as possible, and I did not need to spare expense. I decided to go to St. Louis for curtains and chairs, for beds and lounges, chests and bureaus. When the last of May came I set out for the city.

CHAPTER XIV

This June weather in Illinois! Such glorious white clouds floating in the boundless hemisphere of fresh blue! The warmth and the vitality of the air! The glistening leaves of the forest trees! The deep green shading into purples and blues of the distant woodlands! The sweet winds, bending the prairie grasses for miles and miles! Glimpses of cool water in little ponds, in small lakes, in the brook! The whispering of rushes and the song of thrushes, so varied, so melodious! The call of the plowman far afield, urging the horses ahead in the great work of bringing forth the corn! The great moon at night, and the spectacle of the stars in the hush of my forest hut!

I was superbly well. And for diversion went farther into the woods to hear a fiddler and to have him teach me the art which fled my dull fingers and the un-wieldy bow. And this fiddler! His curly hair, always wet from his lustrations for the evening meal; his cud of tobacco; his racy locutions; his happy and contented spirit; and his merry wife and the many children, wild like woodland creatures, with sparkling eyes and overflowing vitality! Many evenings I spent at this fiddler's hut. And such humbleness! Only the earth for a floor! Only one room where all his family ate and slept and lived!

In going to St. Louis I took the same stage that had brought me to Jacksonville. This time I rode on the *City of Alton*, a better boat than the one that had brought me from La Salle to Bath; but all the conditions were the same. There was the same roistering and sprawling crowd; the same loudness and profanity; the same abundance of whisky and its intemperate indulgence; the same barbaric hilarity of negroes, driven and cursed. And now many goatees, and much talk of politics, of Whigs and Democrats.

St. Louis was languid, weary and old. The buildings had an air of decay. The stream of life moved sluggishly, not swiftly as in New York or Buffalo, or even in the village of Chicago. There were luxury here and wealth. There were slaves and a slave market. I went to it, saw the business of selling these creatures, saw a woman of thirty, no darker than Zoe, sold to a man with a goatee, evidently from further south, who took her and led her away submissively. Whatever the institution might be of necessity and even of gentleness in good hands, here no less was the vile business of the sale. What would become of Zoe, was constantly in my thought. I turned away from the slave market to continue my shopping; but I could not drive Zoe from my thoughts.

Here was I in St. Louis and necessarily withdrawn from care of Zoe. I could not always watch over her. Even if I did, what was her life to be? How could she establish herself? With whom, and where? I was glad that I had not left her at the hut during my absence, that I had taken her to Sarah. Nothing could happen to her while she was with Sarah. Sarah had need of her too. Sarah's baby was soon to be born. Dorothy Clayton, Reverdy's sister, was coming to Jacksonville from Nashville to be a part of Reverdy's household for a time; and the house had to be set in order for her arrival. Turning Zoe over to Sarah was, therefore, a great help to her at this time.

I completed my purchases, arranged for their transportation and returned to Jacksonville. I arrived in the evening and went at once to Reverdy's. I had been gone a week. All were here to greet me. But Zoe was subdued in manner. Her smile was forced. She avoided me, going in and out of the room about the work of clearing the table. She did not pause to listen to the story of my trip. Was she perhaps ill? Reverdy and Sarah prevailed upon me to stay over night. And I did; but early the next morning all of us went to the country together; for Reverdy was now pushing the house to completion.

When we arrived at the hut, as Zoe remained silent and subdued, I began to question her. She protested at first that nothing was the matter; but I knew better, and I persisted in my attempts to draw her out. She began to cry at last. She came to me and rested her head on my shoulder. "Tell me now," I urged. And she relieved herself of the secret in broken words, in half-formed phrases.

She had gone walking one night with Lamborn. He had led her into the woods in search of a rabbit's nest he said was there. He had seized her, put his hand over her mouth, threatened her with harm, with being sold down South. He had overcome her. She had returned to Reverdy's afraid to tell him what had happened. She did not know what Lamborn would do to her if Reverdy went after him. She felt that she was in the wrong for having gone walking with Lamborn, and that she would be blamed by Sarah. Therefore she had not told her secret before. She was sure that neither Sarah nor Reverdy suspected it.

What was I to do? I could not conceive of a wrong like this going unpunished. But my brain refused to plan, to think out what was best to do. I did not know the community well enough, nor enough of the laws to make a decision by myself. I decided that I must consult with Reverdy. I hurried away from Zoe, telling her on no account to leave the hut; and went to find Reverdy. He was at work on my house, looked at me wonderingly as if to question what had brought me over so soon. I drew him aside and told him what I knew.

Reverdy's blue eyes grew terribly deep. They darkened like clouds in a rapidly gathering storm. They were full of comprehending compassion. They expressed alarm, but also an inexorable sense of futility, as if there was nothing to be done. He was silent. He had fought the Indians; he was used to the rough life of the West. He did not betray fear; rather he acted as if there was nothing to be done. When he began to speak that was the tenor of his words. He revealed to me possibilities that I had never dreamed of. I could see that I was caught in unforeseen circumstances. Some of the dangers involved in the situation he only hinted at. For example, the matter of my living with Zoe. There might be people in Jacksonville who believed that my attitude toward Zoe was not of a brotherly nature. Such a suspicion seemed horrible to me. But Reverdy went on to show me why it might be entertained. This remote country, lacking in opportunity for legitimate expression, held secrets of bestial and gross departures from nature. Here was Zoe, young and beautiful. What did our kindred blood have to do with the matter of my desire? I had not grown up with her, and it would be natural enough if I did not feel toward her as a brother. Incest was common enough around here. As to Lamborn, Zoe was a nigger, and the spoil of any one who wanted her. These were some of the things that Reverdy hinted at. If I prosecuted Lamborn, the countercharge would be made that I had been intimate with Zoe myself. If she had a child I would be proclaimed its father, especially if I raised an issue, and tried to fix the paternity upon Lamborn. If I went to see the state's attorney and asked him to act, there was danger that he would not wish to do so, because the present state's attorney was about to lose the office. He would not wish to start a social hostility that would react upon himself. In fact, Douglas was now trying to supplant him. I was known as a friend of Douglas'. Perhaps I would be trying to involve the state's attorney in an unpopular prosecution. If the prosecuting attorney refused to act that refusal would be known, and credit might be given to any reports that might arise that Zoe was mine before she was Lamborn's, if she ever was his. And if I resented the prosecuting attorney's refusal to act, then I might be accused of acting with Douglas in his ambition to get the office. Above all, under the law of Illinois, Zoe could not testify against Lamborn, a white man. Thus, in any prosecution that was to be made, evidence independent of Zoe's word had to be procured. Where was such evidence? That really settled the whole matter. But I had gone through the whole range of deliberation before finding out that Zoe's word would not be received in court.

But why had Reverdy not warned me against taking Zoe to live with me? There was the matter, too, of my equal division of the estate with Zoe. I had done this with the purest of motives. Now the edge of it was turned against me. For why would I surrender so much when I did not have to?

What was I now to do? Should I send Zoe away? Should I keep her in my household and let the tongues wag, as they were doing, or clatter if Zoe should have a child? The secret would be out soon. Lamborn would be sure to betray the fact that he had captured Zoe. There seemed nothing to do then but to settle down with British tenacity to live it out, and brave whatever came to me out of the complications. I was sure of the friendship of Reverdy and Sarah.

With these reflections I went back to the hut. Zoe was still in tears. She asked me if she had not better go away. If I would give her some of her money she would leave and never come back. "No," I said. "I am going to see you through, Zoe. We will face this out together; only do you consult me about what to do, and help me to stand by you."

I sat down and began to think it all over again. Here were all the pretty things I had bought in St. Louis soon to arrive, and the house would be ready to occupy in a few days. Yet these happy events were clouded for me. There was real bitterness in my cup now.

CHAPTER XV

The house was done. My furnishings were delivered. There were curtains to make, many feminine touches were needed to settle the rooms. Sarah did all that she could, but Dorothy Clayton had come. She was just a year younger than I, and of charming appearance and manner. We had become friends almost at once. She was with me daily, as we put the house in order for occupancy. Reverdy thought that Sarah must be apprised of what had happened to Zoe. She was terribly wounded and distressed. But she approved of my course in keeping Zoe with me.

On my birthday, June 18th, we had the housewarming. I gave a party, inviting all the young people from Jacksonville and the country around: those that I knew and those that I didn't--all but Lamborn. The omission would be notable, but I could not invite him. The matter was promptly gossiped about. Lamborn himself was stirred to talk now. He made the most detestable references to Zoe and me; and I was told of them. At the party Douglas drew me aside and confided to me that Lamborn was in an ugly rage.

Douglas was quite the life of my party. He mingled freely with all the company, making himself charming to every one. He danced with every girl present, and more than once with Dorothy. His short figure gave him a certain comical appearance. But he was graceful and adept at the dances. And his wit and good humor kept every one in high spirits. Reverdy, too, participated in the joy of the occasion with generous enthusiasm. Altogether, we were a merry crowd. I had strengthened my hold upon the affections of the community. For the time I had forgotten my embarrassing troubles. They came back to my mind after the guests had departed. And there was something else to disturb me. Dorothy had gained more than my passing interest.

Work was now my salvation, and I had plenty to do. I had learned in this year a vast amount about running a farm; and I was blessed with excellent health. But meanwhile Zoe! It was not long before it was certain that she was to bear a child; and it would not be many months or even weeks when she could not walk out or go to town without betraying her secret to the world. But then what should the explanation be? Should I tell what I knew? Should I remain silent?

Except for engrossing duties, with time to think and brood, I should have been thrown into tortures with the possibilities. There was always the chance, too, that Zoe in the desperation of the moment might run away from me. She had the English blood of my father in her veins, venturesome, perhaps reckless. Perhaps it was well that she had no control of the profits of the farm which had thus far been allotted to her, nor her share of the ready money which my father had left. I had had Reverdy appointed her guardian, making myself accountable to him. I deemed this the fitting thing; and I was also brought to do it because I might be absent at times in the future when she would need money. But if Zoe should run away what would become of her? The chance of her being kidnapped and sold into slavery filled me with terror. Yet the days went on without change.

Except that Sarah's boy was born! What a father Reverdy was! So wondering and gentle. And he guarded Sarah like a lover and father in one. Zoe was wild to see Sarah's boy; but that was out of the question now. She wanted to deed some of her land to the boy, or better perhaps, to Sarah. But she would have to wait until she became of age to do this.

The birth of Sarah's boy affected Zoe profoundly. She was now about two months advanced in her own pregnancy. She was beginning to think of the ordeal herself, of the fate of the child, what it was being born to…. What, indeed? I noticed that Zoe had hours of deep depression. Would it not be best for me to have a woman in the house with Zoe? Mrs. Engle knew of a widow about fifty whose husband had been killed in the War of 1812. And I got her, a Mrs. Brown. Zoe was now free of the housework. She had a companion when I was away on my work about the farm. And I felt relieved. But my mind and heart were full of problems. There was always Zoe! There was always Lamborn, skulking in the shadows of my speculations. How would I unravel this tangle with him?

Then there was Dorothy. Some of the talk must reach her eventually. It might come to her as a smudge upon me. Then I could not expect to continue my attentions to her without explanations. How could I go into explanations with Dorothy? But even if Dorothy only knew that Zoe was my sister, what would she think of me? Could she have an interest in a man with a family relationship of this sort? Could Dorothy, bred in Tennessee, look with favor upon my attentions? Had Reverdy and Sarah kept this relationship from Dorothy? Had some one else told her? But if she had not found these circumstances a reason for turning from me could she tolerate the rest of my difficulties?

And one night I came home to find Zoe in bed. She was in great pain and very weak. She was scarcely able to talk. She took my hand and pressed it, only saying: "I have done something for you. If I die, it will be best anyway. If I live it will be all right. I could not bear to bring you such shame and trouble. Don't worry ... don't."

Mrs. Brown came in and stood by the bed. She did not speak. She looked at me as if to say that sometimes desperate things have to be done. I understood. I acquiesced. Did Mrs. Brown do it? I never asked. Zoe's sufferings were very great. All this for Lamborn's drunken madness. And then Zoe began to mend. She was out of her difficulty. She became herself in a few weeks. But her spirit had changed. She was wiser, more self-possessed. She was more a woman. A great load had been lifted from me; yet I now faced a new Zoe. What would this mature Zoe do to me?

CHAPTER XVI

There was the law against Zoe taking this step, and against any one having any part in it. Still would it be known? I was content to wait for developments and meanwhile to put the whole thing behind me. Work helped me to do this.

I had Sarah's boy to interest me too. They had named him Amos. I had taken five twenty-dollar gold pieces and tied them in a package, bound them with a ribbon, and placed them in his tiny hand. I could not foresee the time when I should touch his hand on an occasion of very different import and with Zoe standing by. Zoe had made Amos some pretty little things and sent them by me. Sarah's only regret was that her grandmother could not see the boy. Her great happiness was wholly beautiful. And Reverdy seemed impressed with a greater dignity and a more gracious heart, if that were possible. I had found Mrs. Brown well adapted to my household. She liked the place; and the prospect was that she would be long in my service. Life was moving on.

I kept in touch with affairs in England and Europe through the London *Times*. I was also a subscriber to Greeley's *New Yorker*; and I did not slight the local paper, which belabored Douglas in proportion as he increased in popularity and power. I read many books as well.

For I felt the stir of a new age. I saw the North, the country around me, growing in wealth and dominance. I saw old despotisms giving way and new ones coming to take their place. The factory system was arising, due to machinery. Weaving and spinning processes had improved. The cry of women and children crowded in the factories of Pennsylvania began to be heard. The hours of toil were long. And if the whip descended upon the back of the negro in the South, the factory overseer in Philadelphia flogged the laborer who did not work enough to suit him, or who was tardy at the task. Women and children there were feeling the lash of the whip. Just now there was talk of a machine which would cut as much grain in a day as six men could cut with scythes. I ordered two of these machines for the next year, for I was farming more and more on a big scale. But what seemed most wonderful to me was an instrument now being talked about which sent messages by electricity. It was not perfected yet. It was treated with skepticism. But if it could be! If I could get a message from St. Louis, a distance of more than a hundred miles, in a few minutes or an hour!

Douglas came out to see me one night to tell me what was on his mind. He wanted to be the prosecuting attorney. Consider the straits of a young man who must make his way and get a place in the world! Is there anything more desperate at times? What was the law business in this community, divided, as it was, by eleven lawyers, shared in by visiting lawyers? Douglas had to live. Youth is forced to push ahead or be crushed. I know he has been accused of manipulation in having the law passed by which he could be appointed to the office and supplant a rival. Well, if he had not had the gifts and the energies to do such things, how could he have served the country and maintained himself? The next February before he was twenty-two, he was state's attorney for the district. No wonder that lesser men railed at him. But what one of them would not have done the same thing if he could?

And now I was seeing much of Dorothy. What did it mean? Was she only my friend? Reverdy, her brother, was my most intimate friend. Did she receive my attentions on account of the relations between him and me? If she knew anything about Zoe she never betrayed it to me. Surely she could not be in Jacksonville so long and be ignorant that Zoe was my half-sister. At last I decided to explore Dorothy's mind. I went at it forthrightly. Did she know that Zoe and I had the same father?

She had heard it. That was a common enough thing in the South; not common there, however, for a colored mother to be the wife of a white father. "I have suffered on account of this," said Dorothy. "You knew nothing about it and had nothing to do with it. It is too bad--too bad, Jimmy!"

There remained Zoe's misadventure. How could I approach that? But if Dorothy had heard of it would she continue to receive me? If she knew about it would not the present association of ideas bring it to mind and bespeak it to me by change of color or expression? I looked at Dorothy quizzically. I discovered nothing in her face. Then I began to think of the certain probability that some one had come to her breathing rumors upon her. So I said: "Promise me something, Dorothy. If any one ever tells you anything about me, say, for example, that I haven't been perfectly fair with Zoe in every way, and honorable as far as I know how to be, will you withhold belief until you give me a chance? Do you promise me that?" And Dorothy stretched her hand to me in a warm-hearted way. "You are Reverdy's friend, aren't you, and he is yours. Well, I promise you. But it isn't necessary, for it would have to be something that I could believe you capable of. Then Reverdy would have to believe it, and then I might have a mind of my own after all. Why, how could anyone say anything about you? You have been as good to Zoe as if she were as white as I."

And so Dorothy didn't know. I left the matter where it was. I could not go on. You see I was nineteen and Dorothy was eighteen and the year was 1834.

But Lamborn. I had made an enemy of him. Rather, he had turned himself into my enemy. He was running with a gang of rough fellows called the McCall boys. They drank and fought, using clubs or stones or knives. They were suspected of trying to rob the stage when it was driven by the poor wretch who had died of the cholera two summers before. That driver was noted for his courage, his ready use of the rifle; and he had frightened the marauders off, and had wounded one of them, who limped away until the trail of his blood was obscured.

Every time I came into town I was subjected to wolfish leers from some member of this gang. Evidently they had taken up Lamborn's cause. Something was preying upon him. He was drinking more heavily. Perhaps he was tormented with the thought that I knew his secret and abided some vengeance upon him. Perhaps his conscience tortured him. At any rate he had become a skulking figure of hatred, showing his teeth and snarling when he saw me and sidling away like a wolf. He had muttered curses as he hurried to one side. "Bloody Englishman" and the like were his remarks. Something told me to watch him, to watch the McCall boys. I began to take pains to guard my house in the country, sleeping always with my rifle by my side; and I had provided my men with rifles, instructing them to shoot if trespassers approached during suspicious hours or when warned away.

The autumn was the most delicious weather I had experienced since coming to America. Enough of the summer was carried over into October, and even November, to keep the days warm and full of sunlight, while the nights were clear and frosty, and always over this boundless prairie the far scattered stars. I had bought an astronomical chart and located the constellations, in which Zoe had joined me in increasing wonder. Then I had a taste of real hunting. Reverdy and I had gone to marshes a few miles away for wild geese and ducks; and we had come back loaded with game for ourselves and friends. There were many parties and what were called "shucking bees," where the company set to to assist the host in ridding the corn of its sheath; and quilting bees; and apple parings. These were occasions of festival, the local rituals of Dionysius. Earlier in the fall I had gone to a county fair and had seen the products of the field on display; and had studied the people: the tall angular gawks, the men carrying whips, the dust, the noise, the cheap fakirs and gamblers, the fights, the drunkenness, the women tired and perspiring carrying their babies and leading a brood. To me it was more like a cattle pen befogged with dust than an assemblage of human beings. And there was no happiness, no real joy; only barbaric breaking away from hard labor and the silence of the farms; only a reeling and a howling and a war dance; and only here and there a flash of breeding and fineness, and intelligent use of the occasion for sweeter joys and fuller life.

The winter came down; but I was better prepared for it than I was the year before. My house with its walls a foot thick of solid oak and tightly plastered against the penetrating winds kept out the cold. And my fireplaces built under my very eye threw a steady heat into the rooms. I was giving parties from time to time and attending them as well. Douglas always came. He was unfailingly the life of the party. He had reenforced his political successes with a genuine hold upon the hearts of the young people and the older people. He was attacked weekly by the Whig newspaper. But he was not without defense. Almost upon arriving at Jacksonville he had written a letter of praise to the editor of a newly started journal. The editor was greatly pleased at this spontaneous expression of interest and had become Douglas' friend and stanch champion. Ah! Douglas was only manipulating. He had written this letter to win a newspaper to his support. The wily schemer! "Genius has come into our midst," wrote the editor. "No one can doubt this who heard Mr. Douglas expound Democratic doctrine in his wonderful debate with John Wyatt. This country is richer for having attracted Douglas to it. He is here to stay. And he will be one of the great men of the country as President Jackson is now the greatest figure since Washington; and Illinois will send him forth as her son to speak and to act on the great questions that are already beginning to fill the minds of the people."

Douglas often came out to stay for the night or for a day or two. He had little law business, but his energies were always employed in shaping his powers toward a participation in the politics of the country. His superhuman energy was intensified by the fact that he had been deprived of an opportunity to educate himself. It was the gadfly that drove him forward with such restless industry. I could see that he had no patience for a detailed study of the law; that he might be ignorant of the technical steps to be taken in the collection of a promissory note, but he would know something about the resources of a treaty; that if he did not know how to settle the title to a farmer's field, he had considered ways to put at rest any claim of England to the territory of the Oregon. Yet he had to live as a lawyer before he could flourish as a statesman. And he had become the prosecuting attorney. His enemies said it was by a trick; that he had had the state law changed so that the legislature could appoint him state's attorney for the district of Jacksonville. The accusation proved too much. Douglas was not quite twenty-two when he reached this office. He had been in the state but two years, not quite that. How had such a youth first won the confidence of enough people who wished to give him this office and were able to do it; and then won the legislature to do the extraordinary thing of changing the law to give him the office, while at the same time supplanting a seasoned and experienced man in the place? How? Was every one corrupt, people and legislature? But it was February and he was the prosecuting attorney for the people.

He came out to see me, and we drank his health and fortune. It was on this occasion that Douglas talked to me with the greatest freedom about my own affairs. His frankness and sincerity, his friendship for me, relieved this broaching of my intimate interests of intrusiveness. I felt no inclination to resent it. He had glanced at Zoe who had come into the room once or twice, remarking that she was an unusual young woman. Then he said: "Your father must have been much of a man. I think his marriage worked upon his feelings ... and Zoe. Don't let this get on your imagination. You are handling it in the right way ... just go on. Let me warn you. The McCall gang is a desperate one. Do not on any account come to an issue with them. There are too many of them. They will sneak up upon you. They carry grudges ...

and another thing, there's Lamborn ... as bad as the McCalls. He's been talking too, making threats against you. I tell you this for your own good. He has been boasting of Zoe's interest in him ... to speak euphemistically of the matter ... but just be careful." Whatever else he had in his mind he communicated it to me by the look of his speaking eyes, keen and blue. Then he arose and went.

Dorothy had returned to Nashville for the winter. She expected to take her place again in Reverdy's household in the spring. And we were writing. I had thought of proposing marriage to her the night before she left. But I could not bring myself to do so. I needed some one in my life. But I was just twenty, and Dorothy seemed so much more mature and wise than I. Then always there was this matter of Zoe. I lived in the expectation that something would come out of Zoe's misfortune; and if it did my name was bound to be connected with it. What would Dorothy say if in the midst of our engagement, if she engaged herself to me, the word should be brought to her that I was the father of Zoe's aborted child and that by some one, perhaps Mrs. Brown, Zoe had been saved the open shame of giving birth to the child and while an inmate of my house? I could see the probative force of these facts against me. This is what kept me from speaking to Dorothy on the subject of becoming my wife and having it settled before she went to Nashville. And then something happened that made my situation infinitely worse before it was any better.

The spring had come on early and I had much to do. I was buying machinery. The mowers that I had ordered were soon to be delivered and I had need to be in town almost daily. There were always loafers about the streets; and among them, not infrequently, the McCall boys or Lamborn. Reverdy had told me that Lamborn had been talking in the barber shop, saying that I was living in a state of adultery with my nigger sister. At the same time I knew, and Reverdy knew, that Lamborn was trying to get Zoe to meet him. He had sent her a note to that effect, which Zoe had turned over to me. Once he had accosted Zoe as she was coming from Reverdy's to join me at the courthouse preparatory to starting home. Reverdy thought that the fellow was eaten up with insane jealousy and had brought himself to the belief that I had taken Zoe from him, if he could be said ever to have had a right to her.

It is an April day and I have come into town and am rushing from place to place attending to many things. Reverdy has met me at the bank to tell me of another opportunity to buy a team of horses and some oxen; for we use the latter mostly to draw the plows that turn up the heavy sod of the prairie. Reverdy has just told me of Lamborn's threat to come to my farm and take Zoe: that when a girl was once his she was always his. He had said these things at the barber shop. Something came over me. I resolved that this intolerable state of affairs, of anxiety for Zoe, of misunderstanding for myself, of dread of the future, of a sort of brake on my life as of something holding me back and impeding my happiness and peace of mind ... all this had to end somehow and soon. I could not live and go on with things as they were.

We stepped from the bank. And there, not ten feet away, stood Lamborn. His mouth became a scrawl, he uttered a growl, he swayed with passion, he moved his hands at his side in a sort of twisting motion. And I thought: there are Zoe and Dorothy, and I may create a feud against me that will follow me for years ... yet this man must die. And I drew my pistol and fired ... Lamborn sank to the ground without a groan. Some of the McCall boys ran out. I fired at them. They fled. I walked forward a step or two. Then I asked Reverdy if he had seen Lamborn reach for his pistol. Reverdy had seen this. I had not. In fact, Lamborn did nothing of the sort. But if Reverdy saw this he could swear to it and help me. The excitement of the precise moment was now over. I felt weak and anxious. I wanted to see Douglas. As state's attorney he could help me. Douglas was soon on the scene. He had heard what I had done. I wanted to talk with him. He waved me off saying: "You must have counsel of your own. You must not talk to me. I would be compelled in the discharge of my duty to use against you anything you might tell me." With that he walked away.

He could not be my friend in this hour of need! What was I to do? Yes, there was Reverdy. But when it came to the matter of locking me up Douglas said: "If Mr. Clayton signs the bond ... make the bond $1000 ... don't lock him up. Get a coroner's jury."

There was not a member of this jury who had not been exposed to some of this vile talk about Zoe and me, in the general contagion of the village gossip. How should this examination be managed? Of course the single question, they told me, was the manner of Lamborn's meeting his death. But the coroner's jury had the power to bind me to the grand jury for an indictment, and that I wished to escape. Well, I had been threatened, to be sure. But why? If Lamborn wanted Zoe and I had her in my house and kept him from seeing her, was it for a good or a selfish reason? Were we not rivals for the same favor? Did one have her and one lose her? Had I killed Lamborn for jealousy, or in self-defense? The single fact that I had shot him stood against the background of all this gossip and village understanding, and was necessarily read into it for my undoing or my freedom.

There was the note that Lamborn had written Zoe! That proved that Lamborn was seeking her; but it might be used to prove that I resented his pursuit. And why? As Zoe's brother, or as her unnatural lover? My brain was in a whirl. I could not think for myself. I talked these subjects over with Reverdy and with Mr. Brooks, who was my counsel. All these things were done the day of the killing. The next morning, with the body of Lamborn lying in the room, I mounted the witness chair in my own behalf, after Reverdy had testified that he had seen Lamborn reach to his pocket, and that it was not until then that I drew my pistol and fired.

Was Douglas turned against me? He plunged into the matter of Zoe almost at once in his cross examination of me. And at last I told the whole story ... with but two exceptions: I did not produce Lamborn's note to Zoe and I did not tell of Zoe's illness and its cause; of returning from St. Louis and finding Zoe in tears, of what she had told me, of the embarrassment I then found myself in, of my perplexity, of my failure to invite Lamborn to my housewarming and the reason for it, of Lamborn's attitude toward me after that, his menacing looks, his growling insults when he saw me ... of all these things I told with full circumstantiality under the examination of the new state's attorney, and with the whole of the countryside looking on, Whigs and Democrats, and with the audience permeated with slavery and with slavery feeling, at least so far as the present case was concerned. What would Douglas now do? He rose and in his deep voice, with perfect command of himself, looking over the audience as if it was a great instrument whose keys he knew, he spoke these brief words: "Gentlemen, it makes no difference to me whether this girl is white or black; if you bind this young man over to the grand jury, I will do what I can to prevent an indictment; and if the grand jury indicts him I will do what I can to have him acquitted. This dead man here met his just fate."

The audience cheered. The jury acquitted me without leaving their seats. I walked a free man into the soft air of April. Douglas came out. His manner was changed. He spoke to me in freedom and in the old tone of friendship. "The boil is now open," he said. "The cut place will heal."

And he walked with me down the street followed by a cheering crowd. Douglas had won the people; and I was free!

CHAPTER XVII

I began to see myself as boring through opposition with lowered head and indomitable will. I was strengthened by the fact that I had never swerved from my duty to Zoe. And now that the beast was out of the way who had caused her so much agony, my whole life seemed cleared. The McCall gang might cause me trouble, but they would need to come prepared, or to catch me off my guard. The opening up of the whole case had had a wholesome effect upon my reputation. The brotherly innocence of my relation to Zoe was the generally accepted one. Reverdy assured me of this. Douglas was a valiant friend to me in this clarification of my nature and my character before the community. The whole atmosphere of my life was now freer; but it had cost Lamborn his life to make it so. It seemed best, however, that I should leave town for a while. I decided to go to Cincinnati and then to Nashville. I wanted to see Dorothy. I felt that I must make myself clear to her, and face to face.

Having made all arrangements for Zoe and Mrs. Brown to keep the house while I was gone and having laid out the work for my men, I set forth for Vandalia, the capital of Illinois, by stage. There I took the Cumberland Road, passed through Indianapolis, a small place; arrived in good time at Cincinnati, a city of more than 30,000 people; a busy place of manufacturers, distillers, and pork packers, since Kentucky, Ohio, and Indiana shipped their hogs to this market to be converted into hams and bacon and lard. I saw the town, the residence of the great Nicholas Longworth, who had grown fabulously rich by making wine. And at the hotel, this latter part of April being warm, I was treated to the spectacle of the men in the dining room taking off their coats and dining in their shirt sleeves amid the not inelegant appointments that surrounded the table. But I was becoming Americanized now and was not as sensitive as formerly to deportment of this sort.

The vastness of America came over me as I descended from Cincinnati to Nashville. Yet there was the southern territory still south of me; and beyond the Mississippi the unsettled empire of Louisiana. Cincinnati had something of the activity and the character of other northern cities; but as I passed through the domain of Kentucky and Tennessee I could not help but see that here was an agricultural country which owed its prosperity to slavery. But what was all that I saw here of industry and utilization of the resources of the land compared to what I saw growing up as a system around Jacksonville?

Yet the loveliness of the country around Nashville enchanted me. I was in a mood to be won, to be sure; for I was completely captivated by Dorothy and the delightful hospitality that was accorded me. Dorothy's mother treated me with such gentle and thoughtful attention, as if she received me not less upon the basis of my friendship to Reverdy than upon my own appeal to her. And as for Dorothy--she was as kind to me as a sister; and yet....

I loved the country and this little city of 6000 people on the hills above the Cumberland valley. Still, so many negroes. In this whole state of about 700,000 people, nearly 150,000 were slaves, so Dorothy told me. It amazed me. Negro slavery, so far as England was concerned, had never to me been a visible thing. But here in America, here in Tennessee, and in this city, it struck one at every turn. It entered into all the daily thinking and plans of every one. It was omnipresent. It touched every life.

This was the town of James K. Polk, whose name meant nothing to me; but Dorothy spoke of him as a leading man in Congress from Tennessee. Here also was the residence of President Jackson, a place called the "Hermitage," a few miles into the country. Dorothy and I drove to it. These were the places of interest to see; and everywhere the southern mansion: the upper and lower porch in front, the spacious windows, the Dorian or Ionic columns, as the case might be; the great entrance door set between mullioned panes at either side, and beneath a lunette of woodwork and glass. The Clayton house was like this, for Dorothy's father had been a man of wealth, a slave owner too in his prosperous days. He had failed and died, Reverdy had gone to the newer country of Illinois to seek his fortune, leaving Dorothy and the mother to the possession of the diminished property which Mr. Clayton had left.

But above everything in the way of delight, for the beauty of the prospect, for the opportunity it gave me to be with Dorothy, were the hills that overlooked the Cumberland valley and the river. We climbed here daily and sat beneath the lovely oaks that shaded the richness of the grass. To the west and north the river flowed to its confluence with the Ohio. Around us the hills. The valley between. The silence of nature, the intensity of unfolding life around us. Always on my mind was the thought of Dorothy as my wife. And why not speak my heart? I could not tell why. Was it Zoe; Dorothy's knowledge of Zoe? Was I investing Dorothy with my own thoughts, putting into her mouth the objections that I could make against myself? I could not tell what Zoe might bring into the life of the woman I married, as well as my own. Surely I was not very robust, very hearty in my speculations. For Dorothy had received me. There was nothing lacking in the warmth of her hospitality ... and yet I sensed at times such a temperate feeling in her glance, in her voice. Even her frankness had that character, or enhanced it perhaps.

And one afternoon as we were walking along the river I spoke what was in my heart. I had this competence. I had built the house. I could make a fortune in time. I was beginning to need some one to help me, to be with me. And no sooner had I spoken than I saw myself: Zoe was my half-sister and I was proposing marriage to a girl who had no feeling that did not bespeak to her the inferiority of the colored skin, no matter if it were lightened, no matter by whom. Dorothy's attitude was that of the high-bred and kindly southerner: the negroes must be kept in slavery as a solution of the social question and for the prosperity of the South; but at the same time the negro should be treated with kindness. And here was Zoe, the half-sister of the man who was asking her to be his companion for life. To what extent, then, the associate on a basis of equality with Zoe too? This was not all. My name had been coupled with Zoe's. Above all, I had killed a man, my rival or Zoe's hunter, as one might choose to believe.

Thus I saw myself. My very hair began to rise and to tingle. How had I dared to make this proposal to Dorothy? And as Dorothy was silent, and looked down as we walked, poking with her parasol at pebbles in the road, I was in a tense anxiety to know with what words she would break the oppressive pause between us. "I could see," she said, "that you liked me; and of course you wouldn't come so far to see me if you didn't. And you must know that Reverdy's friendship for you makes a difference. Do you know...?"

Dorothy lost her voice. The tears came out of her eyes. As she did not speak I began again, trying to say for her what she did not say for herself. "There's Zoe," I said. And then Dorothy quite lost control of herself. She wept piteously. And then she grew calmer. She had faced the reluctant fact when I spoke Zoe's name. We had stumbled up and over that roughness in the road. Any rut or obstacle in it might now be easier endured ... if worse was not to come.

Yes, these stories about me. Had Dorothy heard them? And the life I had taken for Zoe's sake. I was sure Dorothy had not heard of that. Even the first was a subject difficult to approach. I was twenty, Dorothy was nineteen. But the greatest obstacle was the age in which we lived. Women now draped themselves in mystery. There were whole realms of subjects that were not talked between the sexes. We managed things by mild indirections, by absurd circumlocutions.

I began to think of the letter that Lamborn had written Zoe. I was carrying it in my pocket. Did it not prove Lamborn's interest in Zoe? I handed it to Dorothy, thinking that it would disprove my interest in Zoe, of which I had been made self-conscious by the accusations; and not realizing that Dorothy probably knew nothing of all these charges. "Read this," I said, handing it to Dorothy.

Dorothy took it in at a glance, for it was only a few lines beginning "Dear Zoe." It was an invitation to Zoe to meet Lamborn again at the same place. Dorothy's face turned crimson. She handed the note back to me without a word. I had to struggle with the tough materials of the revelation that I wished to make. And I went on to tell Dorothy that the author of the note was Lamborn. "You remember him?" I asked. Dorothy nodded her head. "Well," I continued, "he is dead, thank God. I killed him."

Dorothy was overcome. She reeled. After a moment, in which she found her breath again, she faced about and began to walk toward the town.

I followed, hurt and crushed; for Dorothy had suddenly changed her whole manner. Her face was impenetrable; and it had paralyzed my hope with its expression of self-withdrawal, something almost of anger. I could not go on now and tell my story: that I had killed Lamborn because of his offense against Zoe, because of his menacing attitude toward me, because of the vile things he had said about Zoe. No! nothing I could say now would be in place. I had blundered, perhaps. We walked to the house, silent all the way.

Dorothy went to her room, leaving me in the hands of her mother. Mrs. Clayton, thinking that we had had a lovers' quarrel, endeavored by extra attention to me to overcome Dorothy's absence, and to say to me in this way that she did not share in Dorothy's attitude.

And so it was that Mrs. Clayton and I dined together; and I now had opportunity to tell her of little Amos, of my life in England, of my farm, my new house, my plans for the future. Mrs. Clayton was outspoken enough. She said that Reverdy admired my father for many things, and did not particularly censure his marriage. As for that it was a common enough thing in the South for the planters to have children by negro women, or by the prettier quadroons and octoroons. For herself she hated slavery, but did not know what would be done if the negroes were free.

Dorothy did not appear. We rose from the table and went out to sit under one of the great trees in the yard. I thought I saw an opportunity. Why not talk to Mrs. Clayton? She could tell Dorothy what I was unable to say to her. I set my will to the task.

"You seem to know about my father, Mrs. Clayton. And I want you to know about me. I want Dorothy for my wife. We had a kind of a flare-up this afternoon. I was trying to make my case clear, and Dorothy fell to crying. That's all. You see I came to America in ignorance of everything. No one had told me about my father's marriage; and I blame my grandmother that she did not tell me. Well, I got to Jacksonville and was terribly ill, almost died. Zoe took care of me. And that won me. But in addition to that she is as much my father's child as I am. I found that out as soon as I got up. Then I took her to live with me, to help me with the house, without thinking that there would be talk, not only by those who didn't know that she was my sister as well as by those who did know it. I went to St. Louis to buy furnishings for my new house. While I was gone a man named Lamborn wronged her. This made great trouble for me. And one thing led to another. He was saying vile things about me and about Zoe. And my life was getting more and more unendurable day by day on account of this fellow. And at last I was coming down the street with Reverdy one day, and this Lamborn suddenly confronted me. I drew and killed him. The state's attorney, Mr. Douglas, brought out all the facts before the coroner's jury. The jury acquitted me before leaving their seats. Mr. Douglas told the jury that he would not prosecute me if an indictment was found against me. And so..." I was about to say that I had come to Nashville to get away from the circumstances. But I caught myself and forebore.

Mrs. Clayton had followed me with rapt attention, leaning more and more toward me as my story progressed. She put out her hand to take mine. I could not tell whether it was the hand of pity or admiration. Her eyes were kindly, but they searched me. She seemed to say: "What difficulty in this boy's life is he trying to mingle with my daughter's life?" She spoke. "It is too bad. You are too young to have such tragedy." That was all. Then we went in.

As I arose the next morning I began to wonder what reception would be accorded me by Mrs. Clayton, not to say Dorothy. No one was astir but the colored butler and the maids. Yes, slavery was very well for them. I could see that all that was said in favor of the benevolence of the institution had verification in them and perhaps in all slaves doing like service. But what of the field hands, the heavier workers? I was thinking of these things, but mostly of the desperate situation I was in and of this day ahead of me. Would Dorothy see me again? Would I be the honored guest of yesterday? This silence of the mansion made me feel that its hospitality had cooled toward me. But in a little while Mrs. Clayton appeared on the stair and descended to find me rather restlessly pacing the room.

I could not specify any change in her manner. Perhaps as a matter of breeding I was to be bowed out with all possible courtesy. She smiled me a "Good morning," said that Dorothy would not be down until later. We two went in to breakfast.

I began to feel embarrassed. I could not be at ease. Mrs. Clayton sensed my diffidence. We managed the conversation in broken sentences and forced remarks. My pride asserted itself. I had done nothing myself for which I could be blamed. For the rest, if I was not wanted I should go my way. I asked Mrs. Clayton when I could get a boat to St. Louis. She did not know, but one ran almost every day either directly, or I could change boats at a place called Freesland on the Ohio River. Accordingly, after breakfast, I went to the steamboat landing to make inquiries ... and without seeing Dorothy.

A kind of rebellion and resentment were rising in me. Dorothy was Reverdy's sister; but surely she was of a different spirit if she disapproved of me for what I had done. Perhaps it would be well to be free of my love for Dorothy, to be once more without any feeling that my life needed completion by uniting it with a woman's life. I had offered myself. I was not accepted. My dignity, and place in the world, as I saw them, were dishonored.

When I returned to the house Dorothy had appeared. She smiled gently in recognition of me. I broke the silence by telling her that I could get a boat the next day, and that I must be off. She made no reply.

Later we went to the yard, under one of the great trees. Dorothy was evidently tortured in her mind and did not know what to say to me. She looked worn and as if she had not slept. I searched her face. A tear stole down her cheek. She averted her eyes and clasped her hands together nervously. I could endure the suspense no longer.

"It is best for me to go," I said. She made no reply. "I am sorry that I have made you suffer. Let me erase everything by withdrawing what I have said to you." "You can't," said Dorothy. "You are Reverdy's friend; you know how I love him. You couldn't suppose that anything that has affected you so deeply would not affect him and therefore me. I never believed that I could be so unhappy. You are going and that leaves me to think and think."

My heart took fire again. I stretched my hand to take Dorothy's. She removed hers gently out of reach. "Go your way, my friend," she said. "Later I may write you. You are only a boy yet ... and many things may happen. But be sure that I suffer, and that I remember and that I need help."

She arose and preceded me back to the house. Mrs. Clayton seemed to direct her influence toward smoothing our way. But nothing could be done. I had met defeat and I wished to depart.

The next day I was on the Ohio but not bound for St. Louis. I had decided to see New Orleans. Change of scene might allay my thoughts.

CHAPTER XVIII

I did not tell Dorothy where I was going. I left her to suppose that I was returning to Jacksonville.

In passing to the boat landing I stumbled and fell, bruising myself painfully. I was hurrying to get away and in my haste and sorrow I was oblivious of my surroundings. As I limped along on the deck, I was approached by a kindly man who offered me some ointment which he said was made from the oil that escaped over the surface of the water in the salt wells of Kentucky and elsewhere, in spite of anything that could be done and much to the inconvenience of the business of getting salt. This man said that the oil was being subjected to experiments for use in illumination. As an ointment it was magical, and in a few days my lameness disappeared.

Both on the Ohio and the Mississippi we saw flatboats tied together heaped with coal, which had been loaded into them from the sides of the hills of the Alleghanies and elsewhere. They were being floated down to New Orleans. I had found coal in several places on my land in Illinois. Sometimes one could dig it out of the surface of the ground. But no expeditious means were yet in use in Illinois in mining it.

The Mississippi is a wonder scene to me. The river is full of islands and the boat winds about in endless turns of the stream. There are swamps, and melancholy cypress and funereal live oaks. There are the solitary huts of the woodcutters, and bars of sand covered with cane brake, and impenetrable forests, and the forbidding depths of the jungle. Farther on there are the sugar plantations, and the levees, and the great houses of the planters, and the huts of the negroes, and the vivid greens of fields of sugar cane standing many feet high; and around these the cypress swamp. And on every side in the midst of each plantation the tall white towers of the sugar mills. It is all novel and wonderful to me; and it helps me to forget my insistent thoughts of Dorothy.

The steamer stopped to get wood. It was at a creole plantation. There was a procession of carts here, each drawn by a team of mules, driven by negroes, laughing and joking with each other. They were slaves hauling wood to the sugar mills. We were soon off again on the silent river, which had now broadened to the dimensions of a great lake.

Then we saw steeples, a dome; then the masts of numerous vessels, and steamboats, and tall chimneys. Then we reached the levee of the city. The boat was fastened, and I walked upon the streets of New Orleans. The heat was no greater than I had felt in Illinois. And at night a breeze stirred briskly from the harbor and the gulf beyond. This city of 50,000 people had immediate fascination for me.

In the evening I went to the Place d'Armes where a military band was playing. There were races during the day just out of town. The cafes were filled with people smoking and drinking, playing billiards and dominoes. Ladies in gay costumes sat in the balconies, making observations on the scene, the players, the passersby. French was spoken everywhere. And everywhere was the creole beauty, with black eyes and long silken lashes, and light skin faintly suffused with rose. I plunged into these festivities in order to forget Dorothy.

I went to the Spanish Cathedral the next day, and saw on the porch groups of gray-haired negroes waiting for alms. There were candles on the altar, paintings of the stations of the cross on the pillars, and confessional closets near the door. And here the lovely creole knelt side by side with pure black descendants of the African negro.

Not anywhere did I see the negro treated worse than in Illinois, except on one occasion. I was loitering on the dock looking at the steamboats being loaded by slaves. A negro driving a wagon almost collided with a wagon being driven by a white man. I saw the whole of it. The white man was at fault. Yet he began to curse the negro, who laughingly spoke the truth, that the white man had suddenly veered. With that a man, apparently an officer of some sort, stepped from a patrol box carrying a rifle and with an oath and a vile epithet commanded the negro to drive on. And he did quickly and without returning a word. There was something about the injustice of this that aroused my resentment. It was a partiality that had nothing to do with the circumstances, but only with the persons.

I visited the slave market and again saw the auctioning of human beings, some as light of color as Zoe and of as much breeding. Again I began to speculate on Zoe's future. What would become of her? How would her fate tangle itself with mine? If Douglas had taken an impetus in life from his uncle's failure to educate him, what direction had my life been given by my father's marriage and Zoe? Already I had killed a man for Zoe's sake; and I had been rejected by Dorothy because of Zoe, or because of the circumstances which Zoe had created around my life.

Wherever I wandered on Canal Street, on the wharves, in the French quarter, out to the battlefield where Jackson had won a victory over Packenham, Dorothy was habitually in my thoughts. But always a door closed against any communication with her; anything to be done for her as a remembrance of her generosity; any step to be taken toward making whole what I conceived to be our wounded friendship. Should I write Dorothy? But what? So many exquisite things in the shop windows: jewels, artistries of silver and gold. How I longed to select something for Dorothy! But the door was closed against it. In the antique shops lovely tables, chests, writing desks! If I could only buy many of such things for our home--Dorothy's and mine. But was that home to be? The door softly closed.

And thus I went about the city. It was so colorful, so gay, so continental, so unlike anything I had ever dreamed of. And all the while I was trying to order my thoughts, wondering what I should do. And if ever Douglas in his political ambitions got entangled, to his own undoing, with this mass of human beings, white and black, moving about the carcass of life, what was to be my fate, both on the score of my individual lot, and as one of the units in this racial hostility, and the political and economic forces that generated it?

I tried several times to write a letter to Dorothy. I could not find the exact thing I wanted to say, or the words with which to express it. What should I say? Should I urge Dorothy to a marriage with me? Should I attempt to argue down her misgivings? Should I tell her that I would return to Jacksonville and send Zoe away? Should I write Dorothy that I relinquished any hope of making her my wife? I wrote letters of these various imports and then destroyed them. A kind of paralysis was upon my thinking. And then I would leave my room and wander into the streets, visit the cafes, and find temporary forgetfulness in lively scenes and gay faces.

And one night when I was in the French quarter at dinner I became alert to the conversation of two men sitting at a near table. They spoke familiarly to each other, almost as brothers. But I sensed that they had been separated for some time. At last one of them made references to France and England, and I concluded that he had been abroad. Both were typical planters, with goatees and broad hats, coats of elegant material but widely and loosely tailored. As I followed their words almost the whole condition of America unfolded itself to my understanding.

The tenor of the talk was concerning cotton, the demand for it abroad and at home, and the effect that that demand had upon the South and the whole social and political life of America. Within thirty years past all the Northern States but Delaware had abolished slavery. What would have kept slavery alive after all except for the cotton gin and Eli Whitney, what but England's great machinery development for spinning and weaving, which made the demand for cotton more and more?

The demand! Where there is a demand it must be supplied, and everything must give way to the processes of furnishing that supply: land, slavery, what not. Then there are general references to life and to labor. After all, all labor is slavery they say. Apprentices, farm hands, factory workers are slaves. All this struggling mass of toilers must, in the fate of life, be consumed in the great drama of furnishing clothes and food and roofs for those who can pay. But cotton needs more land. And is not the territory of the United States, the great commons and domains of all the states, North and South, to be used by them for their several and common benefit, for the intromission of property: slaves or cattle or utensils? It seems to me, now that I hear these men talk, that I am compelled to listen everywhere in America to schemes of trade, material progress, the accumulation of money. These planters go on to ask why lines should be drawn across the territory of the United States forbidding slavery north of the line and permitting it south of the line. This territory had been paid for equally by the treasure and blood of all the states. Blood for land! Then slavery on the land to raise cotton! And was not Jefferson prophetic when he wrote that the extension of this divisional line in 1820 alarmed him like a fire bell at midnight? It betokened sectional strife: the North against the South. And about trade! For as the Southern States grew richer they would have more political power, could dominate the North. Some one must dominate. There must be a supremacy. And what would this growing hostility lead to? What would future inventions do to exacerbate it? What of the steam engine, what of machinery, what of unknown developments?

I could not help but think of the bearing that all of this had on my own life.

But finally as they paid for their dinner, lighted cigars, and became less energetic of mood, one asked the other: "Have you ever heard from the girl?" The reply was: "Not a word. How could I? I didn't leave my name. It was best to close the matter by leaving no trace of myself." And the first asked: "Wasn't your name on the draft?" "I had gold, a bag of gold. I simply turned it over to the new husband and went my way."

I was all ears now, studying, too, the face of the man who was confessing to the bag of gold. Was there a trace of Zoe in him? I could not be sure. I seemed to see something about the eyes, but it faded under my scrutiny. At best this man was only Zoe's grandfather; and my father's blood was nearer to Zoe than his.

They started to arise from the table. I wished to follow them. But I had not paid for my meal. I beckoned to a waiter. While he was coming the two planters strolled leisurely from the cafe arm in arm and in intimate conversation.

I was hurrying to be away and to follow them--I scarcely knew why. They were gone when my waiter came. I asked him who the planters were. He didn't know their names; only knew them as rich planters who often visited the cafe. I left the cafe and tried to find them, but they had disappeared. And I stood on the curb watching the iridescent ooze of the sewage in a runnel of the street seep along like a sick snake.

Creole beauties, negroes, planters, roughs, gamblers, passed me. The streets were noisy with trucks. The air was hot and lifeless. The scene about me suspired like the brilliant and deadly scales of a poisonous reptile. I was sick at heart. I was overcome with terrible loneliness. I was in love with Dorothy and I was Zoe's brother. I was caught in this great dramatic ordeal of America without any fault on my part. What should I do? Yes, my ambition. To get rich. That was labor enough. And there was my farm back in Illinois. Why was I here after all? Was it some dream? I would wake myself. I would return to my place, my duty. What else could I do? I went to the wharf to find a boat to St. Louis.

CHAPTER XIX

I was listless all the way home. Passing through Jacksonville I seemed to sense a coldness in the manner of some of the people. Even where there was a smile and a bow, to which I could take no exception, I interpreted an attitude which said: "The Englishman: the fellow who killed Lamborn."

Was the town dividing as to me? I was sure of Reverdy and Sarah, and Douglas, and the president of the college and his wife, and some others; but for the rest I suspected that envy had seized upon a pretext for its exercise. For I was rich; I had availed myself of mowers and all the new machinery for farming and I was a competitor, a man possibly growing more and more in the way. My reception in many quarters seemed distant.

I went directly to the farm. There was my house which I had built with many hopes. There was the hearth to which I longed to bring a wife. But here it was, only for me, for my habitation and rest from labors in the ambition to be rich! Mrs. Brown opened the door and welcomed me with a diffidence. "Where is Zoe?" I asked. Mrs. Brown replied quickly: "Zoe has not been seen nor heard of for more than a week. I got up one morning, and as she didn't appear I went and called her. She was gone. I saw Mr. Clayton about it. The last I heard no one had seen her."

My feelings were mixed of regret and relief. I was fond of Zoe. My sense of justice was enlisted in her behalf. I was fearful for her future, both for the misfortune that might befall her and for the complications that might accrue to me in her living away from my guidance. For there was Zoe's property. But on the other hand, if Zoe were completely out of my life I might win Dorothy.

I walked reflectively toward the fireplace. Should I not write to Dorothy and tell her of Zoe's disappearance? For surely Zoe would not go away unless she meant to stay. She had roving, adventurous blood in her, and an English will. Could I rely upon the hope of her staying away, and that she would not figure in my life in the future except as to the land, the money? Yes, here my hands were stuck as in honey. And when could they be freed and cleaned of it? While I was reflecting upon these things Mrs. Brown walked to the mantle and taking a letter from it handed it to me. It was from Dorothy.

"Dear James," the letter read, "I was never more depressed in my life than I was after your departure; you must know that I would be. In the first place, Reverdy is so very fond of you and esteems you so much, and that counts with me. For he is the best and truest man I have ever known. And I am sure that you are honorable and kind; and you have asked me to be your wife, and any woman worth noticing is moved by a request like that if she has any respect for the man whatever. But this seems to me the most terrible situation that a girl could be placed in. I have thought it over until my mind goes around in a circle, and I cannot relate things clearly any more. And of course I have talked it all over with mother. You can be sure I would not take the pains to do this, nor the pains to write you in detail, if you had not entered my mind in a serious way. Frankly the only misgivings I have of you, and I beg you to forgive me for saying this, is the fact that your father would do such a thing. I cannot understand it, my mother can't. What was he that he could do such a thing with the prospect that he would injure you, his son by another marriage, in so many ways and so deeply? He could not have overlooked these things; nor the feeling that exists in America, particularly in the South, against such an alliance. But putting these things out of mind, you cannot possibly assure me, or any other woman, against the future. There are the property interests; but if these were out of the way there is the relationship. And I blame myself deeply, for I knew that Zoe was your sister almost as soon as I first came to Jacksonville. With this knowledge I should not have come to your parties or put myself in a way to be liked by you. I should have only been polite to you when you came to Reverdy's house. For any other association, I ask you to forgive me. I have written you many letters, and then torn them up. Perhaps I shall send this one. It is as good as I can do. It says everything now except that I am profoundly unhappy, that I shall never see you again--and to wish you happiness under the circumstances fills my throat with a kind of suffocation. And so I write farewell--and can hardly mean it--and yet it must be farewell."

A kind of calmness came over me as I read the last word. There are anxiety and fear, and stir and ministration while the sick are alive. But with death there is quiet in the house. Calmness comes to those who have striven to heal and to save. And with the words "farewell" before my eyes a dumb resignation came into my heart. Dorothy was gone from me and forever! But here was my life left to me to work out, and my ambition to pursue. I grew suddenly strong and full of will. I walked to the door and gazed for some minutes over the prairie. Then I saddled a horse and went to find Reverdy.

It was something to see the brother of the woman I loved; but I must find Zoe if possible.

Reverdy was off somewhere with Douglas. Douglas was working upon the plan of introducing the political convention system in Illinois, as it prevailed in New York. He wished to step from the state's attorneyship into the legislatureship. He had newspaper supporters; he had many friends, as well as many foes. But he was fighting his way.

I talked with Sarah of my trip to New Orleans and played with little Amos. I asked Sarah at last about Zoe. Reverdy had already done all he could to trace her. The stage driver had been questioned, but knew nothing. Some one had seen a girl, probably Zoe, walking north from town. Outside of that nothing had been heard. The facilities for finding her were so primitive. How could posters be sent around, how phrased? How could constables and sheriffs in the surrounding counties be notified? And if an advertisement should be published in the local newspaper where would it reach? Upon what basis could I seek to regain Zoe, if she did not wish to return? Sarah and I discussed these problems. But if she had met foul play how could that be discovered? I seemed quite helpless, yet since it was the best I could do I placed an advertisement with the newspaper. Then telling Sarah that I wished to see Reverdy, I returned to the farm.

CHAPTER XX

I had much to do, and work kept me from brooding. It was three days after I had gone to find Reverdy that he came to see me, bringing Douglas. My first words to Reverdy were concerning Zoe; but Douglas at once took a hand in that subject. She would either turn up after a little wandering about the country or she was gone for good. If she had met her death it would be known by now, in all probability. I could be sure that she knew better than to go south. Her likely destination was Canada, or northern Illinois. There was much going on in Chicago to attract an adventurous girl. Should I not go there for her? But it was only a chance that I would find her. What of her property, her interests? Let them rest until an emergency arose.

In truth Reverdy and Douglas had not come to see me about Zoe, but to enlist my support in Douglas' ambition to go to the legislature. Douglas was now twenty-three years of age. He had been in Illinois just three years. During that time he had become a lawyer, had had the law changed so as to be appointed state's attorney. He had only held that office from February to April of this year, when he had organized a convention at Vandalia to choose delegates to the national convention for next year. He had fought down opposition to the convention system; he had successfully managed a county convention in which he had been nominated for the legislature. Now he was out upon the stump, speaking in behalf of state policies like canals and railroads; and there was the question too of removing the state capital from Vandalia to Springfield, which might constitute a leverage for a vote for internal improvements. Douglas was in favor of both. While slave interests were seeking land for cotton, the agrarian interests in Illinois were awake to the need of transportation facilities and markets. As I had wheat and corn to sell besides cattle and hogs, and would have them in increasing quantities, I should use my influence in behalf of these measures and in behalf of Douglas, who had a vision of their need and a practical mind for securing them. Douglas did not hesitate on the matter of internal improvements. He believed that they should be made by the state. That obviated the centralization flowing from national aid. Let Illinois use its own resources for building canals and railroads. Let the state's credit be pledged. What state had greater natural riches? The Illinois and Michigan canal must be completed. The rivers must be made navigable. At least two railroads must be constructed, which should cross the state from north to south, and from east to west. The credit of the state must be pledged for a loan of money; and the interest on the loan should be paid by the sales of the land, which Illinois had been granted by the Federal government for the canal.

Douglas was full of youthful enthusiasm for this work of building up the state. I could see his great energies moving like a restless tide through them as he talked these projects over with Reverdy and me. I was only too glad to lend him my help. It was to my interest. I trusted his judgment, too. I saw moderation and wisdom in his policies.

Already it was apparent that Douglas stood upon no idealistic immovability when the main thing was at stake. And hence, when the bill which was brought in on the subject of railroads, appropriated the money for eight railroads instead of Douglas' two, and bestowed consolations here and there to counties in order to get their support, Douglas showed his reluctance, but gave his vote. The state capital was moved to Springfield as a part of the give and take of logrolling.

But on the occasion of this call Douglas stood for a very moderate program, as I have already said. When he was elected and had legislative power he surrendered his moderation in order to get the railroads. In fact the people were moving in this direction; there was much magnificent dreaming and hazardous experimentation and the general result could not be prevented.

I had gone to see Reverdy, partly to inquire about Zoe, partly with the hope that I could gain help as to Dorothy. Now he had come to me with Douglas; and all the talk was of politics, with no chance to draw Reverdy aside for a private word. When they arose to leave Reverdy took my hand. His eyes grew wonderfully deep and sympathetic. Then with a slap upon my back and a congratulation that I would help Douglas, the two departed.

Then I began to think whether I should write Dorothy. Yes, her letter demanded some reply. As I sat down to write, Dorothy's view became mine in a flood of emotion of love's willingness to sacrifice. And I wrote:

"Dear Dorothy: The only thing I can say in my own behalf is that I found myself suddenly placed in this position as Zoe's brother, without understanding, or only understanding gradually what it meant to me, or would mean to any one else. I have been learning all of these things; and your letter makes them clear to me. I did not come straight home but went to New Orleans; and your letter had been here some days when I returned. I must tell you that Zoe disappeared in my absence. I don't know where and cannot learn. I am fearful for her; and there are many possible complications. But I am powerless to do anything at this time. She may never return. She may fall into strange hands and make some new relations which will come back upon me and upon any one I cared for with embarrassing results. I am in a position where I can make no assurances. I feel like asking you to forgive me for causing you any suffering or anxiety. I should not have asked you to marry me. It was thoughtless; but I could not with my experience and knowledge of things understand all that my request might mean. As you are Reverdy's sister I can't help but feel a tender and protecting interest in you, whatever may come of it. And I hope life may deal with both of us in such a way that any harm I have done you will be overcome by some good that I may be to you. And without asking to see you again I still keep the hope that fate will be good enough to let me meet you sometime when a clasp of the hand will be welcome to you and with no consequences that are not pleasant."

And then I sealed the letter for mailing and retired; but not to sleep, rather to turn restlessly for some hours in the night.

CHAPTER XXI

Fortunately for my peace of mind I had much to do and much to interest me. The country was developing rapidly under my eyes. Thousands of farms were coming into cultivation. The prairie grass was vanishing before the corn. Villages were springing up everywhere. Jacksonville was growing. A furor of land selling, the selling of lots and blocks in the newly formed towns, swept over the state. And my own farm had increased in value, both because of the care I had given it and because of the growing population. For in truth, while Illinois had about 160,000 inhabitants when I came to it, now as we approached the year 1837 it was estimated that there were nearly 400,000 souls within its borders.

Douglas had no sooner become a member of the legislature, as it seemed to me, than he resigned to take the office of register of land in Springfield, which was now the capital of the state. He was reported to me to be making a great deal of money now, sometimes as much as $100 a day. I saw him in the summer. He was a figure of dash, self-possession, energy and clear-headedness. He confided to me that he intended to run for Congress. He was now twenty-four, a political leader in his party, fearless, dreaded, and resourceful.

Douglas had advised me to read political history. Accordingly, during the long evenings at the farm, I had gone through Elliott's *Debates* and the *Federalist*. My grandmother sent me De Tocqueville's ***De la Democratie en Amerique***, which I read in French.

But now I began to see that abolition sentiment was growing. Societies were being formed and had been for about two years in the northern part of the state. Here in Jacksonville the agitation of the slavery question was frowned upon; but it was fermenting under the surface of southern sentiment.

I was now treated to an American panic, and times were hard. The East wanted a tariff to protect its manufacturers; the South wanted land and slaves. Texas had been filling up with Americans since 1820. She seceded from Mexico and declared her independence now; and General Houston, a Virginian by birth, a Tennesseean by residence, had taken command of the Texas troops, and after the Alamo massacre, had defeated the Mexicans with terrible slaughter in the battle of San Jacinto. The New England conscience excoriated these things and attributed them to the machinations of the slavocracy. But while Douglas had no mastery of the tariff question in its details, his mind shot through to the general philosophy of it. He often said to me that books and works of art should be admitted free of duty. He was wont to laugh at the New England conscience which could swallow the tariff and the growing factory system, and yet reject with such holy loathing cotton and slavery. He could not handle statistics, but he was a master of principles.

As my grandmother was writing me regularly of affairs in England, of the progress of events, of the building of railroads, of Charles Wheatstone's electric telegraph, and of the new books of moment, I on my part was attempting to keep her informed of my life, and of the swiftly moving panorama of Illinois life. And here I insert one of my letters to her because it covers so much of the ground of this time of my life.

"Dear Grandmama: I have before written you of my friend Mr. Douglas who came to Illinois just a little while before I did, and who has had such a phenomenal rise in life in this new country. He is now making ready to go to Congress, and I am to be one of the delegates to the convention which is expected to nominate him. Having resigned a very lucrative post in the Land Office, he has gone into the practice of law and the pursuit of politics. For the latter he has a positive genius, as his whole mind is taken up with visions and plans for the development of the country, and for the aggrandizement of the United States. He is honest and outspoken, courageous even to audacity; but he is sometimes accused of devious ways, and of taking up anything that has a stomach in it. But no one can say that he changes his principles; rather he avails himself of opportune conditions, which are many, to advance himself and the things he believes in. The country has no truer friend. Though I am an alien I am a resident, and therefore I can participate in political affairs and help him without being naturalized. At the present time Douglas is in Springfield, and is much in the office of one of the newspapers there, to which he contributes editorials sometimes. Recently the office was attacked by some men who had been accused of trickery of some sort by the newspaper. Douglas was present; and, though he is a little fellow, he helped to beat off the attacking parties; and in the general assault the sheriff was stabbed by one of the editors; but the matter has all blown over.

"My own unfortunate affair has the appearance now of dying down.

"A very terrible thing has happened in the killing the Reverend Lovejoy at Alton, a town not far from Jacksonville. He was running an abolition newspaper which was offensive to the slave interests or the peace interests, if you want to call them that. And persisting in his agitation of the slave question they undertook to destroy his press. In the altercation Lovejoy was shot. There is great feeling over the matter.

"It is impossible for me to convey to you the intellectual atmosphere of the country. It is so full of contradictions and cross currents. For example, you come to believe that a Whig is against slavery. Then some one comes forward to propose a certain General Harrison, a leading Whig, for President in 1840; and some one arises to show that when he was Governor of Indiana, when it was a territory, he tried to introduce slavery, contrary to the Ordinance of 1787. I wrote you of this Ordinance before. Then there are the most numerous groups of people of every sort of weird convictions; some organized to oppose Masonry; others to curb the Irish and the Catholics; others to prohibit the use of wine and all intoxicants; others to advance the cause of free love; others to socialize the state. There are also religious societies here of every description, such as the Millerites who are now preparing for the Second Advent of Christ which they believe will take place in 1843. They are already making ready to leave their business, get their white robes, and await the Epiphany. In this state, at Nauvoo, a group called Mormons, who came here from Missouri, founded their faith upon a new revelation brought to light by two miraculous stones, said to have been discovered by a man named Joseph Smith. They practice polygamy, as in patriarchal times. They are already stirring up opposition to themselves, for where every one is so good and in his own peculiar way, hostility must result. And in this Democracy, so-called, all the really good people are in the business of forcing others to their own way of thinking. I must tell you also of a branch of the Presbyterian church which separated from the old church on the question of predestination and infant damnation. Of Baptists, Methodists, and others there are numerous sects, which in England would be frowned upon as various forms of ludicrous non-conformism. De Tocqueville's book, for which my thanks to you, dear grandmama, will preserve a very faithful picture of America of this day.

"And it is refreshing, strengthening to the mind and clearing to the eye, to see Douglas and to hear him talk about all these things. He stands so clear, so pure of stock so to speak, amid all this variegated growth of political and social heresy. The other day when I was in Springfield I looked him up. Here he was talking of the Lovejoy matter, which led him into a cataloguing of the abolitionists, the anti-Masons, the Spiritualists, the Mormons, free lovers, old centralists, with the Whigs. I think he is proud that he has no hobby in the way of an ideal or ism. He seems unmagnetic to all such things. If he does not look with suspicion upon the reformer and accuse him of masking some selfish purpose, he is likely to think that the reformer is something of a fool. He gazes with an eagle's eye over the whole of American activity; he sees the South interested in cotton, the North concerned with its growing factories. Steam, iron, coal, and land figure in his deductions. He sees the country rising to power on them. And he sees men--whatever their professions--trying to advance their own interests. Hence he laughs down these queer political and religious groups; and while he deplores the death of Lovejoy, he takes it as a matter of course; the wringing of the nose brings forth blood. He is kindly and most loyal, fearless, clear-minded, and powerful; but he is unmoral. He sees the play of life. He sees the stronger getting more, Texas coming eventually to the United States, though blood be shed. The drift of things is impelled by great forces of ancient and world-wide origin. He believes with all his soul in the superiority of the white race, and that it must rule. At the same time Democracy is the thing, but Democracy let loose only after the philosophical channels have been cut. Notwithstanding his laughter at Mormonism, for example, he would not suppress it. He would let it work out its own fate. Free thought and free speech will kill it, or it will survive in spite of them because of its inherent strength, if at all. All together Douglas is very admirable to me. I think he is a genius; one of those human beings who was born old but who will always be young. And here he is in a country that is changing and growing like a village crowd upon a stage. Already Chicago has more than 4,000, and we are soon to have canals and railroads, thanks to Douglas more than to any other man in Illinois. 'The Great Northern Cross,' a railroad, is soon to be built starting at Meredosia on the Illinois River and running to Jacksonville.

"As to my own affairs, dear grandmama, I have nothing to wish for in the way of material progress. Upon my return from New Orleans, whither I went in order to think down an unfortunate love affair, I found that Zoe had run away. I do not know where she is, and cannot learn by any means at my present command. Though, if Douglas is nominated for Congress, I mean to go about with him through the state. That will give me opportunity to search for her, particularly if we go to Chicago. Do write when you can, as letters are especially welcome to me from you here in this somewhat lonely life."

CHAPTER XXII

Because of the gossip concerning Zoe, and the fact that I had killed Lamborn, opposition was made to me as a delegate to the Congressional convention. I was an alien too; but that did not count. I was a resident and a large land owner.

Though Douglas was but twenty-four years of age, he was already a giant. Opposition gave way before him; he stepped on his foes; he brushed tangles aside. A Mr. May, who was now in Congress, wanted to return. But he found he could not simply assume the nomination and place the responsibility for the assumption upon the request of "many friends"--a vague and specious way of covering up his own seizure of the honor. He had to face the convention system which Douglas had introduced into Illinois politics. And Douglas had Morgan County, his first home in Illinois, back of him; and Sangamon County, his home since he had gone into the legislature and the Land Office. Douglas was nominated.

A cry went up. An experienced Congressman, Mr. May, had been ruthlessly put aside for the sake of an ambitious stripling! The Whigs rejoiced and said that no nomination than that of Douglas could suit them better. And the Whigs were powerful enough. They were coquetting with the Abolitionists; and they stood for the tariff and the bank. Besides, times were hard. It had been said that Jackson had set the tide of money scarcity to flowing; Van Buren had increased it. There were also disgruntled factions because of Douglas' so-called high-handed tactics in capturing the nomination.

Then to make things worse the Democrats nominated a state ticket upon which two of the candidates had been in the Land Office. So had Douglas. Hence the cry: the Land Office Ticket. Douglas had made money, therefore down with him! Only poverty and humility deserved honor.

I not only opened my purse to Douglas, for he was not in fact affluent; but I decided to travel with him in the campaign. True to his courage and his self-confidence he met his Whig opponent, Major Stuart, face to face in joint debate at Springfield. I was greatly thrilled with this contest. Major Stuart was very popular, an old resident, an officer in the Black Hawk War, and a brave one, Reverdy told me. He was of powerful physique, standing more than six feet, and equal to an arduous campaign. At Springfield Stuart and Douglas came to blows. Stuart tucked Douglas' head under his arm and carried him around the square; meanwhile Douglas bit Stuart's thumb almost in two. As a debater and campaigner Douglas was his superior. He made friends by the hundreds everywhere. He went down among the gay and volatile Irishmen who were digging the Illinois and Michigan canal, and won them to his cause. I was with him, watching his methods, marveling at his physical resources, his exhaustless oratory, the aptness and quickness of his logic.

In the midst of the summer we decided to go to Chicago. Douglas' clothes, his boots, his hat, were worn almost to pieces. We were driving a single horse hitched to a buggy. The horse was weary; the harness was a patch of ropes. We could have made these things good with purchases along the way, but Douglas put off the day. At last we decided to make them in Chicago. He was loath to let me use my money for such needs as these, seeing that I had already contributed so much to campaign expenses. But I overbore his wishes.

We were a comical pair driving into the hurly burly of the new city of Chicago. It had recently received a charter. But what a motley of buildings it was! Frame shacks wedged between more substantial buildings of brick or wood. Land speculators swarmed everywhere; land offices confronted one at every turn; lawyers, doctors, men of all professions and trades had descended upon this waste of sand and scrub oaks about the lake. Indians walked among the whites; negroes as porters, laborers, bootblacks, were plentiful; there were countless drinking places and new hotels; there were sharpers, adventurers, blacklegs, men of prey of all description, prostitutes, the camp followers of new settlements, houses of vice, restaurants, gardens. And with all the rest of it evidences of fine breeds, and civilizing purposes in some of the residences and activities. After all a city was to be built.

And here we were--a sorry pair indeed! Douglas, worn from his campaigning, battered and frayed; myself, dusty and unkempt, entering Chicago behind a horse dragging its body harnessed in patches to a rattling buggy. We laughed at ourselves.

Douglas and I went to a clothing store where I insisted upon fitting him out with a suit and a hat. We bought a new harness for the horse. Then we set forth for meals and drinks.

Somehow I felt that Zoe might be in some concert hall singing for the means of life. A darker idea crossed my mind, but I put it away. I told Douglas that I meant to find Zoe, if I could. After our meal we went from place to place in this quest. Douglas did not try to dissuade me, but he looked at me keenly as if he wondered why I wished to find Zoe. Why, after all? As years elapsed I would be rid of all associated memory of her in Jacksonville. Might not Dorothy come back to me if she knew that Zoe had wholly vanished from my life? Yet something of a sense of responsibility, and something of an affection for Zoe kept my mind fast to the idea of finding her. Up and down the streets of Chicago Douglas and I walked, looking for Zoe.

Once I heard a woman's voice singing "Annie Laurie." I rushed into the place whence the voice came, followed deliberately and patiently by Douglas. There stood a woman on a sort of platform. She was garishly dressed. There were idlers and drinkers at the table. When we came out Douglas said that the search was useless; that if Zoe was in Chicago she might be in a place so secret that I would never find her, except by chance. Yes, I understood. And if it had come to that, what could I do with Zoe, if I found her?

Chicago was not long in discovering that Douglas, the marvelous boy, was in their midst. He must make an address. They erected a platform and billed the town. I stayed near until Douglas rose to speak. He looked fresh and tidy in his new suit, and with freshly shaven face. I heard his great voice roll out over the large crowd collected to hear him. I heard the applause that welcomed him, that responded to the first thrill of his fluent eloquence. Then I stole away to look for Zoe.

I walked up and down the streets. I stood in drinking places. I entered a few places of vice. I stopped at the rear of a hotel, where the maids were gathered together resting and talking after the day's work. But no Zoe.

At last I went down to the shore of the lake, rather to the shore of the sluice through which the Chicago River widened into the lake in a southerly direction. I sat here on a rude settee. The air was warm. There were sounds and voices floating over me from the town. Occasionally I could hear the organ music of Douglas' oratory, as it drifted indistinguishably to me. I was thinking, wondering about my own life; enthralled at the vision of this new country, which I could see taking form before my own eyes. Then I became conscious of a couple on a settee near. I had not noticed them before. I got up and walked past them. And there was Zoe!

It was dusk, but she knew me. She gave a quick start, put her hand to her mouth. The man was silent, looking at her, unconscious of my presence. I divined that she did not want me to speak to her. I heard her say to her companion: "Go back. Leave me here awhile, I want to be alone. I will return soon."

I walked on a distance of a hundred yards or more. Then I looked back. I thought some one, Zoe, or both of them were still on the settee. I could not be sure. I retraced my steps. When I came to the settee the man was some distance away, going toward the town. Zoe motioned to me to walk the way I had come. I did so; loitered and returned. Zoe was now alone. I sat down beside her; Zoe took my hand.

My first thought was who was the man. Zoe proceeded to tell me that she was working as a domestic, that this man was a voice teacher who had recently arrived in Chicago from New York. I looked at Zoe, as if to ask her what was the nature of the intimacy that would lead her into this association at night in this secluded place by the lake. I followed this by asking: "Are you very good friends?" "He is kind to me," Zoe said. "He teaches me and we walk out together and talk."

Well, were there not then the usual consequences? Zoe was remarkably beautiful; Zoe's morale had been broken by a terrible experience. She had gone through the disintegration natural to my own difficulties, of which she was the occasion; the killing of Lamborn, the whole condition at Jacksonville. And now, what was Zoe? I could not penetrate her reserve. She stroked my hands affectionately. The tears started from her eyes.

I changed the key by bringing up her interests. "Reverdy is your guardian and I am putting your property in his hands. Don't you need money? Why haven't you sent for money?" "Because," Zoe answered, "I meant to go out of your life, and stay out of your life. Now that you have found me it does not matter. All I could do would be to run off again. But why? This is a wonderful place. I love the excitement, the stir here. And I am in no danger here from being kidnapped. I don't want to go into the country again. I will be all right, James, be sure. But if you want to send me some money I will be glad. Only don't come for me; don't have me known in your life again. I am out of it now. You can't do for me what you could if I was white. Why try? Facts are just what they are. I will be all right here. I am learning to sing. Mr. Fortescue says that I have a voice. That's his name. He is a good man, you can be sure." "He loves you?" I interrupted. Zoe did not answer. "He wants to marry you?" I said, half interrogatively. "I don't believe I am made for marriage," said Zoe. "Where do you work?" I asked.

Zoe was silent for some seconds, as if thinking. I repeated the question. "Don't ask me that, Mr. James, don't," she said. "I know where you are, I know where to find you. And if you need me I will come to you if I can; but don't ask me where I am." "How can I send you money?" "Send it to the post office. Send it to Laurette Toombs. That's my name here. But don't try to find me again. I just pray God all the time that I may never be of any trouble to you; and I am afraid all the time I may." "Why?" I asked quickly. "Oh, I don't know; just because things are what they are. I have already made you a world of trouble. And you have been just as good to me as a brother could be. I just pray God not to make you any more trouble. I must go." Her voice had grown full of pathos. "Where?" I asked. "Don't follow me, Mr. James, just let me go. I am a grown woman. I must lead my own life. Just be good to me as you have been--don't you understand? I grieve. So be good to me, let me manage myself and manage our meetings, whatever they are. Sit here now while I steal away. Promise me."

Zoe got up, stretched her hands to me, then hurried through the darkness to the town. I followed her with my eyes until she was lost to view. The voice of Douglas by a sudden swell of the air was borne to me. One articulate word fell upon my ears. It was "slavery." His voice lapsed into the silence of the receding breeze. I sat alone for a few minutes. Then I arose, and went to the place where Douglas was speaking. He was just finishing. In a burst of impetuous and impassioned eloquence he was pointing to the future glory of the United States, when Great Britain would own no foot of soil from the North Pole to the Gulf. The audience applauded tumultuously. Douglas stepped from the rude platform into the arms of bewitched admirers. He freed himself and came to me. He brought with him a Mr. DeWitt Williams who had prevailed upon Douglas to accept his hospitality for the night. As Douglas' traveling companion, I was invited to share in the entertainment.

CHAPTER XXIII

I had no opportunity now to tell Douglas that I had found Zoe. Her own injunctions to keep her whereabouts a secret appealed to me. Perhaps her going away, the changing of her name, her determination to keep her life free from mine, made for a real solution. Perhaps she could continue in this way for years, taking from me what I might send her. Perhaps I could marry Dorothy eventually. Perhaps all would be well. Perhaps!

When we were driving toward Springfield the next day I was on the point several times of telling Douglas that I had found Zoe. I wanted to discuss the possibilities with some one. Prudence, however, dictated silence--and silence I kept.

Mr. Williams was a prospering lawyer and land speculator. He had been in Chicago for two years. His household consisted of Mrs. Williams and two children, and a Miss Walker from Connecticut, a sister of Mrs. Williams. The house was new and of some architectural pretentions, of brick, in the style of the houses I had seen in New York. It was well furnished. There were two servants; altogether an air of elegance about the establishment.

We had a gay hour at breakfast, for Douglas was in one of his most engaging and talkative moods. Mr. Williams was a man in the middle forties, and seemed colorless and unschooled in comparison with Douglas. He shared Douglas' political opinions, looked upon him with a certain awe; while Mrs. Williams and the children kept a reverential silence.

But Miss Walker! I saw that she was disposed to match wits with Douglas. She was exceedingly fair of complexion, with lovely brown hair and gray-blue eyes, which had a way of fixing themselves in an expression of intense concentration. Like sudden spurts of flame they lighted quickly upon the barely suggested point of a story or an argument. She laughed freely in a musical voice that encouraged

Douglas to multiply anecdotes. Douglas enjoyed this admiration. But after all his attitude toward women was wholly conventional. He did not use his gifts to win them. The idea of making conquests, even through his growing celebrity, did not enter into his speculations. He was a man's man. If he was ever to be interested in a woman it would be in the practical way of making her his wife. He could be a husband, never a lover. His genius, though fed by passion and virility, entertained no visions of romantic ecstasy. His instinct was for the laws.

Miss Walker was to Douglas only a delightful auditor, an apt interlocutor. She looked Douglas through and through. She dropped words of dissent. She expressed her abhorrence of slavery and the South. In referring to South Carolina's attempted nullification of the tariff law, she said that if they ever attempted to secede they should be pushed out of the door and not held. I thought her critical of Douglas, in spite of the amazement which her eyes betrayed for his conversational gifts, his self-assurance and brilliancy. Once she said that there was a right and wrong about everything. And when Douglas glanced up at her quickly, her eyes fixed him steadily. Douglas took up this challenge by saying: "Yes, but who is to decide what is right and what is wrong; or what is to decide it? The progress of the country or the opinions of fanatics?" "The minds of big men," retorted Miss Walker. "And since you have spoken of a great territory for the United States let me bespeak big men for it instead. Persia you know was a big country." "Why make the two inconsistent?" asked Douglas. "You can have both." "No, not where you make material progress the never-ending thought of every one."

Mr. Williams had many things on his mind, that was apparent. His haste in eating, his self-absorption showed that. Yet after breakfast he lingered for half an hour; and during this time Miss Walker, who had noticed me no more up to now than as one of the persons at the table, came to a seat near me in the living room. She was lovely to look at, but in a way half prim. The whiteness of her forehead, the fineness of her hands, her air of clear and quick intellectuality, made her a person to inspire something of deference. And yet I felt myself captivated by her. Surely in every thinking man's heart there is a biological groping toward a woman of mind. Shadowy forms rise undistinguished before him. They are the children that such a woman can bear. He does not know that this is the urge; but nature knows. On Miss Walker's part, I saw her appraising me. She had come west where life was luxuriant and the accidents of fortune abundant and men were strong. She had now over-stayed her visit with Mrs. Williams. Was to-day her day of destiny? Here before her were the rising statesman of Illinois and a man who had increased a fortune.

She was coming to Springfield shortly to visit. Would I be there? Did I know the Ridgeway family there, of which Edward Ridgeway, the founder, had been prominent in the affairs of Illinois, now dead some five years? If I came to Springfield she would be glad to have me call upon her. Well, perhaps she liked me and did not like Douglas after all. Was I drawn to her? I felt some definite interest in her, that was sure. But I was not forgetting Dorothy. Dorothy could not be obscured by a light as white as Miss Walker's. And yet I had to confess that I was thinking of Miss Walker in a half serious way.

CHAPTER XXIV

Douglas' hard campaign was ended when we arrived in Springfield. His humorous remark was that he had the constitution of the United States. He was never so wholly fatigued that a drink or a meal would not pull him up to a zest and a capacity for a further task. A little sleep restored him to a new exuberance. Truly, he was one of the most vital men who come into the world for a restless career.

On the way back we noted how rapidly the country was changing. The influx of settlers was very great. Villages, towns were springing up everywhere. Farmhouses were multiplying. Douglas was enthusiastic over the great prosperity which was evident. As an empire builder his imagination was stirred. If he was not elected to Congress he would have to go back to the practice of law. At this period of his life he was the eager and ambitious youth pressed in the matter of money. I saw his career influenced, if not largely shaped, by material necessity. And as it turned out in the election in August he was defeated by thirty-five votes in a total poll of 36,000. We did not know the result of the election until several weeks later, due to the tardy facilities for communicating news.

He had fought against an able and experienced campaigner. He had the handicap of extreme youth. He had to meet the slurs of "interloper," and the charge of being a pushing newcomer. And yet he was almost elected. There were discrepancies in the count, too. He was urged to contest the election. But the expense was too great. He was poor.

There was much about Douglas to remind one of Napoleon: drive, will, resourcefulness, exhaustless energy. Too bad to remit such a man to the business of getting clients. He was not a plodder. He was a mind who saw men in large aggregations bound to each other by policies and interests. He knew how to handle them as material in empire building.

On that ride back to Springfield he talked to me of many things that gave me an insight into the workings of his mind. For the dreamer, the visionary, he had no patience; he felt contempt for the agitator and the radical. In a theory preoccupying the human mind he saw something akin to madness. Mormonism, abolitionism, all the various forms of propaganda which made American life so clamorous, found a common classification in his tabulation of men. What was really before the country? Truly, the conquest of the wilderness, the production of wealth, the development of national power; but always the rule of the people too. "There are two things in my life," he said to me. "One is the fact that I got mad at my uncle, and the other is the inspiration that I get out of these prairies. Add to these what mind I have, and the sum is myself."

When we parted in Springfield, and I was about to return to my farm in Jacksonville, he could not thank me enough for what I had done for him. But I was his friend, and why not? I saw him later when a dinner was given at Quincy in honor of the Democratic governor-elect whose success Douglas had done so much to bring about. All the speakers paid tribute to Douglas amid storms of applause. They assured him that his firm integrity, the high order of his talent had endeared him to the people; and that he would be remembered in two years with another nomination.

As soon as I saw Reverdy I told him that I had found Zoe and all the circumstances and about Fortescue. Reverdy thought that I should send Zoe money for living expenses on the first of each month; and so I began.

But neither Reverdy nor myself could work out any permanent program for Zoe. After all, what was humanly possible? Zoe was now about nineteen. If she was dealt with justly as to her property what more could I do? If there was danger from Fortescue, or any one else, I was powerless to prevent it. Since she did not wish to live with me, I had no power to make her do so.

In November Reverdy and I went to Meredosia to see the locomotive which had been shipped from Pittsburgh for Illinois' first railroad. All of the horses and oxen of the neighborhood were required to pull the huge iron thing up the banks of the river; and scores of men in ant-like activity worked about it to place it upon the rails. Douglas was in the crowd, happy and enthusiastic. He joined the party, headed by Governor Duncan, in the first journey that a steam train ever made in the state. He tried to make a place for Reverdy and me; but the Governor had filled all the seats with his friends: so we stood as spectators, while the new wonder moved on its way, pulled by the queer locomotive, amid the shouts of the crowd, responded to by the calls of those on board.

Going back to Jacksonville I ventured to talk to Reverdy about Dorothy. He knew well enough what my feeling was for her. He knew the story; he knew her attitude. He did not share in her fears, in her feeling about Zoe. He was frank to say that Zoe could do nothing, could be nothing that need affect my life in any way more serious than if her skin was white. But he explained that Dorothy had the southern view; and if I wished to wait and see if she could work herself out of doubts, well and good; and if I could not further hope he could understand that too. I wanted to write to Dorothy to tell her that Zoe was still away and that I thought she would never return. But perhaps after all Dorothy's attitude was founded in an innate prejudice against the relationship to which she would make herself a party by marrying me. Was this not perfectly unreasonable? It made me distrust Dorothy's nature at times. What was she after all? Finally, however, I wrote to Dorothy as best I could and after many ineffectual trials at expressing myself. Promptly enough a letter came back. It was not lacking in kindness, but it offered no hope. Hurt and listless I tried to turn my thoughts to other things. There were always my growing enterprises--and yet to what end? To be rich, to be richer.

When December came I had a letter from Miss Walker. She was in Springfield at the Ridgeway mansion for a visit through the holidays. There were to be parties and dances. Why did I not come over? And I went.

I looked up Douglas at once. He was making some headway at the practice of law, but his energies, for the most part, were absorbed in perfecting the organization of his party. He was putting together a compact machine. He was on the very edge of being the leader of the Illinois Democracy. What infinite details there are to any given end! If it is the building of a house, tools must be bought, trees felled, foundations dug. A carpenter's finger must be bandaged so that he can go on with the work. Cloth must be found for the bandage and a string with which to tie it. And so Douglas was engaged in infinite talks on the corners, at the newspaper office; he was making short trips; he was writing dozens of letters, he was inserting editorials in the newspapers. But he had time for the gayeties of the season.

He was always the gallant, the amusing wit, the ready raconteur. We were such friends! Again Miss Walker had both of us for attendants; but upon such widely different footing. I was a suitor with many doubts. Douglas was not a suitor at all. He came to her to enjoy the keenness of her mind.

But as I was English, and as Miss Walker thought herself the next thing to it, she took me aside as an understanding confidant as to the life around us. Springfield was almost a mudhole. She was offended by it, but also she found much in it to make her laugh. There were the gawks; the sprawling ill-bred men; the illiterate young women; the mushroom life; the haste, the crudities of living; the ugliness and the disorder; the unsettled, ever restless, patchy catch as catch can existence; the attempt, in a word, to make life, to build a town, a capital. All this shocked or amused her. Did I not see it with English eyes used to tranquillity and order? She wondered why Douglas had left the East. He could have risen there in time; and when he should have done so it would have been an eminence. Had he not acquired brusqueness, vulgarity since coming west? A man of undoubted gifts, she conceded--yet. Perhaps I was her favorite after all.

To test her out, I put my own story around the life of a friend, telling her of a man who had married an octoroon, leaving a daughter of color and a son by a previous marriage with a white woman; also describing the consequences that had ensued. Miss Walker heard me with interested attention. She admitted that the complications were serious. Undoubtedly, many women in the West would care nothing about such a relationship, there was so much indifference here to form and breeding; anything for a husband, anything to get along in the world. Well, if Miss Walker from Connecticut could see my relationship to Zoe in such a light, could I blame Dorothy from Tennessee for judging it more seriously? Perhaps after all this was a woman's reaction to my story.

Later I had a party at my house, inviting all the young crowd of Springfield to come over. Douglas came too, and Reverdy and Sarah and Mr. and Mrs. Sturtevant. It was just after Christmas. We had a roaring fire in the fireplace. We popped corn and pulled candy. I brought in my old fiddler from the woods to play for us. We danced. These festivities were in honor of Miss Walker, and she entered into the fun with great zest. Day by day we were better friends. When she came to go back to Springfield she was no longer Miss Walker to me, she was Abigail. I was not in love with her--there was Dorothy still in my heart. Yet I was very fond of her. I thought she approved of me. As we parted she asked me why I did not come to Chicago. It was fast growing into a city. What better field for making money? Vaguely the idea entered my mind and began to mature.

CHAPTER XXV

The truth was that the loneliness in my life was depressing me; it was in a sense work without hope--only the hope of being rich. While I could not doubt Abigail's fitness as a mate for me, and though I was in desperate need of a companion, Dorothy would not out of my mind and my heart. My indomitable will had asserted itself in the pursuit of Dorothy. Even if my judgment had favored Abigail I could not have given up Dorothy. To surrender the hope of Dorothy was to leave something in my life unfinished; and that was contrary to my tenacious purpose. I could not hear Abigail's voice without comparing it to the softer modulations of Dorothy's. I could not be in the presence of Abigail without feeling that there was something more kindred to me in the personality of Dorothy. And yet I had to confess on reflection that I was not sure of this. Dorothy wrote to me on occasion, but there was really nothing in her letters to keep hope alive. All the while my life was going on in labor, in planning, in building, with Mrs. Brown to keep my house. Even Zoe did not write to me. I knew that she was receiving the monthly allowance from the fact that my letters were not returned. However, at last one was sent back to me.

Then in the late winter I was surprised one day by the visit of a stranger--and a strange character he was too. He introduced himself to me as Henry Fortescue of Chicago--and as Zoe's husband! I remembered; he was the voice teacher with whom Zoe was sitting on the lake front. He began by saying that he had come with very unwelcome news and upon a sorrowful mission. Zoe was dead! Zoe had met her death by foul play. She had been found strangled to death in her bed.

I glanced in horror at this unknown character. He went on to tell me that suspicion had fastened itself upon a half-breed who came to the house where Zoe lived. He had been arrested, was soon to be tried. As to Fortescue's visit here, he had come to see about Zoe's land and interests. He had married Zoe some weeks before her death. Without knowing much about such matters I went at once to the point.

I asked Fortescue what proof he had of the marriage. I began to suspect Fortescue of being the murderer himself. So many desperate deeds were done in this country; so many dishonest expedients resorted to for money, for land. My question gave Fortescue embarrassment. He stammered, colored a little, then went on to say that he had witnesses to the marriage; that the ceremony was not performed by a minister, but that he and Zoe had entered into a common-law marriage. I did not know exactly what this was and at once determined to see Douglas about it.

Meanwhile I was compelled to suffer Fortescue to wander over the farm. He took it upon himself to do so; and I scarcely knew how to forbid him. I did stay him, however, from looking through my house. I saw that he was a hungry dog, an impoverished wanderer who had fallen into means, if, indeed, he was Zoe's husband.

The question now was, how to get him away; how, without denying he had any rights, to keep him from assuming an attitude of proprietorship. I thought it best to go with him. Accordingly, as I had proposed that we go to Springfield at once, we rode partially across the farm in going to Jacksonville. I told Fortescue frankly that I would have to look into his proofs, and that I meant to go to Chicago, and that it was my duty to see to it that Zoe's murderer was punished.

I stopped a few minutes to talk to Reverdy and Sarah. Reverdy was all sympathy and wondered what misfortune would befall me next. Sarah wept for Zoe's fate and for the trouble that it involved me in. She went to the window and looked out. There was Fortescue waiting for me, apparently glowing for the good fortune that had come to him. And here was I in the house of Dorothy's brother and unable to put out of mind the hope that Zoe's death would change Dorothy's decision, even while I was grieving for Zoe. Like a spider at its door Fortescue was waiting for me. Whether he or I should be more benefited by Zoe's death remained to be seen. As I left I asked Reverdy to write Dorothy and tell her what had happened to Zoe.

When we got to Springfield I left Fortescue to his own ways. I looked up Douglas and asked his advice. As always, he was busy in politics. He was now master of his party's organization. But as I had tortures because of my position he had anxieties because of the lack of means. The law business did not bring him a great deal; it could not, for his mind was on other things. He was trying to be secretary of state in order to supplement his earnings as a lawyer. He was catching at whatever offered to float himself along. His life was, therefore, patchy. Would it ever be a whole, well-fitting garment to his great genius?

I took up with him at once the matter of Zoe's common-law marriage. There was first the question whether Zoe could enter into any marriage with a white man. But I had settled that with Mr. Brooks, when going into that matter of my father's marriage with Zoe's mother. Zoe was not a negro, not a mulatto; she had less than one fourth negro blood. Therefore, she did not fall under the inhibitions of the Illinois law forbidding marriages between persons of color, negro or mulatto, with a white person. Douglas confirmed what Mr. Brooks had told me; and he gave me the opinion that a common-law marriage was legal, but that Fortescue would have to bring witnesses to Jacksonville to testify that he and Zoe had taken each other as husband and wife; and that this had been followed by an assumption of the marriage relation.

Douglas advised me to look carefully into the proofs. Well, why should he not return to Chicago with me and help with the investigation? He was willing. Meanwhile Fortescue was waiting for me. When I told him that I was coming to Chicago with a friend he looked suspicious, as if he thought that I was trying to evade him. As he began to press me then, saying that we could all travel together, I forgot myself for the moment in a rise of temper. "The land can't get away; nothing can run away; and you can't get anything until you prove your case. I am going to Chicago with a friend. I will see you there. You can go your own way." Fortescue acquiesced apologetically; and having done with him for the time, I turned again to visit with Douglas.

I had never seen him in a more interesting mood. He wished for good fortune to befall him so that he could do something for the education of the young, since his own opportunities had been limited. In this connection he spoke of the grants of land which had been made to Illinois for institutions and schools of higher learning. And while talking of the Louisiana territory which Napoleon had granted to America, and of Texas whose recent independence the United States had recognized, his imagination glowed before the future power and glory of the country. He was delighted that so many Germans and Irish, fleeing from disorder and oppression in Europe, were seeking freedom and opportunity here, and filling up the new lands. But while my inheritance of a few thousand acres was already perplexing me, Douglas was still free of the great calamity that would befall him because of the new domains! If Zoe as one of the numerous persons of color had already involved my life, how terribly would the curse pronounced upon the descendants of Ham fall upon this Titan, this nation builder! Douglas indulged his satirical talent in an amusing description of General Taylor who was now talked of by the Whigs for President. He charged the Whigs with cunningly picking rough and ready characters, pioneer types, for their appeal to the plain people--pioneer types who really entertained monarchistic principles. There was already much talk that Texas was being drawn toward the United States by the slavocracy. Well, what of it? The main thing was to get Texas. What is this sanctimonious talk in prose and verse in England about Texas? Douglas was very contemptuous of all of this.

Fortescue took his way somehow to Chicago. Douglas and I traveled together. The first thing that Douglas sought to do was to look into the evidence as to the murder of Zoe, and this with reference to Fortescue's possible part in it. To this end Douglas sought the assistance of Mr. Williams. Though he kept a law office, his larger interests were real estate dealings. But he dropped everything to assist Douglas and me in arriving at the truth. We went to the jail and saw the half-breed who was charged with killing Zoe. The state's attorney had the half-breed's confession. Though he was half insane from drink when he did the deed, the prosecutor intended to ask for the death penalty. He was a half-breed!

We intended to look up the witnesses, to learn from them the circumstances which attended the murder. The prosecutor, however, was disinclined to let us do this, and refused to give us their names. He stood on a matter of pride that he had the case in hand himself and had procured the confession. Douglas seemed to think it was unnecessary to pursue the matter, and that was Mr. Williams' attitude. In the hurry of these hours, dinner time having arrived too, we got into a haze--at least I did--about getting anything more definite. Douglas thought that the real question was the common-law marriage. If I wanted to prosecute Fortescue for the murder I could do it any time. In the meanwhile Fortescue would have to prove the marriage in order to derive any benefit from Zoe's death.

We asked Fortescue what evidence he had of this marriage. "For one thing this," he said, bringing forth a ring which had the words, "to my husband Henry from Zoe" and the date engraved in it. Douglas wished Fortescue to produce the witnesses who were present at the marriage. This Fortescue refused to do. He became suddenly stubborn, almost sullen. In a bold way he said to us: "If you are not satisfied with this, I'll prove my case." "You will have to do that anyway," said Douglas, "and perhaps as this matter goes on you will not be so confident." Saying that he would come to Jacksonville with his proofs Fortescue left us and disappeared.

Then Douglas turned to the talk of politics with his friends. Mr. Williams went to his office. I was left alone. Had we accomplished anything? I went back to see the state's attorney by myself, and asked him if he did not suspect Fortescue. The state's attorney said that the case was perfectly clear against the half-breed; that my only interest in the matter was the marriage and to go back and defend that if I chose, though he felt sure that Fortescue would amply prove that he had married Zoe. I dropped the whole thing and called upon Abigail.

She began at once to urge me to come to Chicago. This was to be a city. The opportunities here were infinitely rich. The life was increasingly more interesting. She knew of my troubles, knew of the murder, for it had been the talk of the town. She urged upon me a new life. I did not need to sell my farm--leave it. Come to Chicago where fortunes were being made and where greater fortunes would come to men of vision and energy. We took a walk by the lake, which in reality only came to the shore far south of the town--south of the mouth of the river. Here the waves rolled upon the sand. What purity and blueness in the sky! To our right as far as we could see wastes of yellow sand, dunes, brush, small oaks and pines! Back of us a ragged and wild landscape being broken or leveled by builders, by the opening of streets and roads.

Abigail was truly my friend, wise and sympathetic. Her clear-cut thinking sheared away accidental things, fringes of irrelevancy. I was so glad to get her opinion on the various things that perplexed me. She advised me to make the best fight I could against Fortescue. After that come to Chicago whatever the result. We parted with a clasp of the hand. Then I went to find Douglas.

CHAPTER XXVI

At times afterward I reproached myself for not doing more to fix the guilt of Zoe's death upon Fortescue. Particularly as it became clear to me that his freedom from that responsibility energized his descent upon me for Zoe's interest in the farm. What had my generosity, foolish and boyish, come to after all?

But on this trip to Chicago, whatever our resolutions were on the way, they melted or scattered when we found the half-breed had confessed; also when we talked to the witnesses. Douglas, too, though he had not slackened his interest in my behalf, had politics to occupy his mind. The presidential campaign was on. He was the leader of his party in Illinois; and his presence in Chicago was opportune.

The half-breed was quickly tried, convicted, and hanged. And before I was scarcely ready Fortescue had come to Jacksonville with his witnesses to prove the marriage. I tried to engage Douglas as my counsel, but he was deep in campaigning. Accordingly I turned again to Mr. Brooks. There was nothing left of defense to us but the cross-examination of these unknown persons who came to swear that they were witnesses to the wedding. That Zoe and Fortescue had lived together as husband and wife there was little doubt. Had I not seen them together on the lake front in Chicago? Had not Zoe then hidden herself behind a suspicious reticence? These things corroborated the witnesses.

Mr. Brooks' cross-examination was not very acute. Perhaps there was not much to ask. But we had no witnesses with whom to rebut Fortescue's claim. I could not conceive how I could find any such witnesses; but I had gone to Chicago and left without trying to do so. And neither Douglas nor Mr. Williams had suggested it.

If some six men and two women were willing to swear that they were present to hear, and did hear, Zoe and Fortescue pledge themselves to each other, what could break the evidentiary effect? Fortescue had paid the expenses of these witnesses to Jacksonville; there was no attempt to hide that. But why not a formal marriage? They did not wish it that way. Was not this marriage as valid as any? To be sure. Then the ring! We made little of a defense. Mr. Brooks seemed overcome by the emphatic answers. We lost. And Fortescue came into my life as a co-tenant, a brother-in-law.

Of course I inherited from Zoe too; but here was Fortescue, sharing in every acre, in every piece of timber in my house. Only a division by a court could set off to him his share and leave me in individual possession of mine.

He came to Jacksonville to live. He went into possession of the hut. Whether I would or no, I had to confer with him about various things, fences, taxes, road service. He knew nothing of farming. He often came to ask me what to do, and I could not rebuff him. He brought strange characters about him, particularly some of the witnesses who had helped him to sustain his claim. He sent to borrow utensils, household necessities. He visited with my workmen, wasting their time, putting disturbing ideas into their minds. He was a consummate nuisance. And as usual I had much to do and to think of, and I spent lonely evenings when I did not see Reverdy and Sarah or the old fiddler.

It was now left to me to institute a partition suit to divide the land between me and Fortescue. Mr. Brooks managed this admirably for me. There was danger that Fortescue might compel a sale of the whole farm and a division of the proceeds. There was my house, the attractive improvements around it, bright to the envious eye. Fortescue only had the hut. But at last acres were set off to him. I kept my house and the remainder of the land. And this was ended.

But nevertheless I thought more and more of selling the farm, of moving to Chicago. Fortescue was an impelling cause to this step. I should in that event leave Reverdy and Sarah and little Amos. I should see less of Douglas. But I began to be desperately annoyed by my situation. I could not wholly live down the killing of Lamborn. There was the memory of Zoe. There was now Fortescue. And in Chicago there was Abigail, to whom I was writing. She had become a very close friend. She was urging me constantly to take up my residence in Chicago. But I could not leave without selling the land. I did not wish to sacrifice it. I did not think it wise to rent it. Indeed I could not rent it and derive the same income from it that I could by working it myself. I had not yet found a purchaser who would pay what it was worth.

It was now the autumn of 1840. Sarah had two children beside little Amos, a boy born in August whom they had named Jonas. Dorothy had come from Nashville to help Sarah with the heavy household burdens that were now upon her.

I saw a good deal of Dorothy at Reverdy's; she came to my house on occasions when I entertained. She was as lovely as ever, but she did not have Abigail's mind. She was luxurious in her temperament, aristocratic in her outlook and tastes. She did not stimulate me as Abigail did, but she involved my emotional nature more powerfully. Something of resentment fortified my present neutral attitude toward her. Why, after all, need Zoe have affected her so profoundly? Perhaps my own thinking was toughened by my experiences. I had killed a man for Zoe; I had been through a trial with Fortescue. Surely if there had been any bloom on me it had been rubbed off. Why had not Dorothy seen in me a practical, courageous heart, who took his fate and made the best of it? Was there something lacking of depth, of genuineness, in Dorothy's nature?

There was much stirring now in the country due to the campaign. The log cabin was apotheosized; hard cider was the toast to America's greatness. The hero of Tippecanoe, the pioneer soldier, Indian fighter, the plain man, the Whig, was pitted against the well-groomed and resourceful Van Buren. Reverdy, because of his admiration for Douglas, was for Van Buren; and Dorothy had no thought of any other allegiance. We made up parties to attend the rallies, to see the marching men, to hear the speeches. Douglas, who was campaigning with tireless energy, came to Jacksonville to address the people. He was now twenty-seven and a master. He controlled the party's organization in Illinois. Practice had given solidity and balance to his oratory. He moulded the materials of all questions favorably to his side. Audiences rose up to him as if hypnotized. He swept Illinois for Van Buren. But Harrison and Tyler were elected. The vote of Illinois was a personal triumph for Douglas.

CHAPTER XXVII

A few days before Dorothy returned to Nashville we spent an evening together, first at Reverdy's home, later in a walk through the country. It was moonlight of middle November, and the air was mild with a late accession of Indian summer. I sensed in Dorothy a complete erasure of everything in my life that had stayed her coming to me as my bride. It was not so much what she said as it was her attitude, her tone of voice, her whole manner. But my own troubles had formed a nuclear hardness of thinking in me, which like a lodestar attracted what was for me, and left quiet and at a distance what was not mine.

I was delighted to be with Dorothy, but I did not stand with her on the basis of my former emotional interest. In a way she symbolized the false standards, the languorous aristocracy of the South. She was a presence of romantic music, a warmth that produces dreams. She was not the intense light that shone around Abigail. I had a letter from Abigail in my pocket. Parts of it wedged themselves through Dorothy's words as she rattled on more and more. I might as well have been thinking of my troubles; but in point of fact it was of Abigail.

Dorothy was not like Reverdy, nor was she like Sarah. If she had only been! A pathos was on me in this walk. The wind was blowing. The forest trees murmured like agitated water. The moon sailed high, and Dorothy walked by my side and talked. There was an evident struggle in her to bring me to her, to evoke the old ardor which had reached for her. But we returned to Reverdy's at last, and there had been no touch of hands, no tenderness. She stood momentarily at the gate. I gave her my hand, and with an impassive goodnight, she turned to the door and I went my way.

Then regret came over me. Had I wounded her? And if I had, could I win her back? Did I wish to? I could not entirely bring myself to relinquish Dorothy for good. But did I really care for Abigail? I took out her letter and began to read it again in order to clear my thoughts: "Dear James: You must be beginning to perceive that day by day you are accomplishing certain things and thus forming your life. I admire greatly the way you took hold of the farm and the success that you have had with it; and I admire too the loyalty with which you have stood by your duty. Now I cannot help but urge you to come to Chicago. I feel something of a draw at times to return to the East; but, on the other hand, this growing town has an increasing fascination for me. It is already enlivened and bettered by many eastern people; and you would find a more interesting atmosphere than where you live now. I think some of the southern people who have settled middle Illinois are as fine as any one I have ever known; but I do not like the habits and the principles that go along with the southern institutions. If you could sell the farm you could use the money to make a very large fortune in Chicago. The campaign has interested me very greatly; it has been riotous and colorful and full of extravagance. There is no real truth in all this business. It is the lesser reality of deals and bargains, wheedling, persuasion, and vote-getting. And no one has the gift of specious logic and stump hypnotism better than Douglas. To me he is one of the greatest of small men. Have you read Emerson or Lowell yet? Here are new men of real thoughtfulness whose minds are upon the truth which does not fade with passing events. These questions about Texas and Oregon, about tariffs, about Whigs and Democrats, what are they but the cackle of the moment? And yet there is something pathetic about Douglas. Why does he not settle to the solid study and experiences of the law? Why this catching at this and the other opportunity? Mr. Williams says that Mr. Douglas has just accepted the Secretary of Stateship for Illinois. What an absurd thing for a lawyer to do! His career is so changeable, so flashy. He leaves himself open to the charge of scheming, grabbing, all sorts of things, though all the while he may be doing the best he can. Forgive my opinions, I love to express them to you. I look upon you as a fresh mind who can value the truth of things about it. Douglas may become a very great figure; but I can't help but believe that his restless life may bring him to disaster. Let us hope it won't. Meantime I wish for happiness for you. Your letters are very interesting and I am always glad to get them. Write me as often as you can, give me pictures of your life, the people. And do move to Chicago. Your friend,

Abigail."

I read this letter over more than once with reference to its characterization of Douglas. I could not share her opinions. Why could she not see that Douglas had always done his best? After all, what of the law? Douglas could not be patient with the rules that related to a land title while his thoughts were far afield in plans for the territorial greatness of his country. Meantime he had to earn his bread. He had never stooped to dishonor, to chicanery. He had caught at the driftwood of supporting offices in his swimming of the new stream of primitive life. He was poor. He had enemies. His eye was upon an eminence. He had to make the best of the materials at hand.

I understood Douglas' difficulties because I had had difficulties of my own. I had not faced the world with poverty. But I had faced it with Zoe. I had not battled in issues which were influenced by the negro, but I had a social experience which Zoe had made and complicated for me. If Douglas was now in an office that belittled him, I was sorry, for I was his friend in all loyalty.

CHAPTER XXVIII

Scarcely had Douglas settled as Secretary of State, when he resigned the office to become Justice of the Supreme Court of Illinois. Abigail wrote me a most amusing and ironical letter on this sudden shift of his activities. "What do you think now?" was her query. "I think he is as well fitted to be judge as to be Secretary of State, which is not at all."

When I wrote to Abigail I had news to tell her with reference to the farm. I believed I had found a purchaser in Springfield; and my trading talks with Washburton, for that was his name, had taken me over there a number of times. On one of these occasions I saw Douglas. He had been presiding over a proceeding that had something to do with the Mormons, in which he favored them. He was charged with placating their interests to win them to his political fortunes. "It was nothing of the sort," said Douglas. "I only did my duty. What have I to gain by favoring them? There are a great many more people who hate them than those who have any use for them. Even my enemies know that. Do you know they say, Jim, that I grabbed this judgeship by some high-handed method. It's all a lie. I can do nothing to please some people. They don't like my conduct on the bench. You know how crude things are here. My throne is a platform with a table; and the audience sits so close to me that I can almost touch them. The other day I walked off the platform and sat for a moment with one of the spectators, an old friend. Somebody wrote this up for the newspaper and made a terrible fuss about it. I cannot please some people, no matter what I do."

It was the winter and spring of 1841 that I was visiting Springfield about the sale of my farm. President Harrison had died after a month in office, and John Tyler had become President. Douglas was elated over this. "Tyler is a Democrat," said Douglas. "And we have taken victory out of defeat after all. He has vetoed the new bank bill true to the principles of Jackson; and he has been read out of the Whig party for doing so. Every member of his Cabinet but Webster has resigned, you know. The Whigs are getting nothing out of the triumphs of log cabins and hard cider. They are all a humbug. Their sins are finding them out. We will put in a thorough-going Democratic party in 1844."

Douglas was talking the annexation of Texas. "Think of it," he said. "A territory 750 miles broad added to the domain of this country! The whole continent by right belongs to us. Do you think, if we once get it that there will be any whining that we should give it up? You have seen Illinois filling up; you have seen canals and railroads make their beginning here. Let's do the same for Oregon. I want you to rid yourself of any feeling for Great Britain, and use your English will to the making of America. Do for America what you would do for England, if you were living there. She would take the whole earth if she could get it. Let us take all of North America.

"I am planning to run for Congress again. I am stifled in this little life. There is not enough for me to do here. I am restless to get out and help build up the West."

I asked Douglas if I should move to Chicago. His eyes brightened. "Yes," he said in his quick way. "That is a place of great opportunity. Go there, Jim. I will be there myself, eventually. You can become very rich there with the capital that you have for a start."

Then I told him that I was trying to sell the farm; that I had about matured my plans to move. He was delighted. "I'll miss you here, but a friend is a friend to me, even up there. Go and build. You can help make a city. I want to see this state come into its own. I want to see schools everywhere, giving the advantages to the young which were denied to me. This is the most wonderful of states. Be glad that your destiny brought you here. At the present rate of immigration the population of Illinois will soon be a million. When you came here the population of the United States was about twelve million; now it is about seventeen million; it will soon be twenty million. Do you appreciate these figures? Look at the New Englanders, the Irish, the Germans that have poured into Illinois. Some of them come here with ideas that I find hostile to my ambitions. I have to win them to the liberty of the Democratic party, and keep them from stopping halfway, contented with the fraudulent liberty of the Whigs. I take them in hand at political gatherings; I love to persuade and shape them. I will fill this population of Illinois with love of Democratic ideas. What have the Whigs to offer? Look at the mixed blood of the Whigs, at their tainted ancestors. I take the greatest pleasure in exposing them. It is my fun and my work."

With all this intellectual activity, Douglas was not a reader. I had found Emerson through Abigail; I read the ***North American Review***, and Cooper's novels as they appeared. But Douglas had contempt for the moral idealism of New England. He thought it impractical. "You can't have a brain without a body," said Douglas. "Let the country develop its bones, its muscles, attain its stature. These men think the world is run by righteousness, especially if you let them prescribe the righteousness. But it isn't. It is run by interests. Roofs, clothing, and food must be taken care of; then cities. These men get preconceived ideas of God, and then want to force them on the great impulses of life. But they can't do it."

I ventured to say that the two ran together. His reply was that nothing of idealism counted that did not harmonize with material interests. There would always be war so long as interests conflicted. The lesser had to give way to the larger. War was a factor in the game of supremacy, of life. If Great Britain stood in our way, fight her. If Mexico made trouble about Texas, conquer her. War is the execution of the law of progress. Reason can go only so far, and then the sharpness of the sword is necessary.

CHAPTER XXIX

I sold the farm at last and moved to Chicago. It was with sorrow that I broke up my association with Reverdy and Sarah, and their little family. But I was much relieved to be out of the situation that had been so full of annoyance to me. I had friends to be sure, but I was English; I was a little reserved even yet; I was a driver, a money maker. Then there had been Zoe and Lamborn. Besides, the life on the farm was monotonous. The end of the day marked lonely hours for me. And I was looking forward to much association with Abigail.

I saw her frequently now that I was in Chicago. She was teaching school. Mr. Williams, his wife, their children, were my first friends, the beginning of my new associations.

I began at once to speculate in real estate. Mr. Williams proved an invaluable counsel in these ventures. I made money faster than I could ever have believed it possible to me. I was now very well off at twenty-seven. But was life nothing but money making?

As I had sold the farm on partial payments I was compelled to make frequent trips to Springfield to collect the purchase money notes; and I always saw Douglas unless he was away campaigning. By the new census of 1840 Illinois was entitled to seven Congressmen instead of the four which it had hitherto been allowed. A legislature had reapportioned the state in such a way as to give Douglas a chance to be elected. Douglas' friends had called a convention. The re-apportionment of the state was charged to be arbitrary; the convention was styled "machine-made" with a view to Douglas' nomination. Had he had a hand in this--the young judge of the Supreme Court? If so, many others had had a hand in it.

In the convention Douglas' friends rode roughly over the other aspirants; and when he received the prize they withdrew and accorded him their support. All of this was the perfection of party organization, to which Douglas, with a leader's genius, had directed his party from the moment he had set foot in Jacksonville. Douglas found an opponent in a Whig of Kentucky birth. A Democrat from Illinois, a Whig from Kentucky--such was the anomalous situation. And both agreed about taking over the Oregon territory. But Douglas was the better campaigner, the more winning personality, the more indefatigable worker. Like Napoleon, his sleep was intermittent, his meals eaten on the run. He made speeches for more than a month of successive days. And he was elected. A member of Congress at thirty!

I could see that the hard life was wearing upon him. Perhaps he was too convivial. There was hard drinking everywhere about him; and he did not abstain. He had supreme confidence in the lasting character of his own vitality. He might be ill for a few days occasionally, but he was soon up and actively at work again. His "integrity is as unspotted as the vestal's flame--as untarnished and pure as the driven snow," said a local newspaper when his methods were assailed, and no one could face him without believing that he had courage that would have its way without stooping to meanness, and vision that saw its objective through the hesitant dreams and sickly qualms of lesser strength.

When I went to Springfield in the fall about my farm I found that Douglas had been seriously ill for some weeks. The campaign had exhausted him. There was more gentleness in his manner now than was his wont. He held my hand warmly and was visibly grateful that I had come. He was heartened by this fresh evidence of my affectionate interest. He talked of his plans. He wished to visit his mother in New York State as soon as he could be about. He said that he was entering upon a new stage of his life--upon the beginning of his real career. He wished to have his mother's blessing before taking his seat in Congress.

When I next went to Springfield I found him gone. The place was lonely to me. I collected my note and wandered about idly; passed the Ridgeway mansion where I had met Abigail; went through the new state house. The years between seemed so brief but so full of events. I was twenty-eight, Douglas was thirty; Reverdy had passed forty; Zoe was dead. My farming days were over. It all seemed a dream. My grandmother in England was now in the middle sixties. There were steamships crossing the Atlantic, the first one four years before. Great forces here and in Europe, movements of peoples, and interests were flowing to carry Douglas along for some years, and to carry me and all others in their sweep. I was lonely in Springfield on this trip. Douglas was gone! His career here seemed finished, as if he were dead. Like a camper he had foraged upon the country, made his tent and taken it down. And now he was gone! Everywhere there was talk of war with Mexico. Had Douglas gone forth to bring this about in realization of his dream of America's greatness? A man must be made president who would annex Texas. If there should be war let it come. The land is ours. Our people have gone there. We must seize the whole continent north of the Gulf.

Now that I was separated from him how should I follow him day by day? I got Niles' ***Register*** in order to keep in touch with him.

CHAPTER XXX

L arge mercantile establishments were building in Chicago. Elevators and pork-packing plants fronted the Chicago River. The harbor was being improved by the Federal government. The population had risen to more than ten thousand people. Great labor was necessary to keep the facilities of life equal to the growing demands upon it. The first water works had been installed at a cost of $95.50, and consisted of a well alone. Now the city purveyed water through wooden pipes, laid under the ground. The Illinois and Michigan canal, which Douglas had done so much to originate, was nearing completion. The thousands of Irish laborers engaged upon the work added to the liveliness and colorfulness of the city life. We had excellent mail service. Long since the drygoods box had disappeared which had served as the only depository of mail. The hogs had been barred from the main streets, so that in my boarding place at Michigan Avenue and Madison Street I was no longer disturbed by grunts and squeals as they fed and wandered through the city.

Mr. Williams and I had formed a real estate and brokerage partnership, and we were making money at a phenomenal rate. The air was vibrating with the ring of the trowel and the hammer. Gardens and roadhouses had appeared in the pleasanter places out of town. Everywhere in the central part of the city were livery stables, restaurants, saloons. The harbor was full of sailing craft. Every day saw the tides of emigration pour upon this hospitable shore. I felt the stir of the new life, the growing city. I was fascinated with the money making. I had found new friends. My change of life had brought me happiness.

Abigail and I saw much of each other and we talked of many things, and much of Douglas. I saw him as the symbol of this intense life, this miraculous development. He seemed to me the man of the hour, the man even of the age.

No sooner was he sworn in as a Congressman than he proceeded to make his presence felt. He did precisely what he had done in Illinois when he came to Winchester, penniless and unknown: he seized an opportunity. He admired Andrew Jackson with an almost unqualified heart, and he rose to Jackson's defense in Congress.

I have said that I was reading Niles' **Register**. Through it I was able to follow Douglas' career in Congress from the beginning.

Abigail had made friends with a certain Robert Aldington, who had also come west to teach school. And when we met at the Williams' residence of evenings there were sharp exchanges of opinion between us about life, books, the new city of Chicago, the destiny of America, and Douglas. Aldington was keeping abreast with all the new books in America and England as well. He too had read De Tocqueville; but he was also familiar with Rousseau, Voltaire, the French Encyclopaedists; with Locke. And he assured me that Calhoun, the Senator from South Carolina, had written a treatise on the philosophy of government which for depth and dialectic power, was a match for Locke. He also knew the poets Shelley and Byron. He had studied the French Revolution. He was watching the feverish developments of Italy and Germany. The tide of emigration into Chicago and Illinois furnished him material for infinite speculation. What would this hot blood, seeking opportunity and freedom from old world restraints, do for the new country? He admired Douglas to a degree, but he disliked what he sensed in him as materialism.

We were reading together the proceedings in Congress concerning the fine which had been imposed by court upon Jackson at New Orleans when he was in military charge of the city in 1812. Douglas had taken this as his occasion to make himself known to the House and to the country at large. He was nothing in Congress because of his achievements in Illinois. He had to win his spurs. He had contended with great force and brilliancy that Jackson, in declaring martial law, had not committed a contempt of court; that if Jackson had violated the Constitution in declaring martial law the matter was not one of contempt or for a local court to judge. "Do you see," said Aldington, "his mind runs in a channel of pure legalism, and then it escapes between freer shores." Aldington continued: "The trouble with Douglas is that he does not see that idealism is as real as realism. Douglas is something of a sophist. I do not mean to disparage his value to the country. But he is a genius in making the course of Jackson consistent. He has applied the same art to justify his own conduct. He will always prove an elusive debater; and you see, after all, this makes against his candor. This is not the sort of stuff of which a thinker is made. There are men who will not trifle with facts. They are your Shelleys, your Emersons. These men make the brain of a nation. Douglas may make its body, if you can make a body without making a brain."

"That's exactly it," said Abigail. "But it is not possible to have a statesman as clear in his logic as Emerson, though dealing with coarser material than philosophy's. Surely there is a chance now for some mind of deep integrity, of real spirituality, to do something for this chaotic, vulgar mass of humanity that is grabbing, feeding, trying to foment war with Mexico. I am sure of it. Why this contempt of his for the idealist, the reformer? He classes all sorts of grotesque, half-insane people with the high-minded thinkers of the East. And now that he is in Congress, and will have to face some of them, Adams for example, I expect him to find a match."

I tried to have my friends understand Douglas, as I understood him. What was he doing in Congress now? Trying to get appropriations for the rivers and harbors of Illinois. "Won't that ensure his reelection?" asked Abigail. "Yes, but do we not need the harbors?" I replied. "Why pursue Douglas with arguments like these?"

Abigail's argumentativeness made me turn to Dorothy. Did I want a wife who had such definite opinions about masculine questions such as these? But now how to find Dorothy again? She had been back and forth between Nashville and Reverdy's. We had exchanged only a few letters, with long silences between. I began to depreciate myself for allowing Zoe or anything connected with her to thwart my will with reference to Dorothy. These meetings with Abigail and these conversations and arguments had clarified my mind both as to Dorothy and as to Abigail. I wanted Dorothy and I did not want Abigail. This being the case why should I not go to Dorothy and tell her so? If I went to her with the same will that I took up the matter of the farm, could I not win her?

It was not many days before I had the rarest opportunity in the world to go to Nashville upon an interesting mission. Douglas suddenly appeared in Chicago. The session of Congress was over. He was going to Nashville to see Andrew Jackson. He asked me to go with him; and I took this opportunity to see Dorothy.

CHAPTER XXXI

I had heard much of Jackson and all his works of wonder: as the victor at New Orleans, the greatest hater of England, as the firm friend of the Union against the rebellion of South Carolina, as the foe of the bank, as the most picturesque figure in America. He was living in retirement at Nashville. And to see this man! To see Douglas with him! Abigail laughed at me for my enthusiasm. But also I was to see Dorothy, and to make up my mind once for all--rather, to get Dorothy to do so.

When we arrived in Nashville, making arrangements so that I should not miss the visit to Jackson's house and the meeting between Douglas and Jackson, I went to see Dorothy. Mrs. Clayton met me at the door. She was greatly surprised. But there was wonderful cordiality in her manner. Dorothy was out for the time but would soon return. In the meanwhile Mrs. Clayton was eager to hear about my life and about Chicago. I told her more or less in detail the circumstances which had forced me to sell the farm. As to Douglas, she was devoted to him for his defense of Jackson. Jackson was a demigod to her and to the people of Tennessee. She wished she could be present to see Douglas and Jackson meet. Why could it not be arranged and for Dorothy too? They all knew the General very well. He had been a friend of Mr. Clayton's. Where was I stopping? Would I like to come to their house? My visit to Nashville was to be brief; besides I wished to be with Douglas. She would like to entertain him too. And thus we talked until Dorothy came in.

Dorothy knew before many minutes that I had not come especially to see her. She had heard of Douglas' arrival, of Douglas' mission. Between her mother's recapitulation of our talk and my own additions in her presence, she learned of the events of my life that she did not already know. I could see that she was very happy. And for myself it was an easy reunion.

She too wished to see Douglas and be present at the "Hermitage." Why not? She and her mother could easily presume upon the General's hospitality. Still, would I not be kind enough to arrange it? I stayed to the noonday meal with Dorothy and her mother. Then I went to the hotel to tell Douglas that I would come to the "Hermitage" with them. I did not find him at first. He had gone to pay a call upon Mr. Polk, who had been nominated for the Presidency as a young hickory to Jackson's "Old Hickory." He returned soon and was glad to have Mrs. Clayton and Dorothy come to the "Hermitage." Then I went back to spend the intervening time with Dorothy. She was truly lovely to me now. Her hair was more glistening and more golden; her eyes more elfin; the arch of her nose more patrician. She was gentle and tender. It seemed that all misunderstandings between us had dissolved. We did not mention any of the disagreeable things of the past. We communicated with each other against a background of Zoe being dead, of my being gone from the farm. Chicago, its growth, its color, its picturesque location by the great lake, made her eyes dance. She could not hear enough of it. She had outgrown the Cumberland hills. Her life was monotonous here. As I talked to Dorothy I had a clearer vision of Abigail. I felt sure now that Abigail had no magnetism for me. At the same time I began to recall what I had thought of Dorothy: her southern ways, her aristocratic ideas, her leisurely life, her cultural environment making for the lady, for the Walter Scott romanticism. Chicago had blown the mists from my eyes. I had lived under a clear sky, breathed rough and invigorating breezes. Yet I was drawn to Dorothy. My mind was poised in a delicate balance. And as I had impulsively given Zoe half the farm, I now suddenly proposed to Dorothy while turning from Dorothy to Abigail and from Abigail to Dorothy.

The afternoon was warm. The soft breeze was stirring the great trees, the flowering bushes on the lawn. A distant bird was calling. The Cumberland hills were dreaming beyond the river. And Dorothy suddenly looked at me with eyes in which supernatural lights were burning brightly. It was the look which in a woman comprehends and accepts the man who is before her; it was the secret and sacred fire of nature illuminating her vision and asking my vision to join hers in an intuition of a mating. With that look I asked Dorothy to be my wife.

Her hands were lying loosely clasped in her lap. Her head was leaning gracefully against the tree back of the settee. She closed her eyes; gave my hand a responding clasp. "Be my wife, Dorothy," I repeated. "Do you really love me?" she asked. "With all my heart," I said. And I did. It had come to me in that moment. "Do you love me?" I asked. "I have always loved you," she replied. "I have always admired you. I have waited for you. I did not expect you to come. You see I am now twenty-seven. I have not been able to care for any one else. I could not marry you before; and I could not marry any one else in the interval. Now I am very happy that you really love me." "I do love you, yes, Dorothy, I have always loved you."

Dorothy sprang to her feet, clasping her hands and laughing. "Let's tell mother, come." "What?" I asked. "Why, isn't there something to tell?" "You haven't promised to marry me." "Oh!" exclaimed Dorothy, "does it have to be by so many words? Very well, yes." She took my arm and we ran to the house. We burst upon Mrs. Clayton and told her. "Oh, you children!" exclaimed Mrs. Clayton, half crying and half laughing. "After all this delay. I am so happy."

She took me by the shoulders, looked at me, drew me to her, and kissed me. "Come," she said, "it's time to go to the 'Hermitage.'" And we got into the phaeton hitched to a gentle old horse which Dorothy drove. We entered the "Hermitage" and saw Douglas and the company and the hero of New Orleans.

I presented Douglas to Mrs. Clayton and Dorothy. Then we went forward to greet Jackson. I was introduced to him and I saw Douglas taken into the arms of the great warrior and masterful President.

He was now in his 78th year, thin of face, spare of frame, his body all sinew and nerve, his eyes brilliant with unextinguished fire. I loitered near to hear what he would say to Douglas. He seemed to have a paternal pride in the young Congress-man. He entwined his arm with Douglas', patted Douglas on the knee, looked into his brilliant and youthful face. And after assuring Douglas that his whole life had been a devotion to the law, he expressed deep gratitude for Douglas' defense. "I have always had enemies," he said. "Now I am an old man and can do nothing for myself, and so I am thankful to you."

The old hero's voice shook, his hand trembled. And Douglas looked down, glowing with pride and saying: "I am proud to be your defender. You are and always have been the object of my greatest admiration."

Mrs. Clayton, with a woman's tact, sought to relieve the tension of the moment. She brought Dorothy and me to the General and said: "General, my daughter has betrothed herself to this young man, Mr. Miles."

Jackson was seated upon a sofa. He arose, though with some difficulty, and taking Dorothy's head between his hands, he pressed a reverential kiss upon her brow. "I knew your father; he was a good man, a good friend. Take my blessing." And to me he said: "Mind that you are always a man with her and for her, and against all the world for her. She is worth all your devotion."

The circumstances seemed to affect him profoundly. He turned away from us, as if to hide his tears, leaving us standing in a group. Douglas joined us and extended his congratulations, and we departed together, Douglas to confer with Mr. Polk and the rest of us to return to the Clayton mansion. For there was the wedding now to consider. I wanted to take Dorothy back to Chicago with me.

Mrs. Clayton invited Douglas to take the evening meal at her house. Dorothy joined in the request and I ventured to put in a word. Douglas had to arrange then for a later call upon Mr. Polk.

CHAPTER XXXII

This dinner was the most delightful of occasions. Dorothy was in brilliant spirits. And Mrs. Clayton shared in her daughter's happiness. The colored servants, all slaves, affectionate and interested, manifested their joy in all sorts of lively and profuse attentions. I could hear them laughing in the kitchen. Mammy, the old cook, was singing; Jenny, the maid, came in and out of the dining room with dancing eyes, which she cast upon me, and scarcely less upon Douglas, who was talking in his usual brilliant way. It was pleasing to me to hear Mrs. Clayton agree with him about so many things. She was disturbed by the slavery agitation. She feared for the peace of the Southern States. She dreaded a negro rebellion. She commented upon the fact that even the domestic slaves sometimes sulked or slacked; and that this was due to the talk of the Abolitionists. It was hard enough to keep paid laborers in good discipline; how much easier to encourage the negroes to inattention to duty by attacks upon the system of slavery. But after all, what was to be done?

Douglas referred to Calhoun's attempt to exclude abolition writings from the mails. He referred to this without approving of it. For Calhoun had conceded the lack of power in the Federal government to interfere with the freedom of the press; but he contended that the states as sovereign powers could prevent the distribution of such literature within their borders. Everywhere it seemed to me the slavery question divided reason and thinking against themselves and brought great minds into absurdity.

Douglas wanted the slavery agitation to cease, but on the other hand he did not wish to interfere with the freedom of speech and of the press. Mrs. Clayton now recalled Harriet Martineau's visit to America of some eight years before. She had read **Society in America** and **Retrospect of Western Travel**. Did I know that Miss

Martineau had stopped in Chicago and had described Chicago as it was then?

Douglas returned to the subject of the Abolitionists apropos of this, because Miss Martineau had made herself much disliked by siding with them. He began to talk of Horace Greeley who had helped the humbug Whigs into power in 1840 by his publication, *The Log Cabin*. It was now merged in the weekly *Tribune*, in which all sorts of vagaries were exploited: Fourierism, spiritualism, opposition to divorce and the theater, total abstinence, abolitionism, opposition to the annexation of Texas. Douglas referred to a certain Robert Owen who had thought out a panacea for poverty, who had founded an ideal community at New Harmony, Indiana, which had proven to be not ideal and had failed. Then there was a certain James Russell Lowell who was writing abolition poems and articles for the Pennsylvania *Freeman* and for the *Anti-Slavery Standard*. Douglas classed all these agitators and dreamers together in his usual satirical way. The ponderable move of national interests would crush their squeaks. Here he made one of the most humorous classifications, separating Democrats and nation builders from the ragged and motley hordes of Fourierists, Spiritualists, Abolitionists, loco-focoes, barn-burners, anti-Masonics, Know-nothings, and Whigs. He was inclined to think that the infidel belonged with these hybrid breeds. Though he did not speak of God and had never joined any church, something of a matter-of-fact Deism was subsumed in his practical attitude. The Democratic party stood alone against these disorderly elements. Nationalism and the rule of the people were his lodestars. He was the son of Jackson in the principle of no disunion, and he was the son of Jefferson in the principle of popular sovereignty.

The talk turned to Mr. Polk. As he was a resident of Nashville, Mrs. Clayton, on that ground as well as for political agreement, was heartily devoted to him. These two talked of Mr. Polk's record as a Congressman from Tennessee and later as Governor of the state. "Well," said Douglas, "he is sound on the bank, he is against the tariff, he is in favor of annexing Texas and settling the matter of Oregon. As usual the Whigs are vacillating, because their leader, Mr. Clay, is himself vacillating."

What had all this to do with Dorothy and me? We had happier things of which to think. We could commune with each other undisturbed while Douglas and Mrs. Clayton settled Texas and Oregon.

The meal was over and Douglas arose to depart. As I intended to marry Dorothy before leaving Nashville, if she would consent to do so, I was wondering what I should do about not returning to Chicago with Douglas. Accordingly I asked him if I could see him the next morning. He fixed the hour at ten o'clock, saying that a boat left for St. Louis at noon. With plans thus vaguely left, so far as they affected both of us, he departed. Mrs. Clayton said: "Reverdy has told me so much of Douglas. Now I have seen him, and he is all and more than I was led to believe."

When she left the room I asked Dorothy if we could not be married the next day. Well, but she had much to do to get ready; put the wedding off until December, or later. "You can get everything you want in Chicago," I persisted, "and I want to take you back with me." Dorothy had not talked this matter over with her mother. She was not sure that her mother could be won to a plan so hasty. "Let's see her," I said.

For the whole evening we discussed the subject. Since Mrs. Clayton's household would be broken up by Dorothy's departure, she had to readjust her life. She was thinking something of making a visit of some months in North Carolina. She could not make ready for that immediately. Why not come to Chicago with us, make her home with us? She could bring the colored servants. We talked until one o'clock. Then Mrs. Clayton advised a night's rest on the matter.

CHAPTER XXXIII

The next morning I awoke with such a feeling of repose, of being at home at last. I was lying in a poster bed, which Mrs. Clayton had told me was an heirloom from North Carolina. In my view was a lovely bureau of mahogany; on a stand a vase of roses; at the windows snowy curtains; on the walls pictures of Mr. Clayton in his soldier's uniform, and of Reverdy as a young boy and of Dorothy.

I stretched myself between the comfort of the linen sheets, and turned over on my side to smile to myself, as I looked out of the window into the trees. I was at home at last! I thought back over my voyage across the Atlantic, of the long journey from New York to Jacksonville, of Reverdy at Chicago with his Indian pony, of my illness and Zoe. All my troubles had faded away.

There was soon a knock at the door and Jenny's voice called to me that she had brought me water. I arose, dressed, and went down to the living room. Mrs. Clayton bade me such a kind good morning, kissed me on the cheek. In a moment Dorothy entered, radiant from her night's rest, and with a lover's kiss for me bestowed so happily, yet with something of mischievous reserve--all so charming!

Our thoughts were fresh for the discussion of the marriage. Mrs. Clayton thought that the wedding might take place at once, within a day or two, at least, if I would not insist upon returning to Chicago for a few weeks, or until she had opportunity to close the house preparatory to her visit to North Carolina. This arrangement quite suited me. I wanted to have Douglas present at the wedding. So I hastened away to tell Douglas what my plans were.

I found him making ready to depart, but in consultation with politicians. He was running for Congress again in Illinois, and the presidential campaign was on. But when I told him of my desire he thought for a moment, and consented. He was being importuned to make an address at Nashville. Now he would stay to do so and attend the wedding. I was very happy over these fortunate circumstances and returned quickly to Dorothy. If only General Jackson could be persuaded to come, and Mr. Polk. We had many things to do. I set about running errands for Mrs. Clayton. Dorothy was notifying her friends, getting her veil, her dress into readiness. Mammy and Jenny were cooking all sorts of delicacies; they had requisitioned old Mose who was the slave of a neighbor, Mr. Parsons, and the wedding preparations progressed with speed. I had traveled hither without the slightest expectation of this sudden consummation and therefore had no clothes suitable for the occasion. I had to attend to that as best I could.

The hour came. Douglas arrived with Mr. Polk, who had also been a friend of Mr. Clayton's. But General Jackson was unable to come. He was not strong. He sent a bottle of rare wine and a bouquet and his hearty congratulations; all by a colored messenger who was excited and voluble. General Jackson! It was less than a year when he passed from earth.

Mr. Polk was a full-faced, rather a square-faced man, with broad forehead, packed abundantly at the temples, rather intense eyes, and lines running by the corners of his nose, which slightly looped his mouth upward in an expression of decision and self-reliance. He was already called a small man. But I did not see him so. He was of pleasing presence of distinguished decorum, and chivalrous manner. But after all Douglas was the center of attraction. Mr. Polk escorted Mrs. Clayton to the wedding breakfast, and Douglas took in Mrs. Rutledge, an aunt of Dorothy's.

So we were married, and I was happy. I had found a wife and I had found a mother. Douglas departed, promising to see me in Chicago soon. The guests went their way. I was here with Dorothy, with Mrs. Clayton, Mammy, and Jenny.

There is something good for the soul in being for an hour, even if for an hour only, the central thought of every one; in having one's wishes and happiness the chief consideration of interested friends. And here were Mammy and Jenny, who had no thought but to serve me and Dorothy; here was Mrs. Clayton, who strove so gently to attend to my wants, whatever they were, to put herself at the disposal of these first hours of Dorothy's new life and mine. Mose was at the door with the horses and the carriage, loaned by his master, to drive us into the country and over the Cumberland hills. Mrs. Rutledge lingered a while in evident admiration of me, and with happy tears for the radiant delight which shone in Dorothy's face.

We set forth with old Mose, who was talking and pointing out to me the places of interest, the hills, the huts, the houses which were associated with stories or personalities of the neighborhood. And here was Dorothy by my side, scarcely speaking, her beautiful head at times, as we drove in secluded places, resting delicately upon my shoulder, her eyes closed in the beatitude of the hour.

Mrs. Clayton's position came into my mind. What was this visit to a sister? Was it not a pure makeshift, an expedient in the breaking up of her life, the first step in an accommodation to Dorothy's loss? I had such ample means. Why should she not come with me? Why separate Dorothy from her? Why leave Mammy and Jenny behind, who had served nearly the whole of their lives in this household? I had learned to like the colored people. What heart could withhold itself from Mammy and Jenny? These humble devoted souls whose lives and thoughts had no concern but to make Mrs. Clayton and Dorothy happy, and who had taken me into the circle of their interest! What were the colored people but the shadows of the white people, following them and imitating them in a childlike, humorous, innocent way? How difficult for selfishness, seeking its own happiness, to understand Mammy and Jenny, whose whole happiness and undivided heart were in giving happiness to Mrs. Clayton and Dorothy!

I spoke my plan to Dorothy, "Come, let's take mother, Mammy, and Jenny with us. Close the house for good. I want all of you. We can transfer all this happiness to Chicago. I will get a big house. I have some one now with whom to share my riches. This sharing is the beginning of my real satisfaction in life."

Dorothy took my hand, pressed her cheek against mine. "Oh, my dear, my dear!" was all she said. I felt her cheek moistening with tears. Then drawing her to me I said: "Yes, my dear, that is my wish. Let us drive back now and tell mother."

Mrs. Clayton was silent for some seconds. Then she said: "Aren't you best alone? Take Mammy and Jenny if you wish. But perhaps I can't be a mother to you, James; perhaps you won't want to be a son to me as time goes on. These things must come to mothers and fathers. The daughters find new homes and go away. I did that. And now Dorothy has the same right."

"No," I said, with emphasis, "I want you. I want to transfer this whole atmosphere to Chicago. I want all of you with me. I do not wish you to wander off on this visit. After that what, anyway? You should not be separated from Dorothy. Come, and if you want to go on a visit from Chicago, well and good."

If this was to be, there was much to do. Could we wait until the house was rented, or at least placed with an agent, the furnishings stored if necessary? Yes, I could wait and Dorothy could wait. And day by day both of us importuned Mrs. Clayton to come with us. She saw at last that it was our dearest wish. And she yielded.

In the meanwhile Dorothy and I were driving about the country or sitting under the trees in the yard, living through great rapture, mothered by Mrs. Clayton, and so constantly served by Mammy and Jenny and Mose.

Then the day came. The house was rented. Mrs. Clayton stored some of her furnishings. The choicest things she gave to Dorothy--lovely mahogany and silver.

On a morning, with Mammy and Jenny in our traveling party, with Mose helping us to the boat, hiding his saddened spirit under a forced humor, with Mrs. Rutledge and many friends to see us off, we took our departure. Again the musical whistle of the boat; again the stir and vociferous calls of the pier; again on the waters of the Ohio bound for St. Louis. Again the great Mississippi.

But Mrs. Clayton left us at St. Louis to visit Reverdy and Sarah. She would come to Chicago later.

CHAPTER XXXIV

I took a house in Madison Street, some two blocks from the lake. There was first the business of having Mammy and Jenny registered, something similar to a dog license. But Mr. Williams helped me about that.

I had not seen Abigail yet, but of course she knew that I was married. A vague faithlessness accused me. And yet I had never spoken a word of love to her. It was my admiration for her and hers for me, rising up to ask me why I had married Dorothy. Did I really know myself?

Dorothy was entranced with Chicago. She thrived under its more bracing air. She loved the bustle, the stir. We were now in the midst of the presidential campaign, and Mammy and Jenny saw political enthusiasm in a new phase. Marching men passed through the street. There were shouts, torches, many speeches on America's greatness.

Mrs. Clayton came to Chicago before the election and was all delight over the new life which had come to her. The pulsations of great vitality in the rapidly growing nation were well exemplified in Chicago's development. The country was bursting with commercial expansion; it was lusty with the infusion of strong blood from Europe. Nearly a million Irishmen and Germans had been added to the population since 1840. Illinois, as a garden spot, had received her share of these virile stocks.

The iron production, which was in a primitive stage when I arrived in America, had now grown to be a great industry. There was anthracite coal, which was first mined in Pennsylvania in 1814 on a very inconsiderable scale; and now the output was more than five million tons a year. It was supplanting wood in the making of steam. The Chippewas had ceded their copper lands on the south shore of Lake Superior, and the mining and manufacture of copper had become an extensive industry. Gold was taken in large quantities from the Appalachians. There were about five thousand miles of railroad in the country as compared with the something more than one thousand miles which it had in 1833. The telegraph was following the railroads. For in this very year, under the administration of President Tyler, $30,000 had been appropriated by Congress for the building of a telegraph line from Baltimore to Washington. But above all, the country thrilled with the prospect of acquiring Texas and settling the territory of Oregon. Douglas was at once one of the creators and one of the most conspicuous products of this great drama.

He had been reelected to Congress by a plurality of over 1700 votes over his Whig opponent. The Whigs opposed the annexation of Texas. Clay was against it. New England preached and sang against it. But Tyler had tried to negotiate a treaty for it. It had failed. He devoted much of his last annual message to Congress to the Texas subject, soliciting "prompt and immediate action on the subject of annexation." Douglas, during the campaign in Illinois and in Tennessee, had denounced those weaklings who feared that the extension of the national domain would corrupt the institutions of the country. As to war with Mexico because of Texas, let it come. The Federal system was adapted to expansion, to the absorption of the whole continent. Great Britain should be driven, with all the vestiges of royal authority, from North America. "I would make," he said, "an ocean-bound republic, and have no more disputes about boundaries or red lines upon the maps."

These words sent a thrill through the country. What had Clay to offer as a counteractant, as an equal inspiration to the pride of this lusty nation? Surely not the tariff. This imaginative impulse had carried Mr. Polk to the Presidency; but before Mr. Tyler laid down his office he was able to send a message to Texas with an offer of annexation. It was accepted, and in December of that year, 1845, Texas became a state of the Union.

Mother Clayton had come on to Chicago at last, and we were fully settled with Mammy and Jenny to run the house. My life was ideal, divided as it was between money making and participation in Chicago's development. We had Mr. and Mrs. Williams and Abigail and Aldington as a nucleus for new friendships. I could see more clearly than ever that Dorothy and Abigail were as dissimilar as two women could be. Nevertheless, they became friends. Mrs. Williams and Mother Clayton found much in common. My business relations with Mr. Williams were altogether agreeable.

I resumed my readings with Abigail and Aldington, although Dorothy was not greatly interested. Poe's **Raven** went the rounds this winter and created an excitement. We read Hawthorne's novels. Emerson's **Essays**, the second series, appeared. Then the first discordant note came between Dorothy and Abigail. For Emerson said: "We must get rid of slavery, or get rid of freedom." Abigail exclaimed over this epigrammatic truth. Dorothy looked at Abigail disapprovingly, apparently seeing in her face evidence of a different spirit than she had hitherto suspected. Aldington joined Abigail in praise of Emerson. And for the sake of a balance, I sided with Dorothy and Mother Clayton against them. Though none of us had anything to do directly with the matter of slavery, it thus cast its shadow upon our otherwise happy relationship.

In these readings too I was following with great care the career of Douglas in Congress, in which Abigail and Aldington were not so warmly interested. Douglas' early life, his adventure into the West, had put him through an experience and into the possession of an understanding which were alien to the eastern statesmen. The West was for the enterprise of the young. It was a domain of opportunity for youth, divorced from family influence and the tangles of decaying environment. Hence Texas must be assimilated, and California taken eventually, and the Oregon country acquired. An ocean-bound republic!

As for slavery, it did not enter into Douglas' calculations. I knew, however, that in spite of what any one said, he was not a protagonist of slavery. He simply subordinated it to the interests of expansion. He was willing to leave it to the new states to determine for themselves whether they should have slavery or not. With the impetuosity of his thirty-two years he slipped into a recognition of the Missouri Compromise, and was willing that slavery should be prohibited north of this line. He was generating a plague for himself which would come back upon him later.

But if Douglas' advocacy of the Texas expansion exposed him to charges of a slave adherency, nothing could be said against his cry for the taking of Oregon. The Mormons whom he had befriended without any dishonor to himself had set forth into the untraveled land of Utah. Already a band of young men from Peoria had gone into the Far West. Therefore, when he now spoke for Oregon he had a responsive ear among his own people in Illinois. If the eastern people, the dwellers in the old communities, did not kindle to Oregon, it was because they had neither the flare nor did they see the urge of this emigration and occupancy. With the rapid extension of railroads, how soon would the whole vast land be bound together in quick communication!

So it was, Douglas was offering bills in Congress for creating the territory of Nebraska, for establishing military posts in Oregon, and for extending settlements across the West under military protection. He advocated means of communication across the Rocky Mountains. He thought of his own unprotected youth. He would have the young men from Peoria and from every place feel confident in the knowledge that as builders of the nation's greatness they had the friendship and the strong arm of the government around them.

What was Great Britain doing? Reaching for California, hungering for Texas, eyeing Cuba. She hated republican institutions. She would gird them with her own monarchist principles, bodied forth in fortifications and military posts. It should not be. Douglas had said: "I would blot out the lines of the map which now mark our national boundaries on this continent and make the area of liberty as broad as the continent itself. I would not suffer petty rival republics to grow up here, engendering jealousy of each other, and interfering with each other's domestic affairs, and continually endangering their peace. I do not wish to go beyond the great ocean-beyond those boundaries which the God of nature has marked out. I would limit myself only by that boundary which is so clearly defined by nature."

Meanwhile President Polk was saying: "Our title to Oregon is clear and unquestionable." He was urging the termination of the treaty for joint occupation with Great Britain of Oregon. War! Yes, but Douglas did not fear it. At the beginning of the thirties of his years, he was leading Congress in the formation of an ocean-bound republic.

These were his words: "The great point at issue between us and Great Britain is for the freedom of the Pacific Ocean, for the trade of China and Japan, of the East Indies, and for our maritime ascendency on all these waters."

I watched these proceedings to the end, and until the Oregon territory was settled by the fixing of the 49th parallel as the boundary between Great Britain and the United States. Douglas had striven with all his might to extend the boundary to the 54th parallel. He had failed in this, and was bitterly disappointed. He had been accused of boyish dash and temerity in affronting English feeling with a larger demand. It had come to the point where I could not discuss, particularly in Dorothy's presence, these questions with Abigail. She saw nothing in these labors of Douglas but vulgar materialism. That, of course, was the farthest thing from the minds of Mother Clayton and Dorothy.

But before the Oregon compact was signed, two grave matters disturbed our peace and brought their influence into our happy household. Congress had failed to pass the bills to protect the settlers in the Oregon territory. And we were at war with Mexico.

I felt irresistibly drawn to the war.

CHAPTER XXXV

Dorothy was in terror. We had been married so short a time. Our happiness had been undisturbed. We had found such perfect enjoyment in our home. We had taken such delight in the life of Chicago.

But Mother Clayton encouraged me with bright and admiring eyes. I felt that I owed this service to Douglas. He had mapped out the boundaries of Texas. Should I not carry the sword to defend and establish them? The dream which was Douglas' had also taken possession of me.

Abigail saw nothing in the Mexican War beyond an ambition of the Southern States to extend slavery. It was a fight for cotton. The Eastern States did not like the war, the Whigs opposed the war. Illinois had many enemies of the war.

But these were the facts: Mexico had announced that the annexation of Texas would be considered an act of war. She had broken off diplomatic relations with us when we offered to annex it. She had prepared to resist the loss of Texas with force of arms. Our people were in Texas. They could not be abandoned. "How did they get there?" asked Abigail. "By pushing and adventuring where they did not belong."

President Polk had sent troops under General Taylor to defend Texas; he had sent commissioners to Mexico to make a peaceable solution of the dispute. Besides, he was anxious to get the Mexican province of California, as Douglas was, including the wonderful bay and harbor of San Francisco. Would Mexico sell them without a fight? Mexico had declined. General Taylor was therefore ordered to advance to the Rio Grande. There was war! Its shadow entered my household. Dorothy was in tears. Mammy and Jenny were shaking with fear. For I had resolved to enter the fight.

And Chicago was afire with the war spirit. The streets echoed to the music of martial bands; orators addressed multitudes in various parts of the city. Trade was stimulated. The hotels were thronged with people. The restaurants were noisy with agitated talkers. Douglas' name was on every one's tongue.

Volunteers had been called for. But Illinois could send but three regiments; she offered six to the cause. Many companies were refused. I organized a company, financing it myself. But it could not be taken, and I joined the army under the colonelcy of John J. Hardin. He it was whom Douglas had supplanted as state's attorney. Now he was to lead troops, to the vindication of Douglas' dream.

Dorothy was inconsolable for my departure. She could not have sustained the ordeal except for Mother Clayton. There were fear, anxiety, and mystical foreboding in Dorothy's heart for a different reason. She was soon to bear a child. She was loath to have me away from her in this ordeal. Yet I had to go. A whole continent moved me; great forces urged me forward. I was now an American. Martial blood stirred in me. All concerns of home, of Dorothy, sank below the great vision of war. The aggregate feelings and thoughts of a people make a superintelligence which may be mistaken for God. Of this superintelligence Douglas' voice was the great expression. I broke from Dorothy's arms, after vainly attempting to console her.

The six Illinois regiments assembled at Alton, where I had been so many times before. I was to see this town again in the most dramatic moment of my life, how unimagined in this terrible time of war. We hurried on to join General Taylor, who had already, as we learned later, won the battles of Palo Alto and Resaca de la Palma. Characters later to figure momentously in the history of the country were here to settle the title of Texas with the sword. Robert E. Lee, a lieutenant, was brevetted for bravery in the battles of Cerro Gordo, Contreras, Churubusco, and Chapultepec. Captain Grant had come with a regiment and joined the forces of General Taylor. He took part in the battles of Palo Alto, Resaca de la Palma, and Monterey; and then being transferred to General Scott's army, he served at Vera Cruz, Cerro Gordo, Churubusco, Molino del Rey, and at the capture of Chapultepec. Here too was Colonel Jefferson Davis, who led his valorous Mississippians, who put to flight Ampudia at the battle of Buena Vista. Lee, Grant, Davis, Taylor, the next President, all in arms for the ocean-bound republic of the young Congressman from Illinois!

Our Illinois troops with those from other states, numbering in all 5000 men, proceeded to Monterey, thence to Buena Vista where we were confronted by

20,000 Mexicans under the command of General Santa Anna, who had no doubt of a speedy victory over us. On Washington's birthday, Santa Anna sent a message to General Taylor to surrender, saying that he did not wish to inflict useless slaughter. General Taylor declined, and we fought.

I shall never forget my feelings, but how shall I describe them? My nerves were tense; they rang taut with unexpended energy. I felt death near me. I thought of Dorothy constantly, but I was living with fate.

The line of battle was formed where the valley was narrow. The lofty mountains were on either side of us. Torrents had gullied the plain. The Kentucky volunteers were posted at the left; the Indiana volunteers were stationed near. Our regiment, together with a Texas company, formed the remainder of the line which ran from the plain to the plateau. Extending from these towards the mountains were placed other troops from Illinois, from Indiana, and from Arkansas. Up the valley came Santa Anna, with his 20,000 Mexicans.

He had sent General Ampudia to climb the mountain and fall upon our troops at the left. The battle began in the afternoon and lasted till night.

At dawn Santa Anna advanced his troops in three columns in front of us. And the battle began to rage. The Indiana troops retreated in disorder. But the Illinoisians stood their ground, pouring forth sheets of flame upon the Mexicans. We had to retreat. We were pressed back to the narrows. Then General Taylor, hastening up, took command. Batteries were opened. Grapeshot and canister were poured into the advancing Mexicans. The cannon belched deadly fire. Colonel Davis had routed Ampudia at the left. The Mexicans began to waver in front. We from Illinois and Kentucky started in pursuit. We drove them into a deep ravine.

Here suddenly they were reenforced by 12,000 men. They shot us down like sheep. It was a slaughterhouse. But we fought like madmen. Our riflemen, the squirrel hunters of Kentucky and Illinois, picked off the Mexicans unerringly. Our batteries began to thunder again. Again the Mexicans broke order. They started to run. We pursued them through the valley, under the shadows of the great mountain. Night came.... The silence of night and of our victory.

We had won the battle! The Mexicans fled southward. Then we started to bury our dead. Our losses were terrible. So many boys from Illinois were hearsed in this bloody soil. Colonel Hardin was killed; but we were commissioned to bring his body back to Jacksonville.

This ended the war in northern Mexico. But meanwhile, as President Polk could not buy California, he seized it. He ordered an American squadron to take San Francisco and other harbors on the California coast. He sent General Kearney with a cooperating force to this end. Kearney occupied the city of Santa Fe and organized a temporary government for New Mexico. The President also sent General Scott against the city of Mexico and Vera Cruz and Cerro Gordo. These were taken; but they were used only as levers in the settlement.

What had been accomplished? We had fixed the Rio Grande as the Texas boundary; we had added California, Nevada, Arizona, New Mexico, Wyoming, and Utah to the American domain. With Oregon acquired Douglas' ocean-bound republic was realized. Was it to prove his lasting triumph, or his undoing?

I had been gone less than a year. I was eager to reach Chicago, but I had to stop off at Jacksonville to help bury the body of Colonel Hardin. We made his grave near the grave of my father and not far from Lamborn's.

What had happened in my absence? How should I find the home that I had left? If Dorothy should be dead, or Mother Clayton, or Mammy or Jenny?

I rang the bell. Jenny came to the door. She gave a cry. Mammy came hurrying through the hall; then Mother Clayton, flinging her arms upward in dumb delight. Then Dorothy, lovely in her young motherhood, carrying our boy, the tears running down her cheeks. She could not speak. She could only rub her cheek against mine, press her lips to mine, hold our little boy's laughing and uncomprehending lips to mine. We cried. We uttered broken words.

I entered. The door closed behind me. I was home. All was well. I sat down. All looked at me. Jenny and Mammy loitered in the room. I wanted to speak. But what had I to say? Nothing! Such happiness at being home! So we sat until I broke the silence by asking: "When was the baby born?" Mother Clayton replied: "He is five weeks old to-morrow." Then we all laughed. We had broken this heavy silence with such simple words. And after that, many words, much laughter; and later a wonderful meal prepared by the delighted hands of Mammy and Jenny.

CHAPTER XXXVI

But what of Douglas? During the war I had been entirely out of touch with him. What was he doing? What had he accomplished? What was now stirring in his restless imagination? They all had news for me about him and of varied import, according to their attitude.

For one thing he had married while I was in the war. Mother Clayton approved the marriage. Abigail mocked it. For his wife was a southern woman, the owner of many slaves in Mississippi. Douglas had announced that he would have nothing to do with her property, especially with the slaves. But how was he to escape a derivative gain? So Abigail asked. I knew that he disliked the institution; but here it was touching him again in a peculiarly intimate way. Texas soiled him with its influence and now his marriage identified him with it. He might regard it, if he would, as a domestic matter like the liquor business, which Maine had just now laid low by a prohibition law. As he would not be a liquor dealer, so he would not be a slave owner. But he was the next thing to it in the circumstance of his marriage.

But in my absence he had moved to Chicago, and this gave me great happiness. I should now see much of him. He was speculating in land and growing rich. He was advocating the immediate construction of the Illinois Central railroad. He had been triumphantly reelected to Congress. The Mexican War had helped to do that for him. He was only thirty-four, but a great and growing figure.

Chicago had changed in my absence. The second water system, consisting of a reservoir at the corner of Michigan Avenue and Water Street, and a pump, operated by a 25-horsepower engine, was soon to be supplanted by a crib sunk in the lake 600 feet from shore, from which the water was to be drawn by a 200-horsepower engine. The lake traffic had increased enormously. The Illinois and Michigan canal was soon to be opened.

Mother Clayton had saved for me the copies of Niles' **Register** and had marked passages in Douglas' speeches in Congress, particularly his effective retorts to the aged J. Q. Adams, who pursued Douglas with inveterate hostility. It was all about the slavery question.

I looked Douglas up as soon as possible. We invited him and his young wife to dinner. Surely he had found a charming and interesting mate. We now had so much of life in common and of mutual memory to draw upon. He was eager to hear of the war, the battles I had been in. He was very proud of me and happy beyond measure that I had come out of the war without a scar.

How strange about Colonel Hardin! "An able man, that," said Douglas, "but I don't believe he ever forgave me for taking the state's attorneyship from him."

Abigail and Aldington were also at our dinner. Mrs. Douglas found herself quite at home with Mother Clayton and Dorothy. I could see, however, that she did not like Abigail.

After that Douglas and I had many meetings. He was full of ideas and absorbed in various activities. He was pugnacious and energetic. But what friends he made! He passed in and out of my view frequently, now that we lived in the same city. And before I knew it, scarcely before there was any talk of it, he was selected as United States Senator from Illinois.

It was in December of 1847. He was within some four months of his thirty-fifth birthday. He had now had an uninterrupted career of political triumph. His one defeat for Congress, when he ran the first time, could scarcely be counted against him.

But to my English eyes, in spite of all my admiration for the man, I saw much imperfection in his intellectual make-up, due in part I think to the haste with which he had lived. He had an adroitness and a fertility of mind which were altogether amazing. Yet he was like Chicago: of quick and phenomenal growth. His protective coloration was like Chicago's, which covered its ugliness and its irregularity with bunting and flags on a holiday. He was growing up rapidly, as Chicago was growing up. Chicago was facing greater problems as its population increased; and as Douglas rose into higher power, thicker complications entangled him. He dragged after him the imperfect education of his youth, the opinions of his immaturity. He was now enmeshed in the problems of the new territories, and always, slavery. Prepared or

not, he would fight for his principles. If defeated he would rise quickly; if trium-
phant he advanced.

As leisure was possible to me, and because of Dorothy's somewhat frail health,
we decided to give up the Chicago house this winter and spend the season in Washington. We would take Mother Clayton, of course, and Mammy and Jenny. I would
thus have the chance to watch the contests in Congress in which I was so profoundly interested. I wished to witness Douglas' part in these great affairs. Some of the
old giants were still there: Calhoun, Webster. How would Douglas face these great
men? Above all, the shreds of a decaying past were stretching themselves forward
to enter the texture of the new weaving. How would the two pieces be connected?
Would it be a patchwork?

Douglas had come to me offering an appointment in Illinois. When I declined
this, he suggested a consulship on the continent, or in London. But I could not see
my way clear to leave America. I had too many interests now, and I wished to see
the unfolding of events here.

CHAPTER XXXVII

We found Washington much as Dickens had described it seven years before. The avenues were broad. They began in great open spaces and faded into commons equally unbounded. They seemed to lead nowhere. There were numerous streets without houses. There were public buildings without a public. There were thoroughfares that had no markings but ornaments. The residences had green blinds and red and white curtains at the windows almost without an exception. Grass grew in the avenues. The distances were great, separating the new public buildings from easy access. Brickyards were in the center of the city, from which all the bricks had been taken, leaving only dust, which was stirred by gusts of wind filling the air at times to suffocation. Pennsylvania Avenue was grotesque with its big and little buildings, its small and impoverished shops set between the more splendid windows of jewelry and fabrics. It was in such sharp contrast with Chicago. No noise here. No smell. Instead of lumbering drays, many carriages; instead of bustle, leisure; instead of commercial haste, languid strolling along Pennsylvania Avenue. And there at its head stood the unfinished Capitol; and at its other end the executive mansion now occupied by President Polk, and soon to be the residence of the hero of the Mexican War, Zachary Taylor; and soon of Millard Fillmore.

Dorothy and I and Mother Clayton visited the places of interest at once. We went to the Patent Office and saw the model of the Morse telegraph. We looked at the Declaration of Independence displayed in a glass case at the Department of State. We stood before Trumbull's pictures of the celebrated men of an earlier day. We went to the room of the Spring Court, saw the judges in their black robes, the thin intellectual Chief Justice Taney at the center. We went to the slave market, where the capital of the republic trafficked in human flesh for itself and the surrounding country. Lottery tickets were openly sold. Negroes thronged the streets. They were the domestic servants, the laborers, the hackmen. A raggedness, a poverty, a shiftlessness, characterized external Washington. Washington was not Chicago.

We found that Douglas had settled himself handsomely with his young and charming wife. He entertained a great deal, and was entertained in turn. We dined back and forth with each other. And because of Mrs. Douglas' friendship Dorothy found her social pleasures assured and advanced.

Washington like other cities in America was struggling out of the earth. The whole country was in a similar throe. Everywhere were great dreams partly realized. One could not help but imagine what the nation would become, just as one could not look at the unfinished Capitol at the end of Pennsylvania Avenue without completing its lines in imagination.

We had come to New York City by boat, as I had gone to Chicago by boat in 1833; but in New York we had taken a train to Philadelphia, claimed our baggage at the station, transferred to another station, and taken another train through Baltimore to Washington. The cities of the East were now in telegraphic communication with each other: Washington with Baltimore and New York; Philadelphia and Newark were joined. Polk's election had been flashed by the telegraph. And news now came to Washington on every subject: markets, fires, catastrophes, elections. The public press was very active. The country was in a ferment. The great West agitated the more sensitive, the listening East. From beyond the Atlantic news of thrilling import poured upon us. In truth the whole world was trembling at the threshold of a new era. Douglas was keenly conscious of these world changes. They occupied my own thoughts.

In France Louis Philippe had been dethroned, a republic had been established with Louis Napoleon as President. The ideas of the revolution had worked a democratic triumph as to the suffrage and the form of the government. This was February, 1848, the same month that Douglas made his first speech in the Senate.

This February revolution in France had lighted the fires of liberty throughout Europe. In England there was agitation and violence. The people there were demanding the right to vote. In Italy there was a cry for reform and free constitutions. Mazzini was proclaiming the fact that the people in Spain, Hungary, Germany, Poland, Russia, were oppressed. He called the cause of all peoples a common cause.

The French Revolution had announced the liberty, equality and fraternity of individual men; the new revolution should proclaim the liberty, equality and fraternity of nations. Cavour and Garibaldi were getting ready to bring about the unification of Italy. The Germans had gained some liberties in 1830. But when Paris broke into shouts for freedom in 1848, the news went across the Rhine and the German liberals arose and demanded a constitutional government. Metternich was obliged to flee the country. The Emperor Ferdinand abdicated in favor of his nephew, and the people's constitution was granted. There were rioting and bloodshed in the streets of Berlin.

As a result of all this, thousands of Europeans were fleeing to America, the land of the free. Yet there were the slave markets in Washington, New Orleans, all through the South. And Congress was about to consider the new territory which had come as a result of the Mexican War and the Oregon settlement. How would Douglas react to these world movements? How would he interpret them? Who could stand against this world-wide avalanche? With the North now greatly the superior of the South in wealth, in railroads, mines, in agricultural productiveness, what could the South do for her slaves and her cotton? What would the Titans--iron, coal, gold, copper, wheat, corn--do to the Giant of cotton?

I heard Douglas' first speech in the Senate and interpreted it against this background. He had already been made chairman of the committee on territories, and thus placed in the very midst of the fight touching the annexations. The great Webster was here. He had opposed the annexation of Texas and the Mexican War, and was the spokesman of the Whig party. He had split metaphysical hairs with Calhoun, also here. Calhoun declared that the Constitution was over the territory and by that fact carried slavery into it; no imperialism in America. To this Webster rejoined that the territory was the property of the United States and not a part of it. Hence the Constitution was not over it and slavery could be kept out of it. This was implied powers in favor of liberty. Calhoun's doctrine was: Constitutional government in the interests of slavery. To such dialectics had the matter come. Mazzini might contend for liberty, equality, and fraternity for individuals and nations. Here in America the questions were more subtle. Clay was not here but soon to be here. Hale of New Hampshire was here, an astringent personality, eager to challenge young Douglas from Illinois.

The question was the Mexican treaty. Senator Hale injected abolitionism into Douglas' speech. Calhoun characterized Douglas' retort to Hale as equal in offensiveness to Hale's remark, which elicited the retort. The battle was on. We now had occasion to be proud of our friend. He stood forth with such self-possession, such dignity. With great emphasis he announced that he had no sympathy with abolitionism; but neither did he look with favor upon the extreme view of the South. "We protest," said Douglas, in his great musical voice, facing the southern Senators, "against being made puppets in this slavery excitement, which can operate only against your interests and the building up of those who wish to put you down. In the North it is not expected that we should take the position that slavery is a positive good, a positive blessing. If we did assume such a position it would be a very pertinent inquiry, why do you not adopt this institution? We have moulded our institutions in the North as we have thought proper; and now we say to you of the South, if slavery be a blessing, it is your blessing; if it be a curse, it is your curse; enjoy it--on you rests all the responsibility. We are prepared to aid you in the maintenance of all your constitutional rights; and I apprehend that no man, South or North, has shown more constantly than I a disposition to do so. But I claim the privilege of pointing out to you how you give strength and encouragement to the Abolitionists of the North."

Mother Clayton had been long schooled in the questions which vexed the matter of slavery. She thought Douglas showed great courage in these words, but she was not satisfied with them. She felt that the South had not been protected in its rights and that Douglas owed it to the South to stand with the southern Senators. His position was not definite enough to suit her. He should say that slavery went into the territories by law, or was kept out by law. Douglas' thesis might be judicial but it laid him open to doubts.

This was our talk as we walked away from the Capitol. Dorothy was fatigued by the experience. She was interested, but the debate exhausted her. What she wished more than anything was peace for the whole country.

CHAPTER XXXVIII

I had had a delirium in the serious illness through which Zoe had nursed me, in which a blue fly crawling up the windowpane, sliding down the windowpane, buzzing in the corner of the frame where it could neither climb nor get through nor think of returning into the room--in which this fly took on the semblance of Napoleon. My imagination was then full of Napoleon; and my father had suffered because of him at the battle of Waterloo. And as I sat in the gallery of the Senate, Webster, Calhoun, Hale, Cass, and Douglas reminded me of this hallucination. They seemed to me like flies at the windowpane of Texas and California and Oregon, beating their wings against the dark glass of the future. They were like insects, caught in the rich gluten of circumstances and buzzing as they sought to make their way.

This winter sad news came to me of the death of my dear grandmother, whom I had planned all along to see again. Now it could not be. My life had been hurried forward with such varied events, and with all the rapidity of America's development. I had worked with great industry in putting the farm on a paying basis. I had run at high speed in Chicago. I was still living fast in plans and activities. Douglas was full of the subject of railroad extension, and I was drawn into that. He was trying to formulate a plan for the Illinois Central railroad; and my interests in Chicago drew me to that plan. He was also talking of founding a university in Chicago. These were the subjects of our many talks. Our visits took place at his house or at mine, as he rarely went with me to the places of amusement which I frequented.

A theatrical company had come to Washington from New York which was playing in repertoire, *Jack Sheppard*, *Don Cesar de Bazan*, *His Last Legs*, *London Assurance*, *Old Heads and Young Hearts*, and some other dramas. Dorothy and Mrs. Douglas were devotees of the theater. I enjoyed *Richelieu* and *Macbeth*, and I had seen Forrest as Sir Charles Overreach and Claude Melnotte; but for many of the plays I did not care. Douglas was indifferent to the theater. He was himself too much of a player on the stage of American affairs to be illusioned by any mimic representation.

On a night when Dorothy and I were dining with Douglas and Mrs. Douglas, Dorothy and Mrs. Douglas conceived the idea of going off to see the play of *Charlotte Temple*; for we had overflowed the lesser talk at the dinner table by our discussion of railroads. Accordingly they left us, and Douglas and I settled down to an intimate evening, of which we were beginning to have many. We set a quart bottle of whisky between us, drinking from it from time to time as the evening progressed. Both of us had a fair capacity. And without either of us becoming more than well stimulated, we nearly consumed the bottle by the time Mrs. Douglas and Dorothy returned.

This evening I studied Douglas with more than usual care. I had been struck at dinner by his great devotion to Mrs. Douglas. He treated her with a high-bred chivalry, a constant kindness. I was really trying to get at the emotional side of his nature as to things that did not relate, for example, to an ocean-bound republic. After all, his attitude toward men was one of guarded friendship. He attached men to himself with ardor and loyalty. In turn he gave loyalty and a certain ardor too. But he was really analytical of men. He was suspicious of disinterested friendship. He saw selfish considerations as the social bond. Hence he had less and less patience with New England. The radicals who talked God and benevolence and fraternalism were anathema to him. They had nothing to lose; therefore, they could chant a goodness as to the loss of others; they could praise self-sacrifice, having nothing themselves to sacrifice. As for human love, what was it but the feeling evoked by consideration? Pay a man well and he will love you. Give him good working conditions and he will tolerate the service. Put him to the test by short pay or bad conditions and he will hate you. All of this pointed to the love of men and women. I tried to draw him out on this. I do not know what the lack of his mind was, whether of subtlety or imagination. At any rate it was a realm of thought to which his face was a blank, and to which his mind seemed to have no reaction.

He turned now to the Oregon settlement. He was still furious over it, still indignant at Polk. He had stood for 54:40 as the northern boundary; he was chagrined

at the 49th parallel. Why had Polk fulminated first for 54:40 and faded off to the
49th parallel? England! He hated my mother country with a deep and rancorous
hatred. Coming from Vermont he had taken into his bones a poison for the British atrocities of the Revolution; he loathed England for her conduct of the War of
1812, the ruthless burning of Washington, with all its priceless records of the early
days of the republic. He was eager, restive to fight England. England's invulnerable-
ness tantalized him; her habitual luck infuriated him. Her ownership of the right
thing at the right place and time mystified him. Concretely now there were the
Mosquito Islands off the coast of Honduras which England claimed to own, but
Douglas thought without any right. He was advocating the cutting of a canal across
Nicaragua. What would England do? She would try to use the Mosquito Islands as a
basis of agreement for joint control with the United States of the canal--in spite of
the Monroe Doctrine. Why would not all statesmen rise with him in the assertion
of a title to the whole of North America? Was America in the business of pirating
around the shores of Europe to pick up islands, or promontories like Gibraltar?
Not at all. Then why should England be tolerated in this Western Hemisphere?
What divided the American imagination? The old loyalists and royalists who had
become the Federalists under Hamilton, who were now the Whigs with the same
banking scheme, the same old tariff, the same old hatred of democratic government, the same hypocrisy, the same disingenuous and devious policies. There was
but one American party, one pure-blooded party, good for the East and the West,
friendly to every just thing that the East desired, understanding the West; that was
the Democratic party! It stood for America. It envisioned the needs of the greatness of America. It had fought the war against England and Mexico. It had created
the American domain. And now these old defeated and crooked monarchists who
had stood in the way of America's progress were seizing upon a moral issue, upon
slavery, with which to befool a democratic electorate naturally responsive to the
arguments of liberty. They had opposed the Mexican War; they had brought up the
slavery question at every important juncture to confound counsels and perplex otherwise easy solutions. But what one of them would give back Texas, New Mexico,
California, to Mexico? Would Webster? Would Hale? No, not one of them would
do this.

The campaign of 1848! What would the Whigs do? They would use this Democratic Mexican War to get into power. They would appeal to the war spirit which they had dishonored; they would use a national gratitude for service in the despised war to get the offices and control the administration. Would Clay win the Whig nomination? Not at all. It would be Zachary Taylor, the hero of the Mexican War, the slave owner of Louisiana. This party was over virtuous on the slavery matter, lending an unofficial ear to Garrison and other agitators, but it had been careful not to take a party stand on the question. It would continue to play with the subject. It would put forward a southern slave owner to catch the southern Whigs, and at the same time use his war record to move the pure-blooded and American vote.

Would the Abolitionists put up a ticket? Perhaps. What would come of arraying section against section? Suppose slavery could be put to a vote. In 1840 the Abolitionists had polled 7,000 votes in the country. In 1844, 60,000. This proved that it was not difficult to throw a firebrand into America's affairs. Suppose this vote grew and an Abolitionist President should ultimately be elected? What of American progress in such a contingency? What of a wrecked republic before the greedy eyes of England, the envious hands of kings? Why should such folly be? Let the slavery question alone. Keep it out of the way of American development. Let the territories decide for themselves whether they would have slavery or not; let the states coming in do so, with slavery or without, as they chose.

We took a drink every now and then, and Douglas turned to the subject of railroad extension. He told me of a certain Asa Whitney. Whitney had lived in China. He had returned to America in 1844, urging that a railroad across the continent would bring the trade of China to the United States and enable American merchants to control it. If a canal were built, supplemented by a railroad across that part of the Isthmus of Panama not traversed by the canal, about 115 miles, the distance between New York and San Francisco would be shortened by 1100 miles, and from New Orleans to San Francisco by 1700 miles. This related to the proposed Tehuantepec canal. Ah! but England had already got an interest in this route. So Whitney proposed a railroad from Lake Michigan through the Rocky Mountains to the Pacific. He had laid this plan before the Senate in 1845, showing that if a railroad were built the journey from New York to the mouth of the Columbia River could be made in eight days, and to China in thirty days. A naval station on the Columbia River, but eight days from Washington city, and the Pacific could be commanded;

next, the Indian Ocean and the South Seas. Oregon would become a great state at once. The commerce of China, Japan, Manila, Australia, Java, Calcutta, and Bombay would be ours. What would England say to this? Oh, yes, the Abolitionists might object! Freedom for the negro at any sacrifice. "Let us have a drink," said Douglas, with a laugh.

"I am for this plan," said Douglas. "True, he wants $65,000,000--that is, he wants to raise that much and has asked Congress for a grant of land sixty miles wide across the continent with which to get the money. He is on a lecture tour now, I hear, and has got the Boards of Trade of New York, Cincinnati, Louisville, and some others to favor his plan. As usual, like all other things, the rivalry between the North and the South will affect the route. The Mexican annexations make it necessary to run the road farther south. There is to be a convention in St. Louis soon about the matter, and I intend to go to it."

"What do you think about gold being discovered in California? Now I wonder if Webster does not want to give California back to Mexico. A good joke on us if the Whigs win the next election. How can they play with things in this way?"

We heard some one at the door. Douglas stood up, poured himself another drink, and said: "To the University of Chicago."

Then Dorothy and Mrs. Douglas entered. Mrs. Douglas pointed to the nearly empty bottle and said: "You have had a good time I see." She sat on the arm of Douglas' chair and began to smooth out his unruly locks. "You missed a good play," she said. "We had a very good drama here," said Douglas. Dorothy was pulling at me to go home.

When we arrived we found Mother Clayton laughing and scolding over Dickens' *American Notes*.

CHAPTER XXXIX

Our stay in Washington had come to an end and the campaign was on. I was building a business block in Chicago, which had come to a tangle owing to labor conditions. Throughout the country there was a movement for the ten-hour day, and there were many strikes, particularly in the East.

We decided to return to Chicago by way of New York. Dorothy was in great anxiety about Mammy and Jenny lest they be kidnapped along the way. Desperate characters were about who picked up negroes in the North and sold them in the South. It was as common a matter as robbing a bank or picking a pocket. We kept a close watch on Mammy and Jenny. In New York we rode together in a carriage. But this was also made necessary by the fact that negroes were not permitted to use the street cars.

The city now had half a million people; but I found the old places, like Niblo's Garden, and again walked to Washington Square whither I had taken my lonely way so many years before. Leaving our boy, Reverdy, with Mammy and Jenny at the Astor House, Dorothy and I spent much time in sightseeing.

Broadway was our particular delight. Though it was poorly paved, and dimly lighted at night, it was a scene of great fascination. It was the great promenade. Omnibuses, cabs, hacks, trucks rolled through it all day long. There were footmen in livery; luxury was displayed in the equipages. There were crowds of foreigners; and ragged boys and girls who sold matches or newspapers. New York had the penny newspaper. We looked out upon the street in the early morning, when the workers streamed to their tasks. We saw it at breakfast time, when the bankers hurried toward Wall Street, and the lawyers were going to court, or to their offices in Nassau and Pine streets. In the afternoon ladies, richly dressed, dandies, and loafers crowded the sidewalks. There was fashion in abundance; wonderful silks, ermine cloaks, furs, feathers, gorgeous costumes of all sorts. Gold had been discovered in California! The Mexican cessions and Oregon could be felt on Broadway. In the shops articles from every part of the world were for sale. There were ladies' oyster shops, ladies' reading rooms, and ladies' bowling alleys.

We drove to the new residence districts, like La Fayette Place, Waverly Place, Washington Square, and lower Fifth Avenue. We went down to the Battery from which I had looked with lonely eyes on the ships and the bay fifteen years before. The sailing vessels were giving way to the steamship. The Cunarder *Canada* was in port, 250 feet long, of 2000 horsepower, and with a speed of eleven knots an hour. Everywhere we encountered the New York policemen who had taken the place of the night-watch of 1833. They were all in uniform too. They had made a fight against the uniforms, upon the principle that all men are free and equal, and that they would not be liveried lackeys. But they had come to it. We also attended the theater frequently, like the Chatham and the Olympic. But most wonderful of all was Barnum's Museum, in which that great showman had collected dwarfs and giants, fat women and human skeletons.

I felt impelled to hurry to Chicago, but Dorothy wanted to shop and so we stayed on. One day I had an agreeable surprise in meeting with Yarnell as we were entering the Astor House. I had not seen him since I parted with him in 1833, on my way west. He was now about forty-five years of age, but looked as youthful as when I first saw him, and was more of a dandy. He touched my arm as I passed him. I recognized him at once and presented him to Dorothy. As Dorothy was anxious to return to our son, she left me with Yarnell who wished to join me at luncheon.

He took me to the Hone Club, which was the resort of good livers and men about town. After ordering the meal we set to the comparison of notes. He was eager to hear about the West and of Chicago. He could scarcely believe that Detroit and Milwaukee had a population of about 20,000 each, and that Chicago had distanced them with 30,000. I told him of our canal, which was done, and of our great shipping. Illinois had more than 300 miles of railroad, and we were building more at a rapid rate. This led, of course, to Douglas. Yarnell wanted to hear more of him. I told Yarnell of the beginning of my friendship with Douglas; how he had helped me from the stage to Mrs. Spurgeon's house in Jacksonville; of our friendship since that time, and of our winter in Washington. Then we fell to talking of Webster and Seward. Seward was a power in New York, now about forty-seven years of age; but Yarnell did not like him. Webster had wavered, particularly before the logic of Calhoun. But, after all, was not Webster cribbed by his New England environment? Seward had since been an anti-Masonic, had attended its national convention in 1830. Then he had joined the Whigs, in order to oppose Jackson. Nearly all lunacies had gone into the composition of the Whigs. What about this observance of the law, the higher law included? Why did not Seward honor the requisition of the Governor of Virginia for the return of a fugitive slave? Then we took up Greeley. His daily *Tribune* was now having an enormous circulation. Greeley and Seward were not friends, but there was much of spiritual kinship between them. We grew humorous over recounting the new movements: Spiritualism, women's rights, and temperance. "Do you know what happened right here in New York?" said Yarnell. "The Millerites got ready for the Second Advent of Christ, and there was a shop in the Bowery which displayed a large placard with the words 'muslin for ascension robes.'"

"Don't you see how clearly Douglas' compact mind stands out against all this folly?" "Yes," said Yarnell, "but how is Douglas going to stand out against it? These various reformers never get tired, and they are so numerous that they will overwhelm any man. Besides that, you find able minds like Seward and Greeley taking up with them. Is it the same way out in Chicago?" "Not so much so," I said. "We have many foreigners out our way, and they give a different quality to the civilization. Come out and see."

Yarnell walked with me back to the Astor House, and we parted.

I found Dorothy in tears, almost hysterical. Jenny, in her absence, had stepped from the room for a moment. She had not returned. She could not be found. I went on the streets, I searched everywhere. I drove to the open squares, to the Battery. I enlisted the aid of policemen, but they were none too friendly. I went to the *Tribune* and inserted an advertisement. The hotel employees took a hand. But no Jenny. She was deeply attached to our boy. She could not have willingly wandered away. She must have been kidnapped.

Dorothy cried herself to sleep. I sat through half the night at the window, looking out upon Broadway, listening, at last, to the stir and sounds of dawn. Jenny had been in the Clayton family almost from her birth; an associate of Mammy's for many years. The affection that existed between Dorothy and Jenny was intimate and tender. Dorothy depended upon her for everything. I went to Dorothy and took her in my arms, trying to console her. She was as deeply affected as if she had lost a sister. All that day we searched for Jenny. The days went by, and we did nothing but try to find her. Our loss became the talk of the hotel. The newspapers took up the story. Where was Jenny; in whose hands; what fate had she met? Our boy cried for her, and Mrs. Clayton was inconsolable. But at last we had to move on to Chicago. Was Jenny kidnapped? We never knew. We only knew that we never saw her again. This was the sordidness of slavery, its temptation to the meanest passions, the lowest lusts. The loss of Jenny made me hate it.

CHAPTER XL

I had many business vexations on returning to Chicago. But also the campaign of 1848 was on, and I was deeply interested in it. I had passed through the panic of 1837, but I was not then conscious that a labor movement was on. That panic had stayed it, for a mason or a carpenter was glad of work in those hard days. Then prosperity had revived and now it was in full tide due to a world condition; but in America also due to expansion and railroad building. Mr. Van Buren, in 1840, then being President, and seeking, as his enemies said, to influence the labor vote, had issued an executive order to the effect that laborers and mechanics need work but ten hours a day. Soon after this the bricklayers of Pittsburgh formed a union, the journeyman tailors of Washington opened a shop of their own; the workingmen of Philadelphia got into politics with an Equal Rights party. The laborers everywhere were advocating organization and cooperation and strikes as a means to good wages. In New York the laborers' union association had demanded a dollar a day, made out a political program, which involved opposition to any candidate who did not support the interests of workingmen. Sometimes the militia had to be called out, as in 1846 when some Irish workers on a strike were supplanted by Germans. Horace Greeley had naturally taken a hand in this movement. It attracted the humanitarian mind. The revolutionary processes in Europe of this year, the success of the socialists in France, had a marked influence upon the conditions in America. Meetings were held to congratulate the Chartists in England, the followers of Louis Blanc in France. Strikes were on in Boston and Philadelphia. I was caught in this world drift. I had a strike on my building in Chicago.

I had left my affairs in the hands of an agent manager, who did not assume authority to meet the terms of the strikers. Upon my return I was obliged to settle it myself. I did this by promptly acceding to the demands made upon me. What was a quarter of a dollar more a day to me? I wanted my building to be finished.

One could not escape observing all this rebellion abroad and in America, this awakening of the worker, this fight for human rights upon slavery in the South, even if he did not have it brought to his mind in the concrete way that I did. Slavery might be wrong, that was one thing; it might cut into the rights, first or last, of the free worker; but if the negro was owned in body and in energy, and his labor taken for nothing, except the food, shelter, and clothing required to keep him efficient, was that anything but just a matter of degree from the case of the white man who was paid so much a day, enough to give him food, shelter, and clothing, and thus keep him a fit machine? Thus there was a moral sympathy between the white workers and the black workers; all were making money for an upper man. If it was wrong to appropriate all the black man's labor, it was wrong to appropriate too much of the white man's labor. The Declaration of Independence was a hard nut to crack. While only a few hare-brained agitators wanted negro equality, even Douglas did not like slavery.

The new lands of the West brought fresh troubles to Douglas and desperate struggles to the South. The emigration of revolutionaries from Europe added to the enemies of the slave system. It was hard for them to understand that the Declaration of Independence did not include the negro.

This was the state of affairs in the campaign of 1848. The Democrats had nominated Mr. Cass, of Michigan, for President, and presented him to the people on a platform which placed the responsibility for the Mexican War upon the aggressions of Mexico; it congratulated the American soldiers of that war for having crowned themselves with imperishable glory; it tendered to the Republic of France fraternal salutations upon the success of republican principles, upon the recognition by the French of the inherent right of the people in their sovereign capacity to make and amend their forms of government. It spoke for American Democracy, a sense of the sacred duty, by reason of these popular triumphs abroad, to advance constitutional liberty, to resist monopolies. It advocated a constant adherence to the principles and compromises of the Constitution. It praised the administration of Mr. Polk for repealing the tariff of 1842, and making a start toward free trade.

And not a word about slavery. The convention voted down a resolution which favored "non-interference with the rights of property of any portion of the people of this confederation, be it in the states or the territories, by any other than the parties interested in them."

What of the Whigs? They made no declaration of principles whatever. Complete silence. They nominated General Taylor, as Douglas had predicted, upon his record in the Mexican War, the war successfully prosecuted by President Polk, and through which California, with her gold, had come to the United States. Taylor, the slave owner of Louisiana! But this was not the end of Whig cunning. Millard Fillmore was nominated for Vice President. He was from New York, had been in Congress, had opposed the annexation of Texas, was a tariff man, had fought side by side with J. Q. Adams for the abolition of slavery. But also he had been the Congressman who had carried the appropriation of $30,000 for Morse's telegraph. A mixed man! His good was Taylor's evil. Taylor's evil was his good.

Well, the native Americans had a ticket in the field; the Barn-burners had a ticket in the field; and the Abolitionists. Mr. Van Buren was running for President as a Barn-burner on a platform which declared that there should be no more slave states, and no more slave territory. Where was I to stand amid all this confusion and contradiction? Naturally with Douglas. But I wanted to see what he had to say.

It was not long before he came to Chicago and our interesting association was renewed. He had had something of a quarrel with Mr. Polk, but it had been patched up. Before now he had proposed that the line of the Missouri Compromise be extended to the Pacific Ocean. Was he, too, becoming uncertain of mind? Sometimes I thought he was overworked, that his energies were concerned with too many subjects. He was making speeches; he was talking railroads; he had his own political fortunes to watch. The Whigs were gaining ground. He scoffed at them. He derided their hypocrisy. He laughed at their piebald character. Yet he saw a cunning plot in this presentation to the electorate of men who appealed so diversely: Taylor of the South, and of slavery; Fillmore of the North, and of free soil, backed by the powerful mercantilism of the North, like the bank and the tariff. Both were using Jefferson to win the mob, and Hamilton to satisfy the strong.

It was in the fall just before the election that Reverdy and Sarah came to visit us, bringing Amos, now about fourteen, and Reverdy Junior, about twelve, and Nancy, who was ten.

The Douglases came to dine with us, and after the dinner Reverdy, Douglas, and I retired to the library. Again we had the bottle between us, but Reverdy was an abstainer. He was satisfied with Douglas' personal attitude toward slavery; Douglas' evident wish that the institution was not among us; his refusal to have anything to do with Mrs. Douglas' slaves. Reverdy was a man of peace and believed that Douglas' non-interference policy would ensure peace. He approved of leaving the matter of slavery to the people of the territories. He feared a war, and he opposed the agitation that might bring it. At the same time, he preferred a free soil and a free people. Reverdy was typical of many men in America. And indeed, my heart went with Reverdy in these things, even while my thinking went with Douglas.

Douglas was now the master of his party in Illinois, and it seemed to me that no one could dispute his leadership in the nation. He had perfected the party organization in the state from the small beginnings of which I have told. He was proud of his work and the strength and discipline of his party. He looked forward to victory this fall over the hermaphroditic ticket of Taylor and Fillmore. He was never more brilliant than he was this evening. He was compelling to look at, not when standing, for then his short legs caricatured and belittled his great body. But when he was seated his wonderful face and majestic head truly represented his nature.

Outside the house, in the streets, we could hear the cries, "free soil, free speech, free labor, and free men!" Douglas looked annoyed, ironic lights passed across his face. He said in a satiric way: "Just listen to that." These cries could not be met by direct denial, by an epigrammatic retort. One could not so aptly say "slave banks, slave tariffs, slave labor conditions." These required arguments to expound. If labor conditions presaged slavery for white men were they freed by negro slavery? Was not this roar outside of the house a part of the tumult in Germany and France? Was not this America hailing Europe? Had not this crowd caught up the Democratic platform which congratulated the republicans of France? What would the German vote do, the Irish vote, all the foreign vote? Had not the Whigs, marching through these streets of Chicago, captured all the effective thunder of the Democratic party?

As Douglas sat before us I saw him as a giant around whom great forces were gathering. The light played a curious trick with his forehead, throwing part of it into fantastic shadows. There was a moment's silence in which the deep brilliancy of his eyes flashed upon me. Then his great voice spoke again: "It is easy to have a war--among ourselves." Reverdy looked at Douglas in a sort of terror. Just then Amos came to the door to call us to see a political parade which was passing the house.

We three arose, joining Mother Clayton, Dorothy, and Mrs. Douglas who were already watching it. It was a demonstration of Free Soilers. Douglas had voted against the prohibition of slavery in Texas. This was the answer. These banners, bearing the words "Free Soil, Free Speech, Free Labor, and Free Men," were the challenge. The men who bore them did not know how to apply their principles to anything but the negro. Douglas knew this. At the same time he knew that he had helped to create this demonstration, that he had been influential in initiating this new momentum.

I looked at Douglas to see what effect the shouts, the pushing, running, limp-stepped throng would have upon him. A smile flitted across his face. His eyes were intense and concentrated. He made no comment. The last men of the parade passed with shouts. A drunken marcher fell. The lights faded. We turned into the room. Douglas was laughing.

CHAPTER XLI

W hat was the result? General Taylor had 1,360,099 votes and 163 electoral votes; Cass had 1,220,544 votes and 127 electoral votes. The Abolitionists polled 300,000 votes in the country. The Free Soilers had polled 291,263 votes in the country. Illinois was lost to General Taylor. The Free Soilers had swept the northeastern counties. There had been great Democratic desertions. Voltaire and Rousseau were still at work. These fermentations of Europe had bubbled and exploded around Chicago. The concrete thing known as negro slavery heard the rumble of the ground. The tariff, the bank, imperial power in Congress unwittingly renewed their strength--unwittingly on the part of the Free Soilers.

A slave owner had become President; a man of the fresh blood of the northwest of Michigan had been defeated. A New Yorker, wedded to the tariff, had been put in place to be President by the death of General Taylor. And Douglas found the forces that were to embattle him drawing up in line.

The state was saved to the local offices. The legislature was Democratic, but it proceeded soon to instruct Douglas as Senator to procure the enactment of laws for the territories for the exclusion of slavery from them. The members from Egypt, however, sustained Douglas in his position against the Wilmot Proviso, which sought to keep slavery from Texas. The state was thus disrupted. The opposition to the extension of slavery dated from 1787, from the work of Jefferson in 1800. However, let the people of the territories decide the matter. Local self-government was a popular cry. Between saying that Congress could keep slavery out of the territories, thereby treating the territories as property, not as subordinate sovereignties, and Congress sending slavery into the territories, because the Constitution was over them, what juster pragmatism were possible than to let the people of the territories decide the matter for themselves? If the general government was one of granted powers, where did it get the right to prohibit slavery in the territories? No such power could be indicated.

Oh, well, there was opportunity for infinite speculation. At the same time, here were the territories and here was slavery. The powerful North was assuming a definite opposition to a weaker South. Iron and coal were stronger than cotton. What was to be done by a man who had the burdens of leadership? How should the whole people be at peace? Since slavery could not be removed from the states, why not let its tendrils creep into the territories and there flourish or wither according to the soil? Since it was practical, not radical policy to confine it to the states, and not to abolish it in the states, it was practical and not radical policy to let the territories decide the matter for themselves. If the first course aroused the fury of the Abolitionists, the second course found no favor with the Free Soilers, and ambitious Whigs, drawing upon abolitionism and free soilism for food, for northern mercantilism and for a larger slavery of both blacks and whites.

I had now lived so long in America, seen so much of the country, read so extensively of politics and history, that I was able to follow the questions involved in this crisis. All the while I had the benefit of Douglas' association, who talked to me intimately of his own plans and of persons and issues, as they arose. There were calls upon him now to resign the Senatorship; but he had no intention of doing so. His fighting blood was aroused. He was hardened to contests and to misunderstanding and abuse. He had been berated for coarseness and charged with the half-culture of the West. His sagacity had been caricatured as cunning; his presence of mind taken for vulgar audacity; he was held up as a half-educated debater, filled with a miserable self-sufficiency. He was attacked as a demagogue. The East held itself aloof from him in unctuous self-righteousness, because of his stand in the Mexican War. His fight for Oregon had aligned against him the friends of England in America. Yet men were in power because of him. A Whig had been elected President upon a war record of a fight for Texas. Who wished to part with Texas, New Mexico, California, or Oregon?

If Douglas had the slavocracy back of him and catered to it, he did not have plutocracy back of him. If he had been a demagogue he would have done the bidding of some faction. He did the bidding of no faction. His mind was budding with railroads now, for the Far West. What he was now doing made for a money control of the country in the future; but that was not apparent to him. What one of us saw that we could not make an ocean-bound republic without a supremacy of wealth, even if it was brought about by a plebiscite? This did not make it democratic.

It was at this time that Mother Clayton's health began to be frail, and Dorothy was by no means strong. The winters in Chicago had been very trying upon both of them. Just now I had so many interests that I could not leave the city. But Mother Clayton wished to return to Nashville for a few months, and Dorothy decided to go with her. Our boy was not as robust as we should have wished. Mammy, by no means to be left out of our consideration, was aging and longed for the old scenes of Nashville. We closed our house, and I went to the hotel. Then Abigail and Aldington were married. They went abroad to study European conditions. Thus the most of my associations were interrupted. All but those I had with Douglas.

To go to Nashville was an inconvenient trip, but I made it on several occasions. Once on a mission of deep sorrow. Mother Clayton died in June just as she and Dorothy were preparing to join me in Chicago. I was thinking of going to California on account of the gold discoveries. So I brought Dorothy and Mammy back, although Mammy was very old and could not be of much service.

Thousands were turning their faces to the West. How to get there, how to equip oneself, were the questions. Some went by Cape Horn, some by the Isthmus of Panama, some by the overland route. Thousands joined companies. Others bought ships or chartered them. The wildest of rumors spread of the richness of the discoveries. Fabulous reports of fabulous prices and wages in California were scattered broadcast. I wanted to go. But why, after all? I could get richer, but why get richer? Besides, there were my interests and Dorothy. I felt the adventurer stir within me, and talked with Douglas about going. He did not wish me to leave Chicago. What soil could be richer than that south of Madison Street? Besides, he was working on the Illinois Central railroad project, and that would mean all the money that I would care for, if I would take advantage of the opportunities which the railroad would create. Then there were the transcontinental lines to be built. A convention was soon to be held in St. Louis, and Douglas wished me to go along with him.

It was held in October and I went with Douglas to attend it. The proposition was the construction of a railroad from the Mississippi to the Pacific. The delegates were mostly from the Mississippi valley, more than 800 in number, and Douglas made me a delegate from Illinois. He was promptly elected to preside over the convention. The first thing proposed was the construction of an emigrant route on the line of the proposed railroad. This was in the interest of the gold seekers. A delegate who said he had constructed more than 7000 miles of telegraph offered to string a wire to California if Congress would lend its aid. There should be stations along the way, with troopers to defend the emigrants against Indians. The troopers could carry the mails, thus insuring the delivery of a letter from St. Louis to San Francisco in twelve days. Another delegate advised the convention that Charleston and New Orleans would soon be joined by telegraph. As a means of communication, he proposed that for the sending of messages from Washington to Oregon, it could be done in fifteen days by transmitting a telegram by boat from New Orleans to Laredo, and thence by telegraph to some point on the Gulf of California; thence to San Francisco and to Washington or Oregon again by boat.

It was a vital, noisy assemblage of men; and Douglas was a perfect talent as a presiding officer. His great voice could easily be heard over the entire hall and it seemed altogether fitting, since he had so long been interested in binding the country together with railroads and telegraphs, that he should be the spokesman of this body of men, who were inaugurating this magical transformation of America.

The lobby of the hotel was full of faces of all descriptions. The millionaire was there, the countryman, the slave dealer, the man with the goatee. The barrooms and corridors were noisy with excitement, loud talk of politics, of railroads, of trade, of slavery; denunciation of the Whigs, curses for the defeat of Cass. I saw bloodshot eyes, reeling steps, coarseness, cruelty, wastefulness in drink. Yankees and Dutch were denounced as trash and as cowards and traitors. They had defeated the Democratic party the previous fall. Plans were made on the moment among various excited groups to go to California. A transcontinental line must be put through at once.

Amid this motley throng stood Douglas. He glowed in the admiration he received. He was acclaimed, cheered; his hand was taken in a rough and hearty manner by scores, wherever he stood or walked. One moment he was talking with a group of men from Tennessee; again he was exchanging salutations with Captain Grant, who was here now without prospects, drinking too much, quite a sorry figure, lounging about waiting for something to turn up. Not so with the dignified

Major Sherman. He had been to California, on field duty in the Mexican War. Now well groomed and of fine bearing, he stood about the lobby interested in the projected railroad. Douglas, Grant, Sherman,--all had a definite relation to the Mexican War, and the new territory. Douglas seemed to be taking renewed life from this interesting experience. I was his companion all the time, loitering near as he talked to various notables. I looked over this mass of humanity and thought of America as a whole, and wondered what it would do with its rich possessions, and its problems. Its fate seemed hopelessly entangled, in spite of the material prosperity--perhaps because of it.

CHAPTER XLII

I felt now the truth of Webster's picturesque words that "the imprisoned winds were let loose." We might have a transcontinental railroad, and Douglas' Illinois Central might connect Chicago with the Gulf of Mexico. All of this building might go forward successfully. But at the same time the slavery question would not down. Even railroad building was a bone of contention, for as to a line to California it had been debated whether it should start from Chicago or from St. Louis. Hence it was that every activity of Douglas had to reckon with the negro. There were now great things to be done at Washington. And as Dorothy had enjoyed herself so much during the winter that we had spent there, she was urging me to return. I had my affairs now under better management, and communication with Chicago was rather convenient; besides Dorothy was not well. The loss of Jenny and the death of her mother had visibly affected her health. I decided at last to spend the winter in Washington.

The trip from Chicago to New York by boat and by train was as wearisome as before. When we arrived in New York, Dorothy had to take to her bed and rest for two days before proceeding to Washington.

We took a house again, keeping Mammy for intimate service and supplementing her with two colored women who fitted in fairly well. Our boy Reverdy was put in school.

I began to attend the sessions of the Senate, taking Dorothy when she wished to go. Clay of Kentucky, after an absence of eight years, was back; here were also Webster and Calhoun, the lions of an earlier day. They were enacting their last parts, trying to re-imprison the winds of destiny, which the events of the Mexican War had set to roaring over the land. Young America, in the person of Douglas, faced the hierarchy of the earlier republic; and Seward of New York, older than Douglas by some twelve years, but less versatile and attractive, stood now as a spokesman for a new party.

If there were pessimists who believed that the Union was in danger at this time, Douglas was not of them. He could not see the South, if reasonably accommodated, interfering with his ocean-bound republic. He had elasticity, a fresh edge. The coldness of dying arteries was not upon him, as in the case of Webster, Clay, and Calhoun. He had great projects to forward, such as grants to secure the construction of the Illinois Central railroad. He knew what railroads meant to the country. He was of the West and he understood it. He was quick to offer a bill in the Senate for a grant of land for the construction of this railroad from Chicago to New Orleans, and it was passed. In the debate over the bill Douglas of Illinois faced Webster of Massachusetts. It was a dramatic antithesis. Douglas, young and devoted to the prairies, Webster, old and fixed in his admirations for the East. The old question of disunion arose. If we would have liberty and union forever, railroads would insure them. Douglas had said that if the North should ever be arrayed against the South, the pioneers of the northwest and the southwest would balance the contest. Webster had spoken slightingly of the West which Douglas so greatly loved. And these were Douglas' inspiring and prophetic words in reply:

"There is a power in this nation greater either than the North or the South--a growing, increasing, swelling power that will be able to speak the law to this nation and to execute the law as spoken. That power is the country known as the Great West--the valley of the Mississippi, one and indivisible from the Gulf to the Great Lakes, and stretching on the one side and the other to the extreme sources of the Ohio and the Mississippi--from the Alleghenies to the Rocky Mountains. There, sir, is the hope of this nation, the resting place of the power that is not only to control but to save the Union. We furnish the water that makes the Mississippi; and we intend to follow, navigate, and use it until it loses itself in the briny ocean. So with the St. Lawrence. We intend to keep open and enjoy both of these great outlets to the ocean, and all between them we intend to take under our special protection, and preserve and keep as one happy, free, and united people. This is the mission of the great Mississippi valley, the heart and soul of the nation and the continent."

Did these words have any definite meaning to Webster? He knew nothing of the West. He sat with his leonine eyes fixed upon young America in the person of

Douglas. No, as for that, Douglas did not know how truly he was speaking. He could not see in what manner time would fulfill his words. No, not even though there was thrilling conviction in his great voice, which filled the Senate chamber.

On the subject of the territories Douglas had offered several bills of his own. I can't remember their order, their substance, beyond the fact that they looked to the territorial control of slavery. But I remember a very cutting reply that he made to one Senator who interrupted him to ask by what authority a territory could legislate upon slavery. "Your bill conceded that a representative government is necessary--a government founded upon the principles of popular sovereignty, and the right of the people to enact their own laws; and for this reason you give them a legislature constituted of two branches; you confer upon them the right to legislate upon all rightful subjects of legislation, except negroes. Why except negroes? I am not therefore prepared to say that under the Constitution we have not the power to pass laws excluding negro slaves from the territories. But I do say that if left to myself to carry out my own opinions I would leave the whole subject to the people of the territories themselves."

In a sense Clay was the center of attraction, both because he had returned after a long absence and because he was expected to use his conciliatory power toward a settlement which would satisfy both the North and the South. He had come to Washington expecting to be received with open arms by President Taylor. He had been disappointed. He was not overstrong, being in his seventy-third year. But his old charm had not faded, his power over men had not abated. He had loved a drink, a game of cards; he was a slave owner, from a slave state; he had not been consistent in his thinking and his preachment. True to his peculiar gift of leadership and negotiation, he had framed a compromise which provided for the admission of California as a free state. This contradicted the doctrine of the right of the state to come into the Union free or slave, as it chose. The bill provided further for the admission of Utah and New Mexico with or without slavery as they might choose. This impugned the admissional doctrine of California. It provided for the abolition of the slave trade in the District of Columbia, and for the passage of a fugitive slave law, such as would satisfy the South. A motley bill! Calhoun was against it. He demanded the extension of slavery into the territory acquired from Mexico, and proposed an amendment to the Constitution providing for two presidents, one from the South and one from the North, with a veto over each other's acts. Any absurdity for the sake of slavery! Perhaps disease had something to do with this unreason. He died in April before any law was passed.

Webster supported Clay's bill, thus standing for the admission of Utah and New Mexico with or without slavery as they might decide. Douglas in the discussion, with his eye for the concrete, pointed out that the ordinance of 1787, and the Missouri Compromise as well, were practically dead letters. As to the free law respecting Oregon, Oregon had previously fixed the freedom status for herself. As to the fantastic proposition of striking a balance between the North and the South, giving them equal new states of freedom and slavery, he pointed out that that was a moral and physical impossibility. The cause of freedom had steadily advanced, the cause of slavery steadily failed. "We all look forward with confidence to the time when Delaware, Maryland, Virginia, Kentucky, and Missouri, and probably North Carolina and Tennessee, will adopt a gradual system of emancipation. In the meantime we have a vast territory, stretching from the Mississippi to the Pacific, which is rapidly filling up with a hardy, enterprising, and industrious population, large enough to form at least seventeen new free states. Now, let me inquire, where are you to find the slave territory with which to balance these seventeen free territories, or even any one of them?"

This was not exactly placating the South. Douglas missed his opportunity as a demagogue.

Turning to Webster Douglas said: "California came in free according to those laws of nature and God to which the Senator of Massachusetts alluded. It would be free under any bill you may pass or without any bill at all." And Seward spoke for a law higher than the Constitution. Well, there were many laws of justice, mercy, and ethics which the Constitution did not comprehend. Still, if it came to a question of law, what law was to be observed? The laws that were written, the laws relating to the progress of the country, the laws that worked for peace among the American people? If Webster could vote for this compromise, surely Douglas could. Both might have to return to their homes, there to face hostility arising from a different vision of the questions than that these men had, acting upon their responsibility and attempting to reconcile many interests.

In point of fact, Douglas returned to Chicago to find a storm of disfavor rising about him. His enemies were multiplying. His own state was disappointed in him. The South distrusted him. But he had infinite confidence in his own strength. Webster was declining, both he and Clay were soon to die. But Douglas was only thirty-seven. More than thirty years yet before he would reach their age. Clay's Compromises had become a law. The slavery question was settled. Now for the Illinois Central railroad.

CHAPTER XLIII

We returned from Washington to New York, for much was going on in the metropolis. The newspapers day by day were full of Douglas and his difficulties in Chicago. The common council had adopted a resolution censuring Douglas, calling the Clay Compromises a violation of the laws of God. The aldermen of Chicago must have been affected by the religious psychology which was now sweeping the country.

We read that Douglas had heard that a mass-meeting was about to indorse the resolution of the city council; he had gone to the hall to defend himself and had been greeted by hisses and catcalls. He had faced his hecklers, forced them to adjourn until he could address them; then he had addressed them, carried them by storm and procured the resolutions to be expunged.

Evidently the city council did not understand the Clay Compromises. Or had Douglas' oratory swept them off their feet? It may not be a pleasing sight to see a slave returned to its master, but what are you going to do with the law? Are you willing to violate the Constitution for the negro? A heckler asked him: "Are not the provisions of the Constitution respecting the return of a fugitive slave a violation of the law of God?" Douglas was quick to reply: "The divine law does not prescribe the form of government under which we shall live, and the character of our political and civil institutions. Revelation has not furnished us with a constitution, a code of international law, and a system of civil and municipal jurisprudence. If this Constitution is to be repudiated for the law of God, who is to be the prophet to reveal the will of God and establish a theocracy for us?"

I began to think of this law of God. Men are always reaching for it. Sometimes it is only a club for interest or revenge. You have offended me. God will punish you. If God was opposed to slavery he could have prevented it in the beginning and He could terminate it now. Perhaps Douglas thought of this when saying that God had not provided a code of municipal law. If He had, He could have written freedom into the Constitution. Douglas was at least sure that he knew as much about the law of God as Garrison or Seward, or abolitionist lecturers in back halls.

De Tocqueville had written that "America is the country of the whole world where the question of religion has asserted the most real power over the souls of men." The ringing of church bells, church going, revivals, the calling upon God to note and punish sin, pervaded the country and the cities. The Bible was a textbook of God's thinking. It justified slavery in the South; it encouraged abolitionism in the North; it suggested interference and regimentation; it counseled forgiveness and vengeance.

At this time in New York one could not turn or pick up the most casual publication without finding something in the nature of a moral propagandum. At breakfast I read from the **New York Independent** that "Rum, profaneness and Sabbath breaking always go together." The editor was "sorry to find that the stockholders of the Saratoga railroad still run their cars upon the Sabbath. It is an odious and monstrous violation, not only of the laws of God, but of all the decencies of Christian society. And yet I had noticed ladies traveling in them, thundering into Saratoga on the Lord's Day. Women traveling in a public conveyance on the Sabbath. There is something in this peculiarly degrading and shameful. It ought to be only the lowest of the sex that would stoop to such debasement." And another paper said: "We are sorry to learn that the directors have established an accommodation train for Sunday morning between this city and Poughkeepsie, in addition to the mail train to Albany. Mr. James Boorman, through whose efficient service as President the road was mainly built, has resigned his office as director and has addressed a firm remonstrance to the Board against this impiety."

This was the time in which Douglas was now working. Every one knew what the law of God was. Every one appealed to the Bible as God's word. For much of this Douglas had perfect contempt; and he was quick to sense a taint of it in Seward, or any one whom it had infected. Such men as Stephens of the South were insisting now that the real intellect-of the North cared nothing about slavery, and only used it to masquerade their centralizing plots. If local self-government could be extinguished for the purposes of abolition why not for anything, in behalf of which a moral enthusiasm could be evoked? Why not a constitutional amendment establishing a state religion? Why not a state religion under the present constitutional clause which makes provision for the general welfare?

One day when Dorothy and I were seated at Niblo's at luncheon I felt some one touch my shoulder. I looked up and saw Aldington, back of him Abigail, who was laughing at my expression of surprise. We all broke into exclamations. They had just returned from Europe. They joined us in the meal; and there was scarcely enough time to tell back and forth all that was of mutual interest. He saw me with the ***Independent*** and began to rally me. "Did you know," he said, "that the early Puritans in New England were the progenitors of one third of the whole population of the United States by 1834? They constitute one half of the population of the states of Ohio and New York now, and they have gone into the northwest. They will make trouble for your Douglas. I admit that they have blighted art and hobbled literature. They have expurgated Shakespeare, they have fought the theater, they are always ready for the moral battle. They know what God wants better than anybody. In a sense they are hounds in pursuit of a lot of things in the great hunt of life. They are a stubborn lot. It will be hard to take away from them anything that is their own, and also to keep them from destroying anything that they don't want."

"Well, now don't you see," I asked, "that Douglas is against all these people and that he has all these influences to fight? For example, these Puritans cannot rule if popular sovereignty is adopted everywhere. They are numerically too inferior. How, for example, can you stop the railroads on Sunday if you let communities, states, control the matter? But if these fanatics get into control of the Federal government, they can do it. Don't you see the point? This is what Douglas is thinking about. He knows that you can have freedom about life only where every man has a say."

Then we began to talk of the religious revival. Periodicals were noting the great turn of the public mind to religion. "Fruits of the spirit" were extolled. Great and glorious works of divine grace were wrought in Maine. A village in Massachusetts had enjoyed "a heavenly refreshing from the presence of the Lord." In Cincinnati there was "an outpouring of the spirit." In the woods of Michigan men rode into a village to obtain mercy, having heard that the Lord was there. In New York City noon prayer meetings were held. A conductor found salvation suddenly while operating his horse car in Sixth Avenue. A sailor saw Christ at the wheel. Christ was met in parlors, in places of worldly gayety. An actor had been rescued from his wicked calling. Harriet Beecher Stowe wrote: "We trust since prayer has once entered the counting rooms it will never leave it; and that the ledger, sandbox, the blotting book and the pen and ink will all be consecrated by heavenly presence." Her brother, the pastor of Plymouth church, had converted one hundred and ninety souls. A theater was used for a place of worship. Actors were called upon to repent: You who have portrayed human nature before the footlights, fall on your knees and acknowledge God! Rum had been driven from a saloon near this theater. "Thank God," said Beecher, "let us pray silently for the space of two minutes. What a history has been here. A place of fictitious joys but of real sorrows has been reformed. It is open for God's people to sing and pray in. God be thanked that Heaven's gates have been opened in this place of hell."

Garrison saw the point. Of the revival he wrote that it had "spread like an epidemic in all directions, over a wide extent of country. Prayer meetings, morning, noon and night; prayer meetings in town, village, and hamlet, North and South. The whole thing is an emotional contagion without principle. This revival, judging from the past, will promote meanness, not manliness; delusion, not intelligence; the growth of bigotry, not of humanity; a spurious religion, not genuine piety."

Theodore Parker denounced the mania too, and was attacked for it by Methodists and others. He sew that the North had its rain gods, its prosperity gods, its bread and butter gods, its rituals and devotions for these gods; and that the South had the same number of gods.

What then of the law of God? Douglas was at one with Garrison and Parker in this criticism of the religious mania.

Thus we talked along together. The principal thing about Abigail was that she despised the South, but for the reason that there was nothing there but the political mind and that it was concerned almost entirely with the negro. It had no literature. Longfellow, Emerson, Whittier, Lowell were producing works of merit; and the South was doing nothing. Poe was born in Boston, had lived South, but had written out of nowhere. He had died about a year before, discouraged and broken.

The most silent voice at the table was Dorothy's. She did not really enter into these discussions. Her softer, altogether feminine nature was disturbed by these things. Abigail began to laugh. "Why," she asked, "does every one say here 'how's your health' instead of 'good morning' as they say in England? People look care-worn to me in America; they are spare and pallid. Not many ruddy complexions. Why all these sharp-faced, lantern-jawed, lean, sallow, hard-handed people? Why this depression of spirits? Perhaps they really get a thrill out of religion after all. Why all these advertisements of quack remedies, why all this calling on God? This is a place of bright sunshine and exhilarating air. After all, I do not understand it."

"All due to the habits of life," said Aldington. "Look at the fast eating--look at them here. Too much hot bread and sweets--too much pie for breakfast. Too much pork. Too much living at hotels and boarding houses. Too much drinking before meals; not enough wine and beer with meals. Too much tobacco chewing. No exercise. Only the farmer, the laborer works. They go too far. But where do you see outdoor sports? No cricket, no rowing. Nothing but trotting around in buggies. Recreation consists of lounging around on sofas at Saratoga. All the public men ill. I hear that Toombs is indisposed. Sumner is in poor health. Douglas, the little giant, is losing strength. What a curious people, aged and young, corrupt and idealistic, candid and hypocritical, religious and materialistic, hoarders and spenders, self-righteous, licentious, Puritanical." "Like all others," I interjected.

"Like no other," Aldington rejoined. "Go back to your native England and see. You have forgotten some things. There is such a thing as a definite stock. And if you call the English bulldogs, for example, your America is a mixture of the wolf, span-iel, lapdog, shepherd, and about all breeds; and according to the occasion any one of them, with quick changes. Abigail and I have been here for a number of days and we have been entertained by some of her splendacious friends, to use Thackeray's adjective for American fashion; and the impression it all makes on me is beyond de-scription. I want to see a better thing made of Chicago. I really hate it here, all this striving for money--but of course no place can beat Chicago for that--but also the idlers here, the worship of Mammon, the dullness and the gloom of elegant people, the extravagant dressing, the liveried servants, all this imitation. And all this talk here of America being the only religious, free, and enlightened people in the world. Why, they are not free at all. The mind must be free before the man is free, and the mind cannot be free in a despotism. The slavery of the North is just as bad as the slavery of the South. For look at these people; slaves to fear, slaves to stupid customs, slaves to superstition, slaves to foreign ideas of dress, fashion, wealth; slaves to all the vices by which money is made, and all the tricks and hypocrisies by which it is piled up and invested with rulership; slaves to absurd ideas; slaves to every foolish reform. Why, sometimes as I think of it, I see the negro in the South as the freest man in America. He is only a slave as to his labor. Every one must work. Instead of receiving money he gets clothes and a hut. He can't go away from the plantation, but why go away? One must be somewhere. And as to these other things, he is not a slave at all."

"Yes, and that's not all," I said. "A money power is fast growing up in this country which will rule the country so thoroughly that the small dictation of the cotton industry of the South will not be a comparison. Slavocracy is only one of the scales on the tail of the dragon of plutocracy. Gold and silver, tariffs, subsidies, colonies, banks of issue--these are the claws and teeth of the big slavery."

"So says Adam Smith," Aldington interjected.

"Exactly so, and it's all true. Every one of the old timers knew these things, Washington, Jefferson, Hamilton. I am beginning to think that Franklin, Payne, and Jefferson were the truest thinkers and greatest planners for a republic that America has had. And what do you think of Douglas now? He is a Nationalist with Jackson, and a Republican with Jefferson; a let-alone philosopher all the time."

"Oh, yes, but Douglas is not educated. He is not really sound. He is not deep enough. He is not--I hate the word spirituality--but he hasn't the right heat, the right light. I may not be able to put my finger on the exact fault--it is not exactly demagogy--but I see him using blocks of people, who are bound together by a common emotion or idea, as a man might use a block of stone for his house. He picks them up and puts them in the place that suits his own ambition. There is one thing, however, with which I am inclined to sympathize with Douglas. His appeal is really more intellectual than emotional. You see an ocean-bound republic requires imagination to get the thrill out of it, but you can catch anybody in America with a military uniform. And while Douglas may be a war man, so to speak, he is really too honest to play that game. I'll grant him that much. I think that the Whigs are out-playing him. And it looks to me that the emotions of America--what some people might call the conscience of America--are being drawn away from Douglas by this slavery matter. Just now territory and railroads are not so strong, or will not be so strong pretty soon as the cry for emancipation." "I am glad to hear you say these things," I said. "Douglas is only thirty-seven; he will not fully mature his powers for ten years yet. I have talked with him many times and have known him intimately and I think I understand the man. He is distrusted in the South simply because he will not bend all law making to the slave interests. He has just been written down in Chicago on the law of God doctrine. And yet he stands his ground against both the North and the South without flinching. He defies his enemies. He has the very sanity that you have extolled here at this table. I think he has the only rational solution for this slavery question. He is a very great man in my opinion."

"What do you think of Barnum?" asked Aldington. Abigail looked up and said: "Yes, I would like to hear a little about Barnum and less about Douglas. I hear that Jenny Lind is coming to town." "It's to-day," said Dorothy. "And don't we want to see her arrive? I do, let's go."

And we all hurried forth to witness the greetings given to the Swedish nightingale.

CHAPTER XLIV

Barnum had been taken by De Quincey as an epitome of America: "A great hulk of a continent, that the very moon finds fatiguing to cross, produces a race of Barnums on a pre-Adamite scale, corresponding in activity to its own enormous proportions."

Barnum had resorted to daily advertising, a great sensationalism to keep up interest in the arrival of the singer. We went from our table to the pier to see her descend from the steamer. Triumphal arches of evergreens and flowers had been erected over the way she passed. A great crowd had collected. Bands were playing. Her face came into view. Shouts arose. She bowed and smiled to the wild throngs about her as she rode with Barnum to the Astor House. Here the Swedish and American flags floated in her honor. New York was in a frenzy of delight. But the tickets to hear her! All this excitement had been worked up for use at the box office. And Aldington could not afford the price. We wished Abigail and Aldington to be with us. I therefore submitted to the Barnum extortion for the whole party.

Jenny Lind sang at Castle Garden, where I had sat nearly twenty years before, when New York had about half the population. The crowds pressed around the entrances. Those who could not afford to enter hoped to get a glimpse of her anyway. It was an enormous audience, and all of distinguished New York was there. Senator Webster had been one of those to receive her at the pier, and he was in the audience too. We were all deeply moved by this wonderful voice. Poor Dorothy was frequently drying her eyes. And when she sang one of her own national airs, Webster sat entranced. At its close she courtesied to him. He arose and bowed to her with the majestic manner of a great monarch. The audience went into a fury of applause. Every one spoke of her as good of heart, sweet and natural of manner. She had given her share of the proceeds of this concert to various charities in New York

City. A feeling of uplifted life spread over the metropolis. She melted the souls of thousands, and purged the craft of money getting. We came away from her as from a higher realm. "What," said Abigail, "is anything in the world, money or statesmanship, what, of all these things of which we have talked to-day can be compared to an art like that, a divine influence like song?"

After this we started on a round of the theaters. I prevailed upon our friends to prolong their stay, to be our guests. We saw Burton and Edwin Booth. We went to the Opera, saw the ballet which Fannie Ellsler had previously inaugurated. The *Independent* was denouncing the theater as an unmitigated evil; the ballet was a shocking exhibition of legs. Still they had come, and New York had them.

We dined at Niblo's, at Castle Garden. We drove about the city. We went out to see Trenton Falls where Jenny Lind had been taken as part of her entertainment, and where she had sung in the woods and been answered by the birds.

I began to notice that Dorothy was unusually quiet. She complained of fatigue, of pain. We had done too much perhaps. One morning she could not arise. Abigail and Aldington were returning to Chicago. We had expected to go with them. But Dorothy could not travel now--she could not stand that terrible journey of boats and cars, of changes and delays. So we bade adieu to our friends.

Dorothy did not rally, as I had expected. She grew weaker day by day. She became gravely ill. In the midst of the extra labor thrown upon Mammy, she too was compelled to take to her bed. I was forced to look about for servants, finding two Irish girls at last. Then quite suddenly Mammy died. She was very old. And thus we were cut off from all our past, Nashville, the old days. And I stayed almost constantly by Dorothy's side, trying to bring back her strength. It entered my mind at times that after all I was not as tender a husband to Dorothy as I should have been. I was with her a good deal, to be sure. At the same time, I was much preoccupied. She did not like politics, and could not share my interest in that direction. The condition of the country really distressed her. She had seen slavery in its benign aspect, and she was impatient with any criticism of the institution.

It was months before Dorothy sat up and began to walk again. I could see that she was frailer than before and might never be strong again. Our boy Reverdy was not robust. And the winter was coming on. At the same time Dorothy did not wish to return to Washington. She wanted to hear no more of politics. I had to select her books for her, something that soothed her, led her into dreams. ***Uncle Tom's Cabin*** was now appearing in serial form. I was reading it with great amusement. But I dared not show it to Dorothy. I had heard Beecher and knew his sentimental attitude. This book had for me the same quality. Yet it helped me to pass many hours while watching by Dorothy's side. Somehow I felt that it would produce a storm akin to the religious psychology which was sweeping the country. Critics were already noting its moral effect. Mrs. Stowe was hailed by Sumner as a "Christian genius," a Joan of Arc. Garrison said that it would make two million abolitionists. In Paris it was compared to Dumas' ***The Three Guardsmen*** as a popular ***tour de force***. Others detected in it a resemblance to Rousseau's ***Nouvelle Heloise***. One pleaded for the liberty of the slave, the other for the rights of the peasant. But I knew that the book was not really true. It forefronted the brutality of slavery, it minimized the benevolent aspects of the institution, which I had myself seen. It was written with intensity of feeling, with the revivalist's method and emotion. It was like her brother's sermons, and equally unauthentic. Yet how strangely was this book received. It won Macaulay and Longfellow and George Sand, and stirred the heart of Heine. It exasperated the South. The winds of destiny previously let loose were blowing madly now.

In the midst of my own cares I awoke one morning to read that Douglas was on his way to Cuba. The thought went through my mind, why not take Dorothy and go in order to give her the benefit of this summer climate through the winter? As Douglas had traveled by way of New Orleans he had stopped in Memphis and I read in the ***Tribune*** what he had said to the people there: "If old Joshua R. Giddings should raise a colony in Ohio and settle down in Louisiana he would be the strongest advocate of slavery in the South; he would find when he got there that his opinion would be very much modified; he would find on those sugar plantations that it was not a question between the white man and the negro, but between the negro and the crocodile. You come right back to the principle of dollars and cents."

At New Orleans he had uttered the God of nature doctrine: "There is a line or belt of country meandering through the valleys and over the mountain tops which is a natural barrier between free territory and slave territory, on the south of which are to be found the productions suitable to slave labor, while on the north exists a country adapted to free labor alone. But in the great central region, where there may be some doubt as to the effect of natural causes, who ought to decide the question except the people residing there, who have all their interests there, who have gone there to live with their wives and children?"

No recognition of a right and a wrong, to be sure. But no express advocacy of a wrong. I could not see then, and have never been able to see since, why Douglas with this practical facing of the business of life could not fare equally well with public opinion as Hamilton has fared with it, who advocated corruption in government as a means to a national power.

I went to Dorothy with my plan about Cuba, telling her that Douglas had gone there. It stirred her languid spirits. She was all eagerness to start. We took passage from New York, sailing around Florida, at last around Morro Castle into the harbor of Havana. The blueness of the water, with the balmy wind blowing almost incessantly began to restore Dorothy. The Spanish city lying before our eyes, yellow and continental, awoke her interest. At the dock there were crowds of idlers, Spaniards, negroes, to see us fasten and disembark. With Dorothy and our son and two maids we made our way to a hotel near the water. I was anxious to look up Douglas; but it was impossible the first evening, owing to Dorothy's indisposition. She had been seasick and the journey had fatigued her. Nevertheless we went to the roof of the hotel together and sat there until nearly midnight, inhaling the luxurious breeze from the gulf and gazing up at the brilliant stars of this tropical sky.

The next morning I was down to breakfast early, leaving Dorothy to be served in her room. The hotel was drab and decayed exteriorly; but the dining room was a continental elegance of marble, gilt, and mirrors. Douglas was not stopping here, as I had already learned. I concluded that he would be at one of the better known hotels on the Prado, and I hurried thither as fast as I could. I soon located him; but he had gone out for a few days, was making something of a tour of the island, including a visit to the celebrated cave of Matanzas. Leaving a note for Douglas which apprised him of my hotel, I hurried back to Dorothy. The city was so brilliant under the golden sunshine, and the air so delightful, that I wished to spend these wonderful hours in seeing the city.

Havana was as novel to me as to Dorothy. It was Spanish, therefore having no resemblance to London or any other English town. It seemed to me to be about the size that New York was in 1833. We spent three days driving through the Paso de Paula, along the Malecon, up and down the Prado lined with laurels and distinguished for fine houses and clubs. We visited the parks, the Exchange, the old churches, the navy yard, La Fueza, built by De Soto, the old markets of Colon and Tacon, the Palace; and we stood in the Cathedral before the medallion which marked the burial place of Columbus when his remains were removed here from Santa Domingo in 1796. We dined about the cafes and hotels, and attended the theater, and walked, when Dorothy felt equal to it, through the parks, or along the wall of the sea which stretched from the punta.

I have already recorded so much of wrangling politics and the debates of infuriate minds that one might infer that I was leading no life of my own. Do you think that I am only a shadow or a registering machine, and that Dorothy is not flesh and blood? Sometimes it occurs to me that I am not treating her as a woman in spite of my desire to be thoughtful. A vast world of rich imagination, of vital emotion was in truth moving about me all the while, and in breasts that I did not comprehend. For all my life up to this time and beyond it, as you shall see, was occupied with money making and with watching principally the epic development of America. But I was later to awake as from a day dream or from a life in a shell, to the consciousness of a brighter world of sunlight and of wings. I was at peace now, and with Dorothy, whose frailty required my watchfulness and my care, and whom I delighted to please with lovely things. That was the extent of my emotional life. And so we drove, and visited the shops in Opispo Street. For I was waiting for Douglas. I wanted to take him off to a bull fight or a cock fight. And I was eager to hear him talk of his plans, of America, of anything that came from his fluent and restless mind.

One evening when Dorothy and I were in the comfortable lounging chairs on the roof of the hotel, looking over toward Morro Castle, counting the largest of the richly brilliant stars, Douglas came upon us. He had returned from his trip only that afternoon. Finding my note, and leaving other engagements, he had come over to call, delighted and surprised to find that we were in Havana. Cuba already had a railroad, but it was not of much extent. He had been traveling by carriage, and in the hillier localities in a vehicle of two enormous wheels, drawn by horses driven in tandem. He had seen the cave, the pineapple fields, the sugar plantations. His imagination was already at work for America.

He went on to say to me that whenever the people of Cuba should show themselves worthy of freedom by asserting their independence and should apply for annexation to the United States, they ought to be annexed. And that whenever Spain should be ready to sell Cuba, with the consent of its inhabitants, the United States should accept the chance. With spirit he exclaimed that if Spain should transfer Cuba to England, or any other European power America should take Cuba by force. "It is folly," he said, "to debate the acquisition of the island. It naturally belongs to the American continent. It guards the mouth of the Mississippi River, which is the heart of the American continent and the body of the American nation." This led Douglas to speak, and with bitterness, of the Clayton-Bulwer treaty, which had given England joint control of any canal across the Isthmus of Panama. "I was disgusted with this treaty as I was disgusted with the settlement of the Oregon boundary. Just look at it! Here the Monroe Doctrine has been an avowed policy for thirty years, declaring that no European colonization will be permitted in America. And what happens? Whenever there has been no opportunity to enforce the doctrine, because there has been nothing at issue, we have cock-a-doodle-dooed; and whenever a chance has arisen to enforce it we have beaten a retreat, frightened to death by the awful consequences if we do enforce it. Frightened by our own spokesmen, Senators and others. Frightened by England in the main; for truly we have no other power to fear. So when the Clayton-Bulwer treaty came up I fought it as I fought Polk on the Oregon boundary of '49. I said then, and I say now, that the time may come when we shall want to possess some portion of Central America. It has come to the pass that I can't stand for America as to new territory without having the Abolitionists charge me with favoritism to the South. But it's a lie and history will vindicate me. But if I want Cuba or Central America for slavery I want them also for America. And what does England want them for? For freedom, I suppose, for the good of America! The agreement not to fortify the canal was not reciprocal, because England holds Jamaica, which guards the entrance to the canal. What rights did England have to the Mosquito Coast? Well, her title is at least doubtful.

"But what I hate about the canal treaty is the recognition of the right of European powers to intervene in American affairs. We contracted with England to protect any canal or railroad across the Isthmus; and not only that, we invited other

European powers to join with us in that protection. And that lets in all the kings of Europe, and where's your Monroe Doctrine? It vanishes into air. Study it out; you will see all these Whigs and all these motley groups joining the Whigs, pulling together by a sort of momentum started by the old crowd which sided with England against America in the Revolution. They are the same crowd that tried to break down the American system when they were banded together as Federalists. They tried secession at Hartford, when they didn't like the War of 1812; then they held up their hands in horror when South Carolina threatened to secede over the tariff. They called on God to avenge the Mexican War; then they grabbed this slavery matter to give them a moral push into power. They elected a President, but were afraid to formulate a platform. All the while they had played with England, skulking and running and fawning upon England, when our vital interests were at stake, and siding with England on the canal and on Oregon. They are better than other men! They are more holy! They are pure, just, broad! They love God! They are the only Christians! There is only one evil and that is slavery! But there are many gods, of which banks and tariffs are not the least; yet I notice that they do not give away Texas and California, those unholy fruits of a wicked war for which you fought, my friend. They like the gold and the wheat. And in order to ride into power they put forward old Taylor, and blow hot and cold with him and Millard Fillmore."

The great organ-like voice of Douglas poured forth a steady stream of talk as we sat together under the wonderful stars of a clear sky, with the soft breeze from the Gulf blowing around us. Dorothy had fallen asleep. I got up and looked at her, and finding her resting peacefully I returned to my chair. It was now near midnight. We could hear the rattle of cabs on the cobblestones, the cries of strange voices in Spanish; and we saw the lights in the harbor, the lights in the Prado, over the city which was still feasting and playing. Then Douglas confided to me that he was going to be a candidate for President in this next campaign of 1852.

The prospects were very good, he thought. If he could get two or three western states to speak out in his favor he would win. He wondered if I could not go to Iowa for him. He hoped to have the leading politicians of Illinois as delegates at Baltimore. He wished me to be a delegate, not that I was a leading politician, but I counted for as much since I was an old friend and a sympathetic adherent. I told him to use me in any way that would serve him.

Having all these enterprises on his hands he was leaving for Mobile in the morning. No time to see a bull fight. "I'll not say good night to Mrs. Miles," he said. "Let her sleep." He got up to tiptoe away. "Good night, Senator," called Dorothy. She had aroused at the cessation of our talk. Douglas returned and in his most gallant manner bade Dorothy good night. Then he strode away, stepped through the trapdoor, began to descend, disappeared. I looked up at the great stars. Then lifting Dorothy into my arms, I carried her to the stairs and on my back to our room.

CHAPTER XLV

Dorothy and I lingered in Havana until we were sure that spring had come to Chicago. Then we took a boat to New Orleans; and once again I ascended the Mississippi to St. Louis, and thence to Chicago by the Illinois River and the canal.

It was still cool in Chicago, the air fresh and vital. Great spaces of deep blue stood far back, cool and thrillingly serene; against these spaces the white clouds coming over from the far west and disappearing into havens over the lake and into Michigan. The lake was roaring to the stiff breezes of the blustering spring.

Chicago was a thrilling spectacle. The Illinois Central railroad was being built. The railroad mileage in the country had now risen to more than ten thousand miles. The short roads with steamboat connections were giving way to the trunk lines. Boston was now connected by rail with Montreal. There were nine hundred miles of railroad in Ohio; six hundred in Indiana; about four hundred in Illinois. The Michigan Central connected Chicago with Detroit. The Michigan Southern was opened, and the first train from the East had entered Chicago. A train had started west from St. Louis on the first five miles of the Pacific railroad. Telegraph lines stuck forth everywhere into the great spaces of the country, like the new shoots of a tree.

The breech-loading gun had been invented. The fire-alarm telegram system had come into use.

Thackeray had come over from England to smile upon us genially, to lecture at the rate "of a pound a minute," as he had expressed it. Young America was putting old America behind her.

Calhoun was gone. Clay, defeated in his life's ambition to be President, had crept to his grave. Webster was a dying man. The slavery question had vexed and shadowed his dying years. He had supported the Compromises of 1850 and had been bitterly denounced for it. Whittier had expunged his name from the list of the great and the good. He had wanted to be President too. Men like General Harrison had secured the prize over his head. He was reduced to the rejection of the proffered Vice Presidency. He had been Secretary of State under Harrison, Tyler, and Fillmore. He had supported the bank, the tariff, implied powers, and Hamiltonism. He had followed Clay's leadership. Still he had risen to great heights of oratory and legalistic reason. Carlyle had called him a logic machine in pants. His debate with Hayne, however, was to furnish the material for one of the greatest of state papers, to be written less than a decade from this day. From the hills of Massachusetts he failed to see the West. Young Douglas had fronted him and told him of the power of the new and growing country along the Mississippi River. Old America was passing. The West was asking for the highest recognition. Douglas was thirty-nine and seemed to be the man for President.

I did not pretend to be a politician, but only an observer and Douglas' friend. I read everything that was written about the questions of the day, the newspapers, the ***Congressional Record***. It was clear to me that the Democrats had been split in 1848 by their attitude toward the Wilmot Proviso, which was intended to keep slavery from the Texan territory. Then came the Compromises under a Whig administration. The Compromises were hated by the South and cursed by the Abolitionists in the North. The Democrats were united by an acquiescence in the Compromises. And now the Whigs were divided because of them. They had played foxy in '48 by a no-platform. They were unable to have one, because they had no united voice. The Free Soil party had collapsed in Illinois. Altogether hopes ran high for the Democrats. But who should be the candidate?

Douglas! He seemed to me the ideal man, as Webster seemed the ideal man to admiring Whigs. But Douglas, like Webster, was doomed to fail, at least in this convention. The prize was captured by Franklin Pierce, whom no one knew, but it was not until the forty-ninth ballot. On the forty-eighth ballot Douglas had thirty-three votes to Pierce's fifty-five. Then there was a stampede to Pierce. The West had lost. Young America was put aside for a fair-sized man from New Hampshire.

The Whigs met the same month in Baltimore. Webster, soon to die, was again a candidate. The platform was made and submitted to him. He approved of it. It indorsed the Compromises. But again there was an old soldier in the field, in the person of General Scott. He had fought the British in 1812. He had made treaties with the Sauk, Fox, Winnebago, and Sioux tribes after the Black Hawk War. Yes, he had made a brilliant record in the Mexican War. In mental stature he was up to the knees of Webster, and no more. But Webster had no imaginative appeal. He could only pull twenty-nine votes on the first ballot, as against Scott's one hundred and thirty-one votes. Webster never had more than thirty-two votes. On the fifty-third ballot Scott was nominated. And in a few months Webster died, and left the tangles of statecraft to other hands.

Who was Franklin Pierce? Pretty soon Hawthorne, whose romances I had enjoyed so much, put forth a life of his long-time friend. "When a friend dear to him almost from boyhood days stands up before his country, misrepresented by indiscriminate abuse on the one hand, and by aimless praise on the other, it is quite proper that he should be sketched by one who has had opportunities of knowing him well and who is certainly inclined to tell the truth." These were Hawthorne's words. Pierce was a gentleman of truth and honor, devoted to his family and to his country, accomplished, of fine appearance, and always Democratic. But how could this man win against an old soldier? Webster and Douglas had lost the nomination, how could a gentleman win the election?

I returned to Chicago and to my business. But Douglas' term for Senator was about to expire, and he necessarily entered the campaign with vigor. He traveled from Virginia to Arkansas, from New York to Illinois and all over his own state. He mocked Scott's letter of acceptance, attributing its composition to Seward. His physical endurance seemed exhaustless. All the while he was living and confraternizing and drinking. Pierce was elected. Douglas won the legislature for another Senatorial term. In the midst of these excitements Mrs. Douglas died.

She had been to our house but recently. If I had prophesied between her and Dorothy I should have believed the end would come to Dorothy first. Dorothy was so frail, so incapable of effort. Already I was beginning to think of a milder climate for her for the winter.

Douglas now seemed to lose heart. His temper became bitter. His dress was slovenly, his manners familiar, his associations indifferent. He was drinking too much. In his public utterances he was more emphatic, more caustic of tongue. If the loss of the nomination had disappointed him, the death of Mrs. Douglas had over-whelmed him. He was not interested in his Illinois Central. He was doing nothing with his large tract of land three miles south of Madison Street. He was very well off. But he had no heart to enjoy his prosperity. He was doing nothing about founding his university. He was a giant sorely smitten, ready to rouse from irritability into fury against his enemies. He was in a poor way to master his own spirit and future.

I suggested to him a trip to Europe to forget his sorrows, to recuperate his spirits. He liked the idea. But first he had to return to the Senate. There he spoke of Cuba and its annexation, almost in the same words he had used when talking to me that midnight on the roof of the hotel in Havana. Bitterly he denounced the Clayton-Bulwer treaty. Audaciously he excoriated England. Almost immediately he was off to visit England, but not to see Queen Victoria, although invited to her presence. He went to Russia, saw the Czar. He visited the Crimea and Syria. From New Orleans I followed his travels. I had taken Dorothy there to escape the Chicago winter.

CHAPTER XLVI

New Orleans had grown to be a city of 170,000 people. Its commerce was enormous. It was the great entrepot of the continent's sugar and cotton industries.

Day by day I stood on the wharves, watching the steamers unload and load, gazing over the busy mass of humanity back of which was labor, black and white, slave and free! The great Mississippi, broad and foul, waking from its sleep in the lowlands above, gathering speed here, feeling the call of the sea, begins to move with increased life. Across from the city are lowlands, sugar refineries, smoke stacks. The negroes call to each other, laugh with spontaneous, childlike humor. The wharf officers, the brokers, pass with intense faces. It is hot. Sweat drips from black faces and from white. Whips crack. Mules trot and stumble over the loose and resounding boards. Heavy wheels rumble. And the life of gambling, drinking, pleasure, crawls about the French quarter, along Canal Street, on Royal Street. The bell in the Cathedral rings. I catch the whiff of flowers. Gulls fly over the muddy water.

I think of Douglas far away in Russia, of all my life in its early days, now growing so misty. I am more than thirty-seven; and sometimes I feel weary. I grieve for Dorothy. She has wound herself with tenderness around my heart. But less and less can she share life with me.

I go to the Place d'Armes to see the equestrian statue of Jackson which has been erected here since my last visit. It is now called Jackson Square. The St. Louis Cathedral has been largely rebuilt. I wander through the Cabildo again, visit the old cemeteries, read the names of the dead. The scent of strange blossoms affects me poignantly. I stroll through the parks, and I visit the life in the French quarter.

Dorothy can drive with me at times, but not for long. Our boy distresses her;

and a governess keeps him away much of the time. There are memories all about me. La Fayette has been here. He was in this very Cabildo. The old hero of New Orleans, who blessed Dorothy and me, walked these streets. Now he is long gone. Clay is gone, Webster, Calhoun. The country is at a pause. Hawthorne's friend is President. And Douglas is in St. Petersburg, riding a horse grotesquely, and bringing his western ways into the very presence of the Czar.

Sometimes I wonder if Zoe is not alive, if some kind of consummate trick was not played on me. Fortescue did not kill her. He did not seem to me like a man who would commit murder. Why would any one murder Zoe? Might she not have been sold for her loveliness to some man desiring a mistress? No! Zoe would write to me if she were living. Yet I went everywhere in New Orleans searching for Zoe.

Often I visited the St. Louis hotel, for there young quadroons and octoroons on sale, tastefully dressed, were inspected by men with all the critical and amorous interest with which a roue would look upon the object of his desire. Their eyes were gazed into, their hair stroked, their limbs caressed and outlined, their busts stared at and touched. Men went mad over these beauties.

A story went the rounds that a young man in Virginia fell in love with an octoroon slave while on a visit to a country house. The girl had gone to her mistress for protection, and received it, against the man's advances. But he had returned, saying that he could not live without the girl. The mistress had sold her to him for $1500. Did Zoe meet that fate, and not violence?

So I searched the cafes, the places of amusement, the bagnios for Zoe. And into every octoroon's face in which I saw a resemblance to Zoe I peered, hoping that it would be she. For with Dorothy so much ill, and with no one in the world of my own but Dorothy and our boy, I had hours of profound loneliness. In New Orleans this winter I was more lonely than I had ever been in my life. I no longer had to strive, I had money enough. And all the while my real estate investments in Chicago doubled and trebled while I traveled.

There were many French in New Orleans; there was reverence there and memory for Bonaparte. There was gladness and exultation now that Louis Napoleon had accomplished a coup d'etat and established a throne upon the ruins of the republic. His soldiers were in the Crimea, fighting as desperately as if great wealth or fame could be won by their valor and death. But it was all for the glory of the French throne! A French monarchy again, after the struggles of Mirabeau, after the agony of Marat, and after the rise of republican principles which Douglas had hailed with delight! If these things could be done with honor and applause, did Douglas deserve the hostility which was rising up against him? Was America so immaculately free that Douglas' subordination of the negro to the welfare of the republic at large should be so severely dealt with?

On the bulletin boards in great headlines, the progress of the Crimean War was heralded. The French soldiers were winning imperishable glory. The Light Brigade had died for God and the glory of England in the charge at Balaklava. Cavour had sent the Sardinians to help France and England against the Russians; these were soon to fight for the liberty of Italy. Always liberty and God! Russia had gone to war against the Turks because of a quarrel between the Greek and Latin Christians at Jerusalem. Then the Czar demanded of the Turk the right of a protectorate over all Greek Christians in the Ottoman empire. It was refused. Hence war. And England and France and Cavour's Sardinians are fighting Russia. Perhaps the Latin church is the inspiring cause. Minds and noses concur, and the result is conscience.

America is in a distressed condition and growing worse. Politics raves. Malice, destroying forces are abroad. Always war with or without the sword. The Greek Christian must be protected; but the Turk must not be vanquished, his country taken by Russia. Louis Napoleon would win a little glory. England needs the Turk, because she lusts for Egypt and India. France wants Algeria and Morocco. In America the North wants power; the South wants power. Men are anxious for office. Labor has interests at stake; so has manufacturing. Farsighted money makers, imperialists, deploy these factions; parties are formed; the populace is fooled with war records and catch words. Men must be destroyed in order to achieve results--for God and liberty. Among others, Douglas must be destroyed!

He has risen from obscurity to be the first man in America in the realm of state-craft. He has been a cabinet maker, a lawyer, a legislator, a judge, a Senator, then a leader, now chairman of the committee on territories. He has perfected political efficiency, introduced the convention system, done for representative government what the reaper has done for the harvest field. He has done this all himself without wealth or family to boost him. He is charged with being clever and resourceful, but no one points to corruption in his life. Is there a statesman in Europe or one in America with a cleaner record? His whole energy has been devoted to the development of the country. He has worked for schools, for colleges, for canals, for railroads, for the quick dissemination of intelligence, for the rule of the people on every subject, including slavery, and for that rule in places of maturing sovereignty, like territories, and in places of complete sovereignty, like states. He is spiritually hard, hates the sap-head, the agitator, the simple-hearted moralist. He is indifferent to slavery, when it stands in the way of his republic building. He knows that slavery cannot thrive in the North. He knows that prairies of corn, hills of iron and coal, fields of wheat are as alien to slavery as the tropics are alien to polar bears and reindeer. He sees a God who works through climate; and he sees that the cotton calls for a certain kind of worker, and corn for another. He did not read and he did not know much of anything of the work of Marx and the Revolutionary Manifesto of 1848. He did not need to. He sensed the materialistic conception of history. He had no horror of slavery, knowing exactly what it was; on the other hand he was falsely accused of trying to plant it in the territories.

He was hunted and traduced! Moralists prattled of his lack of a moral nature; envy tracked him, shooting from ambush! He had become rich and famous. He was the first man in his party. He was young and full of power. He might be President. The sanctimonious quoted Scripture against him. "Where a man's treasure is, there will be his heart also," said an enemy in the Senate, referring to the fact that Douglas had married a woman who was a slave owner. Douglas had replied in these manly and tender words: "God forbid that I should be understood by any one as being willing to cast from me any responsibility that now does or has ever attached to any member of my family. So long as life shall last and I shall cherish with religious veneration the memories and virtues of the sainted mother of my children--so long as my heart shall be filled with paternal solicitude for the happiness of those motherless infants, I implore my enemies who so ruthlessly invade the domestic sanctuary to do me the favor to believe that I have no wish, no aspiration to be considered purer or better than she, who was, or they who are slaveholders."

It was while I was in New Orleans that Douglas wrote me a letter regarding the Presidency. "I do not wish to occupy that position," he said. "I think that such a state of things will exist that I shall not desire the nomination. Yet I do not intend to do any act which will deprive me of the control of my own action. Our first duty is to the cause--the fate of individual politicians is of minor consequence. The party is in a distracted condition, and it requires all our wisdom, prudence, and energy to consolidate its power and perpetuate its principles."

It was this letter that stirred my reflections as I went about New Orleans reading of conditions in Europe and foolishly searching for Zoe. Moreover, I was beginning to be tired of everything in America, and particularly worn with New Orleans. I longed to be back in Chicago in the fresh air by the lake, away from the steam, the heat, the sensual atmosphere of this southern city. Yet Dorothy could not just now venture into the changeable climate of Lake Michigan. I was forced to stay on for her sake. I continued my wanderings and my thoughts about the city, guiding my business interests in Chicago by correspondence.

But at last we started.

CHAPTER XLVII

I wanted to stop on the way to see Reverdy and Sarah. I had a call to the renewal of the old days, to an overlooking of the farm, the places I had first known in Illinois. But as Dorothy wished to be home, to settle into a regular life of comfort at once, I had to take her to Chicago and then return later to Jacksonville. Before leaving I had several conferences with Mr. Williams about our joint interests; and we talked of Douglas too.

Mr. Williams thought that Douglas was getting deeper and deeper into trouble. The Compromises of 1850 were only partially satisfactory. They had not appeased the Abolitionists. A new party was growing up around the discontent which those Compromises had created. Mr. Pierce's administration had met some disturbances, though it had sufficed in the main. He had gone into office with the support of many of the best men of the country, as, for example, Bryant, the poet, and of course Hawthorne, his boyhood friend. Since his election the Whig party had gone to pieces. There was no party but the Democratic party. Beside it nothing but factions and groups trying to find a way to unite. Chief of these was the Know-nothings who stood for what they called Americanism, and raised an opposition to Catholicism. Next were the Abolitionists. There were smaller bodies, all inharmonious. I felt that Douglas was destined to drive these lawless resolutes into defeat and become President. He was not in Chicago now; but I was soon to see him. In the meanwhile I thought I would go to see Reverdy and Sarah.

Reverdy was now in the middle fifties, and aging. Sarah looked thin and worn. She was really an old woman. Amos was a man. He had taken up with farming near Jacksonville. Jonas was nearing his twentieth year. The story was for the most part told for them all as one family.

Reverdy and I drove about the country; and it had changed so much. Boundaries had disappeared; forests had vanished. Familiar houses had given way to pretentious residences, many built in the southern style of Tennessee or Kentucky. Great barns dotted the landscape. Yet the pioneer was still here. My old fiddler in the woods had aged, but he was much himself. He played for us. And we went to the log hut, in which I had lived during my first winter on the farm. Here it was with its chimney of sticks, its single room of all uses, the very symbol of humble life, of solitariness in the woods. I had lived here when the country was wild, but Reverdy said that before my coming to Illinois it was wilder still and more lonely. "What do you think," said Reverdy, "of a man and a woman living here in the most primitive days; no church, no schools. No doctors to relieve suffering, or scarcely to attend a birth. No books, or but few. The long winters of snow; silence except when terrible storms broke over a roof like this. Imagine yourself born and reared in such a place; all the family sleeping in this one room in the bitter cold of winter. Sickness without medicine. Imagine Douglas living here. His early youth had its hardships; but after all he has had a comfortable life. He soon became prosperous. Now he is rich. What public man has become so rich? Yes, here is the American cotter's home; and so many boys have come out of a place like this and gone to the wars or into public life. It is America's symbol."

"You do not like Douglas, do you, Reverdy?" I asked, as we turned away. "Yes, I like him, I have always supported him--but somehow I feel that he is not good enough. I don't know what else to call it. You know, I don't like slavery; at the same time I don't know what to do with it. Sometimes I think Douglas' plan is all right, again I am not sure. All the time I feel that there is not enough sympathy in his nature for these poor negroes. I confess that at times I am for letting the territories manage it for themselves; and at other times I am for keeping it out of the territories by law. All the while I like Douglas' plan for the West. He has done wonderful work for the country. I wish I could make myself clearer, but I can't. I saw slavery in the South and know what it is. I am a good deal like Clay. He had slaves but disliked the institution. I have never had any slaves and I dislike it as much. Yet the question is what to do. If you keep it where it is you simply lay a siege about it. Great suffering will come in that way to the negroes of course. It is a kind of strangulation, selfish and small. On the other hand, if you give it breathing space what will become of the country? I know Douglas' argument that it cannot exist in the North. But suppose you have it all over the South, that's pretty big. Besides, what's to hinder new work being found for the slaves? Why can't they dig coal and gold like peons? Why can't they farm? Perhaps not; and yet I am not so sure of Douglas on that. He is the most convincing man in the world when you are with him. But when he goes away from you his spell slips off and you see the holes in his argument."

"You have been reading and thinking, haven't you, Reverdy?"

"Oh, yes, all the time. What I am afraid of is a war. I had a little dab of it in the Black Hawk trouble. But a war between these states would shake the earth. I have two boys, you know. Sarah worries about it. Everybody's beginning to live in a kind of terror."

"I have read about it too, ever since I have been in America. I have applied my philosophically exercised faculties to it. I have talked with Mr. Williams about it many times and with Douglas. I have had dozens of conversations on all these things. It seems to me that I could advance some new arguments myself."

"What new arguments could you advance?" asked Reverdy.

"Well," I said, "suppose I wanted to take a definite stand that slavery is wrong, which these Whigs won't. They only play with the question. They want to limit it perhaps. But why? Is it wrong? Or is it against northern interests? What? But suppose I took such a stand and needed a legal foundation. Couldn't I say that Congress could prohibit slavery in the territories under the power it has to regulate commerce between them? I put this question to Mr. Williams and he hadn't thought of it; but he told me that Judge Marshall held that commerce was traffic. Very well? Isn't slavery traffic? It's buying and selling. It impresses things that are bought and sold--cotton. And slaves are the subject of traffic. Therefore to regulate it--keep the slaves out of the territories where they might be bought and sold after getting into the territories, as well as where they might be sold into the territories--is the regulation of commerce, isn't it? Well now, isn't that better than calling the territories property and subject to the arbitrary rule of Congress as merely inert matter? If you can rule the territories arbitrarily as to slavery, why not as to anything else? Suppose we annex Cuba; under this doctrine we could rule Cuba arbitrarily, just as England ruled the Colonies here arbitrarily. Then take the assumption that Congress has the power to keep slavery out of the territories; just the power, not the express duty; well, it follows that Congress has the power to let it in the territories.

If it can put it in or out of the territories it can leave the territories to put it in or out. And why isn't that best? Right here is the point of my adherence to Douglas. For I see a growing central power in this country not acting on its lawful authority, but upon its own will, dictated by theories of morality or trade or monopoly. If this matter is left to the territories it is left to the source of sovereign power and to local interests; if it is controlled by Congress it means an increasing centralization. What I really mean is that this mere assumption that Congress can deal with the matter in virtue of some vague sovereignty, without pointing out some express power in Congress to do so, leads straight to imperialism. And thus on the whole, having a regard for the future of America and its liberty, I stand with Douglas. I have read Webster in his theories that the territories are property, and can therefore be dealt with under the clause which empowers Congress to make all needful laws and regulations for the territory and other property of the United States. Well, why doesn't he go farther and let Congress at one stroke emancipate the slaves? For a slave is certainly property, and if needful rules and regulations as to the negro require his emancipation, why can't he be emancipated under this clause? But if territory is property, so is a slave. And if territory is property, who owns the property? Why, all the states of course. And if they own the land and own the slaves too, why can't they take into their own land, unless they are forbidden to do so by a majority of the states, representatives legislating under some clause of the Constitution which gives them the right to do so?"

"Oh, yes," said Reverdy, "I have heard most of this before. But I'll tell you: the first man of account who rises up to say that slavery is wrong will be remembered, even if he is not honored. I am not talking about all these agitators and fellows; nor even of Seward or of Hale--they're too sharp and smart. I mean some man who puts the right feeling into the thing like Mrs. Stowe did in her book. You see, I was raised in Tennessee, and I don't care how you apologize for it, or make it look like labor of other kinds, or prove that all labor is slavery, just the same this negro slavery is vile. You can find good reasons for anything you want to do. I don't know where we get our right and wrong--it comes up from something deep in us. But when we get it, all this argument that Douglas is so skillful in simply melts away. I really wonder that so many women in the South favor slavery and that my mother was so wedded to it, and Dorothy now."

We were passing now the house I had built. "Who lives there now?" I asked. Reverdy gave me the name. It was not the man to whom I had sold the farm. I thought of Fortescue. "Where is Fortescue?" "Oh, he lit out from here," said Reverdy. "Do you know," I said, "I have thought it possible that Zoe might not be dead." "How could that be?" "I don't know. I feel that I went through that transaction dazed and without verifying things, as I should have done." "Oh, no, if Zoe were living you would know of it long before now."

After our drive we came back to Sarah and the meal that she had prepared for us. Women reflect the politics of the hour in nerves and anxiety, in anticipated sorrows. Sarah wished all agitations to stop. She longed for peace. She was in dread of war. Perhaps Dorothy's health had been affected by the growing turbulence of the country.

Young Amos and Jonas came in and ate with us. We turned to the talk of railroads and the growth of Chicago. Sarah took a hand now and said: "These things are all right. You won't get any war out of railroads and telegraphs. You men can reason and argue as much as you please about this slavery matter; but I have two sons, and I didn't bring them into the world to be killed in a war; and I won't have it if I can help it--not for all the niggers in the world."

CHAPTER XLVIII

If I were recording the life of an artist I should be dealing with different causes acting upon his development, or with different effects produced by the same times in which Douglas lived. Instead I am trying to set forth the soul of a great man who extracted from his environment other things than beauty; or rather the beauty of national progress. The question was, after all, whether Douglas was helping to give America a soul. What was he accomplishing for the real greatness of his country by giving it territory and railroads? What kind of a soul was he giving it? Who in this time was giving America a soul? Abigail had often hinted at these questions. And I had to confess that they occupied my thoughts.

I run over now with as much brevity as possible the events which led to the crisis of Douglas' life. With the Compromises of 1850 the Whig party began its rapid decline. The South did not like the Whig tariff. The Whig attitude on the slavery question was too ambiguous to appeal to the North. With its dissolution other organizations began to feed on its remains. The Know-nothings arose and disappeared, without accomplishing anything. Greeley said of them that they were "as devoid of the elements of persistence as an anti-cholera or anti-potatobug party would be."

In early 1854 the Whigs, Free Soilers and Anti-Slavery Democrats met at Ripon, Wisconsin, and proposed to form a new party, to be called the Republican party. They took part of the name which Jefferson had coined, dropping the word "national" out. Douglas, enraged by this blasphemy against Jefferson, suggested that the word "black" be put in where "national" had been left out, making the name Black Republican party.

A year later Douglas put through his bill for the organization of Kansas and Nebraska, which provided that they could come into the Union with or without slavery as they chose. He had long before voted against slavery prohibition in Texas;

for the extension of the Missouri Compromise to the Pacific; for the Compromises of 1850, which made California free and left Utah and New Mexico to come in free or slave, according to their own wish. I had to confess that he had no clear constitutional theory himself. He was only growing more emphatic in favor of popular sovereignty as a name for territorial independence on the subject. He compared this popular sovereignty to the rights which the Colonies asserted against England to manage their own affairs, and for the violation of which the Revolution ensued. The principle had appeared in most of the bills that he had sponsored or supported. Now it was the real doctrine. He was like an inventor who, after making many experiments, hits upon a working device. He was like a philosopher, who conceives the theory, then clears it, shears away its accidents or even abandons it. He had long been distrusted in the South. The Kansas-Nebraska bill still further alienated the South. The South wanted slavery carried into the territories by the Constitution, even against the will of the people of the territories. What had Douglas to gain with popular sovereignty? He really overestimated its appeal. He knew that the South did not like it, but he believed that it was sound, and that it would win the majority of the people. He advanced it not only as a solution of a vexed condition, but in the name of Liberty.

He misconceived the case, and here his tragedy began to flourish. I was sorry to witness his discomfiture and his first forensic defeat. Clergymen denounced him; and thinking no doubt that they were the spokesmen of the back-hall radicalism and ignorant morality which he despised, he fought them back bitterly: "You who desecrate the pulpit to the miserable influence of party politics! Is slavery the only wrong in the country? If so, why not recognize the great principles of self-government and state equality as curatives?"

He was burned in effigy and branded a traitor, a Judas, a Benedict Arnold. The whole mob power was used against him. But he was Hercules furious. He was against the wall, but unrepentant. He came to Chicago and announced that he would speak in front of the North Market Hall. It was September, and still lovely summer weather. I could not induce Dorothy to go, so Mr. Williams, Abigail, Aldington, and I went to hear Douglas defend himself. All the afternoon before this evening bells were tolled, flags were hung at half-mast. I got to Douglas, telling him that I feared violence to his person. He waved me off. His brow was heavy with scowls, his eyes deep with emotion. He was like a man ready to fight and die. Finally the hour arrived, and he mounted the platform intrepidly, amid hisses and howls. He paused to let the tumult die. He began again. He was hooted. He stepped forward undaunted, and let forth the full power of his voice:

"I come to tell you that an alliance has been made of abolitionism, Maine liquor-lawism, and what there was left of northern Whiggism, and then the Protestant feeling against the Catholic, and the native feeling against the foreigner. All these elements were melted down in one crucible, and the result is Black Republicanism."

A voice called out: "You're drunk!" Bedlam broke loose. In a silence Douglas retorted: "Let a sober man say that." There were cheers. He went on:

"How do you dare to yell for negro freedom and then deny me the freedom of speech? I claim to be a man of practical judgment. I do not seek the unattainable. I am not for Utopias."

"Topers!" said a voice, and there were yells.

"Nor for topers," resumed Douglas.

"I want results. What have you done with prohibition of slavery in the North by Federal law? You who want negro equality, why don't you repeal the laws of Illinois that forbid the intermarriage of white and blacks, that forbid a negro from testifying against a white man, that allow indentures of apprenticeship, and that require registration of negroes brought into the state, the same as you license a dog? The Federal government does not prevent you. The Ordinance of 1787 gave you the start that you want for Kansas and Nebraska. Yet you have these things; and you don't have slavery. Why? Not because the Federal government says you can't have it, but because you yourself do not want it. I say that this northern country is dedicated by God to freedom, law or no law; if it hadn't been, General Harrison, who introduced slavery into Indiana against the Ordinance of 1787 would have introduced something that would be there now. So much for you Whigs who voted for Harrison in 1840."

A voice:

"How about Kansas and Nebraska?" There were more yells. "I am telling you, if you will hear me. You old Whigs who followed Henry Clay to the end, why do you denounce me when the Kansas-Nebraska bill is the same in principle as Clay's

Compromises of 1850 …"

"How about California?"

"It was a compromise. And as I have said before if the people of California had wanted a slave state they would have had it, any law to the …"

Voices crying: "Benedict Arnold! Judas!" Douglas' voice rose to its fullest power. He was fulminating Black Republicans, Know-nothings, Anti-Catholics, humbug Whigs. I felt sure that he would be attacked. For two hours he fought with this wild and wicked audience. He appealed to their sense of fairness. If he was wrong, what harm to hear him through, the better to see the wrong? If he was right, why condemn him unheard? I could only make out a few sentences from time to time. He grew weary at last. He drew out his watch. The audience quieted to hear what he would say. "It is now Sunday morning. I will go to church and you may go to hell."

He stepped from the platform, walked boldly through the angry mob, ready to assault him. Without a tremor, fearlessly he edged his way along to his carriage, got into it, and was driven away, the mob hooting, bolder rowdies running after him, and covering him with vile epithets.

We walked away slowly without speaking to each other. We were too shamed, too sympathetic with Douglas to tolerate this exhibition of lawlessness. We were disgraced by an American audience which had tried to disgrace an American Senator, who asked for nothing except for the privilege of being heard.

When we arrived at Clark and Randolph streets Aldington and Abigail paused for a moment before turning in a direction different from mine. They said good night and went on. I walked with Mr. Williams until I arrived at my house. Then I went in, to lie awake and to think of the spectacle of the evening.

CHAPTER XLIX

The next day I went out to look at the ten acres which Douglas had given for the founding of the University of Chicago. I walked over the ground, came to the lake. I was thinking that if Douglas' life were ending in failure how futile was my own life! I was rich to be sure, but what had I done? I had inherited money. Douglas had started in poverty and accumulated a fortune. I had done nothing but increase my wealth. Douglas' activities had covered many fields, and now if he was to fall! What was American liberty? How could their devotion to a liberty, bring liberty to him? Douglas' wife was dead; Dorothy was an invalid.

In a few days I went around to see Abigail. That terrible evening remained a subject that must sometime be discussed between us.

Abigail was never more gracious than on this occasion, and seemed to understand that I needed to be lifted out of my reflections. She knew what Dorothy's invalidism meant to me, and she was sympathetic with my devotion to Douglas, in so far as it was an expression of human friendship. She had a point of view about everything, which had been developed and clarified by reading and travel. It came over me that I had been nowhere in Europe, that I had been wandering up and down America. My life in England was by now almost obliterated from my consciousness. We were not long in the talk before she said that a man should have more than one interest, that music or some form of art, or a hobby in literature should be taken up as a relaxation from business. What were politics but the interpretation of business? She showed me some pictures she had been painting. A teacher had opened a studio in Lake Street. Why did I not try my hand? I would find it a diversion from other things. I had always loved etchings. I wished I could do that. Well, this artist taught etching too. She inspired me at once to see him. His name was Stoddard, and she gave me the number. I conceived an enthusiasm for this new activity, thinking that it would take me out of myself and away from the America that was closing around me with such depressing effect.

Then Abigail and Aldington in supplement of each other began to recall the names of men then living whom they characterized as light-bearers. "Really," said Abigail, "there are only a few men of real importance in America to-day. These politicians and orators--Seward, Sumner, even the late Webster--amount to very little after all. They are even less than Lowell, whom Margaret Fuller recently characterized as shallow and doomed to oblivion. Longfellow is an adapter, a translator, a simple-hearted man. Whittier--well, all of them have fallen more or less under the moralistic influence of the country."

"That is what I like about Douglas," I said. "He is not a humbug. I like his ironical voice against all these silly movements, like liquor laws; these ideas like God in the little affairs of men; all this barbarism which breaks into religious manias; all these half-baked reformations. They carry me with him into an opposition to negro equality--all this stuff of Horace Greeley, Emerson, and in which men like Seward and Sumner, and American writers and poets, big and little, share."

"Oh, yes," said Abigail, "but after all you can say Douglas is just a politician. You do not need to grieve about him. He is tough enough to stand anything. He was put down by that mob. But I dare say he was not as much disturbed about it as you were. If he should die to-day what would the world lose? He has no great unfinished books, no half-painted pictures, no musical scores without the final touches. Look over the world, my friend. Do you realize who is living in it to-day? In Russia, Tolstoi and Turgenieff; in Germany, Schopenhauer, Freytag, Liszt, Wagner--Wagner is just Douglas' age too. In France, Hugo, George Sand, Renan, Berlioz, Bizet. In England, Tennyson, Macaulay. These are only a few. What has Douglas written or said that will live? What has he done that will carry an influence to a future day? I want to see you lift yourself out of this. Frankly, you seem to me like a man who has never come to himself. You have lived here in Illinois since you were a boy. You found work to do, and you did it. You wanted to be rich, you have had your wish. But the material you have handled has become you. It has entered the pores of your being, and become assimilated with its flesh. You have gone on oblivious of this greater world. There is another thing, and I have never known this to fail: you were a soldier in the Mexican War, and the causes for which it was fought have burned themselves into your nature. You are like a piece of clay molded and lettered and shoved into the hot oven of war. You came forth with Young America, Expansion burned into you. Douglas, being your close friend, and being for these things, gave interpretations to these words. Your glaze took the reflection of his face; and these words became other words of like import, or imaginatively enlarged by the lights which his winning art cast upon them. Give Douglas wit, humor, and he would carry the whole country. For it runs after greatness of territory, railroads, the equality of man, the superiority of the white race. As dull as the mob is it knows that Douglas does not stand for its morality and its God. If he had wit he could make them laugh and forget the distance that divides him from them. We all understand why he has enemies; why the revolutionaries from Germany, Hungary, Austria, divide in doubt over him. But what has he to carry against them that will be a loss to the world, if he fails?" I felt a little apologetic for my devotion to Douglas as Abigail talked. Had I made a god of a poor piece of clay? No, it was not true. I knew him, I believed in him. He was the clearest voice in all this rising absurdity of American life. But Abigail had given me one idea that I wished to act upon.

I went the next day to see Stoddard and started to learn etching. If I could only transfer to the copper plate what I had seen of sand hills, pines, pools of water, the gulls over the lake, the picturesque shacks of early Chicago of 1833 and 1840; the old wooden drawbridge, which was over the river in 1834, with the ships beyond it toward the lake and the lighthouse, and in the forefront canoes on the shore, covered with rushes and sand grass. After a few days I saw Douglas. He came on an evening when I was just about to go to him. I had been thinking of him day by day, but waiting for the effect of his rough experience in front of the North Market to wear away from his thoughts and mine. He was now himself again, his eye keen, his voice melodious, his figure pervaded by animation. I noticed perhaps for the first time how small and graceful were his hands. The greatness and shapeliness of his head could not be overlooked. From beneath shaggy and questioning brows his penetrating eyes looked straight through me. Had his pride been wounded, his spirits dampened? Not at all. He was willing to face any audience anywhere. He had told the South unpleasant truths. He had satirized the groups that went to the making of the Republican party. "I have a creed," he said, "as broad as the continent. I can preach it boldly, and without apology North or South, East or West. I can face Toombs or Davis, if they preach sectional strife, or advocate disunion. I can continue to point out the narrow faith of Sumner and Seward. I shall not abate my contempt for the ragged insurrectionists who are going about the country for lack of better business, scattering dissension. Am I to be President? There is trouble now in Kansas and Nebraska. Can I help that? I have stood for the right of the people there to have slavery or not as they chose. But if any trick is played on either of them, whether in favor of slavery or against it, they will find me on the spot ready to fight for an honest deal."

Seeing Douglas in all his strength and self-confidence again I was happy. We talked of the old days and drank from the old bottle. I took him to the door, followed his retreating figure down the street, so short but so massive. Then I went to Dorothy, to find her sleepless and unhappy.

CHAPTER L

No way to mark time quicker than by Presidentials. Four years pass in the space of two or less; for no sooner is a President installed than committees meet for reformations and plans. Six months between the election and the installation of a President! When he has served a year the election is nearly two years passed. Thus, as it seemed, the election of 1856 was upon the country before we had time to appreciate what Mr. Pierce had done. Had he had a fair chance in such a brief period to do anything? I was at work attending to my business, trying to etch too, but I could not keep my mind off the game of politics. Among the tens of thousands of men in Illinois who were devoted to Douglas no one was more loyal to his ambition than I, and perhaps no one was less conspicuous. I followed the *New York Tribune*, the *Springfield Republican*, the *North American Review*, the *Independent, Harper's Weekly*, and the southern press, as well as the papers of Illinois. I had made a large book of clippings, which expressed the journalistic thought of the country. All these things put together kept me fully occupied. Our son Reverdy was coming to an age when his schooling would need attention. I wished to send him to England. But that was difficult to do, because, while Dorothy was urging a trip abroad she wished to go to Italy, on account of the climate.

In truth Dorothy was growing more distressed every day over American affairs. She found harshness in Chicago. She did not find sympathy with the ideas with which she had grown up. Her failure to make close friends interfered with her social delights. Mrs. Douglas had perhaps been her greatest intimate. With her death she had seemed to lose interest in other cordial associations. Her nervous organization was badly devitalized. I, too, hoped to see the continent, and particularly Italy. But I did not wish to leave until the campaign was over, owing to my interest in Douglas. I wanted to watch affairs now, but also I wished to help Douglas, if I could.

For the first time the Republicans entered the field. They adopted a platform which incorporated the Declaration of Independence. It was against popular sovereignty, lest the people vote in slavery, or be tricked into doing so. It stood for Congressional control of slavery extension, and implicit in this was the constitutional power of Congress to do so. It had, with the Declaration of Independence, with the invocation of God, and appeals to the Bible, gathered a working force in the country. The press, the platform, had been busy to this end. Seward with his higher law was a contributor. Chase, who was termed by Douglas a debater, where Seward and Sumner were only essayists, was one of the big figures in the new movement. Beecher and Greeley were spokesmen of the new organization. The convention nominated Fremont who had explored Oregon in 1842.

He was of the spirit of Douglas. He was an expansionist. He had gone into California in 1845, and raised the American flag on a mountain overlooking Monterey. He had helped later to conquer California. He had for various audacious and disobedient acts been tried and court-martialed, and dismissed from military service. President Polk had approved the verdict, but remitted the penalty. Then he had resigned. Now he was the object of the highest honor of an American convention. He was made the spokesman for a platform which denounced the invasion of Kansas by an armed force in the interests of slavery. He had gone into California for the slavocracy which engineered the Mexican War, as New England contended. Now he was at the head of the party waging war upon that slavocracy. A strange people, these Americans!

Douglas had said that he did not want the office of President. Perhaps that was an exhibition of political coyness, for he was in the lists just the same! He had 33 votes on the first ballot, of which only 14 came from the South. President Pierce, who was running again, met a wavering fortune. On the sixteenth ballot he had not a vote. Douglas had 121 votes; a certain Mr. Buchanan had 168. On the seventeenth ballot this Mr. Buchanan was nominated. Who was this Mr. Buchanan?

He had been Secretary of State under Polk, had helped to secure the Texan territory. So much for the appeal to Young America. He had been minister to Great Britain. Therefore he was abroad when Douglas was gummed with the poisonous sweet of Kansas and Nebraska. He thought slavery was wrong; therefore, you Abolitionists, here's the man for you. He held that territorial extension of slavery need not be feared; let the people rule. As a Congressman he had voted to exclude abolition literature from the mails; come forward Calhoun-ites and vote for Buchanan. They did. Fremont did not get a vote in North Carolina, South Carolina, Georgia, Alabama, Florida, Mississippi, Texas, Arkansas, Missouri, Tennessee; and only 281 in Maryland, 291 in Virginia, and 364 in Kentucky. But Millard Fillmore, running on a platform of America for Americans, almost divided the vote with Buchanan in those states. He carried Maryland against Buchanan; but of the whole popular vote he was nearly a million behind Buchanan. Fremont had 1,341,264 votes and Buchanan had 1,838,169 votes. The electoral college gave Buchanan 174 votes, Fremont 114, and Fillmore 8. Why could Douglas not have been nominated?

We got the news by telegraph in Chicago. As I studied the bulletins, I was wondering whether the result was symptomatic of transient causes or whether it betokened great changes. Had the Declaration of Independence been approved at the polls? How was Douglas taking it? I did not see him. I wrote to him, but he did not reply. Did he get my letter, or was he consoling himself in convivial ways?

I now prepared to go abroad. I was leaving a country that had changed in almost every way since I had come to it. I was leaving a city that was nothing but a hamlet when I first saw it. I had seen New Orleans and Chicago connected by rail, and the state grow from a few hundred thousand to a million population. I had seen Arkansas, Florida, Michigan, Iowa, Texas, Wisconsin, California, added to the Union. Coal and iron had become barons and were doing the bidding of steam, which was king. The oil that had floated on the surface of the salt wells of Kentucky was soon to be more powerful than cotton. Everything had changed--but man. Was he rising to a purer height, had a glory begun to dawn on America? Should slavery, polygamy, rum, be driven from the land? Then should we be free and happy, and just and noble? France had got schools and the ballot by the Revolution, but now she had a throne again. We had the ballot but did we have freedom? No law could have made a mob hiss Douglas at the North Market. Freedom in their hearts would have given him an audience.

Was I free? Was I happy? I was not free. I was not happy. My life seemed cribbed. Dorothy was an invalid. I went to her from watching the election bulletins. I sat on the side of the bed, took her in my arms. "Let us go to Italy," she said. "I am dying here." She pressed her frail hands around my neck. "Oh let us go--let us go."

CHAPTER LI

We sailed on the *Persia*, 376 feet long, 45 feet of beam, gross tonnage 3300, horsepower 4000, speed 14 knots an hour. As Dorothy knew nothing of ocean sailing craft she was unable to share in my wonder at all the splendor and comfort of this wonderful steamer.

From the first Dorothy was ill. Our boy Reverdy too became seasick. As I was not affected in the least I had the care of both of them. A part of the time the sea was very rough.

One night when we had been on the water three days Dorothy called to me. She had been greatly nauseated during the afternoon. A sudden return of the discomfort had seized her. I arose quickly and made a light. The boat was rocking. A stiff breeze was blowing. We were headed through a great darkness. Dorothy was deathly pale. She was unable to bring up anything more and was convulsed with retching and coughing.

She grew suddenly quiet, her eyes closing, her lips parting. "Dear," she murmured. I waited for what she would say. She had become at once limp in my arms. I shook her gently, pressed my ear to her breast. I could hear no heart beat. I called her, laid her down, wetted a towel, and applied it to her head. She did not rouse. I went from the stateroom to find the physician. He came hurriedly. But Dorothy was dead. That word of endearment was her last.

Without, the sea and the sky were as black as a sunless cave. The water rolled around us, pitching the boat forward and sideways. The timbers creaked, lamps jiggled, the hallways seemed to undulate like snakes. But the heart of the *Persia* pumped with rhythmic regularity. The passengers were asleep, or in various festivities, in cabins or in the dining room. Nothing was stayed for this tragedy which had come to me. On we went through the darkness! Dorothy was lying where I had placed her, her head turned to one side, her face pale in the last sleep. I aroused little Reverdy. He looked at his mother, kneeled by the berth, and sobbed. The physician took us out of the cabin, locked the door, and put us in another. I tucked little Reverdy in bed again; then I went out to look, at the storm, the dark water, the impenetrable sky.

Back of me was America, flattened out like a map in my imagination, lost and sunk like old Atlantis. I sent my mind across it from New York to Chicago, from Chicago to California. What was it? Earth, a continent containing an embattled and disappointed Douglas, millions of struggling people. Ahead of me, over thousands of miles of water, an unknown Italy. I lived over all my life, but mostly now all my life with Dorothy, from those first days in Jacksonville when I was under a cloud because of Zoe and the killing of Lamborn, to our days in Nashville; the ecstasy of first love, our walks and restings among the Cumberland hills, the kindness of Mother Clayton, her joy when she learned that Dorothy had consented to become my wife. I saw again the face of Jackson, his eyes, his reverence when he kissed the brow of Dorothy; his tears and his feeble step when he walked away from us. And I lived over early Chicago, all my days with Douglas. Where was he now on that flattened, negligible map called America? In what soil had Zoe moldered into the earth? What had become of Fortescue? Where were Abigail and Aldington, Reverdy, Sarah, this night? How could the millions storming over slavery and war, territories, sugar and cotton and iron, gold and railways think of these things if they were face to face with a reality as stark as I was, in a boat rolled by dark water, tossing forward toward Europe and with a burden like the dead body of Dorothy? All this night I walked the deck. I saw the dawn come up, ragged and blue, patched with dark clouds, which the wind drove close to the mounting waves.

The captain ordered an autopsy. Dorothy had died of heart failure. Then there was to be a burial at sea. In the afternoon the clouds lifted from the sky. Toward the west the sun burned over the water, making a wake of fire from the boat to the utmost horizon. I took a last look at Dorothy, kissed her cold brow. Then she was wrapped with sheets on a plank weighted with iron, and taken to the stern of the boat. I stood near to see it all, with little Reverdy weeping as if his heart would break.

The body is cast into the water, and in the very golden wake of the sun. I cannot hear the splash; I only see a slight flap of the sheet. The water closes over instantly. A gull frightened into a slight veering off turns to the spot where Dorothy has disappeared. No ripples to mark the place where she has been received by the sea! The boat has gone on without staying. I keep my eyes fixed on the place. Waves cross and recross over it. The sunlight shifts. Tears and the sun blind my eyes. I rest them a moment and then look again. Where was it that Dorothy sank? What great fish started at the splash, the white apparition; and then returned to nibble? To what depths has Dorothy sunk? To what darker waters has she been towed by some creature of prey? The sailors have gone to their other duties. Little Reverdy is by my side, weeping softly. I must write to the older Reverdy back in Jacksonville. He is her only relation in the world. To-night I must sleep, if I can.

But I do not sleep. I wonder if I have been a good husband to Dorothy. What was she doing, how living, in the years past, when I was absorbed in business, following the fortunes of Douglas, studying the books that had no bearing upon her happiness nor, alas, upon mine? I saw her now as patient, sometimes alone, perhaps always waiting for me, but never complaining. How many happy hours had I sacrificed to other things when I might have been with her! Was Dorothy happy? Did she love me? I began to think over the occasions of her demonstrations of affection--after all how few they were! Always tender toward me, but how infrequently were there moments of passion, of ecstasy. Had I awakened all of her nature? Had I been living a neutral life all these years? Was I in some sort a negligible character, without magnetism, of unfulfilled passion? A slumbering nature?

But where now was Dorothy's body? We were fifty miles, seventy-five miles, a hundred miles from the unmarked spot of burial. She had sunk fathoms into the abyss. The bell on the boat had rung the midnight, then one o'clock. I heard it toll for two--then I slept. I awoke hearing little Reverdy sobbing. I stood out of the berth and tried to comfort him. Then we dressed and went to breakfast. Whatever happens there must be coffee and toast. Then I walked the deck and longed for land.

We changed boats at Cherbourg. Then a dreary voyage to Naples. We hurried through the noise and colorful disorder of Naples and drove by carriage to Rome. We entered the same gate through which Milton and Goethe had passed, into the Piazza di Spagna. At the foot of the steps leading to Trinita di Monti--here where the foreigners stayed, the English quarter. I found accommodations in a pension. First there was the unpacking, and little Reverdy had to be kept comforted, if possible; I must start him in school too. Life must always go on. I became sensible of many bells. The strange noises of a civilization wholly unknown to me came up through my window. I looked out upon the Piazza di Spagna, knowing nothing of its history. Who would be my friends here? Back of me was nearly a quarter of a century in America and before me what?

CHAPTER LII

Our pension was all that could be desired. Mr. and Mrs. Winchell were here from America, from Connecticut. She was about twenty-seven; he was nearly sixty. They were on their way around the world, stopping in Rome for some months. She was studying painting under an artist who also taught etching. In this way I came under the instruction of Luca, who had a studio not far from the Piazza di Spagna, and also into daily association with Mrs. Winchell.

First little Reverdy had to be placed in school and given a tutor. Before doing this I took him around the city, and we saw together some of the churches: S. Maria del Popolo, S. Giovanna dei Laterano, S. Angelo, S. Paolo. I took him to the Pantheon, the Coliseum, to St. Peter's, into the Vatican. Thus I gained my first impressions; and on these rounds I found the courier Serafino Maletesta, who became a source of so much interest and delight to me.

My mornings were spent in Luca's studio; my afternoons in sightseeing with Serafino, in which Mr. and Mrs. Winchell joined, though infrequently by him. He was ageing and not well. And often from the beginning Mrs. Winchell and I set off together with Serafino to explore museums, visit the Palatine, drive to the edge of the city where the Alban hills were plainer across the Campagna, as level as a prairie around Jacksonville.

I was struggling with Italian, carrying on such conversation as I could with Serafino, and with Mrs. Winchell, who was growing proficient in the language.

Serafino was something past sixty. He had been with the Carbonari of 1820, and in the Italian revolution of 1830-31. He saw this suppressed. Then when the republican movements of 1848 shook Europe, he had participated in the third Italian revolution of that year; and again he had seen Italy put down, this time by the intervention of the French, whose Louis Napoleon sought by this action to win the friendship of the Catholic clergy in France. The hated Austrians now ruled Lombardy and Venice. In Rome, now that the Pope again had temporal, power, the political affairs of the city were in the hands of Cardinal Antonelli, who suppressed political agitation with great severity. It was not only an American audience before North Market Hall in Clark Street, Chicago, that denied the freedom of speech. Cardinals were up to the same thing, as well as mobs.

Serafino told me calmly, with occasional profanity, of the arrest of large numbers of Italians who belonged to the Unita Italiana at Naples, whose condemnation was speedily followed by hideous dungeons and atrocious cruelties. There was slavery in Italy too!

Italy was under the heel of Austria. Religious bigotry, more subtle and more powerful than the slavocracy of America, was crushing hope from the lives of the Italians, while Mazzini and Cavour battled like Titans against the powerful hierarchy of monarchy and Catholicism. There was little of the history of Italy, of ancient Rome, that was seemingly unknown to Serafino. He had read all his life; and he had been in the actual conflicts of awakening Italy. Now his head shook a little when his face reddened from suppressed wrath. He cursed quietly, but with a terrible energy. He was poor; but there was a refinement in his personal appearance. His worn shoes were always polished, his coat and trousers of many years service were always brushed. He would appear at the appointed hour, bright of eye, cleanly shaven, and always with wonderful suggestions for sightseeing for the afternoon. He lived somewhere near the Forum. Having never married he was continuing a friendship formed long ago with a woman who kept house for him and lived with him. As he was no longer fitted for a battle or strife he was now an adviser to younger men. He was no doubt suspected but he seemed to have no fear. As we went about among priests and soldiers he smiled and spoke to them.

He knew them of old and a certain security seemed to be his. His two interests were politics and art, but art had won him almost completely. What he knew of history and of art, his life-long residence in Rome made him the most interesting of couriers.

Our conversations widened and deepened day by day. Had he heard of Douglas? No. He had read ***Uncle Tom's Cabin***. What did I know of Mrs. Stowe? I ran over the list of our notables. They meant nothing to him. State sovereignty, popular sovereignty, the Missouri Compromise, the Compromises of 1850, the Kansas-Nebraska act were words without significance. But there was negro slavery. "How can that be in your country?" he asked, and laughed ironically. "If all men are created free and equal how about the negro?" he asked.

I went on to tell Serafino, that Thomas Jefferson, when drafting the Declaration of Independence, had condemned George III who had forbidden the American Colonies "to prohibit or restrain this execrable commerce"; but that the clause was stricken out by South Carolina and Georgia. Therefore that the Declaration did not mean negroes when it said "all men." Serafino looked at me with quiet, comprehending eyes which said: "It's the same struggle of money and power everywhere." He added aloud: "Italy will never eat free bread and have enough of it until the Austrian is driven off our back. They make us work and take away our labor in taxes. We are negroes too."

He wanted to know something of Garrison, of whom he had heard. What was thought of Washington in America? But in the midst of these subjects he would stop to point to a broken column, a ruined temple; or he would turn suddenly into an old church to show me some beloved picture. After all, the old life of street brawls, debates, and dungeons had faded out of him with the dying of the rebellious fires of youth. There were only echoes of these thunderous events in his soul. His eye only brightened fully before a picture or a statue. His reverence arose only to some perfection of color or of form.

Once he took me by a quick turn, as if by impulse, into an old church. "There is a lovely Madonna here," he said. "Who painted it?" "Some pupil of Raphael's perhaps." Serafino removed his hat and stood reverently before this beautiful face, so human, so tender. "I have heard you say so much against the Church, the Papacy--I thought you were not in the Church," I said. "No, I am an atheist," replied Serafino. "But what has that to do with this? Look at those eyes, those lips. In '48, when my soul was torn, I used to come in here every day just for the consolation of that face. And now I come for the memory and the peace it brings me." Slow tears were on the lower lids of his eyes. With a rough hand he brushed them away, then asked me: "What do you think?" "I love that face," I replied. "I understand how you feel."

A friendship grew up between Serafino and me. He was not a perfunctory guide. He never grew tired. When five o'clock would come and the day was really ended I would say: "Well I must be back now. Little Reverdy is coming over for an early dinner." "Ah, but just this one picture," he would say, "it will only take a few minutes. I want you to see this. It is a great work and something may happen. I may forget to bring you again." Then we would walk in and out of the cold and gloom of the church after having stared the picture into vividness.

During my morning work my friendship with Mrs. Winchell ripened rapidly. We had an excellent start in the circumstance that we were Americans. We knew of cities, of some people in common. Abigail had come from Connecticut and that, in a sense, laid a foundation for our conversations. We were working together, she with painting, I with drawing and etching. We criticized and suggested concerning each other's work. Or we put down our brushes and pencils and talked of life. In this way at last she knew of my going to America as a youth of eighteen, of the farm, of Zoe, of my marriage, my life in Chicago, my long friendship with Douglas, and lastly of Dorothy's death at sea. Her eyes would look intently into mine. And when I told her that I considered my life practically wasted she said: "Do you know every one's life is wasted; nearly every one. Few find their work and pursue it. Most of us are drawn aside, or tripped, or blinded. Your friend Douglas seems to me to have had a wasted life. As you tell me all this I see you as a man of tremendous will drawn into an accidental path, not his real path. You are an artist at heart. I don't mean that you will ever be a great etcher, though one cannot tell; I mean that all this turbulence, sordidness, American hurry, waste, vulgarity, agitation, politics, did not belong to you. But what right have I to talk? My life is a waste too."

Little by little I learned from her what her life had been, what its central impulse was. She was a poor girl who hungered for opportunity. She had looked with critical eyes upon marriageable men. I wondered if she had been attractive to many men, if many had had the discernment to see what she was. If a young woman marries an elderly man of wealth it is probable that no young man of wealth has come to her at the favorable hour; and probable, too, that no man of merely compelling magnetism has been interested in her. Mr. Winchell was kindly, a noble nature; he gave her a tender, but only a paternal love. But through him she had traveled; she had had the beauty of life for which her heart was insatiable. There were no children; there never would be children, and what lavish, ecstatic affection she bestowed upon my Reverdy! So day by day I learned that she was a teacher in Connecticut when Mr. Winchell came along, willing to give her everything if she would marry him. He had been rather a heavy drinker up to this time, now five years before; when he left off drink for awhile. Then he had begun again, but rarely indulged to excess. It may be that drink had emasculated him before he married her; but now if because of this he tippled occasionally, he was justified in medicine which dulled feelings that he could not be a husband to this radiant woman, who treated him always with such tenderness and devotion, always honored him with such scrupulous attention.

She wanted a child above all things. All of us remember some woman whom we knew in youth who kept canaries, or raised flowers or had some queer little fad. We learn to know why women do this. In her case she expressed her mother's passion in studies, in art, in travel, in friendship, in kindness to every one; above all in devotion to her husband. She mothered him in the most tender and beautiful way. In a little while I knew all her story, as she did mine.

Serafino came for me one morning at the studio. There was an old cafe beyond the walls near the Campagna where the food was wholly Italian and of the best. It was a wonderful place for the rest of the noonday meal, for a view of the Alban hills. The sun was warm, the sky was clear. The intoxication of an Italian day was in the air. I wished so much to share the delight with someone. Mrs. Winchell was sitting near absorbed in her work. But she had looked up and bowed to Serafino, whom she had seen with me so frequently. I turned to her and asked: "Would you and Mr. Winchell like to join me?" "Let us go and ask him," she replied. So we set off to the pension to invite Uncle Tom. That was the name she called him, and I had begun to use it myself.

Uncle Tom had made the acquaintance of some men of his own age from New York. They had begun to patronize a cafe located beyond the American Embassy, where broiled chicken and fresh vegetables were a specialty and where the red wine was of the best. He had an engagement with these cronies and was preparing to leave as we came in. He listened to Isabel's exclamations about the place to which Serafino wished to take us. If she had been his daughter and I had been his son he could not have sent us off together with a heartier laugh, a more undisturbed heart. "You two go," he said. "You get along about pictures and scenery. I am going to Canape's, and play checkers this afternoon. I am too fat to run around like you young folks do. Go on and have a good time."

And we ran down, following Serafino who had preceded us to engage a carriage. Off we drove, the wheels rattling over the stones, past the Forum, past the Coliseum, in view of St. Peter's. Soon we entered a dusty road. The houses were small now, broken and old. At last we drew up into an open space surrounded by little buildings: a blacksmith's shop where the anvil was ringing, little bakeries, markets where vegetables and bologna were vended. Ragged Italian children, gay and soiled with healthy dirt, were playing in the dust, turning somersaults, chasing each other, laughing. Beyond us was the Campagna, the Alban hills. We climbed a rickety stairway to a platform or roof of stone. An eager and obliging waiter brought us a table, spread it, put before us red wine. And Serafino, seeing these things done, disappeared, leaving Isabel and me to dine together under this clear sky with the green of the lovely plain spread out before us to the purples of the hills.

How could I help but make comparisons between Isabel and Dorothy? I had never known any women but Dorothy and Abigail, Sarah, Mother Clayton. I had never come into romantic contact with any woman but Dorothy. Now I was advancing to this relationship with Isabel. I began to wonder if I had given Dorothy love. I had given her perfect loyalty. Was there a form of treason to Dorothy's memory in the fast beating of my heart here in the presence of Isabel, under this sky, in this charming place? Perhaps I had been starved too. Yet because of her personality, the radiant flame which was herself, the laughing and girlish genius which was in her, but above all the spiritual integrity which was hers, I stood in awe of her. But that awe was sufficiently explained by her devotion to her husband. I saw in her eyes honor and truth, and the peace of mind that sometimes comes with them, all the while that I felt the blood surge around my heart and pulsate in my hands. There seemed to be nothing now of which we could not speak. Her interest in children betrayed itself in exclamations over the ragged little Italians playing in the court. I wondered if my heart had ever been profoundly stirred. I had married Dorothy. But suppose Zoe had not been in my life to have offended and alienated Dorothy's interest for a time, and thus to have energized this English will which was mine for conquest of the farm, for the killing of Lamborn--for the continued pursuit of Dorothy? In such case had I married Dorothy? What would life have been to me if I had met Isabel when I first knew Dorothy? This woman of white flame talking of art, of travel, of Rome, of religion, of beauty; giving way to girlish chuckles and laughter. Was she not closer to me, as temperate genius of the North, than Dorothy, out of the languor and the romanticism of the South? Was not Douglas closer to the North, which Isabel seemed to me now to symbolize, than to that South with which his fate had now so long been entangled?

A step is heard. The old stair creaks, and Serafino's head appears above the railing. We look up, aroused from our enchantment. The afternoon lights are slanting across the Campagna. It is time to go. I have overpaid the waiter. He honestly offers to rectify it. Isabel laughs, seeing that I am oblivious of such worldly things. That breaks the spell. And we drive back to Rome and our pension.

CHAPTER LIII

I begin to wonder about my Reverdy. At the school I see him in association with English boys. He is not so strong as they, not so handsome, not so alert and apt. Isabel has never had a child and wants one with consuming passion. This boy is mine, but am I better off than Isabel? My life grows clearer to me. I have receded from it and can see it better. I can look out upon Rome and then close my eyes and recall Chicago. I think of my long years of money making; then I turn to reflection upon art and life. I thrill in the presence of Isabel; then I remember the mild but tender passion which Dorothy aroused in me.

I thrill before Isabel, but I give my feelings no expression. There are looks, no doubt, hesitations of speech, flutterings of the heart, that she may hear. But she is encompassed with flame that bars my way. I do not try to pass. We are all friends together, Isabel, Uncle Tom, and I. No plans are made which exclude Uncle Tom. Isabel and I have no secrets, no stealings away, no intimacies however slight, no quick withdrawals upon the sound of his step. Everything is known to Uncle Tom. I had impulses to all clearness of conduct in the circumstance that Uncle Tom is so much my friend. He treats me like a father; he is always doing generous things for me. He is delighted to see Isabel go with me to a church or a gallery, when he is too tired or too ill to accompany us, and that is often.

And day by day Isabel was happier. She became a creature of glories, shining transparencies. We had books together, music together, our work together. We had the companionship of the morning and the evening meal, sacred rituals between beings who love each other. We had infinite talks together with Uncle Tom or alone, as it happened. If Uncle Tom saw our exaltation, nevertheless he knew all that was between us. For it was beauty of life that Isabel and I shared, and who cannot know between whom this secret exists, if he have eyes to see?

He knew I loved Isabel, if he had not forgotten all that moves in the blood of a man of forty-two. He knew that she loved me--at any rate in some quality of love. For Isabel used this word freely in the ecstasies of her spirit, in the rapturous atmosphere of Italy. "I love James, Uncle Tom--not as I love you; but I really love him! How wonderful that he should come to us. He is like my brother, but he is something more. He is a great friend." Uncle Tom would smile benignantly upon this radiant woman, whom he had married for her youthful vitality, for which he gave the happiness that comes of wealth. Perhaps in his ageing psychology he did not know that there was passion in our hearts. Yet I think he was a great soul, wishing Isabel to have every happiness. I know he was my friend. There was nothing in him of the envy of January because of my younger years, nor reproof for the Maytime sunshine that was in the heart of Isabel.

Isabel and I had been to the Vatican several times. Uncle Tom disliked pictures; above all he dreaded the fatigue of walking and the cold of the churches and rooms where he was obliged to remove his hat. One afternoon Isabel proposed that we go again to the Vatican; there was a face there she wished to show me. We asked Uncle Tom to come with us; but this was one of the days when he did not feel strong enough for anything. He was keeping to his room. Perhaps later he would go to Canape's. "You two go along. You will get on without me."

Isabel took me directly to the suite which was decorated by Pinturicchio for Alexander VI. We looked at the Annunciation, the Nativity, the Magi, and the Resurrection. Somehow I was more moved by these paintings than by anything I had yet seen in Rome. The soul of this painter took possession of me. Then recalling what Isabel had said I asked her: "Where is the face, Isabel, you wished to show me?" "There," she said. "Turn around." I did and saw a bronze bust on a pedestal. "That, you mean?" Isabel nodded. I walked closer to it. It was Pinturicchio.

A deeper emotion than I had ever before felt before a work of art took possession of me. Such wisdom, benignity, genius! What a soul belonged to this man! I looked about to see if we were watched by guards. As we were alone I put up my hands to caress this face, moved by some unknown impulse. Touching the silken surface of the bronze my whole imaginative power seemed to awake; my life spread out before me. I know not what it was; memories of so many things; not least of all Isabel's presence understanding what I felt. My eyes blinded; my shoulders shook a little. Isabel came to me and gently put her hand on my arm. We walked away. "Who was Pinturicchio?" I asked of Isabel. And she told me. I took a guide-book out of my pocket and began to read. "There is a story," it said, "that Pinturicchio was starved by his wife during his last illness." I closed the book. After all had not Douglas been starved in the finer part of his genius by the life to which he was wedded? How would his face look in bronze, ridged with reason and controversy; what could ever bring him out of the dust and noise of the levels where he was battling, even to the plateaus to which poor Serafino had climbed?

After that I looked at everything of Pinturicchio's I could find in Rome. We found his Coronation of the Virgin, his frescoes of St. Antonio. But Isabel, who had already been to the Villa d'Este with Uncle Tom, began now day by day to plan another excursion there. She had not gone up to Tivoli, nor seen the cataracts; we could do all of this in an afternoon if we did not stop to wander through Hadrian's Villa. This time Serafino went with us; but Uncle Tom was again indisposed, and laughingly bade us to go on and leave him to an afternoon at Canape's with his cronies.

Serafino rode on the box with the driver, and that left Isabel and me to something like a privacy, as we drove by the quarries of travertine where the slaves of old Rome went blind and died hewing out the stone that went to the building of the Coliseum and the theaters of Marcellus and Pompey. We passed the little stream whose waters were blue with sulphur, filling the air with its odor. The grasses and herbs were green; here and there an almond tree was in blossom. The dark cypresses of Hadrian's Villa stood like spires of thunder clouds against the wonderful azures of this uplifting sky. Before us were the mountains, pine-clad, vineyard-clad; and far up the gleam of a cascade shone like a bent sword in the sun.

Serafino took us through the room of the d'Este Palace telling the driver to meet us at one of the entrances to the grounds. When we emerged and descended to the Hundred Fountains he turned away giving us the directions to reach the carriage. He knew that this was a place where lovers would wish to dispense with a guide.

We walked through the avenues of great cypress trees and came to the farther end of the pools whose curbs were decorated with flowering urns. There we looked at the palace and listened to the song of the merles. Beside this all was silence, only the stir of the wind against the soft strings of the trees--the most melodious harp in the world! We climbed to an eminence, stood by an iron fence and gazed down upon the fisheries surrounded by graceful bushes and trees. Then we found the Fontana dell' Ovato, and a seat before it. It was a semicircle of stone perforated by arches over which the water musically poured. Here we rested, listening to the merles, the falling water, the whispering of the wind. Ghosts of dead delight seemed to pass us; unseen presences of passionate gallants and capricious loveliness, hungering hearts wounded by life, by beauty, by desire, spoke to us through the murmuring water, the stir of the wind, the intense silence when all sounds were turned away by the veering of the delicious air.

And Uncle Tom was in Rome at Canape's drinking with his American cronies! Only myself knew my starved heart, but surely he knew the heart of Isabel. What was the attitude of mind in allowing this free association between Isabel and me? Does the heart of age become deadened? Does it understand; does it but partly divine these secrets; does it for any of these reasons cease to be sensitive?

Then suddenly, as Isabel and I sat there in these enchanting surroundings, an uncontrollable emotion seized me, one that had no regard for a future, that sought only to realize wholly and at once an ecstatic present. For what could be between us? I could not marry Isabel; and what could be? Blindly, without a thought of any of these things, I took Isabel's hands and drew her to me frightened and trembling. Instantly I saw what I had done. Our life of frank companionship fell away from us. A new birth was ours; but of what wonder and terror and danger! Isabel exclaimed: "Oh, my friend!" Then she lost her voice and whispered, "My friend!" She became relaxed, leaned back her head, closed her eyes. Tears crept down her cheeks. And I was silent, in a kind of madness of fear, passion, regret, nameless sorrow. What could I say, to what could she listen? There was a long silence. Then Isabel began to speak.

"Help me, my friend," she said. "How can I tell you how to be my friend? Still it must be. I care for you so deeply. Let me speak, but understand me as I try to speak, and help me. You are young and strong. You are so companionable; I never grow tired of you--but you must know that I am not different from you in all impulses, imaginings. But be my friend. Take into your being the beauty we have together; these flowers of friendship attend and keep for our garden--our Villa d'Este. Let it be open to the sky and wind as this is, a place where innocence and kindness may come, where children may play and the old rest. Ah, my friend, you have lived and now be strong for me. Uncle Tom is so fond of you. Think of all you have. You have had a wife, and you have a son. Be noble, be understanding, for really you see I am poor and you are rich. If possible these hands of passion which you have placed on mine must change, and my hands must forget what you have done. Otherwise what is the future to be?"

Isabel began to sob, between her words crying: "Oh, be my friend!" How could I comfort her? The very comfort that her heart craved was that which her sorrow strove to deny me the giving. I drew out my watch; we had long overstayed our time, for we were to lunch at the Sibylla in Tivoli. We walked slowly to the entrance where Serafino waited for us with the carriage. He was smoking a pipe, calm and happy, and in companionable conversation with the driver.

At a table near the Temple of Vesta here on the Castro Vetere, the waterfalls below us, Horace's Villa above us, we dined and became happy again.

When we got back to the pension Uncle Tom was there to greet us and to receive Isabel's kiss upon a mischievously yielded cheek, and to hear her rapturous account of the afternoon.

And I went forth with little Reverdy in the Borghese Gardens; afterwards to continue my studies of the etchings of Piranesi.

CHAPTER LIV

Isabel now took Reverdy into her heart with an ardor that could not be mistaken. She often went to bring him from school to the pension. She took him in walks about the broken columns of the Forum. They clambered together over the galleries of the Coliseum and to the heights of the Palatine, exploring the ruins of the palaces of the Cesar's. They had walked out to the Appian Way, and gone to listen to the merles and the golden wrens among the cypresses of the Protestant cemetery.

Reverdy had begun to call Isabel "Mamma Isabel" and Isabel addressed him as "son." Uncle Tom fell into the same way. The kinship between us was strengthened by these endearments.

But I observed something of deeper, more mystical import; Reverdy was attached to Isabel with an intense and curious filial passion. He would rush into the room and kiss Isabel, flinging his arms about her with ecstatic joy. She evoked this demonstration in some secret, maternal way. And now as I tried to remember I could not recall that Dorothy had ever caressed Reverdy--not that she was cold toward him. She was the soul of kindness. But whenever had she held him to her breast with demonstrative heart-hunger and expression; whenever had she played with him, walked with him, entered into his life of game or studies? She had never done so. Perhaps Reverdy had never had a mother after all. Now he had one in Isabel, who seemed to direct something of the energy that she had channeled into art and into travel to this boy of mine. But she did not in any way withdraw her interest from me.

I was wondering after our day at the Villa d'Este if she would place herself again in a like intimacy with me, if we should go about together as before. No, there was no change as to program; but her eyes were so clear, so innocently bright, her smile and laugh so gentle, yet free of direct invitation, above all her devotion to Uncle Tom was so noble, that I felt loath to make my approach more intimate. What I craved and what I was glad to keep was our daily association. And now while she always invited Uncle Tom to be with us and he more and more went his own way, Isabel turned to Reverdy and arranged for him to accompany us about Rome and into the country, once to Hadrian's Villa, once to Ostia where we looked upon the sea. It did not seem to me that Isabel sought to keep me at a distance and to bring in Reverdy as an influence to that end. She took such great delight in having him with us. It seemed only to happen that he went with us. It was not always so. And it was all quite natural.

We had thus become friends in the profoundest sense. Once she referred to Pinturicchio saying: "If you feel that you could have loved that man, don't you see that the same feeling can exist between a man and a woman? I am talking of that unity of two minds out of which the finest emotions come; and in the case of artists the noblest works. Love is not just passional love, just this flame that burns so brightly and then dies. It may be a flame that has no material sustenance, or so slight that we are not subtle enough to discern it; a flame that feeds on flame, unites with another flame and grows brighter for the union; and finds in the flame a substitute for oil. Friendship is what I mean--or love may be a better word. Here in Rome among the old shrines and temples where the anemones and violets bloom so profusely, before the sculptured faces of Zeus and Aphrodite and Apollo and Bacchus, one dreams one's self into intuitions of the old gods, and the lovely faiths of the ancient world. And I go sometimes alone with a book to the Borghese or to the Capitoline and there let my imagination wander in re-creation of the visions of life and the soul that came as interpretations to the ancients. I have lately been reading a book on the cult of Orpheus, the Pagan Christ, one of the loveliest figures of the Greeks. It made me believe somehow that Christ never lived, that he is only a creation of the anonymous imagination of a hungering world. For surely Orpheus did not live, and how closely he resembles Christ as an embodiment of the heart's aspiration to free itself from the material and to rise into a realm of pure beauty, understanding, devotion--all lovely things. My friend, I was thinking of you all the while. And if you could have been a friend of Pinturicchio in the noblest sense, why not of me? I am not trying to play with words or with ideas, or to perplex you, or to excite your doubts or your desires. I think you have never had a friend. What, after all, could you find in a soul so masculine, so lacking in intuition as Douglas; upon whom you have poured your admiration for all these years? Has it not been for lack of some one better to whom you could give your heart? That is why I wish that you and I could find an enduring and inspiring union in a mutual interest in great things. Forgive me, I grieve that all this seems a cruel waste to me--all these years of your life."

"Is your life not a waste?" I asked before I could check the words.

"No," Isabel replied calmly, in no way offended. "After all there is a feeling in my heart for Uncle Tom such as you might have felt for Pinturicchio. What does one derive from love? There are riches in admiration, gratitude, sympathy, filial tenderness, in desire for devotion; yes, even in pity; in the bestowal of comforting hands; in solace given in hours of fatigue and illness; in care for declining vitality. All these expressions I have. And now, my friend, I would be a help to you. I would give you eyes to understand your past; and a vision to choose a better future. If you have ever been Dionysius, which you have not, you are yet an unawakened soul. I would have you become Orpheus, attended by the Muses of all this loveliness with which we are surrounded here. By contrast it makes me think of America, so vast but so without a soul. By soul I do not mean that energy which enforces righteousness, the dream of the fanatic, the ideal of the law fabricator; but the soul of high freedoms, delights, nobilities. For there is just as much difference between those things as there is between Douglas and Pinturicchio. All of this goes without saying, of course; but I am thinking of the application of these things to you. I am your friend, you know."

Was there reality in Isabel's words? Was she not sublimating the materials of our thwarted relationship? Turning to Douglas I tried to tell her what character of thinker he was and how, in spite of any deficiency that he had, he was a brave heart and a thinking mind and a needed builder in America.

"It may be," said Isabel. We were sitting in the Gardens of Adonis once occupied in part by the golden house of Nero, here where St. Sebastian was bound to a tree and pierced with arrows. What material symbols for our thoughts! Ruins of walls, columns and capitols lay about us; and on the air was borne the music of bells and the low murmur of Rome. In this pause of our conversation I heard a cry and looking up saw Reverdy running toward us, throwing up his arms in delight and falling upon the breast of Isabel. She embraced him with all tenderness; then arose and began to run with him about the garden. In a little while we saw Uncle Tom approaching slowly. He was much out of breath and looked definitely ill. How had they found us? Isabel had told Uncle Tom that we might stroll here; and Reverdy had prevailed upon Uncle Tom to drive this way.

In a few days there was to be a service at St. Peter's which Isabel was eager to see. She was talking to Uncle Tom about it, begging him to go, and he was half consenting though reluctant. Reverdy was all delight over the prospect, and it was an opportunity for me to be with Isabel. She had never become a communicant of any church. But she abhorred atheism. It denied the love that she saw in nature, the divinity that permeated the human mind; the law she sensed in growth and decay; the spirit of beauty that reigned everywhere to her imagination. We were at one on this matter of denying a God, but the repugnance that I had had to imperial Catholicism had been increased by Serafino's recitals of Italy's sufferings under the Church and Austria. And in Rome one saw the settled dominance of clericalism. Perhaps the Church was like negro slavery. If the Church ministered to beauty and spirituality, was it not asserted in favor of slavery that it afforded leisure; did it not correspond to the fertilization which enriches the roots of a gorgeous flower? I could see Isabel turning to the esthetics in the Catholic service. "What can you say," she asked, "against a faith that surrounds itself with pictures, sculpture, music, incense, the rhythm of rich Latin, the appeal in words to life renewal, eternal life, purity, glory, tenderness? Say what you will of it; condemn its external sovereignty, of guns and poison and machinations--condemn these as you will--its ritual calls to purer dreams. And perhaps in all our life there must be oppression and particular injustice in order to produce the finest blossom."

Uncle Tom seemed to be falling into more frequent indisposition. He often lay in bed for the greater part of the morning. There were days when he did not leave his room. Again he would go forth to Canape's; and while he was rarely in anything like a stagger, he was often saturated with wine, heavy and sleepy from its influence. Isabel through it all treated him with unfailing kindness; and some of our excursions were interrupted because of Uncle Tom's taking to bed after returning from Canape's; or because he could not arise before noon after an evening with his friends. She would not desert his side. Was there something in my presence with his life with Isabel, our friendship for each other, that woke nerves to suffering which only drink could dull?

The day of the service in St. Peter's we all set forth in one carriage, Reverdy riding on the box, and Isabel, Uncle Tom, and I in the seat. I noticed that Uncle Tom was more than usually self-absorbed. Isabel patted his hand or held it, and talked to him of the objects of interest along the way.

The service was about to begin when we entered. We walked as far as the bronze plate which marks the comparative length of the Cathedral of Milan, and I was looking toward the bronze pavilion with its twisted columns which tents the tomb of St. Peter, through and around these columns at the candles on the altar. Chanting voices echoed, soared in hollow reverberations up and about the arches, the domes; an organ was giving forth soft thunder in some hidden quarter.

Suddenly Uncle Tom steps back, sways, coughs. Isabel utters a slight cry; I look at Uncle Tom and take him by the arm. Bystanders help me support him. He has turned very pale, blue at the lips. With the assistance of two men we take him to a carriage, drive to the pension. We put him to bed and send for a physician.

Reverdy is sent away, and Isabel and I watch. For Uncle Tom is dying. The doctor says it is only a matter of a few hours. Uncle Tom wishes to make a will. Will I write it out for him? His thoughts are clear. He remembers his possessions, his relations. To brothers and sisters he gives handsome purses, all the rest to Isabel.

"Isabel," he says with difficulty. "Yes, my dear," she replies in a voice of great tenderness. "Isabel, I want to give Jimmy something--ten thousand dollars." Before she can speak I interject: "I do not need it, Uncle Tom." He rolled his head in a negative, turned his hand feebly. "I give it to you that you may do something for her. Then it will be from you and from me too." Isabel stifles a sob by placing her hands tightly over her mouth. "Write," says Uncle Tom; and I write.

The will is written. The doctor has come again. Uncle Tom signs the will in our presence. Then he asks the doctor for medicine for his lungs. "I seem to have a cough," he says. But it is not his lungs but his heart. We are standing by the bed. Uncle Tom takes our hands and puts them together. Instantly his head sinks upon the pillow. He is dead. The doctor walks from the room. Isabel and I stand by the bed with closed eyes, holding hands.

CHAPTER LV

Standing beside the dead body of this man a future with Isabel took form in my heart. Love is a great solemnity itself. And in this moment I felt that Isabel shared my vision.

We buried Uncle Tom. Then Isabel began to prepare to sail for America. Of course no trip now around the world. She must go back to Connecticut, but she must go alone. That was her wish. It was understood that I should follow her later. This much was definite between us. Many plans filled her mind. She had a large estate to put in order. There were lawyers and agents to consult. I really wished to return with her in order to assist her. But she said: "It is best for you to stay here for a while. We shall write to each other. Later I wish you to come."

The question in my mind was not shall we be married, but when shall we be married. But Isabel's mood was too serious, too majestic for me to broach these definite subjects now. I looked into her eyes. It seemed to me that my thoughts were silently communicated to her. She pressed my hand gently. And so after some days of packing, in which I helped her constantly, she sailed away and left me in Rome.

I tried to work but the time would not pass. All my drawings and etchings were failures. What after all was art to me except a diversion? Too late! The only art that I ever could achieve was that of giving happiness to Isabel and being worthy of her devotion. Her letters came frequently, always so full of wise observations, striking fancies and imagery; so many with thanks for what I had been to her. She wrote me that Uncle Tom's will, as he had dictated it, had been probated and acquiesced in by every one.

Six months went by. I had gone with Reverdy to Lake Maggiore to escape the heat in Rome. While I was there a letter came from Isabel asking me to come to her. In three weeks I was by her side, having first placed Reverdy in Phillips Exeter. We were together in the great homestead which had belonged to Uncle Tom's father, there in Connecticut. It was full of the treasures of old times. Priceless things gathered on Isabel's travels--a great house set in a wonderful expanse of grounds about a mile from a pretty village. It was October. The earth was aflame with the fires of the forest. Jays cried from the maples. The air was subtle with a delicate scent of pine needles and fallen leaves.

She had other guests in the house. But they dispersed themselves gracefully. We were much alone, reading, listening to music played softly by one of her woman friends at a distance in the drawing room. Our favorite place was the window seat in the library, heaped with pillows and overlooking lilac and rose bushes, where we could see the great elms, the fountain, the country beyond. We had many walks together; and one afternoon we came to a place on a woodland path amid hills, trees towering above us, a brook playing below us. The air was hushed with a passionate Orpheus, and there I sensed her yearning. I heard the rhythm of her flesh singing to me. Her hands were stretched toward me, the pupils of her eyes grew wide as if a vision stood before her. For the first time I kissed Isabel upon the lips.

Hitherto we had breathed the rarefied air of the peaks, seen the white light of the upper spaces, felt the passionless gods about us. Now we were descending the rich valleys, to the clustered vines, to the places of soft sounds and voluptuous air, to havens of sleep, to the replenishment of our souls in the bridal supper.

That night we sat again in the window seat. Her other guests faded here and there. For a time there were shadowy fancies from the piano, then the house was stilled. But outside an April rain was falling. It pelted the windowpanes as softly as driven petals. It made a fairy swish as of far-off waves, and we sat together in a dim light. Isabel's eyes were closed. Her head rested partly on my shoulder, partly on a pillow. Her hand lay limp in my hand. Her whole being was relaxed. We were quite alone.

Isabel was with me body and mind. But a terror crept upon me. My very hair trembled. I pressed her hand to my breast. It seemed only an act of will, however, not of emotion. I drew her head close to my breast. All these actions arrayed themselves before my detached observation. Paralyzing self-analysis preoccupied me. I kissed her upon the brow, the eyes, with pressure and strength upon the lips. I was not acting; I was thinking out these demonstrations. The consciousness that I was deceiving Isabel broke my emotional concentration. Could she sense that my heart was beating, but with terror? Where were the flames that had sung to me ethereally before? Where the song out of the flesh, but too subtle for the ears of flesh? Yet I drew her closer to me, folded her tightly against my breast. My imaginative strength was more and more absorbed in self-analysis, into wonder as to what weakness had taken place in me. For here was Isabel dissolved in my arms and how could I continue this futile demonstration? But why also desist? The sweat began to stand out on my forehead. What should I say? Uncle Tom no longer stood between us. Isabel was my bride. There were no barriers to break down, no protests to overcome. We were both of an age and of an experience where formalities lose their significance. The goddess had descended to me and here was I a witless fool. Finally there flashed into my mind what she had said to me in Rome: "My friend, for this once be Orpheus--Orpheus was once Dionysius. Orpheus, tranquil and inspired, touched the quiet lyre surrounded by the Muses. Orpheus had been Dionysius drinking wine, beating cymbals. Be Orpheus, my friend, and take into your being these beauties of the mind which are given us--these flowers of friendship attend and keep for our garden."

These words ran through my tortured brain. They completed my enervation. But I could utter none of them to Isabel. What fear that hatred was budding in the heart of this woman at my side! I pressed her hands every now and then to see what was moving in her; for as my mind would not cease to analyze, analysis became keener. Always she returned the pressure. Her kisses at first given with ardent emotion were now lisped softly against my cheek. So we sat side by side. The rain pelted the window, the clock chimed. And the night was passing. A proposal of marriage seemed belated, incongruous. Yet it came into my mind as a protective coloration to more immediate expressions of the moment.

Men have lost women because they dishonored them or betrayed them or changed for the time toward them--for a thousand reasons. But look at me. What were friendship, truth, honor, the service of all that I was, love in its highest and deepest sense, understanding, sympathy with all of Isabel's flights of the mind, if I could not come to her with a promise of the future? She was not only the revelation of all that I had desired and of all that I had missed in life, but she was the symbol of a fate that has come past the appointed hour. I was the father of Reverdy by Dorothy, whom I loved with a heart's beginning; and I was the defeated lover of the ideal whom I had found too late.

In these circumstances of myself and Isabel were symbolized the lives of all men who give their devotions to lesser loves, who find their creations and their work imperfect or worthless when the planting season has passed.

As hollow as the words sounded, I nevertheless asked Isabel to be my wife. And Isabel without changing her position and without opening her eyes said in the quietest of voices: "You know I love you. You know I have loved you in every way a woman can. I love you as I loved Uncle Tom; for you are my friend, as he was. But what will the future be? I have been compelled all my life to center my thought upon books and music, friends, travel, and devotion to Uncle Tom. I have developed this power of concentration and self-denial; but would you bring me to live over again what I lived with Uncle Tom? Oh, my friend, no man can understand and fathom the maternal desire in a woman. It is a mystery which she alone knows."

What life remained in me sank down just as a stricken eagle falls into the thickets and is still; and breathes quietly and draws the film over its eyes. I could not answer her. The October air was mild. The house was overheated. A window was open. An entering wind began to stir my hair. I thought of how it must look to another, these beginnings of gray hair. Age had come to me. And I could see Isabel with my feelings alone, sitting beside me so pale, so tender, so sorrowful.

The clock strikes three. Isabel arouses, turns slightly from me, and gradually sits up. "That was three, wasn't it?" she asked. "Your train leaves early in the morning. You must sleep a few hours. I shall not see you at breakfast. The maid will bring it to you. Shall we have a glass of wine together?"

She poured wine for me and we drank. She handed me a lighted candle. Then she stood and searched my face. She offered her lips to me, turned and walked away.

I stood with the candle in my hand, watching her until she passed through the shadows and darkness of the hall. The house was without a sound. No step of her came from the hall or the stair. I still stood with the candle in that silence and fluttering darkness. Then I went to my room.

CHAPTER LVI

B ut I did not retire. I stood for a few moments looking through the window into the darkness. Then I placed my belongings in my satchel, stole softly out of the room, down the great stairs, opened the great door of the main hallway and walked off the porch on to the gravel road, through the iron gate and into the highway leading to the village. I looked back at Isabel's mansion, at the roof dark between the dark trees. Under that roof the most priceless heart I had found in life was beating--but was it in sleep or in wakefulness? I was numbed, stunned, hopeless. I could never return here, never see Isabel again. The Orphic metamorphosis meant a complete disappearance from her life. She had not turned me away or dismissed me; she had done no cruel thing, said no word that wounded or would grow poignant in memory. She had been in every way an angel of light-- and for these reasons I could not see her again. Whatever I was in truth, rid of accidental emotions if such they were, I had filled her mind with fear and doubt. Thus our fate was made, our sorrow was born.

As I walked along in the darkness toward the village, my loneliness in the world came over me. I had not attached many to me; many of those I had won were gone. Was there a home for me? How could I return to the house in Chicago? To what there? I had come from Italy to America; from a city of memories and spiritual richnesses to the tumult of New York. Above all I had found heaven in Isabel and lost it. My life had come to flower only to be withered. I had stepped out of heaven into hell, and from a great light into darkness.

But the soul does not give up while there is breath. If one is ill he looks forward to health; if he is slowly dying he hopes for years of life; if one friend is lost there is another to turn to. No heart so desperate but can imagine a haven, however poor it may be, and go to it.

In this hour my mind turned to Reverdy back in Jacksonville. There could be no truer, kinder heart. There in the prairie of Illinois that I had grown up with he would be my solace. What had I to do with Rome, with art; what with a woman like Isabel? I had ventured on sacred ground and this was my punishment. A god had driven me forth. I had won my heart's desire; but before I could enjoy it a god, ironical but just, intuitive and swift to punish, had sent me down to my place in life. I would go to Reverdy, and stand before him in my familiar guise. He would not see Rome in my eyes; he would not know that I had been in Paradise; that in my heart shone a face that I had put by and should never look on again. Every man is a temple of forsaken shrines, of altars where candles burned replenished by spirits that need open no doors--a temple whose portals are barred.

I went through Chicago, which had grown and changed in my absence so marvelously, straight to Jacksonville, regarding nothing on my way, reading nothing. Like a supernatural being which has girdled the earth in a second, it seemed that I stood before Reverdy and Sarah and their children. I stood before them, but I could hear the bells of Rome; and I saw Isabel as she handed the candle to me and walked from the room.

I supplemented what I had written to them of Dorothy's death; then I told them brokenly of Rome. Where could I begin, what words could I select to express briefly my experiences? But besides, Isabel was all my thought, and of her I could not speak. Then we had the meal. The house, the town, the surrounding country, began to assemble themselves together familiarly. I was back. The old life was slipping on me as one removes his best dress for the overalls of work. Pinturicchio! What light was falling on those soft and tender cheeks in the Vatican? But where was Douglas?

Douglas! Reverdy looked at me as if he had much to say. "He's campaigning," said Reverdy; "already has made about a hundred speeches. He has a fight on his hands. He has a tough rival to handle."

"Who is it?"

"Abraham Lincoln!"

"Who is Abraham Lincoln?"

I had never heard that name before; nor seen it in print. Reverdy went on to tell me briefly that Lincoln had been in the legislature at the same time that Douglas was in 1836; that he had been in Congress in 1847; that he was well known as a lawyer in Springfield; that for many years he had done nothing but practice law, though more active in politics since 1855 than before. That was some explanation of my ignorance of the name.

I repeated it aloud: "Abraham Lincoln. That is a great name," I said to Reverdy. "Well, he's an able lawyer, and he gives Douglas enough to do in the debates they're having." "So they are debating, are they?" I asked. "Yes," drawled Reverdy, "Lincoln was nominated for Senator by the Republicans; Douglas of course is again the nominee of the Democrats. Lincoln challenged Douglas to a debate; and they're at it hot and heavy. We talk of nothing else. It's funny you didn't hear of it anywhere along the way home. This part of the country is on fire, and they say the East is waking up to what is going on here in Illinois. I've got the newspapers here containing all the debates. You've got some good reading ahead of you. To-morrow's the last debate over at Alton."

"We must go," I said quickly. "I wouldn't miss that for the world. We must go." And I was thinking, what better way to forget Isabel? Reverdy was really glad to hear this debate at Alton; but it was necessary for him to attend to some things this day in preparation of being absent to-morrow. In the afternoon he had to drive out to his farm, and I went with him. And when we came within a short distance of the log cabin, where I had spent my first winter on the farm, I was seized with a desire to see it again. There was so much of Rome and Italy fresh in my mind with which to contrast my previous life. And we drove to the cabin.

The door had fallen to one side. The clay between the logs had dried, turned to dust, and fallen away. The roof had sagged. The fireplace was going to wreck. We looked in. Weeds had grown up during the summer through the crevices of the floor. The place was lonely and haunted. "Well," said Reverdy, "this is the kind of a home that Lincoln had as a boy. He was born in a cabin like this; and he's poor now. He has never got rich like Douglas has. And Douglas will soon be as poor as Lincoln if he keeps on at the same rate spending money in this campaign. They say he has mortgaged nearly all his property in Chicago. Everybody's fighting him--the Republicans, all the Abolitionists, and half the Democrats. This campaign means his political death or life."

"You say Lincoln was born in a log cabin. Is this a campaign of the log cabin, hard cider, and war records?"

"Well, perhaps more log cabins, but no war record. Lincoln was never in any war but the Black Hawk. He was against the Mexican War; and when in Congress voted for resolutions that the war was unconstitutional and improper. No, he is not old Harrison or old Zach Taylor. Still the log cabin is in the fight."

Then Reverdy went on to tell me that Lincoln was a clean man and that the Republicans had no abler man in Illinois; that he had been a good deal in politics after all, though quiet for about ten years. That while Douglas had been Senator, chairman of the committee on territories, his name on everybody's tongue, the most prominent man and the most active in the whole country, building railroads, organizing territories, battling with Great Britain, settling California and Oregon, and Kansas and Nebraska, traveling abroad into Russia and Asiatic Europe, and companioning with notables everywhere, making money almost like a millionaire, Lincoln had been over at Springfield practicing law, talking on the street corners, sitting in his office alone in reflection, sometimes reading; but all the while, in a way, resting.

"He's fresh and Douglas is tired," said Reverdy. "He has the advantage of not having committed himself much. Douglas has spoken freely on everything. He's four years older than Douglas, but he's a younger man. He's a temperance man they say; and while I like a drink, I don't like to see a man drink as much as Douglas does. They say he's been pouring it down during this campaign. But as for Douglas' stooping to debate with Lincoln, it's no stoop. They make the fur fly when they talk. What I fear is that there's going to be trouble in this country. I hate slavery, but I hate this agitation too. I don't want to see the North keep on making war on the South. It will breed trouble sure. And this is where I stand with Douglas. He is for non-interference with slavery and his election will be a quieter."

When we got back to Reverdy's house I plunged into the newspapers containing the debates. I read until suppertime, and then late into the night. I read them all. I went to bed and analyzed the arguments.

A house divided against itself cannot stand! This was Seward's irrepressible conflict clothed in Biblical language. The religious revival which had swept the country gave these words a compelling acceptance. But as I read this it came over me that both Jesus and Lincoln were sophists. For a house divided against itself can stand; and irrepressible conflicts rage forever. They may change their ground, but they do not cease. I had seen this in Europe and in Italy, where in the January just past a certain Orsini had attempted the life of Louis Napoleon because he had not acceded to the labors of Cavour and thus hastened the liberty of Italy. And yet Italy was standing and France. Houses are divided everywhere and they stand. Beelzebub is crafty enough to cast out devils here and there in order to confound his kingdom with the Kingdom of Heaven. Of course he does not cast all the devils out--if he did he would lose his kingdom--only enough to make himself appear as one of the divine wonder-workers. A house divided against itself can stand, even as the world can stand with both good and evil in it, with both God and Satan in divided authority over it; and even as man has good and evil in his own nature and still lives and works without becoming wholly good or wholly evil. So could this country stand divided into free and slave states as it was formed at the beginning. There was not the slightest chance that it would ever become all slave, as Lincoln had presented one of the alternatives of a divided house. There was great chance that it would become all free by natural processes, as Douglas had indicated over and over again before the time of these debates.

Here I found that the debaters had split hairs on what the fathers had done. "Why can't these agitators leave the states as they were made by the fathers, slave and free?" asked Douglas. "They were not made," retorted Lincoln, "they were found; slavery was found and was let be as it was." "No," said Douglas, "the fathers organized a republic, adopted a Constitution; and when they made it, instead of abolishing slavery, making it free, they kept slavery and made it slave by the votes of states passing upon and acceding to an instrument of government. And besides, this instrument of government provided for the importation of more slaves from Africa; and provided for the capture and return of fugitive slaves now in the country or thereafter to be imported into the country."

Douglas had attacked the doctrine of a divided house with all possible power and brilliancy. He had insisted that there was no more reason for the house of America to be divided because there was negro slavery in some states and no slavery in others, than because there was prohibition in Maine and whisky in Kentucky. And that there would be disunion if some states warred on other states about the purely domestic affairs of the latter. This was the only sense in which the house could be divided, and caused to fall. That disparate interests in the states should not make hostility between them; and that hostility arising from attacks and agitation should be put down. He went on to denounce the Republican party for holding and preaching a faith that arrayed one section of the country against another; and with great satire and invective he showed that the Republicans stood upon sectional principles which could not be preached in the South and not everywhere in the North. "But now you have a sectional organization," he had said to a theocratic audience at Galesburg, "a party which appeals to the northern section of the Union against the southern, a party which appeals to northern passion, northern pride, northern ambition, and northern prejudices, against southern people, the southern states, and southern institutions. The leaders of that party hope to be able to unite the northern states in one great sectional party; and inasmuch as the North is the strongest section they will thus be enabled to outvote, conquer, and control the South. Is there a Republican in Galesburg who can travel into Kentucky and carry his principles with him across the Ohio?"

Douglas had even shown that Lincoln did not utter the same sentiments in all parts of Illinois. In Chicago where there was a large alien vote Lincoln had said: "I should like to know if taking this old Declaration of Independence which declares that all men are equal upon principle and making exceptions to it, where will it stop? If one man says it does not mean a negro, why may not another man say it does not mean another man? If the Declaration is not the truth let us get the statute books in which we find it and tear it out. Who is so bold as to do it?... Let us discard all this quibbling about this man and the other man, this race and the other race being inferior, and therefore they must be placed in an inferior position, discarding our standard that we have left us. Let us discard all these things and unite as one people throughout this land until we shall once more stand up declaring that all men are created equal."

Douglas had driven Lincoln hard upon this application of the Declaration of Independence with the result that in the southern part of Illinois, at Charleston, Lincoln had uttered these words of a very different tenor:

"I will say then that I am not nor never have been in favor of bringing about in any way the social and political equality of the white and black races; that I am not nor never have been in favor of making free voters of the negroes or jurors or qualifying them to hold office or having them marry with white people. I will say in addition that there is a physical difference between the white and black races which I suppose will forever forbid the two races living together upon terms of social and political equality; and inasmuch as they cannot so live that while they do remain together there must be the position of the superior and the inferior; that I, as much as any other man, am in favor of the superior position assigned to the white man."

Lincoln and Douglas were therefore at one on this. But how about slavery? Lincoln looked forward to a time when slavery would be abolished. How could that be? By not admitting any more slave states? No! For Lincoln confessed that he would as a Senator vote to admit a slave state, if it as a territory had had a free chance to have slavery or freedom as it chose, and if in becoming a state it freely adopted a slave constitution. As to these opinions Lincoln and Douglas were agreed; for Douglas had fought the Kansas constitution because it forced slavery on Kansas; and now the whole Buchanan administration in Illinois was arrayed against Douglas for his attitude on Kansas, and Lincoln was profiting by that.

How would Lincoln abolish slavery? By starving it, girding it about gradually with freedom, keeping it where it was. That was all. What would Douglas do? Referring to Lincoln's looking forward to a time when slavery would be abolished everywhere Douglas said: "I look forward to a time when each state shall be allowed to do as it pleases. If it chooses to keep slavery forever, it is not my business but its own; if it chooses to abolish slavery, it is its own business not mine. I care more for the great principles of self-government, the right of the people to rule, than I do for all the negroes in Christendom. I would not endanger the perpetuity of this Constitution, I would not blot out the great inalienable rights of the white men for all the negroes that ever existed."

What would Lincoln do about the fugitive-slave law? Douglas had denounced attempts to evade it and actual violations of it. Even the Whigs frowned on its nullification. What would Lincoln do? He was not in favor of its repeal. He had said at Freeport: "I think under the Constitution of the United States, the people of the Southern States are entitled to a Congressional fugitive-slave law.... As we are now in no agitation in regard to an alteration or modification of that law, I would not be the man to introduce it as a new subject of agitation upon the general question of slavery."

For the rest, what did it all come to? Like two pugilists Lincoln and Douglas blocked each other's blows, drove each other into corners. Lincoln twitted Douglas about being on both sides of the matter of extending the Missouri Compromise. Then Douglas tripped Lincoln, who had asserted that only slavery had ever disturbed the peace of the Union. "How about the War of 1812, and the Hartford convention?" asked Douglas. How about the tariff and South Carolina in 1832? He might have asked, how about the Alien and Sedition laws and the Kentucky resolutions of 1798. But for the rest, what did it all come to?

Lincoln contended that Congress had the power to forbid slavery in the territories; Douglas worked up from a position, which scarcely denied the power, but rather shrank from its use, to the position that sovereignty abode in the people of the territory; and that as Congress has no express grant of power to legislate upon slavery as to a territory, the territorial sovereignty had the only power to do so. He attacked Lincoln's position that a territory is a creature of Congress as a property, to be clothed with powers or denied powers; and particularly with powers not possessed by Congress itself. This doctrine led to imperialism. Douglas held that Congress had the power to organize territories under the clause providing for the admission of new states; but when they were organized they assumed an organic sovereignty out of an inchoate sovereignty, and had the right to legislate as they chose to the same extent as a state. It was the old fight between implied powers and strict construction.

What in the Constitution forbade slaves from being taken into the territories? Not a thing. Moreover the territories were the commons of all the states, won by their common valor and blood. Could not a liquor dealer from Chicago take his stock to Kansas? Assuredly. Why then could not a planter from Louisiana take his slaves to Nebraska? Liquor and slaves were property. Who said so? The fugitive-slave clause of the Constitution, and the fugitive-slave law of 1850 which Lincoln admitted he would not alter.

But after the liquor was in Kansas or the slave in Nebraska could they flourish? That depended on the territorial law, the attitude of the people. Did Congress have to pass favorable legislation? From what clause flowed the duty and the power? Did a territorial legislature have power to pass favorable legislation? It was not called upon to do so by anything in the Federal Constitution. Therefore, the mere right to take a slave into free territory under the Dred Scott decision, take it as property, was a naked right without local support. "This popular sovereignty is as thin as soup made from the shadow of a starved pigeon," said Lincoln. Nevertheless, it was what it was and no more. And Lincoln's catch question on the legal right to keep slavery out of the territories did not catch Douglas. The mere right to take a slave into free territory could coexist with no protective legislation after the slave was there. It could coexist with unfavorable legislation and social opposition. Let natural processes rule.

What was the difference between this and girding the slave states around with freedom? That could scarcely be done without the aid of natural processes.

But since Douglas did not admit that Congress had to give favorable legislation to a slave owner who had taken his slave into a territory, the South was drawing away from him. He was not their friend to the extreme doctrine of taking a slave into a territory and keeping him a slave against the will of the territory. Was Douglas unmoral? What of the unmorality of taking Kansas and Nebraska from the Indians? Was he syllogistic, analytic, intellectually hard? But was not Lincoln so too? Douglas derived from Jefferson through Jackson; Lincoln from Hamilton through Webster, whatever else could be said of them.

Thus I read on through the night until I had finished all that Douglas and Lincoln had said at the six debates then finished. The next morning Reverdy and I started for Alton.

I could scarcely wait to get my first glimpse of Lincoln.

CHAPTER LVII

Alton, this old town that I had visited so many times before, was crowded with people drawn from the surrounding country, from across the river in Missouri. As to the temper of the audience, it rather favored Douglas. I saw the leering, ugly faces that I had seen in the lobbies of the hotels in St. Louis years before at the railroad convention, when Captain Grant was lounging there and planters swarmed at the bar and cursed Yankees and nigger-lovers.

It was the fifteenth of October, fair and temperate. Thousands swarmed around the speaker's stand in the public square, which was bare of flags or mottoes by express orders of the masters of ceremony. The time arrived. Lincoln came to the platform and took a seat.

He was tall, enormously tall, long of limb, angular, narrow shouldered. His skin was yellow and dry, wrinkled. His hair was black and coarse. His eyes were sunk back in his head with a melancholy expression which could flame into humor or indignation. But his forehead was full, shapely, and noble. The largeness of his nose, tilted a little to one side, gave sculptural strength to his face. His great mouth with its fleshy underlip, supplemented the nose. Both were material for grotesque carica-ture. He looked like an educated gawk, a rural genius, a pied piper of motley follow-ers. He was a sad clown, a Socratic wag, a countryman dressed up for a state occa-sion. But he was not a poor man defending the cause of the poor. There was nothing of the dreamer in his make-up, the eccentric idealist. His big nose and mouth and Henry Clay forehead denied all of this. He sat in self-possession, in poise, clothed in the order of confident reason, unafraid, sure of himself but without vanity, in a wise detachment, on a vantage point of vision. His frock coat, rusty from dust and wear, did not fit him. The sleeves escaped his wrists by several inches; his trousers had hitched up as he sat down, so that one half of his shanks was exposed to view, leaving his monstrous feet, like the slap-boots of a negro minstrel, for ludicrous inches over the floor. His neck was long and feminine, and stuck up grotesquely much above a sort of Byronic collar held together by a black stock tie. I had never seen a man so absurd.

Douglas was as ludicrously short as Lincoln was tall; broad shouldered where Lincoln was narrow; thick chested where Lincoln was thin; big headed where Lincoln was small; of massive brow where Lincoln was full and shapely; of strong bull-like neck where Lincoln was small and delicate; of short, compact, powerful body where Lincoln was tall, loosely constructed, awkward, and muscular. Douglas' face wore determination, seriousness, force, pugnacity, and endurance. But his hair was grayer than mine; he looked tired. He arose and in that great melodious voice which always thrilled me, he said: "It is now nearly four months since the canvass between Mr. Lincoln and myself commenced."

He went on and controverted Mr. Lincoln's "house divided against itself," going over the ground of the previous debate. There was not a sound of disturbance in the audience. They were in a charm, a trance. Oratory could rise to no greater heights. Then after saying that the Declaration of Independence did not include the negro, Indians, or Fiji Islanders, but that all dependent races should be treated nevertheless with fairness, and that it did not follow that because a negro was an inferior he must be a slave, he appealed to the rights of the states and the territories to control slavery for themselves. He closed with these memorable words:

"Why can we not thus have peace? Why should we allow a sectional party to agitate this country, to array the North against the South, and convert us into enemies instead of friends merely that a few ambitious men may ride into power on a sectional hobby? How long is it since these ambitious northern men wished for a sectional organization? Did any one of them dream of a sectional party as long as the North was the weaker section and the South the stronger? Then all were opposed to sectional parties; but the moment the North obtained the majority in the House and in the Senate by the admission of California and could elect a President without the aid of southern votes, that moment ambitious men formed a scheme to excite the North against the South and make the people be governed in their votes by geographical lines, thinking that the North being the stronger section would outvote the South and consequently they, the leaders, would ride into office on a sectional hobby. I am told that my hour is out. It was very short."

Short it was. I thought he had just begun. What would this strange creature now rising to six feet four inches of awkward angularity say in reply to this wonderful oration? He opened his great mouth and spoke. What is this? A falsetto note, a piping instead of the musical thunder we have heard. He poses strangely, his gestures shoot up and out like the arms of a dislocated clothes rack. He rises on his toes with a quick springlike movement, as if he were a puppet loosened by a spring from a box. He sways from side to side to give emphasis to his words. His mouth opens to huge proportions in moments of excitement. His black hair falls over his forehead. His great nose sticks out like a signboard. Is he scoring?

I know, for I have read the other debates. He is wasting no words; he is meeting Douglas point by point, whether successfully or not. He seemed embarrassed, diffident at first. Why not? He is fighting a giant; then there are ugly faces in the audience, men in drink, slave owners from Missouri, Democrats who hate sectionalism and loathe the rise of the Republican party. Whispers are near me: "He amounts to nothing. Douglas has laid him out. He is scared. The Little Giant has choked him."

But Lincoln goes on. His earnestness deepens, his seriousness becomes more impressive. His voice is carrying even though it pipes. He has endurance, too, and courage and fighting will. But Douglas has made it very difficult for him; indeed he has brought Lincoln to his terms on nearly everything--all but the 'house divided against itself' doctrine; and the right and duty of Congress to keep slavery out of the territories. These are issues between him and Douglas still; but is this the real issue after all? He is nearly through. He has been going on as if he were making a statement of a case. It is interjected with argument; but it is largely statement of positions. It is declaratory and follows the form of a poem, not an argument. It assumes premises; he says "I think so." It has reason back of it, but it is the reason of things proven. It is fortified by matters of general acceptance. It has logic, but the logic of things existing inherently, not made. And at last, more earnestly than before, he says:

"On the point of my wanting to make war between the free and the slave states, there has been no issue between us. So too when he says that I am in favor of introducing a perfect social and political equality between the white and the black races. These are false issues upon which Judge Douglas has tried to force the controversy. There is no foundation in truth for the charges that I maintain either of these propositions. The real issue in this controversy--the one pressing upon every mind--is the sentiment upon the part of one class that looks upon the institution of slavery as a wrong, and of another class that does not look upon it as a wrong. The sentiment that contemplates the institution of slavery in this country as a wrong is the sentiment of the Republican party. It is the sentiment around which all their actions, all their arguments, circle, from which all their propositions radiate. That is the real issue. That is the issue that will continue in this country when these poor tongues of Judge Douglas and myself shall be silenced. It is the eternal struggle between these two principles--right and wrong--throughout the world. They are the two principles that have stood face to face from the beginning of Time, and will ever continue to struggle. The one is the common right of humanity and the other the divine right of kings. It is the same spirit that says: 'You work and toil and earn bread, and I'll eat it.' No matter in what shape it comes, whether from the mouth of a king who seeks to bestride the people of his own nation and live by the fruit of their labor, or from one race of man as an apology for enslaving another race, it is the same tyrannical principle."

What had come over Lincoln? He was no longer awkward. A divine grace permeated his being. The October sun threw glory upon his brow, gave us a look into his deeply illuminated eyes, left nothing of the great nose and mouth but their strength, the sculptural impressiveness of stone features in the sides of hills. What would Serafino think if he could hear this?

Then of a sudden I saw Pinturicchio in Lincoln's face, the same gentleness along the sunken cheeks, the same imaginative glow in the whole countenance. Here in this warped and homely face, this face out of the womb of poverty and sorrow, the winter loneliness of the forest, the humbleness and the want of the log cabin, the mystical yearning of humanity on the prairies and under the woodland stars, I saw for a swift moment in the glancing of the sun, as he uttered these words, the genius of the poet who knows and states, who has lived years of loneliness and failure, who has seen others grow rich, notable, and powerful, and who has remained obscure and unobeyed, with nothing but a vision which has become lightning at last in a supreme moment of inspiration. Lincoln had had his hour whatever should befall him.

The debate was over--the debates were over. Reverdy and I walked away with the great crowd hurrahing for Douglas, a few hurrahing for Lincoln.

I began to repeat to myself what Douglas had said years before in the Senate in replying to Webster: "There is a power in this nation greater either than the North or the South--a growing, increasing, and swelling power that will be able to speak the law of this nation and to execute the law as spoken. That power is the country known as the Great West. There, sir, is the hope of this nation--the resting place of the power that is not only to control but to save the Union."

This prediction had now been fulfilled. This West had produced Lincoln and Douglas. One of them was sure to have the responsibility of executing the law as spoken. Of this I was sure.

CHAPTER LVIII

When I got back to Chicago I found a letter from Isabel. It read: "My dear friend: It hurts me to think that you stole off in the darkness. I can see you in imagination walking the lonely way, carrying your satchel. Perhaps it made no difference that you did not stay until morning, but still it hurts me. And what can I say to you now? Are we like two people who are kept from each other by circumstances that they do not control, like friends whom a war separates? I hardly know how to express myself. There seems to be nothing to say; and yet there is so much for which I wish I had words; or I wish some word of mine could alter the circumstances. I am loath to lose your friendship, your association. We have so much in common that can be enjoyed through letters; and I do wish you to write me. Above all you must not think that anything of depreciation or disregard has entered my heart. If this be true, why must you change toward me? Do I speak fantastically when I ask you to try out a marriage of the mind? The experiences through which you and I have passed have enabled me to penetrate the reality of my wishes and so even to have had them. I have known one kind of devotion; and I can fancy disillusionment coming over something more intensely emotional. Can we not think that we might grow tired of each other, and that we are to-day where we would be if we should become disillusioned but without having the bitterness of such an experience? Our poor human natures are cursed with fatigue, and with the loss of beauty and vision consequent upon daily intimacy. Let me say to you then that I love you and shall always love you, and that I have nothing in my heart that would not console you if everything in my heart was frankly expressed to you. If I ever should marry any one you will not lose your place in my affections. I turn to my life which I left for you. And you must see that if you have tragedy, so have I. As far as possible lift yourself out of the disturbing things of politics, and leave lesser personalities with the gods who are fashioning this world in the image of more enduring truths. There is solace to me, and I hope there may be to you, in the fact that we two are in the world together and that I can think of you as my friend and I trust can write to you as I hope you will write to me. Let us face the reality and consider that after all we have the sweetest and best of things that can be between a man and a woman. If I can ever help you in any way I shall be so glad. I sense somehow that you may fear me, thinking that you have become indifferent in my eyes. This is not true. I cannot too often assure you of this. I hope for good things for you and your Reverdy. Give my love to him from 'Mamma Isabel' and believe me, affectionately, Isabel."

And I wrote to Isabel: "Some of your admonitions came too late to me, for I am interested in politics again. I have just returned from Alton where I went to hear Douglas debate against a Mr. Lincoln, a lawyer of Springfield, who has been nominated for Senator by the Republicans. He is as much of a backwoodsman as anybody could be, as much so as Harrison and a good deal more so than Taylor. But he is not to be despised either in himself or on account of his backers. The Republican party in Illinois profits by the feeling of the German revolutionnaires; and Lincoln may be ever so poor and so humble, nevertheless the Republican party has drawn to itself some of the richest and most powerful interests in the country; interests which are far-sighted enough to see that if the Republican party can be put into power the mercantile ambition of the North to control the South and the whole country will be realized. No human being could have been a greater orator than Douglas was at Alton; while Lincoln, in spite of disadvantages of voice and manner and physique, rose to great heights of eloquence. The climax of his speech was when he spoke of the world-old struggle between right and wrong. I was swept off my feet for the moment and seemed to see in his face something of the genius of Pinturicchio. Now I wonder if I was not befooled both as to the value of Lincoln's utterance and as to his kinship with the great Italian artist. After all I do not know what is right and wrong; and I do not believe any one else does. I see that people get worked up into furies over what they think is right and wrong, and kill each other on account of it. Later ages view the matter as of no importance; and the lives that are lost in the struggle are as forgotten as the multitudinous leaves which bestrew the ground of an autumnal forest. I fear I am in a very bad state of mind. It is true, as you intimate in your letter, that I am passing through a certain humiliation of spirit; and I am thus inclined to speculate on the value of all truths and philosophies. I seem to see that material things control truths and influence our human natures in every way. Our experience demonstrates this fact. And in the case of Douglas and Lincoln, Douglas is quick to sense the moralistic hypocrisy with which the Republicans are draping their trafficking ambitions. But, on the other hand, I believe that Lincoln is as honest in his desire to keep slavery out of the territories as Douglas is honest in his plan to let the territories decide the matter for themselves. Both of these men are ambitious. Lincoln is of the industrial faith which is backboning the Republican party, and Douglas is of the vaguer and less materialistic faith which for so long has appealed to American Democracy in terms and promises of all kinds of freedoms and independencies.... I would give my life almost to see you again, but somehow I do not know how to bring it about, while at the same time I am living in hope that it may be so, and trusting that you will see me in a different light, and that I can give you assurances which will justify your vision. I am not very well and have been consulting a physician, since coming West, who seems to think that my nerves are in bad condition and that I am worn by striving and by life. It is curious too that Douglas, though bulky and fat, seems to me a tired man. Perhaps both of us have lost the way; and it may be true that later he will have the true vision as I did in you. I wish you could call me back to you. My mind wavers as I write. Affectionately, James."

With the exchange of these letters I merged my feelings into other things. The roar of Illinois and of the country tended to keep my mind from brooding on Isabel. There was a melancholy resignation in the words of Lincoln upon his own defeat for the Senatorship, which were in key with my own grief and helped me to sublimate it. He had written to a friend who chanced to show me the letter: "It gave me a hearing on the great and durable questions of the age, which I could have had in no other way; and though I now sink out of view and shall be forgotten I believe I have made some marks which will tell for the cause of civil liberty long after I am gone."

The cause of civil liberty! Had not Douglas stood for this too? He had won against the terrific opposition of the Buchanan administration. He had fought the slave constitution of Kansas and he had beaten down in this campaign the enmity which had risen up around him because he had fought that constitution. The Republicans were exceedingly glad that Douglas' contest had divided the support of his own party. They had no thanks for him for what he had done for civil liberty in that regard. They were glad of his election over Lincoln for the sinister reason that Douglas' triumph, since Douglas was almost at one with Lincoln as to the matter of slavery, meant a decline and a division of the Democratic party as a whole. At the same time there was talk now of Lincoln for the Presidency. But Lincoln did not think he was worthy of the honor. Lincoln was writing and saying: "What is the use of talking of me whilst we have such men as Seward and Chase, and everybody knows them, and scarcely anybody outside of Illinois knows me; besides, as a matter of justice, is it not due to them? I admit I am ambitious and would like to be President.... But there is no such good luck in store for me as the Presidency of these United States." There was a pathos about this man Lincoln which won my heart.

I spent some evenings now with Aldington and Abigail. We drove out to see the Douglas property south of the town. A horse-car line was being built from Randolph Street to 12th Street, but beyond that was the waste of sand and of scrub oaks, and the land which Douglas had all but lost in financing himself in this campaign. I was ready to help Douglas with money if he would accept it from me; but just now he was not an easy man to find, and he did not come to me.

The trial and execution of John Brown was another thunderclap. And Abigail showed me what was being said about it. A certain Henry Thoreau, a strange, radical soul living in the woods near Concord, Massachusetts, had compared John Brown to Christ. "Some eighteen hundred years ago," Thoreau said, "Christ was crucified; this morning perchance Captain Brown was hung. These are the two ends of the chain which is not without its links. He is not old Brown any longer; he is an angel of light.... I foresee the time when a painter will paint that scene, no longer going to Rome for a subject. The poet will sing it, the historian will record it; and with the landing of the Pilgrim Fathers and the Declaration of Independence, it will be the ornament of some future national gallery when at least the present form of slavery shall be no more here. We shall then be at liberty to weep for Captain Brown."

Could it be possible that this Captain Brown should have his Pinturicchio? Well, might it not be so since Victor Hugo, living in exile, had also given Brown an apotheosis? Abigail also had Walt Whitman's *Leaves of Grass*, who was preaching the doctrine of brotherhood, democracy, resistance to the law.

"What sort of country is this?" I asked Abigail. "Can every one set himself up as a judge of the laws and disobey them if he chooses? If you had heard Douglas' speech you would be convinced that this sort of mania will cease or there will be war. Even Emerson is among these idealistic rebels, for he says that it is a lack of health to cry 'madman' at a hero as he passes. I think the Bible is responsible for much of this turmoil and foolish rebellion, if not all of it. Lincoln founded his campaign upon the Bible: a house divided against itself cannot stand. And just because Christ is taken as divine, every word and act of his is lived up to by some madman as justification for acts like those of Brown."

In the meantime Abigail had found among her papers the words of Victor Hugo: "He is not a New Englander," she said, "nor an American idealist. And he says--I'll translate it for you: 'In killing Brown the Southern States have committed a crime which will take its place among the calamities of history. The rupture of the Union will fatally follow the assassination of Brown. As to Brown, he was an apostle and a hero. The gibbet has only increased his glory and made him a martyr.'"

Well, was not Douglas a martyr too? Who had done more for his country? Was Lincoln any more radical than Douglas? Lincoln was defeated to be sure, but Douglas was penalized for what he had said in these debates. No sooner had he returned to Washington than he found himself deposed from the committee on territories. He was beginning to be a man without a party. He was paying for his ideas.

A book called ***Helpers, the Impending Crisis of the South*** had at this time woven itself into the clouds of the gathering storm. It had influenced the election of a Speaker in Congress, for although Lincoln was defeated in Illinois, the Republicans had 25 Senators to 38 Democrats; and the House had 109 Republicans to 128 Democrats. A crisis was indeed impending, with Douglas, the greatest man in the country, dishonored and disarmed by the Southern States. What was growing up, and from what source, which should be the master of the destiny of the country? What was giving it strength but some form of materialism? The phrase "the struggle for existence" crept into our conversation, for Darwin's ***The Origin of Species*** had made its appearance this year. We discussed its principles as far as we could make them out from the reports of the book. Every one knew that strength survives. But what is strength? Did the North have strength, or the South? Did moral ideas have strength, or did war? All the while, where did God come in? Abigail said: "He comes in in this very struggle, defeat and devouring. For all the while there is triumph in the realm of the mind, and mind is God. My friend, you can think of Douglas and slavery and politics, and impending war; I know of something that overtops them all and can handle all of them as playthings. That is chemistry."

"Where do you get all these things?" I asked Abigail. "From Richard, from books, from publications, everywhere. I am watching this thrilling thing called life and I can laugh when I see you taking Douglas and Lincoln so seriously; for really they amount to very little. Douglas has given some of his land to found a university. What will they teach in it? Anything of Douglas'? What? No, young minds will read philosophy there and study mathematics and chemistry by which engines, bridges, telegraphs, will be constructed. Here is a funny thing. You remember the Atlantic cable was laid last summer. Poor old Buchanan, the mighty President of a mighty Republic, is so ignorant that he doubts the verity of the message which Queen Victoria sent to him. Douglas and Lincoln! What are their speculations as to whether this ridiculous old document called the Constitution goes into a territory or not? Give me old Bishop Berkeley with his inquiries concerning the virtues of tar water. It takes imagination of some moment to sense, as he did, that tar contains the purified spirits of the trees, of vegetation which can heal and help man. These were dreams worth while. Now a German chemist named Kekule, comes along and develops a theory called the valence of atoms. And who can tell what will come of that? For that matter, Sir Walter Raleigh did more for the world than Douglas. He found petroleum in the Trinidad pitch lake way back in the sixteenth century. And now a well has just been drilled, not for salt as you saw it in Kentucky as a boy, but for the oil for which they then had no use except to make ointment for people who stumble on the pier trying to catch a boat."

I said to Abigail: "I have never pretended that Douglas was a scientist or an artist or that he had a philosophical mind, but now that you bring these things to my attention I want to ask you why he is not a first-class disciple of Darwin, since he has advocated the processes of nature in the solution of the slavery question."

"Nature! Well, are climate and soil any more nature than thought? Can't we use our will and our thought to assist climate and soil, about anything? But after all I get tired of this emphasis of the one slavery, just as you do. Why not include some other slaveries for condemnation? There is Emerson for example. He didn't start out with this John Brown idea. He began with a plea for emancipation intellectually from England; and for emancipation from the slavery of orthodoxy."

"Yes," said Aldington, "I wish to add my plea too, and against the slavery of a lot of things: against the slavery of courts and bad laws and bad thoughts and poverty, and the whole business which we can see growing up in America, and making laws to stimulate it and protect it."

CHAPTER LIX

I was now more lonely than I had ever been in my life, more lonely than I was on the farm. Then I had youth and expectation of wonderful things. I had ebullient spirits which were excited by simple things, the new country, the prospect of growing rich. Now my spirits were on the level of the prairie itself and I could look over the whole of life. I had nothing in particular with which to employ my energies except taking care of the riches that I had acquired. Riches had no meaning to me now. They brought nothing that moderate means would not buy. What I needed was some one in my life. I had lost Dorothy. My boy was away at school. Isabel was denied me. If she had only rejected me so that my will had been raised against her. Then I should have had passion for my thought and action. But it was with gentleness and understanding that she bade me adieu.

Douglas was left to me, but what could he do for me or I for him? He had been my friend with that loyalty which characterized him from the time that he had taken me from the clutches of the law for killing Lamborn. We had seen much of each other along the way. Did loneliness ever come over him? He had married again, but was he happy? He was living a life of much social brilliancy with the new Mrs. Douglas in Washington. But was he happy? Or was he drowning disappointment, the tragic sense of life's inadequacy, in abandoned diversions?

Like myself, he had wished for riches and attained them. He had lost his riches. I still possessed mine. But I was no happier for that. He had married a woman who was a slave owner. On my part, I had been made kindred to the slave blood by the marriage of my father. He wished for land, for wealth, and had taken a purse to marry an octoroon. Douglas had wished for land for his country and had paralleled the course of the slavocracy to get it. I had killed a man because of Zoe; then Zoe had disappeared and a part of the accursed land which had come to me through my father had passed to the unknown Fortescue, who had appeared and disappeared from my life like a thief. I had married Dorothy because my will drove me to it in overcoming her opposition to the fact of Zoe. I had loved Isabel and lost her. Douglas had loved the North and the Great West. Was he to lose them?

Thus Douglas and I seemed to have arrived at the same place in life. He was broken in fortune and without a party. I was burdened with what more and more seemed to me a tainted fortune. And I was as isolated as he was. I could not help but think of him constantly, of his long years of labor, his great struggles, his heroic fight, his undaunted courage. Could anything lift him out of his complication to honor and freedom? He was the most talked of man for the Presidency. If he could only win that now and stand as a master man for nationalism, union, progress, peace, popular sovereignty, all the great liberties for which he had battled. He had already failed twice to be nominated. If now he could not win the prize, what would be his future as against the growing power of the Republican party?

As my heart was set upon Douglas' ambition I set off for Charleston, South Carolina, in April. Anything to alleviate my regret over Isabel.

When I arrived there I sought Douglas and found him deep in consultation with his advisers. He was unmistakably confronted with the severest contest of his life. He was delighted to see me and got me admission to the convention hall. I had tried to come as a delegate; but Illinois had split in a fight over her own son, and there were two delegations, one for and one against Douglas. And I could be on neither.

Douglas' birthday, April the 23d, saw the opening of the fateful deliberations. He was destined to have no peace and no rest. Others might find shelter from the storm. He was compelled after his great labors in the years before to walk through the lightning and have it gather about his head. His doctrines on slavery had alienated the whole South from him. But he had the West, save California and Oregon, which acted with the South. Yet he was their son too. He had strength all through the North, because of the West. That West which he had done so much to create, which he had prophesied would stand as a balance between the North and the South, was for its son and its prophet--save California and Oregon.

But of the whole thirty-three states, seventeen were against him. The West fought the South and fought for Douglas. The South made a common cause of opposition to the North and the West. But the new Giant put through the Douglas principles in the platform.

Then Alabama, Mississippi, South Carolina, Florida, Texas, and Arkansas seceded from the convention. The West had won but it had lost the South. And now in the balloting Douglas could not be nominated. He needed 202 votes, he could only poll 152-1/2. The heat grew intense. The delegates, trying to accommodate their interests, wandered about the old city talking seriously and not excitedly. There was little drinking. The local clergy offered up prayers for the success of the convention, for peaceful solutions. Balloting and balloting! No choice! The twenty-third of May arrived and the convention, exhausted and half disgusted, adjourned to meet in Baltimore, June 18th. Douglas had not been nominated. His party had split just as the Republicans had anticipated when they were congratulating themselves on Douglas' success in the Senatorial contest with Lincoln.

Meantime, the seceders went to another hall, adopted a platform that suited them on the slavery matter, and nominated John C. Breckenridge.

I did not go up to Baltimore to see the end of this melancholy business. I followed the proceedings in the press. Delegates from the state delegations which had seceded appeared there on the scene to gain admission. They were admitted where pledged to Douglas; upon this decision a second secession took place. Then they nominated Douglas; but he was now like a runner who has been tripped along the way, and who stumbles spent and breathless over the goal. He had conjured the West. It was strong enough to adopt his principles, but it could not prevent the convention from dividing. It could nominate him, but could not hold to him the states he needed in this, his greatest trial. And among his bitterest enemies was that Jefferson Davis whom I had seen in the Mexican War and who was now Senator from Mississippi. My hatred of the South nearly reached self-contempt for the way in which my life had been united to its feeling. All my thinking of the country and the terrible events which followed the monumental folly of not giving Douglas a united nomination dates from these days.

On my way west I read in the press of the verbal clash between this Jefferson Davis and Douglas in the Senate. With an insulting inflection Davis had said: "I have a declining respect for platforms. I would sooner have an honest man on any sort of a rickety platform you could construct than to have a man I did not trust, on the best platform which could be made."

Douglas had retorted with telling effect: "If the platform is not a matter of much consequence, why press that question to the disruption of the party?"

Why? But the South had done it. And Davis had done it.

CHAPTER LX

Who should call upon me the next morning after my arrival in Chicago but Yarnell? I had not seen him now for several years. And he was a delegate to the Republican convention.

"How is this?" I asked him. "I remember yet what you said to me about slavery when we came to America more than twenty-five years ago." "Oh," he replied, "that makes no difference. The Republican party is not going to disturb slavery where it is. It only proposes to keep it out from what it isn't. The platform will refer to the Declaration of Independence, and all that. But it will also have a tariff plank. The Democrats have beaten the Morrill tariff bill; and we want a tariff--Pennsylvania wants a tariff for iron. And we will nominate Seward and elect him."

"What if the Southern States secede?"

"That suits us. That will give the Republican party complete control. With the Southern States out, we will have the Senate and the House as well as the President, and we can dominate everything, and gather in all the offices--postmasters, marshals, Federal judges, everything. The northern Democrats will have nothing to say. Your friend Douglas will have nothing to say. He is already a played-out horse. He won't be able to even whinny in the Senate. And the world and the fullness thereof will be ours."

"How about Seward being too radical?"

"No, he isn't. Look at what it comes to. Kansas will come in as a free state. The work is already done for that. California came in as a free state. Minnesota, Oregon, Wisconsin, have all come in as free states under the Democratic party and with Douglas on top as Senator. There won't be any more slave states no matter who is elected."

"That's what I think."

"I only say this to show that this talk of the radicalism of Seward is nonsense. He spoke of the higher law, to be sure, but Douglas has been talking of nature and nature's God. What's the difference?"

"No difference except that Douglas' law of nature means something and the higher law means nothing. We can see what the law of nature is; we don't know what the higher law is, unless you can fathom the mind of the fanatic; of Thoreau, of John Brown, and Garrison. I will tell you something: Lincoln of this state is not so far apart from Douglas. He has rejected the higher law of Seward in a recent letter. He is for the irrepressible conflict, because it is the same thing as the house divided against itself. He must stand by his own doctrine--and the Bible. He is as practical as Douglas."

"That's the point," said Yarnell. "The Abolitionists don't like Lincoln. He said right here in the debates that he was not in favor of giving the nigger a vote or making him a citizen. He isn't for the Declaration of Independence when it comes to things like that. But he is of no moment. He's not known. He's only a local man. He's a country jake, isn't he?"

"Rather so."

"That's what I hear. He's had no experience. Seward, you know, has been Governor of New York, and Senator. He's a famous man. The political machine is back of him, and lots of money in New York City."

Then Yarnell went on to tell me that he himself was connected with the street railways in New York, and that the railways were backing Seward. Wall Street, however, was a little nervous. It didn't want any man elected President who would drive the South into secession. No use to let iron drive out cotton. Let us have both cotton and iron.

We went out to walk through the city. Yarnell was amazed at the growth of Chicago. We wandered over to the Wigwam where the convention was to be held. It was a huge frame structure, seating ten thousand people. The city was swarming with delegates and visitors. All the hotels were filled; the saloons roared with drinking crowds. How many thousand cigars were lighted every minute! Stubs decorated the floors, the spittoons, the sidewalks. The houses of ill fame were riotous with men let loose upon a holiday.

At the Richmond House there was much champagne, for that was the head-quarters of the New York crowd. Yarnell took me here and introduced me about to his friends. He was well known. He had money for the occasion, and was esteemed in that light. It was a different crowd here from that I had seen in St. Louis years before, but its spirit was the same. "If you don't nominate Seward, where will you get your money?" Yarnell was saying this here and there. Some one at our side says: "This railsplitter Lincoln, who carries the purse for him?" "The tariff carries it," is the answer. "There's more money in the tariff than all that Seward can rake together." "Very well, Seward is for the tariff. Give us the tariff and Seward, then we will have the tariff money and Seward's money too."

Yarnell and I left the Richmond House on our way to look again at the crowds. Bands of music were playing everywhere. Men were marching. Tom Hyer, the great prize fighter, was leading a club of rough and handy men. They were preceded by a noisy band. They shouted. The staring crowd shouted. Hyer had come for the purpose of lifting a lusty voice for Seward at the critical moment. He and his men had good fists too to use in a case of doubt on a question of votes or of a right of entrance to the hall. They pass, the band dies away; other marchers follow. Some paraders are carrying rails bearing the banner with the words "Honest Old Abe" That reminds me of something. We go over to the office of the *Chicago Times* to see in the windows some rails which Lincoln split when he was working on the bottoms of the Sangamon River, thirty years before.

"I should think Greeley would be for Lincoln," I said to Yarnell. "I saw the *Tribune* yesterday and it slants toward Edward Bates of Missouri."

"That old slicker," sneered Yarnell. "Why who can depend on him? He's been for every one and everything, and then against them. He hates Seward. We kept him off the New York delegation. Now he's got on the delegation from Oregon, got some one's proxy, and he's here to make trouble. But it won't do him any good. We will put Seward over on the first ballot."

We came to the *Times'* window and looked at the rails. "Well," I said, "if they nominate Lincoln, we'll have another log-cabin campaign."

"Yes, that's what it will come to. What's all this talk anyway about Honest Old Abe? Every man is honest enough, and no man in politics much more honest than another. We don't need that kind of dramatics to elect Seward. There is enough to the man to elect him. We mean to have a clean-cut, high-toned campaign with a great man to lead us, who is known to the whole country. The day is past for this log-cabin business. It's now a stone front and champagne."

I went back with Yarnell to the Richmond House, then turned my own way to study the crowds. Chicago was a carnival of unlicensed spirits. What thousands of blue flies already swarmed upon the fresh carcass of this new political party! A few years before and it was poor, but of flesh that was fresh. Now it was beginning to stink. Tariffs, railroads, all powerful moneyed interests, special privileges, were settling upon it, blowing it full of eggs. All the old Whigs now long hungry, the old Federalists in disguise, the old plotters and schemers long defeated, were here. The motley elements that Douglas had derided as anti-Masonics, Know-nothings, Abolitionists, Spiritualists, where were they? Sunk in silence, out shouted, out talked, outnumbered by office seekers and monopolists. Tom Hyer was bawling, Garrison could not be heard. The New England manufacturers were here. Whittier was singing their songs and did not know it. I began to think of Rabelais, and of life as gluttony, eating and drinking, digestion and evacuation. I had a vision of all these hordes of men dead at last, their buttocks exposed to driving rains, upturned to a dark sky which breathed futility and contempt upon ended plots and hungers!

That night I started out again with Abigail and Aldington. There had not been anything like the same amount of drinking at Charleston. Harlots staggered through the streets, their arms interlocked with those of howling men. Tom Hyer passed, leading his gang of toughs, the gayly liveried band swelling the air with great horns and drums. Again the rails and banners for "Honest Old Abe." Rumors caught us as we passed: the Germans were for Lincoln; Greeley wanted Douglas elected President and was scheming to defeat Seward for the nomination. We went to the Richmond House. I wanted Abigail and Aldington to see the smoking, drinking, gabbling delegates from New York. We ran into Yarnell. He was preoccupied, and was a little in drink. He stood with us for a moment, and then was buttonholed and taken away. We returned to the streets to watch the marchers.

Yarnell was good enough to get tickets for Abigail, Aldington, and me, asking us with a half smile not to cheer for any one unless we cheered for Seward.

It was in the air that Seward would be nominated. Greeley said so, but he was really fighting Seward. We spied the bald head and bespectacled eyes of the great editor moving about the Oregon delegates. The tumult and the passion of the Charleston convention were not as dramatic as this. These men were here to destroy the Democratic party, to take control of the government. The air was of concentrated passion and will. There was a declaration of principles to be formulated out of sagacity and dramaturgy. Principles were to be observed but baits to be dangled; factions were to be conciliated, relative claims adjusted; the higher thought of the nation respected; radicalism tickled but not embraced; wrong censured, but needless offense avoided. Hence state rights got a sop; the tariff was advocated and the Pacific railroad; the harmless Declaration of Independence was quoted at large. Everybody had used it for more than eighty years--why not this platform?

The balloting begins. The expectation is intense. All of us have caught the crowd spirit, the infection of the mob. New England is polled first. What is the matter? She does not give Seward the fully expected vote. Very well! New York is reached. William M. Everetts, hook-nosed and dished of mouth, plumps New York seventy votes for Seward. The convention recovers from its fear. All is going well for Seward after all. What of Pennsylvania and her tariff? She has fifty-seven votes; fifty and one half of these go to a favorite son, Simon Cameron. This is a mere compliment; Pennsylvania will come to Seward now that her favorite son has been honored. Illinois is reached and votes for Lincoln. There are cheers. But he is the favorite son of Illinois. These are his people. The next ballot they will go to Seward. Indiana is reached. All of her vote goes to Lincoln. There are great cheers. But Lincoln split rails once in Indiana. This is a complimentary vote too. Ohio is reached. She has two favorite sons, Chase and McLean. Missouri is reached. Edward Bates is her son and gets the vote. What is this vote of Virginia,--fourteen votes out of her twenty-three for Lincoln? Some one near us whispers: "The South hates Seward worse than any one."

At last the whole vote is announced: Seward has 173-1/2; Lincoln 102. The Illinois River breaks loose; the great shouter for Lincoln, hired for the occasion, storms and bawls above the hubbub of the convention. Where is Hyer the prize fighter? He has been out with his gang. Drinking? We do not know. At any rate he is late, has missed one of the psychologies of the convention. After the noise is subsided, we hear that Bates, Greeley's favorite, has forty-eight votes. "Call the roll!" "Call the roll!" shout hundreds of delegates. Men are going mad with anxiety. Arms are waved frantically, delegates rise from their seats and bawl undistinguishable words. Curses and hisses fill the air. The second ballot begins. Why does Pennsylvania deliberate, why does she retire so often to consult her wishes? There is laughter over it. She changes her vote now. Her favorite son, Cameron, gets two; forty-eight go to Lincoln. What is the matter with Seward? We had heard there was plenty of Seward money in Pennsylvania. Yarnell had told me so. Why doesn't the machinery work? Ohio falls off seven votes for Chase; Bates loses thirteen of his Missouri votes. Vermont throws her whole vote to Lincoln, and the Stentor from the Illinois River bottoms raises a thunder of applause. But Tom Hyer has now arrived and the Seward chorus is working.

The vote is announced: Seward has 184-1/2; Lincoln 181; necessary to a choice, 233. Seward is ruined. Tom Hyer is down. The band, the banners are for nothing. All the Seward money is for nothing. To be Governor, Senator, the leading man of the party for years, the great debater of the Senate, the author of the irrepressible conflict, the most dreaded enemy of the South--all this goes up and out in a second like a poor sulphur match in a gale. Seward is ruined. A country lawyer from Springfield, Illinois, once a state legislator, once a Congressman, has killed him in two blows. What has done it? The irrepressible conflict. It has crushed him before it crushed many more, old and young throughout the land. He is too famous. His words are too well known. The house divided against itself is not so well known. Lincoln is obscure. He is a trim new champion of fifty-one years of age, ready after some fifteen or more years of resting and training, for a great fight.

Yet may not Greeley's Bates still come in? A horse not so swiftly running before now has a chance. Where would Seward's strength be thrown now that he cannot use it for himself? Can he throw it to any one? No! For the third ballot gives Seward 180 and Lincoln 231-1/2. But Seward is still holding on. Ohio has been sticking to Chase. The vote is not announced by the chair. But hundreds of pencils have kept the score. And just about as it is to be announced, Ohio throws four votes from Chase to Lincoln. Lincoln is nominated! The West of Douglas has won.

The convention goes mad. The Illinois River roars like waters over a thousand dams. Lake Michigan shouters make the rafters tremble. A cannon is fired from the roof. But no one inside hears it. We go forth to the street. Masses are yelling and crying with delight. Old Abe from Illinois is nominated. Chicago is delirious with joy. From the Tremont House a hundred guns are fired. Processions start; everywhere men are bearing rails. Bands play. Drink flows like sudden freshets. Yarnell passes at a distance. He is staring straight ahead, hurrying somewhere. What is left for Seward, for his supporters? Virginia had been bought, why didn't she deliver? Ohio was fingered for Seward. Why didn't Ohio yield? Pennsylvania had taken quantities of Seward money. Why this ingratitude? What nominated Lincoln? The Seward men have an answer.

The madness of the crowd for railsplitting! The log-cabin tradition! Genius and statesmanship have been set aside for a popular symbol, railsplitting. A party of moral ideas has reverted to claptrap. These are the bitter comments of Seward's beaten army. Then there are curses for Greeley. Greeley has avenged Seward's lifetime enmity. He has slaughtered the great man of the party. Why? The old traitor wants Douglas elected.

CHAPTER LXI

The press comments of the country on Lincoln's nomination were exceedingly conflicting. He was written of as the man whom Douglas had beaten two years before, and without other distinction; as lacking in culture, in every way inferior to Seward; as a whangdoodle stump speaker of the second class, and without any known principle. What is this talk of Old Abe Lincoln, Old Uncle Abe, Honest Abe Lincoln? Was he not a log roller in the Illinois legislature of 1836? Had he not been driven from position to position by Douglas in the debates? What is honest about him above other men? Why a nomination on the strength of a deceiving nickname? Is he not for the tariff and loose construction? Has he not been a Whig with all the humbuggery of that party, of log cabins and imperial practices?

The Republican press was more favorable. He was hailed as a man of the people, sprung from the people. On a hurried visit with Douglas, he told me that Lincoln was as able as any man the Republicans had, abler far than Seward; and of great integrity, though he loathed Lincoln's political faith. "I'll carry nearly every northern state against him," said Douglas. "The Union must be saved. I know the South. They will secede if Lincoln is elected. It's utter madness of them to think of this; but mad they are. We must handle them accordingly. Wall Street, New York, is afraid of Lincoln. They don't want their business disturbed by secession or even by a hostile South. Cotton is that strong."

Douglas was full of fight and energy. He intended to canvass the entire country. He was going into the South to point out the dangers of a divided country. "They are terribly mad at me down there. But I have never feared an audience yet. I intend to face them--and win them."

No Presidential nominee had ever made a speaking tour before. Lincoln stayed quietly in Springfield. Seward made a speaking campaign, traveling on a special train. At Springfield he stayed in his car and did not show Lincoln the courtesy of calling upon him. Lincoln, without standing on any pride, went to see Seward, edging his way through the crowd to the car.

Douglas fought everywhere to the last. If in his Senatorial days and before he had been complaisant to the slavocracy, the Charleston convention would not have seceded from him. His course now in the campaign silenced men like Hale and Seward who had nagged him for years with their depreciations and suspicions. He went into Virginia and there while speaking he was heckled by a Breckenridge follower. He was asked if the Southern States would be justified in seceding if Lincoln should be elected President. "No," thundered Douglas. "The election of a man to the Presidency of the American people, in conformity to the Constitution of the United States, would not justify any attempt at dissolving this glorious confederacy."

"But if the Southern States secede upon the inauguration of Lincoln, before he commits an overt act against their rights, would you advise or vindicate resistance by force to their secession?" If Douglas had ever prostituted his mind to the South, now was the time to do it again. But this was his answer:

"I answer that it is the duty of the President of the United States and all others in authority under him to enforce the laws of the United States as passed by Congress and as the court expounds them. And I, as in duty bound by my oath of fidelity to the Constitution, would do all in my power to aid the government of the United States in maintaining the supremacy of the laws against all resistance to them, come from what quarter it might. The President should meet all attempts to break up the Union as Old Hickory treated the nullifiers in 1832."

What of the right of revolution? Douglas conceded that, but insisted that the election of Lincoln would not be "such a grievance as would justify revolution, or secession."

I believed this too. Upon large ground if the South had the right to hold the negroes in slavery, the North would have the right to hold the South in the Union. If the South wanted to stuff fate into a small pocket of logic and allow their narrow bigotry to get the better of their reason, I was in favor of licking them in the name of sport and in justification of Darwin's law of the survival of the fittest.

Douglas, in spite of threats against his life, went into the Far South appealing to them to consider the dangers ahead. The Democratic party was hopelessly divided. Some partisan newspapers were carrying two tickets on the editorial page. Others were fighting Douglas bitterly; others supporting with fierce energy Breckenridge of Kentucky. Many were scheming with a view to the contingency that the election would be a tie and that the House of Representatives, in making the choice, would select Douglas.

Chicago was a whirlpool of excitement. In the middle summer Albert Edward, Prince of Wales, traveling in America as Baron Renfrew, came to Chicago on his way hunting in Illinois. The fate of the nation was a passing play to him. While he was here he was a greater object of interest than either Douglas or Lincoln. We heard that he was to stand on the balcony of his hotel to watch the political parades of the evening. Mr. Williams and I went forth to see the future King of England.

The city was thronged with people. Bands were playing everywhere. The Wide-awakes, a Republican organization, were out in force marching as soldiers, dressed in glazed caps and capes, carrying torches. Mottoes and transparencies were borne aloft by hundreds. "Free soil for free men." "No more slave territories." "We do care whether slavery is voted up or down." "Abraham Lincoln cares"--these were the banners. And everywhere the banner "Protection to American Industries." Men carried rails. The crowds cheered and roared. And Baron Renfrew looked on, surrounded by his entourage and a few of the elite of Chicago. We stared up into his face. Did he smile, approve? Was he greatly interested? If America should divide it would be better for England. We saw him turn and smile as he evidently spoke to one of his party.

Then a parade of Douglas men passed. They too carried banners. "Little Giant." "Ever Readies." "Cuba Must Be Ours." "We want none but white men at the helm." "We want a statesman, not a railsplitter for President." "Free Trade"--these were the Douglas mottoes. We turned at last and made our way through the crowd. Hawkers were selling railsplitter pins, Honest Abe pins. The streets were a medley of noise, confusion; the sidewalks were blocked. Drunken men, eager men pushed their way through. Bands played. Far off a stump speaker's voice could be heard. All this waste of sand and scrub oak which I had seen in 1833 was now covered with buildings big and little. It was the battleground between two sons of Illinois.

October came. I grew more and more apprehensive for Douglas' fate. I had had a letter from Isabel gently foreshadowing her marriage. My boy was not advancing in his work at school. Inexorable loneliness was descending upon me.

Douglas came to Chicago on a speaking trip. He had been in Indianapolis where his voice was so hoarse that he could scarcely be heard. Chicago gave him a magnificent ovation. They saw the man now in all his clearness of mind and strength of heart. He repudiated the schemes of fusion.

"Every disunionist," he said, "is a Breckenridge man. As Democrats, we can never fuse either with northern Abolitionists or southern bolters and secessionists. Yes, my friends, I say to you what I said in North Carolina and in the same words: I would hang every man higher than Haman who would attempt to resist by force the execution of any provision of the Constitution which our fathers made and bequeathed to us. You cannot sever this Union unless you cut the heartstrings that bind father to son, daughter to mother, and brother to sister in all our new states and territories. I love my children, but I do not desire to see them survive this Union."

With these words his tired and broken voice fell back into weakness from the great melody and power of its habitual quality. His weary body had risen into fresh strength for this utterance. His face assumed a great majesty. Men and women alike wept to hear him speak so--wept for the dark days ahead, wept for a great man failing in a struggle in which he was yet holding to cherished ideals, now being blown and scattered by the storm of the new era. They saw him surrounded on all sides by enemies. The South hated him. The northern Democrats with southern ideas hated him. The fanatics hated him. The Republican party which he had stepped upon with giant contempt hated him. In eight years of existence it had gathered to itself the contemptible factions that he had satirized. They had united now in the supreme purpose of defeating him. He was appealing for the same principles to which he had always been devoted. He was defending the Union as he had defended it since the days when I saw Jackson put his arm around him, and look with paternal pride in his eyes. He knew the heart and the will of the South. He was trying to tell it to the North. He felt that his own election would prevent disunion. He asked people to believe that he wished to be elected, not to gratify his personal ambition, but for the sake of the Union.

It was all in vain. The avalanche, loosened years before by stray adventurers

building fires for their little kettles, and running thoughtlessly over weakened at-
tachments, was now moving down on Douglas and the Union. The October election showed that he was defeated. Pennsylvania, Ohio, and Indiana were carried
by the Republicans in the state elections. Douglas was speaking in the South. His
life had been threatened. An attempt was made to wreck his train. In Alabama he
was showered with missiles. Not a northern paper published these shameful insults,
which if published would have won him many friends in the North. Amid dangers
and discouragements he went on to the end.

He was in Mobile when the news of Lincoln's election reached him. Before
leaving Alabama he did what he could to prevent that state from seceding.

Undismayed, he went on to New Orleans. There he addressed the business
men, pointing out to them that Lincoln would have a hostile Senate on his hands if
the South would only remain in the Union; that Lincoln could carry out no abolition or unfriendly policy toward the South without a Senate; that all of Lincoln's
appointments would have to be confirmed by the Senate. All of these things he said
to dissuade the South from secession. When they would not be persuaded, he tore
the mask from their faces and told them directly that Lincoln's election was only a
pretext for those who wished to set up a Southern Confederacy.

Lincoln was elected. But Douglas was not dishonored. He had achieved a great
personal triumph. He had polled 1,357,157 votes in the country against Lincoln's
1,866,452. In Illinois he had polled 160,215 votes to Lincoln's 172,161--in spite of
New England and the Germans. He had received 163,525 votes from the South
against Lincoln's 26,430. But he had lost to Breckenridge or Bell fourteen southern states. Protective tariff Pennsylvania had given Lincoln 268,030 and Douglas
16,765. Protective tariff Massachusetts had given Lincoln 106,533 and Douglas
34,372. Douglas had fought the South, he had fought against the disadvantage of a
divided party, he had fought the protective tariff, yet Lincoln had polled but a little
more than 500,000 votes more than he had. No use to say that the populace does
not understand questions of government or that they cannot rise to high justices
and rewards. Douglas' personal triumph had been great, but his remarkable popular
support shrunk to an insignificant twelve votes in the electoral college. He was vanquished and I was more deeply depressed than I had ever been in my life. Lincoln
was elected! And the South seceded.

CHAPTER LXII

It is war! Mars has descended. The irrepressible conflict has taken the sword. The house divided against itself is in the last contest to see whether there shall be two houses or one. The devils are now to be cast out, not by Satan but by the Lord mighty in battle, great in anger. Grapes of wrath are to be treaded now, and a furious wine drawn from the broken flesh of men hitherto growing peacefully on peaceful stems, North and South.

Douglas wishes without ostentation to make himself clear in his friendship and support of Lincoln. No envy, no pique, no chagrin. He has often prophesied this war. For years he has warned the country against sectionalism. He does not now say, I told you so. The war has come. He is for the North, as he told the South he would be if elected himself. He is against disunion with all his heart. His health is broken; he has no future on this earth except to work to bring peace, and to win the South to save the Union. And he labors like a Titan to these ends.

I waver in my plans to go to Washington to see Lincoln inaugurated. In any event I shall devour the report of the proceedings. I cannot keep my mind off the event. I cannot wait to see Douglas to express to him my great admiration, my deep affection. Yet I fear he is beyond the reach of such things. What does he care whether I admire him or not, or whether any one loves him or not? Such things cannot touch him now. But I would see him again. And I would see Lincoln too.

On the morning I am to start I leave my house in Chicago; then I return to my porch and think, holding my satchel. I start again, force myself to go. I drag myself on to the train. Things are changed now. I can go by rail all the way. No need of boats and canals in this late February of 1861.

Washington is in a thrill. It is expected that the crack of a rifle from a tree or a housetop will fell the tall Lincoln from Illinois, as he faces the crowd to take the oath of office. But all was peace. The South only intended to go its way and let Lincoln do what he could, if anything. I stood with the rapt mass close to the stand where I could see every face on the platform. Lincoln came, Douglas came. Douglas was giving notice to the country that he was hand in hand with Lincoln for the Union.

Lincoln has no place to put his tall silk hat, brand new for this occasion. Douglas, gallantly not seriously, thoughtfully not showily, with grace and taste, takes Lincoln's hat and holds it while Lincoln reads his inaugural address.

Lincoln is now becomingly dressed. He is past fifty-two; no gray hairs, no beard, looks clean shaven and youthful, like a man of thirty, prematurely old. He is swarthy, wrinkled. He is powerful, rested, self-possessed, masterful. The cadence of his voice is full of kindness and conciliation. Its rhythms speak in sympathy and respect for the feelings of every one. Some of his words move me like great music. He says in closing so clearly, so beautifully, sounding as of silver trumpets blown by archangels:

"The mystic chords of memory stretching from every battle field and patriot grave to every living heart and hearthstone all over this broad land will yet swell the chorus of the Union when again touched, as surely they will be touched, by the better angels of our nature."

I see Pinturicchio in his face. I hear the reverberations of Beethoven's dreams in his voice. This man is kindred to the greatest souls.

I know about the mystic chords myself. I have been in battle. I fought for Texas. Be that cause good or bad, it has now blossomed in me for the Union. I have followed Douglas for nationalism and progress. I am still with him, and the more so because Douglas is with Lincoln.

The crowd is moved. The great event is over. The railsplitter has disappeared to that house of state from whence he shall never emerge carefree and happy. And Douglas goes to consult with him, to aid him.

Lincoln depends now on Douglas, cannot dispense with him. They have known each other for a quarter of a century, in that Illinois of the West which Douglas prophesied would hold the balance of power in any crisis of the North and the South. That prophecy is fulfilled. It would have been fulfilled by giving Douglas to the Presidency. It had given Lincoln instead; and the prophecy is fulfilled.

Lincoln shows to Douglas his call for 75,000 men to put down the rebellion. Douglas approves of the wording of the order, but says it should call for 200,000 men. He knows the South!

"What do you wish me to do?" he asked Lincoln. Lincoln thinks it would be well if Douglas used his great influence to appeal to doubtful sections, or wavering peoples. In obedience to this suggestion Douglas sets off for Illinois.

I have preceded him. I know what war means. I know the processes, the psychologies, the technique. Bands are playing, men are enlisting and marching in Chicago. Orators are talking, women are singing and sewing. Shrouds and coffins must be made as well as caps and cloaks. Iron must be cast, nitrate dug, thousands of laborers set to work to hammer, to nail, to mold, to fashion engines of destruction. Nurses must be trained, for there will be blood to stanch, wounds to dress, and the dying to comfort. That Captain Grant whom I saw in St. Louis years ago has come to Springfield from Galena, left his tannery for the war. He is training some regiments for the service. Amos, Reverdy's boy, has joined the army, and Jonas too. Reverdy writes me about it. Sarah is full of anger, resentment, terror, and sorrow against this huge thing that has broken over her hearth and taken her sons. I am too old to fight. But I have money to give. I throw myself into the work with the hope of forgetting myself, my losses, my loneliness, my life. What can I do for Douglas? I have this wealth. He is now broken financially. When he returns to Chicago I must open my purse to him. What other use have I for money but to give it to this war, or to Douglas?

Douglas comes back from southern Illinois where he has been speaking. He is going to address a Chicago audience. It is not likely that they will hoot him now. After some difficulty I find him. His face lights up with a certain gladness as he sees me. But he is a dying eagle that ruffles its feathers when food is offered it; then sinks back upon its broken wing when it sees that it cannot eat. What is my friendship now to him? What is any earthly thing to him? He bears the sorrows of earth without the consolation that any Heaven can cure them. His voice is hoarse, his face is worn and streaked with agony. His eyes look through me, over me, beyond me. He sees me, but what am I? His hair is gray--much grayer than mine. He is only 48 but he is an old man. He has no place in life now but to save the Union. All his strength and activity have come to this simple faith, as simple as the faith of a child. He

reaches back into the years when he was 21 and first came to Illinois, to that substance of his being, always inherent and of his genius, which was and is now compact of nationalism, progress, intelligence, the firm union of sovereign states. This
is all he has to sustain him now. He has laid up this food for the last hours, for this
crisis of his soul. All souls must lay up something spiritual, even as they must lay up
food for the winter of life, for the bleak bright hours of the soul's sterile fight.

And this old love which led him to Jackson when I was there with Dorothy,
which led him to Jackson for the great privilege of looking into the old hero's face
is all that sustains Douglas now. He is poor in purse but rich in service and love; he
can never be President if he wished to be. This new era will take all his devotion,
but it will not even make him Senator again. But what need? The office is nothing
now to him. He has no place politically, except as a leader of all men. He is without
a party, but he has a country.

I offer him my purse. He smiles and thanks me. No time now to think of his af-
fairs--later perhaps. Something deeper than money friendship is required to arouse
the depths of him; and only the depths of him are left. Will I come to hear him
speak? I go.

He is on the heights now. The purest fires leap from his being. The eloquence
of great truths flows from his lips, along the melodious waves of that voice of thunder. He has become Orpheus; his Isabel is the Union now embodied in the strength,
the beauty of the North which he has always wooed and never won until now. The
crowd draws toward him, gives its spirit to him, casts its devotion at his feet. He is
on the heights. For Death is near him and Death is the sincerest and most authentic
of inspirers. He has nothing to ask now--only that the Union be saved. He has no
reproaches for any one except disunionists. He has become impersonal on all things
but the Union. I know that the end is near for him. No one can speak so who is not
prompted by Death.

He has fallen ill at his hotel in this Chicago that he loved and dowered with a
university and linked to the South with a great railroad in the interests of peace and
a firmer Union. I go to see him. Mrs. Douglas cannot admit me. He is unconscious
of those around him, but his soul is at work. "Telegraph to the President and let the
column move on." "Stand for the Union." "The West, this great ..."

I go into the mad streets so grief-stricken, so alone. Dorothy is long dead. Isabel is lost to me. My boy is away. My home is haunted with loneliness. I would be rich if Douglas was to be too. Now he is rich, I am poor; he is poor, I am rich. Men are marching, bugles calling. The city roars. At the foot of Clark Street I see the masts of scores of sailing craft. Chicago has become a great mart.

The June sky is blue and cool, and great white clouds sail through it so indifferently. They were here when I first came to Chicago; here when the French explored the wilderness. Here they are now just the same; and Illinois has more than a million souls, and every heart carries the burden of war. Over them this sky, these clouds. They do not care.

It seems but a few minutes and the words go about the streets: "Douglas is dead." The newsboys cry it soon. I am prepared, but the city is not. It is shocked and wounded. Douglas is dead! This voice that spoke to us so lately is stilled. The great man who submerged everything of self in a cause of many is no more. I am dumb, a few tears ooze from my eyes; but on I go through the crowds. Now I shall throw myself more than ever into the work of the war. I pass a theater where speeches are being made. From it I hear a voice singing "Annie Laurie." I stop to look at a sign containing the name of Madam Zante. And I go in to hear her sing. I draw near her to get a seat. It is Zoe!

Zoe! I send up my name by an usher. The word comes back quickly to join her behind the scenes. There she is waiting for me. And we fall into each other's arms and sob. She is all I have left in the world except little Reverdy. I hold her from me. She is majestic, glorious in the maturity of great beauty, intelligence, art. She has long been a singer of note under this name of Madam Zante. What of Fortescue? She ran away from him. What was the explanation of Fortescue's trick? So far as we could guess at it, only that he had used the murder of another woman to get the property that he had learned from Zoe that she had inherited. But we had no time to talk of this now. "Come with me, Zoe, to my house." And Zoe came. But she was soon off again to nurse in the hospitals.

It is November, 1861. Word comes to us that Reverdy's boy, Amos, has been killed in the battle of Belmont. Douglas has now been in sleep five months; now Amos is a sacrifice to the war. He had joined Captain Grant's army against Sarah's fierce protest. He had gone forth happy and proud. Now he was to rest in the cemetery in Jacksonville near the dust of my father, near the dust of Major Hardin, and

Lamborn.

And so it was that Zoe and I stood side by side touching the dead hand of Amos. Sarah was too grief-stricken to be surprised at Zoe's reappearance in our lives. She wailed incessantly: "What is free territory to me? My boy is dead! What is the end of slavery to me? My boy is dead! There was no use for this war, no use, no use! It needed never to be. If they had only listened to Douglas. What are Lincoln and Jeff Davis thinking of? My boy is dead."

And for nights after returning to Chicago I heard Sarah's voice crying: "my boy! my boy!"

The battle of Gettysburg has been fought. That single thing that makes or destroys every man had come upon General Lee and commanded him to follow. In his case it was audacity. He had invaded Pennsylvania and been hurled back. And not long after I heard that Isabel's husband had been killed in that terrible battle. She did not write me. The silence of life had come over us.

I read the Gettysburg address of Lincoln. It moved me like a symphony. But I did not believe it to be true. This government was not conceived in liberty. It was not dedicated to the proposition that all men are created equal. We were not engaged in a strife which tested whether this government so conceived and so dedicated could survive. The South could have set up a separate government and the same liberty and the same equality which informed the union would have remained intact. Isabel's husband, and the other thousands who had died there had not consecrated the ground unless the Union meant something more than a union. It had to mean liberty and more than the emancipation of the negroes for that ground to be consecrated. And a few years later its glory was detracted from by the machinations of merchants who grew fat on the blood of that battle. And yet I was moved by Lincoln's words more profoundly than by anything that I had ever read.

CONCLUSION

It is April 23d, 1900. Three hundred and thirty-six years ago to-day a man named Shakespeare was born. He lived with some gnawing at his heart, wrote some plays, and died. He was wise enough, I fancy, to see that the joke is on those who remain in life, not those who leave it. Eighty-seven years ago to-day Stephen A. Douglas was born. He lived, stormed about these States, talked of great principles, was tossed aside by a squall on the universe of things, and died. It is now thirty-nine years since he summed up his life's wisdom in the words: "Tell my children to obey the laws and support the Constitution." That was about the summation of Socrates' wisdom, this matter of the laws, as he lay in prison opposite the Acropolis. He refused to walk forth free, except by the law. If I live until June the eighteenth I shall be eighty-five years of age. On the score of age I should feel much wiser than Douglas who died at forty-eight and Socrates who died at sixty. I feel that I am a good deal like Shakespeare. I have very little respect for the laws--at least for the written laws. I am not so sure about the higher law, if I am left to determine it. But in truth I am a good deal in doubt as to what is right, and what is wrong, what good and what evil. And I never know what the law is. I have wondered about it all my life. I have thought at times I knew, but I have been for the most part betrayed and fooled.

And why not now? Miss Sharpe, delicate, spiritual, active of mind, lives at the boarding house where I do. She thinks I am a fine old gentleman. She likes my society. I am to her taste interesting because I am experienced. I am richer intellectually than any man could be at an earlier age. She reads to me, often reads to me:

"Grow old along with me, The best is yet to be, The last of life for which the first was made."

How glorious is old age! She comforts me, makes me contented with my state at times; she makes me forget how I feel when I rise in the morning, stiff, bewildered, sometimes wondering where I am. She helps me to establish my mind when it thinks of too many things at once, and cannot choose for paltering and fumbling. I walk with a cane; but legs are nothing. The soul is the prize, the flower. My food does not digest itself well; my heart flutters and stumbles; my eyes refuse to work even with the best of glasses. The doctor says I have an old man's arteries. I know when my memory falters that it is due to the brain which has shrunk, and to the incrusted arteries which do not carry enough blood cells to the brain to give me memory. Still the best is yet to be, and this is now it. I think the law of old age will get me eventually just as the law of the new era caught Douglas and destroyed him.

It is thirty years now since the great Chicago fire swept my fortune away. I saved one lot out of the wreck. A skyscraper wanted it to complete its necessary ground space. So I leased it; and the rental keeps me. The lease will be out in 1989--but no matter for that. Between 1871 and 1890 I had a hard time of it. I tried to repair my fortune and couldn't do it. Then the building of skyscrapers struck Chicago, and I came into an income through this lease. I have a good room at the boarding house and all I wish of everything. Perhaps I shall revise my will and leave something to Miss Sharpe. I should like to depart from the customary bequests to hospitals and colleges. If the University founded by Douglas had not been taken over by the money made by the Standard Oil Company I might give something to it. Some say that the University stands for spiritual hardness, a Darwinian scientific which distinguished Douglas, but I am not sure. Yes, I believe I shall revise my will in favor of Miss Sharpe. Sometimes I suspect that she wants to marry me. She talks of nothing but the soul, as Isabel did in Rome. I am sure I have plenty of soul. I have no one else to give my money to but Miss Sharpe. My boy died in the middle sixties.

As for the rest, they are all gone. Zoe and I lived happily together until the rage of the influenza in 1889; then she died. Mr. Williams, Abigail, Aldington passed away and were buried in a cemetery about a mile north of the river. Then their bodies were removed somewhere, for the cemetery was turned into a park. Lincoln Park it is now. Reverdy, Sarah, gave up the battle years ago. They went to sleep by the side of their son, Amos, who was killed in the battle of Belmont. Their other children are scattered to unknown quarters. I know not if they live.

A strange thing happened yesterday. Mr. Williams' grandson called upon me. He is going to South Africa with a load of mules for the British. Almost every one in America wants the Boers put down. He asked me to go along and for a moment I took him seriously. The adventurer in me arose. Then I became conscious of my stiff legs. Besides was I ever much of an adventurer after all? Why did I not travel in the splendid forties and the leisurely fifties? Still I believe I have had as much out of life as Cecil Rhodes. He started out to be rich. So did I. He got diamonds and gold. I got land. He wished to see England world-triumphant. I wanted to see America an ocean-bound republic. I followed Douglas. He was inspired by Ruskin. For Ruskin had fired young Rhodes at Oxford with these words: "England must found colonies as fast and as far as she is able, formed of her most energetic and worthy men; seizing every piece of fruitful waste ground she can set her foot on, and there teaching her colonists that their chief virtue is to be fidelity to their country, and that their first aim is to be to advance the power of England by land and by sea."

Accordingly Rhodes had set out to become rich; he plotted the supremacy of England in South Africa. And now there is war on President Kruger of the Transvaal, who was at the head of its affairs in the years when Douglas was settling Oregon and California and talking of popular sovereignty. Gold was discovered there, as it was in California; and there was a great exodus of English; and now the question is whether the Ruskin idea will triumph or Kruger's idea, which is derived from the Bible, shall triumph. The Bible is used in many ways and on all sides of everything. Kruger is an abolitionist concerned with abolishing Great Britain. But I think Great Britain will abolish him, and find plenty of Biblical authority for it. Many sacred hymns will be sung, and God will be loudly praised when the end comes.

Rhodes is using his great wealth to assist England in her war against the Boer Republic. He has advocated from a youth up the formation of a secret society with the following objects, as expressed by himself: "The extension of British rule throughout the world.... The colonization by British subjects of all lands where the means of livelihood are attainable by energy, labor, and enterprise, and especially the occupation by British settlers of the entire continent of Africa, the Holy Land, the valley of the Euphrates, the islands of Cypress and Candia, the whole of South America, the islands of the Pacific not heretofore possessed by Great Britain, the whole of the Malay Archipelago, the seaboard of China and Japan, the ultimate recovery of the United States of America as an integral part of the British Empire."

A large lust for land, dwarfing to Douglas' call to American supremacy on the North American continent, the expulsion of Great Britain therefrom, and from all dominance in the Western Hemisphere. It was rather costly to Douglas to take over Texas; and the retention of the old land of the Southern States was the nation's crisis which killed him. For any land-lust that Douglas had, he has paid. Will Rhodes pay for his lust? No, I think he will be paid for it. For he has been a success. He has seen his hopes for England all but realized. So far as the United States is concerned England has recovered it. She rules us in trade, literature, in thought. We elect our own rulers, to be sure; but England controls them, though we pay their salaries.

However, I shall not go to South Africa. I know that I may die in an instant; and though, if dying at sea, I might sink to the depth, where something of Dorothy remains, I would as soon be reduced to ashes and scattered on the shores of this lake that I have known so long. That would be symbolical of my purposeless and wasted life.

The day being fine, this being Douglas' birthday, I have come from my boarding house to the little park which bears his name, and where stands the column to his memory, crowned with a bronze counterfeit of him, standing forthright and intrepid, as I have often seen him in life. It is a clear sky with racing clouds that the statue stands against, and I almost imagine it swaying and moving, such is the illusory effect of the clouds. I enter the park and rest on a settee looking toward the lake.

Chicago has now a population of a million and a half--you will observe that this passion for figures remains with me. To the south I can see the smoke of the steel mills; to the north the towers of granite, tile, and brick of the city, and all between populous quarters. Twenty miles of city north and south; ten miles of city east and west. I am on Douglas' ninety acres, ten of which he deeded to the University of Chicago. Its three-story college building stands to the west of me about one half a mile; abandoned now. The acres themselves have passed to an insurance company on a mortgage. And in the general decay of Douglas' memory and influences this seems fitting enough.

Of course, the Civil War was waged to free the negro; and to do it it was necessary to have a protective tariff, which came into being soon after Lincoln was

elected, and has been the policy of the country ever since. Also for this emancipation it was necessary to revive the bank, and this was done during the war. Not
long after the war was over--about two years--the trust known as the Standard Oil
Company was organized. Its moving spirit endowed the Douglas university and
moved it to the Midway Plaisance. It has continued its uninterrupted graduating
years from Douglas' time till now. It is still Douglas' university--at least as much so
as this United States was Douglas' these United States. It is a university built out of
tariff privileges and railroad rebates; while Douglas' university was built from land,
which Douglas was foresighted enough to buy in anticipation of Chicago's growth,
and the increment in values produced by the Illinois Central railroad. Douglas was
hotly denounced for crookedness and money grabbing in those days of 1858 by the
Abolitionists and Free Soilers. Indeed much is said now in criticism of Mr. Rock-
efeller; but I believe it will pass. Besides he is not running for office, or trying to
found an ocean to ocean republic; and hence criticism does not hurt him so much.

Below me and down behind a wall the tracks of the Illinois Central roar to
the wheels of numerous trains, long trains of ten and twelve cars, sleepers, diners,
parlor cars, bound straight for New Orleans and New York, either place reached in
twenty-four hours from Chicago. I wish Douglas could see this. Still, would he like
to know that the public have no access to the lake at any place where the tracks lie
between the shore and this wall? Perhaps he would see that this occupancy cor-
rectly exemplifies the fate that the free-soil doctrine has met with throughout the
country.

There are sounds of trowels, voices of workmen behind me. A group of masons
and laborers is repairing Douglas' tomb; for it is not scrupulously cared for these
days. Postprandial orators are frequently remarking amidst great acclaim that the
hand on the dial of time points to Hamilton; and if government is as corrupt as the
newspapers say it is, and if Hamilton stood for corruption in government, the hand
on the dial undoubtedly points to him. At this moment a young man and woman
come to a settee near me. The young woman asks her companion: "Who is that
monument to?" "Douglas," he answers in staccato. "Who was Douglas?" "A Senator
or something from Illinois. But why change the subject? You have kept putting this
off, and I have six hundred dollars saved now, and prospects are good. I would like
to be ..." the rest is borne away by the wind. But I know it is the old theme. Soon

his arm encircles her shoulders over the back of the settee. She looks at him and smiles. It is April! The men are repairing the mortar between the stones of Douglas' tomb. Two are masons, two are negro helpers. The negroes are as free as the whites; the whites are no freer than the negroes. They are all wanderers, looking for jobs without settled places, paying board as I do, or living in rented places. One of them may own his house. Some laborers do, not many. They are like the factory workers, the whole breed of workers throughout the land. The Civil War did not make them prosperous, or change their real status. It seems that the God of nature still rules, and that Darwin is his best prophet. These men are free to work or to starve. Some things have changed. It is no longer against the law to send abolition literature through the mail. But it is against the law to incite laborers to strike, whether they are white or black, and it is against the law for laborers, white or black, to organize themselves into unions. The slave owners were pretty well organized once, both financially and politically, but now the corporations are much better organized than the slave owners were. The negro did not dare to rebel against his master. And now the law prevents the laborer from organizing against the corporation. We have freedom now, but of a different quality. It has changed its base, but is there more of it?

A freight train goes by nearly a mile long. It is laden with coal, oil, iron. I can't believe that the soil is free. Coal and oil and iron have too much of it. I think of the banners borne in the campaign of 1860, when Baron Renfrew stood that night on the balcony of his hotel. He will soon be king of England and emperor of India. And some one--either the men who carried those banners or their sons--some one now has a complete overlordship of this United States.

Why did not these banners make free men and a free soil? I suspect that the banner of protection to American industries was as influential at least as the free soil banner. It was easy after the war to force the XIV Amendment on the country, to give citizenship to the negro so far as his color had kept him out of it. It remained for the courts to call the corporations citizens and to fit to their backs the coat of equal protection of the laws, which they told us was cut and sewed for the negro. Hence this long freight train with coal, oil, and iron--all very well, but where are the free men and the free soil that Reverdy's son died for?

Cries are now being uttered of capitalistic America. Also they say the Supreme

Court is always the mouthpiece of the dominant influence. That was what was said when Taney decided that Dred Scott was not a citizen. "The courts are tools of Satan, the Constitution is a league with Hell," said Garrison. He burned a copy of the Constitution on a public bonfire. That could be done then, for slavocracy only interfered with free speech in the South. Now it is not so safe to criticize the Supreme Court anywhere in America. I myself think that coal and iron and oil are more powerful than cotton ever was, and more permeatingly dominant. It would not do to burn the Constitution anywhere in this United and Standardized States. As for mocking the flag, one might be lynched on the spot.

The Filipinos have taken literally the Declaration of Independence, which is the platform upon which Lincoln was elected; and they are fighting us in the name of Lincoln. We have an army over there sustaining the honor of the flag, under William McKinley, President of the United States and Commander in Chief of its Army and Navy. Mr. McKinley was a soldier in the war under Lincoln. He, therefore, knows something about military matters. He has demonstrated that he has something in his head beyond the theory of protection to American industries. He is demonstrating that he knows how to lift the United States out of its isolation, and to carry it beyond its place in the Western Hemisphere with nothing but satellites like the West Indies and Hawaii to be trailed by its gravitational movements. Also he learned how to put down rebellion in the Southern States, and that is the same thing, of course, as putting down rebellion in the Philippine Islands. We have bought the islands. They are ours. They are farther away, to be sure, than Cuba which Douglas wanted for his ocean-bound republic. But though farther away, civilization, our duty, and the manifest destiny of old compel us to hold them. When Alcibiades embarked on his Sicilian expedition, it was said that Athens itself was sailing out of the Piraeus, never to return. And some think that when Admiral Dewey sailed into the harbor of Manila with his fleet he took the old America with him, never to return to these shores; and what was worse, it disappeared there out of his hands and is lost for good.

There is China, where we have set up a Federal judge. There is the trade of the Orient; the Philippine Islands themselves are rich in hemp. To get land for hemp is different from getting it for cotton--for I am sure hemp makes a better rope with which to strangle liberty.

But though the Constitution has not reached the Islands, while the flag has, it may in time reach them. Meantime no mocking of that perambulating and capricious instrument! It contains the power to acquire islands, or the whole of China, by conquest or treaty; and the power to govern them as we choose, limited only by our ideas of Justice. It would not do to let them have popular sovereignty, any more than it would have done in Douglas' day to let Kansas have popular sovereignty. The right to prohibit or allow slavery in a territory goes with the right to extend the Constitution with its XIV Amendment to the Philippine Islands, or not to extend it--and we have chosen not to extend it. Thus the extra constitutional foundations of the Republican party have led to colonialism.

Douglas, in bronze, looks over the lake to the east--to what? Perhaps to the hills of Vermont and his youth, when no forecasting angel could have told him what could come to him and his country. Perhaps he knows now that free souls are better than free soil, since he never had much use for the kind of free soil that was shouted at him.

This morning's paper has long dispatches about the progress of our troops in the Philippines. Perhaps that is the reason why Douglas' back is to the west. Surely he does not mean that he turns his back upon the domain of Mexico and Oregon. It must be only upon the conquests of the new capitalism. I am glad, and more than glad, that negro slavery was abolished. It was nothing but a wooden plow anyway. Our new steel plows work much better and they have this advantage: they accomplish more, they are in themselves more of slaves, and they are creators of time and of greater wealth.

There are strikes over the land. Why? Are not men free? Yes, they are free to choose their work if they know how to do more than one thing, or if they are able to move from the place where they have been employed. But they are not free to organize, to agitate for better wages, or to strike. What is this matter of freedom after all? It reminds me of the steps of a stairway. A step consists of a horizontal board and a vertical board and then another horizontal board. The first horizontal board is the present condition, and the second horizontal is the liberty that is desired, the vertical board is the difficulty in the way. One must overcome resistance to step up. When he does he has achieved the liberty to which he aspires. But he is standing on the same sort of a level that he did before. This stairway goes up indefinitely, and at last becomes lost in the sky of the future, like the beanstalk of Jack the Giant-killer. All this sounds quite materialistic, and as if I was without hope, but I am not materialistic, or despairing of the future. I know that matter cannot be explained without resorting to such concepts as force, causation, action, and reaction. And these are the ideas of the mind. And I think of matter and of history in terms of action and reaction. The mind of man is the most wonderful thing that we know anything about, and its secret is the secret of the universe. Having never been happy myself, I am not a disciple of eudemonism; but I see life as struggle and change; and though I do not know what it means, I know thought will not be at rest, that hopes will not cease, and that dreams of liberty will fascinate the minds of future Lincolns and Douglases.

The masons are eating their luncheon. I arise to go to Douglas' tomb. The young woman says: "I wonder who that old man is? He has been sitting right there all morning."

I wonder myself who I am. I take my way feebly up the stone steps to the grated door of the tomb. I look through. There lies the sarcophagus which contains the bones of Stephen A. Douglas. There was no truer, braver man in his time, and no abler.

I put my spectacles on, for I cannot see well into the tomb. Yes, there are the words: "Tell my children to obey the laws and support the Constitution." No, I do not subscribe to that. I believe in liberty and not law. Douglas' popular sovereignty was more liberty than it was law. These words on his tomb must have been spoken by him with reference to the preservation of the Union. At any rate I do not believe in these words. I accept instead Walt Whitman's admonition to the States: "Obey little, resist much." What shall we obey at all, and where shall we resist? You must decide that for yourself, or ask those about it who still have the capacity for living.

I am old. Now I must go to luncheon and then take my afternoon nap.

www.bookjungle.com *email: sales@bookjungle.com fax: 630-214-0564 mail: Book Jungle PO Box 2226 Champaign, IL 61825*

The Codes Of Hammurabi And Moses
W. W. Davies

QTY

The discovery of the Hammurabi Code is one of the greatest achievements of archaeology, and is of paramount interest, not only to the student of the Bible, but also to all those interested in ancient history...

Religion   **ISBN:** *1-59462-338-4*   **Pages:132**

MSRP $12.95

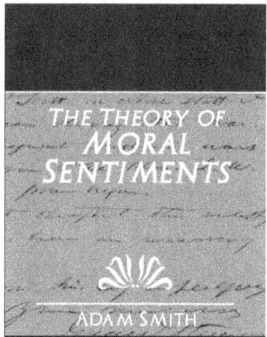

The Theory of Moral Sentiments
Adam Smith

QTY

This work from 1749. contains original theories of conscience amd moral judgment and it is the foundation for systemof morals.

Philosophy ISBN: *1-59462-777-0*   **Pages:536**

MSRP $19.95

Jessica's First Prayer
Hesba Stretton

QTY

In a screened and secluded corner of one of the many railway-bridges which span the streets of London there could be seen a few years ago, from five o'clock every morning until half past eight, a tidily set-out coffee-stall, consisting of a trestle and board, upon which stood two large tin cans, with a small fire of charcoal burning under each so as to keep the coffee boiling during the early hours of the morning when the work-people were thronging into the city on their way to their daily toil...

Childrens   ISBN: *1-59462-373-2*

Pages:84

MSRP $9.95

My Life and Work
Henry Ford

QTY

Henry Ford revolutionized the world with his implementation of mass production for the Model T automobile. Gain valuable business insight into his life and work with his own auto-biography... "We have only started on our development of our country we have not as yet, with all our talk of wonderful progress, done more than scratch the surface. The progress has been wonderful enough but..."

Pages:300

Biographies/   ISBN: *1-59462-198-5*   *MSRP $21.95*

The Art of Cross-Examination
Francis Wellman

QTY

I presume it is the experience of every author, after his first book is published upon an important subject, to be almost overwhelmed with a wealth of ideas and illustrations which could readily have been included in his book, and which to his own mind, at least, seem to make a second edition inevitable. Such certainly was the case with me; and when the first edition had reached its sixth impression in five months, I rejoiced to learn that it seemed to my publishers that the book had met with a sufficiently favorable reception to justify a second and considerably enlarged edition. ..

Reference   ISBN: *1-59462-647-2*

Pages:412

MSRP $19.95

On the Duty of Civil Disobedience
Henry David Thoreau

QTY

Thoreau wrote his famous essay, On the Duty of Civil Disobedience, as a protest against an unjust but popular war and the immoral but popular institution of slave-owning. He did more than write—he declined to pay his taxes, and was hauled off to gaol in consequence. Who can say how much this refusal of his hastened the end of the war and of slavery ?

Law   ISBN: *1-59462-747-9*

Pages:48

MSRP $7.45

Dream Psychology Psychoanalysis for Beginners
Sigmund Freud

QTY

Sigmund Freud, born Sigismund Schlomo Freud (May 6, 1856 - September 23, 1939), was a Jewish-Austrian neurologist and psychiatrist who co-founded the psychoanalytic school of psychology. Freud is best known for his theories of the unconscious mind, especially involving the mechanism of repression; his redefinition of sexual desire as mobile and directed towards a wide variety of objects; and his therapeutic techniques, especially his understanding of transference in the therapeutic relationship and the presumed value of dreams as sources of insight into unconscious desires.

Psychology   ISBN: *1-59462-905-6*

Pages:196

MSRP $15.45

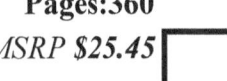

The Miracle of Right Thought
Orison Swett Marden

QTY

Believe with all of your heart that you will do what you were made to do. When the mind has once formed the habit of holding cheerful, happy, prosperous pictures, it will not be easy to form the opposite habit. It does not matter how improbable or how far away this realization may see, or how dark the prospects may be, if we visualize them as best we can, as vividly as possible, hold tenaciously to them and vigorously struggle to attain them, they will gradually become actualized, realized in the life. But a desire, a longing without endeavor, a yearning abandoned or held indifferently will vanish without realization.

Self Help   ISBN: *1-59462-644-8*

Pages:360

MSRP $25.45

www.bookjungle.com *email: sales@bookjungle.com fax: 630-214-0564 mail: Book Jungle PO Box 2226 Champaign, IL 61825*

QTY

The Rosicrucian Cosmo-Conception Mystic Christianity by *Max Heindel*   ISBN: *1-59462-188-8*   **$38.95**
The Rosicrucian Cosmo-conception is not dogmatic, neither does it appeal to any other authority than the reason of the student. It is: not controversial, but is: sent forth in the, hope that it may help to clear...   New Age/Religion Pages 646

Abandonment To Divine Providence by *Jean-Pierre de Caussade*   ISBN: *1-59462-228-0*   **$25.95**
"The Rev. Jean Pierre de Caussade was one of the most remarkable spiritual writers of the Society of Jesus in France in the 18th Century. His death took place at Toulouse in 1751. His works have gone through many editions and have been republished...   Inspirational Religion Pages 400

Mental Chemistry by *Charles Haanel*   ISBN: *1-59462-192-6*   **$23.95**
Mental Chemistry allows the change of material conditions by combining and appropriately utilizing the power of the mind. Much like applied chemistry creates something new and unique out of careful combinations of chemicals the mastery of mental chemistry...   New Age Pages 354

The Letters of Robert Browning and Elizabeth Barret Barrett 1845-1846 vol II   ISBN: *1-59462-193-4*   **$35.95**
by *Robert Browning* and *Elizabeth Barrett*   Biographies Pages 596

Gleanings In Genesis (volume I) by *Arthur W. Pink*   ISBN: *1-59462-130-6*   **$27.45**
Appropriately has Genesis been termed "the seed plot of the Bible" for in it we have, in germ form, almost all of the great doctrines which are afterwards fully developed in the books of Scripture which follow...   Religion/Inspirational Pages 420

The Master Key by *L. W. de Laurence*   ISBN: *1-59462-001-6*   **$30.95**
In no branch of human knowledge has there been a more lively increase of the spirit of research during the past few years than in the study of Psychology, Concentration and Mental Discipline. The requests for authentic lessons in Thought Control, Mental Discipline and...   New Age/Business Pages 422

The Lesser Key Of Solomon Goetia by *L. W. de Laurence*   ISBN: *1-59462-092-X*   **$9.95**
This translation of the first book of the "Lernegton" which is now for the first time made accessible to students of Talismanic Magic was done, after careful collation and edition, from numerous Ancient Manuscripts in Hebrew, Latin, and French...   New Age/Occult Pages 92

Rubaiyat Of Omar Khayyam by *Edward Fitzgerald*   ISBN:*1-59462-332-5*   **$13.95**
Edward Fitzgerald, whom the world has already learned, in spite of his own efforts to remain within the shadow of anonymity, to look upon as one of the rarest poets of the century, was born at Bredfield, in Suffolk, on the 31st of March, 1809. He was the third son of John Purcell...   Music Pages 172

Ancient Law by *Henry Maine*   ISBN: *1-59462-128-4*   **$29.95**
The chief object of the following pages is to indicate some of the earliest ideas of mankind, as they are reflected in Ancient Law, and to point out the relation of those ideas to modern thought.   Religiom/History Pages 452

Far-Away Stories by *William J. Locke*   ISBN: *1-59462-129-2*   **$19.45**
"Good wine needs no bush, but a collection of mixed vintages does. And this book is just such a collection. Some of the stories I do not want to remain buried for ever in the museum files of dead magazine-numbers an author's not unpardonable vanity..."   Fiction Pages 272

Life of David Crockett by *David Crockett*   ISBN: *1-59462-250-7*   **$27.45**
"Colonel David Crockett was one of the most remarkable men of the times in which he lived. Born in humble life, but gifted with a strong will, and indomitable courage, and unremitting perseverance...   Biographies/New Age Pages 424

Lip-Reading by *Edward Nitchie*   ISBN: *1-59462-206-X*   **$25.95**
Edward B. Nitchie, founder of the New York School for the Hard of Hearing, now the Nitchie School of Lip-Reading, Inc, wrote "LIP-READING Principles and Practice". The development and perfecting of this meritorious work on lip-reading was an undertaking...   How-to Pages 400

A Handbook of Suggestive Therapeutics, Applied Hypnotism, Psychic Science   ISBN: *1-59462-214-0*   **$24.95**
by *Henry Munro*   Health/New Age/Health/Self-help Pages 376

A Doll's House: and Two Other Plays by *Henrik Ibsen*   ISBN: *1-59462-112-8*   **$19.95**
Henrik Ibsen created this classic when in revolutionary 1848 Rome. Introducing some striking concepts in playwriting for the realist genre, this play has been studied the world over.   Fiction/Classics/Plays 308

The Light of Asia by *sir Edwin Arnold*   ISBN: *1-59462-204-3*   **$13.95**
In this poetic masterpiece, Edwin Arnold describes the life and teachings of Buddha. The man who was to become known as Buddha to the world was born as Prince Gautama of India but he rejected the worldly riches and abandoned the reigns of power when...   Religion/History/Biographies Pages 170

The Complete Works of Guy de Maupassant by *Guy de Maupassant*   ISBN: *1-59462-157-8*   **$16.95**
"For days and days, nights and nights, I had dreamed of that first kiss which was to consecrate our engagement, and I knew not on what spot I should put my lips..."   Fiction/Classics Pages 240

The Art of Cross-Examination by *Francis L. Wellman*   ISBN: *1-59462-309-0*   **$26.95**
Written by a renowned trial lawyer, Wellman imparts his experience and uses case studies to explain how to use psychology to extract desired information through questioning.   How-to/Science/Reference Pages 408

Answered or Unanswered? by *Louisa Vaughan*   ISBN: *1-59462-248-5*   **$10.95**
Miracles of Faith in China   Religion Pages 112

The Edinburgh Lectures on Mental Science (1909) by *Thomas*   ISBN: *1-59462-008-3*   **$11.95**
This book contains the substance of a course of lectures recently given by the writer in the Queen Street Hall, Edinburgh. Its purpose is to indicate the Natural Principles governing the relation between Mental Action and Material Conditions...   New Age/Psychology Pages 148

Ayesha by *H. Rider Haggard*   ISBN: *1-59462-301-5*   **$24.95**
Verily and indeed it is the unexpected that happens! Probably if there was one person upon the earth from whom the Editor of this, and of a certain previous history, did not expect to hear again...   Classics Pages 380

Ayala's Angel by *Anthony Trollope*   ISBN: *1-59462-352-X*   **$29.95**
The two girls were both pretty, but Lucy who was twenty-one who supposed to be simple and comparatively unattractive, whereas Ayala was credited, as her Bombwhat romantic name might show, with poetic charm and a taste for romance. Ayala when her father died was nineteen...   Fiction Pages 484

The American Commonwealth by *James Bryce*   ISBN: *1-59462-286-8*   **$34.45**
An interpretation of American democratic political theory. It examines political mechanics and society from the perspective of Scotsman James Bryce   Politics Pages 572

Stories of the Pilgrims by *Margaret P. Pumphrey*   ISBN: *1-59462-116-0*   **$17.95**
This book explores pilgrims religious oppression in England as well as their escape to Holland and eventual crossing to America on the Mayflower, and their early days in New England...   History Pages 268

www.bookjungle.com *email: sales@bookjungle.com fax: 630-214-0564 mail: Book Jungle PO Box 2226 Champaign, IL 61825*

QTY

The Fasting Cure *by Sinclair Upton*   ISBN: *1-59462-222-1* **$13.95**
In the Cosmopolitan Magazine for May, 1910, and in the Contemporary Review (London) for April, 1910, I published an article dealing with my experi-ences in fasting. I have written a great many magazine articles, but never one which attracted so much attention... New Age/Self Help/Health Pages 164

Hebrew Astrology *by Sepharial*   ISBN: *1-59462-308-2* **$13.45**
In these days of advanced thinking it is a matter of common observation that we have left many of the old landmarks behind and that we are now pressing forward to greater heights and to a wider horizon than that which represented the mind-content of our progenitors... Astrology Pages 144

Thought Vibration or The Law of Attraction in the Thought World   ISBN: *1-59462-127-6* **$12.95**
by William Walker Atkinson   *Psychology/Religion Pages 144*

Optimism *by Helen Keller*   ISBN: *1-59462-108-X* **$15.95**
Helen Keller was blind, deaf, and mute since 19 months old, yet famously learned how to overcome these handicaps, communicate with the world, and spread her lectures promoting optimism. An inspiring read for everyone... Biographies/Inspirational Pages 84

Sara Crewe *by Frances Burnett*   ISBN: *1-59462-360-0* **$9.45**
In the first place, Miss Minchin lived in London. Her home was a large, dull, tall one, in a large, dull square, where all the houses were alike, and all the sparrows were alike, and where all the door-knockers made the same heavy sound... Childrens/Classic Pages 88

The Autobiography of Benjamin Franklin *by Benjamin Franklin*   ISBN: *1-59462-135-7* **$24.95**
The Autobiography of Benjamin Franklin has probably been more extensively read than any other American historical work, and no other book of its kind has had such ups and downs of fortune. Franklin lived for many years in England, where he was agent... Biographies/History Pages 332

Name	
Email	
Telephone	
Address	
City, State ZIP	

☐ **Credit Card**   ☐ **Check / Money Order**

Credit Card Number	
Expiration Date	
Signature	

Please Mail to: Book Jungle
PO Box 2226
Champaign, IL 61825
or Fax to: 630-214-0564

ORDERING INFORMATION

web*: www.bookjungle.com*
email*: sales@bookjungle.com*
fax*: 630-214-0564*
mail*: Book Jungle PO Box 2226 Champaign, IL 61825*
or PayPal *to sales@bookjungle.com*

Please contact us for bulk discounts

DIRECT-ORDER TERMS

**20% Discount if You Order
Two or More Books**
Free Domestic Shipping!
Accepted: Master Card, Visa,
Discover, American Express

www.ingramcontent.com/pod-product-compliance
Lightning Source LLC
Chambersburg PA
CBHW080953020726
47505CB00009B/2177